Praise for *Shattered Image*

A sparkling debut for Stacy Monson! Vibrant, believable characters leap off the pages into your hearts in this evocative, grace-filled story, and you can't help but cheer them on while shedding a tear or two. Shattered Image *shatters the popular belief that image defines us, and reaffirms that we are much more than the reflection we see in the mirror, that we are God's masterpiece!*

—Brenda Anderson, author of the *Coming Home* series

The heartfelt journey of a woman running from the spotlight and a man reaching for it. Stacy creates warm and complex characters who will live with you long after you turn the last page.

—Sharon Hinck, award-winning author of the *Sword of Lyric* series

A Chain of Lakes Novel

SHATTERED IMAGE

Stacy Monson

His Image Publications
Plymouth, Minnesota

Scripture is taken from the New International Version of the Bible.

ISBN: 978-0-9861245-0-1 (print)
ISBN: 978-0-9861245-1-8 (ebook)

To those who struggle to be themselves—keep your focus on the One who gives you value, who loves you just as you are, and who delights in you as the person He created you to be. He adores you.

And I pray that you, being rooted and established in love, may have power, together with all the Lord's holy people, to grasp how wide and long and high and deep is the love of Christ, and to know this love that surpasses knowledge—that you may be filled to the measure of all the fullness of God.
Ephesians 3:17–19

– 1 –

"I'm fired?" Kiera Simmons' world tilted off its successful axis.

"That sounds so ugly." Margaret, the Paisley, Inc. CEO, crossed her legs and leaned back in her leather chair, tapping her fingertips together. "Since we're paying out your contract, we prefer to call it a separation. In light of the ongoing investigation, we believe your reputation is no longer conducive to representing our fashion line. I'm sure you understand."

Kiera stared at her. Understand being fired? "I wasn't involved in any of it."

"And we're glad about that, of course." Margaret's silken voice oozed condescension. "However, when we signed you as our fashion spokesmodel, we were clear your behavior both on and off camera must be above reproach."

Her dark eyes narrowed. "We're dealing with impressionable young women, Kiera. Being connected to someone like Thomas Ramsey was a poor decision that turned out to be very unpleasant for all of us." She frowned over black Armani glasses. "I pushed to get you signed because I thought you were above this sort of behavior."

Being duped by someone I cared about was bad behavior? The walls of the sterile office seemed to inch closer. Kiera lifted her chin, her breathing uneven. "You're right. I was as naïve as the rest of his constituents to think he truly had everyone's best interests in mind."

Margaret's red lips quirked. "Your focus should have remained on your job." She slid two sheets of paper across the gleaming desk. "Now if you'll sign both of these, we can all move forward."

"Termination Agreement" glowed red at the top of each page. Kiera clamped her hands together in her lap and leaned back. If Christine were here, she'd know what to do, but her former agent was halfway around the world on her honeymoon.

I didn't do anything wrong! The burn in her chest flared as the letters blurred. *They can't do this.* Thomas's actions had humiliated her on a national level, put her private life under a microscope, and almost landed her in jail. Now they were costing her the only job she knew how to do.

"I'm the best spokesmodel you've had." She leveled defiance on the woman who at one time had been her champion. "My ads brought in a fifteen percent revenue increase this year alone."

Margaret dipped her head. "But now that your name is associated with the…incident, we're hoping we don't lose that ground. The Board has decided that putting a fresh face to this next campaign may prevent that."

Kiera blinked. "What?"

"We signed Fiona for the upcoming series."

A strange buzzing filled her ears. "But we finished the first shoot for the campaign last month. Everyone said it's the best we've done. *You* said it."

"Fiona will do a wonderful job as well. She's a young, fresh face." Margaret leaned forward and clasped her hands on the desk, stilted sympathy on her powdered face. "Kiera, I know this is difficult for you, but you'll be free to try something new and…different."

The walls inched closer. Margaret's cloying perfume choked the air from the room. So this was it? Tossed aside like last year's fashion?

The phone intercom chimed once and Margaret pressed a button. "Yes?"

"Your two o'clock is here."

"Thank you. I'll be just another minute." She extended the pen to Kiera. "It's time for all of us to move on."

The craziness that had erupted with Thomas's arrest four months ago had hounded Kiera to this moment. She couldn't breathe, couldn't think. She scribbled her signature on the papers and shoved them back across the desk.

Margaret folded one and slid it inside an envelope. "This is your copy.

And the remainder of your pay. You must vacate the apartment by this Saturday, May 31st."

The apartment? Nausea churned. Of course they'd boot her out. First the job, then her home. Did they want the clothes off her back too?

Margaret stood, her gaze lifting Kiera out of the chair onto stiff legs. "We appreciate the work you did on behalf of Paisley, Kiera. We wish you the best in your future endeavors."

Moments later Kiera stood on the busy Manhattan sidewalk outside the fashion agency's headquarters, squinting against the spring sunshine. Envelope clutched in her fist, she shivered in the breeze, jostled by people hurrying past. Traffic crawled along Fifth Avenue, horns blaring, cabbies shouting and gesturing at each other. Tempted to make her own gesture at the glass office building that loomed over her, she gripped the envelope tighter. Her father had taught her better than that.

After Thomas's arrest, she'd been pursued by paparazzi, given countless statements and depositions, and taken to occasionally wearing disguises in public. The sense of doom that had lurked at the edge of every day enfolded her, pushing her off balance. Legs trembling, she looked around for a bench, for something to stop the free fall.

"That's her!" The girlish squeal scraped across her skin.

Not now. Kiera slipped her sunglasses on and turned away from the voices, wobbling a few steps before a touch on her arm stopped her, followed by a hesitant, "Excuse me?"

With a tiny sigh, she flipped the internal switch and let her face light up, turning toward the voice. "Yes?"

Three teens stood plastered together, arms linked, wide-eyed with excitement. Had she ever been that young, that awed by celebrity?

The tallest girl had a toothy smile. "Are you Kiera Simmons?"

She had been an hour ago, but now... She pulled on her professional face, hoping her smile was more than a grimace. "Yes, I am. Who would you lovely young ladies be?"

It seemed impossible but they squeezed together even tighter in a fit of giggles. Dressed in fashionably ratty jeans and ribbed camis under lightweight hoodies, they could have stepped out of one of Kiera's own ads.

"I'm Anna," the tall one answered. "This is Jamie and Mia. We just wanted to say we love your work."

"Your Paisley pictures are awesome," Jamie gushed. She rummaged through her colorful Paisley backpack and pulled out a magazine, folded open to Kiera's photograph. A deep pink infused her freckled face as she held it out. "Would you, maybe, sign this?"

"I'd love to." Stuffing the crumpled envelope into her purse, Kiera accepted the magazine and neon pink pen and glanced at the ad before signing her name to the bottom. Who was that girl with auburn hair, heart-shaped face, and light dimple in her chin? The smiling, airbrushed exterior masked emptiness inside.

Ignoring the burn in her eyes, she handed the photo and pen back to Jamie. "There you go."

The girls studied her signature, dancing with delight. Anna looked from Kiera to her friend. "Jamie's hair is almost the same color as yours."

Her friend's blush deepened as she wrapped a strand of dark red hair around her finger.

"You have beautiful hair, Jamie." Kiera forced a smile, the tremble in her legs threatening to dump her on the sidewalk. She needed to breathe. To go back in there and fight for her job. Or find a place to hide from her life. The free-fall sensation made her sway.

"Doesn't Paisley have the coolest purses?" Anna asked, then frowned. "But my mom won't let me wear the clothes yet. She says they're for older girls."

"How old are you, sweetheart?"

Anna stood taller and tossed long brown hair. "Fourteen. In three months. That's old enough to wear their stuff, right?" She released a short breath and deflated. "I don't wanna look like my kid sister. Like you said in the magazine, the right clothes can change who we are. And I want to look glamorous and beautiful like you."

I said that? The pleading in the girl's eyes touched something deep inside Kiera's battered soul. There was nothing glamorous about her life. Especially now. And being fashionable only went so far. To be thirteen again with a chance to do it over—do it right.

"You know what, Anna? It's *not* the clothes or makeup that make you beautiful." She pulled her sunglasses off and looked at each earnest face, willing them to believe her words. At some point she'd stopped believing them herself. "It's who you are inside that matters. *That's* what makes you special. Don't ever let other people tell you who you are."

The tremble intensified. "I have to run, girls. I'm so glad we met. Take care, okay?"

"Wait! Could we take a picture with you?" Anna held a sparkly red iPhone.

Kiera hesitated, then nodded. This might be the last time anyone asked. "That would be fun."

The girls squeezed close, surrounding her with giddy excitement and the fruity aroma of body wash and hair gel. Anna extended her arm and snapped the selfie.

"Thank you!" She threw her arms around Kiera. "Thanks for talking to us. You're really nice."

Kiera hugged each girl, then signaled a cab. Once inside she managed a wave and sagged against the backseat. Tears blurred her view of New York. The bright lights and endless possibilities, intoxicating when she'd arrived to start modeling eight years ago, now suffocated her.

She folded her arms tight and closed her eyes. It was time to go home—to Minnesota, to find out who she was away from the lights and cameras. The idea was more terrifying than facing hordes of paparazzi had ever been.

That evening she left a voicemail for Christine with a brief explanation of what had happened, finishing with "I'm hoping this will give us a chance to work together again." Her bravado disconnected with the call. It had been three years since she left Glitz, and Christine, for the Paisley dream job.

Too humiliated to contact anyone else, she passed the rest of the evening in silence as she stared out the floor-to-ceiling windows, watching the sun set on the greenery of Central Park.

Over the next few days, Kiera stormed through the spacious apartment, slamming personal items into boxes she'd gotten from the doorman, telling her plants just what she thought of Margaret, Thomas, and the mess she was in. They listened stoically, though she half-expected them to shrivel up in boredom from her unending rant.

On Friday morning, after another fitful sleep, Kiera rested against the chic couch cushions, fingers wrapped around a steaming mug of hazelnut coffee. The firing still didn't make sense. Following the flight of a distant plane, her eyes narrowed. Was Thomas somehow involved? An unwelcome memory stopped the breath in her throat.

Standing in the courtroom two months ago, Thomas had turned his back to his lawyer and leaned toward her. "I don't know what you think you know, Kiera, but I suggest you keep it to yourself."

She'd lifted her chin in the face of his veiled threat and crossed her arms, thankful there were no cameras in the courtroom. "Unlike you, I prefer the truth."

His eyes took on a hint of steel. This wasn't the same man who nearly a year earlier had charmed her into a high-celebrity relationship. "I'd be careful with that attitude, Miss Spokesmodel. It could end your successful career."

She pushed the memory away and sipped her coffee. "God, I know I haven't made time for you lately," she whispered, "so maybe you don't have time for me but...what do I do now?"

– 2 –

A smattering of applause followed the last chords of the song. "Thank you. You've been a great audience." *All twenty of you.* Peter Theisen squinted to see past the stage lights from his piano bench. "I appreciate you stopping by the Maxim Theater onboard the *Royale* to hear me tonight. I'm sure the ship's casino is calling to you, so here's my last song."

He ran his fingers over the ivories. "I wrote this for my Gram. I miss her like crazy." He forced a smile. "This is 'Pinecones and Clover.' I hope you enjoy it."

The song stirred bittersweet memories of life at the cabin—sunlight dancing across the lake, the lonely call of a loon, shooting stars in a black sky. He'd sung the familiar words almost every night for the past six months, but the melody still evoked her smile of encouragement. No one had believed in him more.

The last notes faded into applause. "Thank you. Enjoy the rest of your evening aboard the *Royale.* Goodnight."

As the small crowd dispersed, a white-haired couple stopped at the edge of the stage to shake his hand and share memories of their favorite songs, a few of which Peter had sung. Hearing them compare his music to Frank Sinatra, Perry Como, and other crooners from that bygone era sent a thrill down to his scuffed dress shoes.

Most of the people who visited his show were friendly, occasionally boisterous, and often tipsy. At the end of long days in the sun, they needed a few drinks and a chance to relax. More than once he'd put people to sleep. He chose to take it as a compliment.

The couple moved on and Peter collected his cheat sheets. Landing this cruise line job had seemed like an answer to prayer after years of doing landscape construction and singing in coffeehouses and dinner clubs. He lived to sing, to make people smile, but twenty-three weeks of the same gig six nights a week had worn him down.

He swayed with the gentle motion of the ship. In eight days he'd be back on land, figuring out what to do next. The thought of another summer hauling landscape boulders made his back ache. He could only hope Bill had something else planned. That's what agents were for, weren't they?

"Nice show, man." A stocky, balding man with a warm smile hopped up on the stage and held out a hand.

"Thanks. Glad you enjoyed it."

"I've enjoyed all of them, actually. I sat in on one part or another every night this week."

Peter grinned and released his hand. "Couldn't find anything better to do?"

The man chuckled. "Actually, I made a point of stopping in. I'm Mark."

"Peter. Obviously." He gestured to a table beside the stage and they settled across from each other. "I appreciate repeat customers."

Mark leaned forward, elbows on the table. His round, bearded face was sunburned, his nose peeling. Green eyes smiled behind wire-rimmed glasses. "I like your voice and your style, Peter. You've got a great mix of original songs and classics with a contemporary twist. Very unique."

"Thanks." He never tired of hearing positive comments. Probably because he'd heard so few growing up. In his parents' eyes, his dream of a singing career had never measured up to the medical and legal careers of his siblings.

"How many months have you been performing onboard?"

"Almost six. I've got one more week. I seriously need to regain my land legs."

"My wife and I have been onboard for five days and I'm starting to feel that way," Mark said with a chuckle. "Peter, I'm impressed with how you handle yourself onstage. You have a relaxed style that resonates with the audience. That's not something you can force. Either they connect with you or they don't. Yours do."

Gram had told him to be mindful of the audience, that performing wasn't all about him. "Thanks. You sound like you know the business."

"I'm a music producer."

"I see." He'd met a music producer in the middle of the ocean?

"You don't have any commercial albums out yet, right?"

"Just the demo. My manager said we'd work on it once I'm off the ship."

"Who's your manager? Maybe I know him."

"Bill Djerf."

Mark's expression remained neutral. "A big name in the music industry."

Peter dipped his head. So he'd been told and not just by Bill himself. "I signed on about eighteen months ago after he heard one of my coffeehouse gigs. He's had me performing in every possible venue ever since. Including this one."

"A good way to hone your craft. You have amazing potential, Peter." Mark settled back and cleaned his glasses with the hem of his polo shirt. "I'm always looking for new talent. I'd like to produce your first CD."

"Seriously?" *Smooth, Theisen.* "Have you been producing long?"

The corners of Mark's mouth twitched. "A number of years now. I think I've got the hang of it. Would you like to give my studio a try?"

"Sure!" His feet tingled. Good thing he couldn't dance or he'd be on the table making a fool of himself. "I need to discuss it with Bill before I give you a firm answer, though."

"Good idea." Mark pulled a business card from his wallet. "Here's my contact info. Talk it over and get back to me. If you're interested, I think I could get you in around the first of June. I have a few other projects pending so if I don't hear back from you in the next two weeks, I'll move ahead with them."

He stood and extended his hand. "I think you've got a great career ahead of you, Peter. Even if we don't work together, I fully expect to hear your music on the circuit soon. Good luck."

"Thanks." Peter watched him thread his way between the tables, then dropped back into the chair, studying the business card. *Mark Simmons, Simmons Music Production.* The name was familiar. Minneapolis, Minnesota? Gram's image leaped to mind, and he smiled. Her cabin was a few hours north of there.

He pulled out his iPhone and Googled the studio. After several toe-tapping minutes waiting to connect, he skimmed the results, mouth open. No wonder the name sounded familiar. Mark Simmons had just received his 13th Grammy Award.

Eyes closed, Peter smacked his forehead. And he'd asked Mark if he'd been producing long. *What an idiot!* While he'd researched producers in Nashville and L.A., he hadn't considered Minnesota. The list of studio clients punched the air from his lungs. *The guy who produces CDs for the amazing NightVision is going to produce mine?*

He shot to his feet, grabbed his folder and hurried out of the empty theater. If he was recording a CD at SMP, he'd better be ready. He needed to write more songs. Practice every free minute. And revisit the song he wrote for Gram before she died. That *had* to be on his first CD.

Taking the narrow crew-only stairs two at a time, he spoke his promise aloud. "Just a little longer, Gram, and I'll prove to everyone you were right to believe in me."

Kiera slung her bag over her shoulder and faced the townhouse as the cab drove away with a spray of gravel. The flight home to Minnesota had been three hours of turbulent emotions. She stood still and pulled in a breath of crisp, late evening air. Spring in Minneapolis meant the sweet aroma of lilacs, stars winking through budding tree branches, the gentle music of crickets. And peacefulness.

No car horns or neon lights. No crowded sidewalks or nonstop, pulsing energy. Every time she came home, she was reminded of how different this place was from Manhattan.

Being the Paisley spokesmodel had kept her living in New York far more than here with Terese. She'd been a lousy part-time roommate, but having this safe haven had ensured her sanity amidst a crazy life. A tiny smile touched her mouth. This was where she needed to be now as she decided what to do next.

Colorful ceramic pots overflowing with petunias, geraniums, and greenery filled the townhome's landing and dotted the stairs. Her smile widened. Yet again, Terese's green thumb welcomed her home.

She started up the sidewalk pulling a carry-on stuffed with the few things that hadn't fit in the boxes she'd shipped home yesterday. When she found the strength, she'd get rid of whatever held bad memories. Which would be most—

The front door flew open. "Girlfriend, it's about time you got here."

Kiera returned her best friend's enthusiastic hug. "Sorry for showing up so late, Tess."

Terese Matsuyama stepped back, hands on her hips, and grinned. "Since when is eleven o'clock late for you New York types? I'm just glad you've shown up period. Here, let me take the carry-on. Ooo, nice purse. Is that a Burberry?"

"Yup. Want it?"

Laughing, Terese led the way inside. "Oh, right. Like you'd let go of something that gorgeous."

Kiera dropped the shoulder bag in the entryway. "I don't want it." If only she could shed the memories as easily.

Her gaze roamed the familiar living room. Contemporary with Asian accents. A floral aroma tinged with citrus. Instrumental music in the background, candlelight casting a gentle glow. She sighed. "Wow, it's good to be home."

Terese stood the carry-on in the middle of the Oriental rug and folded her arms. "I was stunned when you called to say you were moving back. I can't wait to hear what happened to tear you away from the Big Apple."

As dark, almond-shaped eyes searched her face, Kiera looked away. Still processing how her world had been knocked off its foundation, she couldn't admit she'd been fired. At least, not tonight. Uttering the words would unleash emotions she wasn't ready to face.

"But," Terese said, "since you look wiped out, let's get your stuff in your room so you can crash. We'll talk in the morning."

I'm home. The realization echoed through her mind, draping over the chaos like satin, soothing the burn in her chest. Throat tight, she croaked, "Thanks, Tess."

Terese left her with a hug, closing the bedroom door with a quiet click. Kiera stood still for a long moment, listening to the silence of her life. She slid into her worn Paisley pajamas and went into the bathroom to wash her face. Patting her skin dry, she studied her reflection. Without makeup, hair in a disheveled ponytail, it was an unremarkable face. A smattering of freckles against pale skin, a longish nose, a high forehead. Dark eyebrows in need of tweezing.

What had been a face owned first by Glitz and then by Paisley was now the face of someone who had no clue who she was anymore. She smoothed moisturizer onto that face, the way she'd been instructed so many years ago, brushed her teeth the way she'd been told, then shut off the light. She climbed into bed and turned off the bedside lamp. In the darkness, she released the breath she'd held since the meeting in Margaret's office and let the tears come.

– 3 –

Late the next morning, they sat in the sunny yellow kitchen drinking coffee and discussing Terese's wedding details. Her roommate's round, animated face was lit with joy, sending a discordant note through Kiera's chest. Honestly thrilled about next April's wedding, she couldn't imagine ever being this over-the-moon kind of happy.

Thomas had embezzled not just money but her faith in people. And the firing had erased the last of her trust. As much as she loved sharing in the wedding plans, it was yet another reminder of how alone she truly was.

"I'm really glad we went with those colors," Terese said. "I think they'll look great on the three of you. Remember the flowers in old Mrs. Olson's yard? That's what they remind me of."

Kiera nodded. "She might have been the neighborhood's biggest crank, but nobody could beat her gardening."

She watched Terese start another pot of coffee, thankful for this enduring friendship. Since third grade they'd been inseparable. Mutt and Jeff, her dad had called them. Terese's tiny stature and straight black hair was the opposite of her own tall frame and wavy red hair. Terese was direct, funny, a bundle of words and energy.

"A cord of three strands isn't easily broken." Terese often quoted the Bible verse. "Between you, me, and God, we can handle anything. But you have to be willing to let me in when things go wrong."

Kiera released a silent breath. It was the one stumbling block that remained after twenty years of laughter, mischief, and friendship. She needed to admit what really brought her home but, as usual, the words stuck in her throat. Perfection had been drilled into her for so long, the thought of admitting defeat made her nauseous.

Terese refilled their mugs then settled in her chair. Lips pursed, she met Kiera's gaze. "Kier, I'm glad you're home. I didn't want to bring this up on the phone."

"That doesn't sound good." She wrapped her fingers around the mug. Could you get fired from being a best friend?

"It's not bad. Not really. It's just...Jason is being considered for a promotion."

"That's great!" Kiera cocked her head. "Isn't it?"

"It's fabulous. He's thrilled." Terese lowered her chin, looking like she might apologize. "It's in Germany."

Germany? "That's so...far."

"I know. I can't decide if I'm excited or scared or sad. Or all three." Tears filled her dark eyes. "New York was bad enough but at least you or I could hop on a plane to spend the weekend together. Germany is really far. But maybe," she managed a wobbling smile, "you can convince them to do a photo shoot there?"

No job and soon no best friend. There wasn't much left to lose. "When will he find out?"

"September first. If they pick him, he'll work between here and there for the six months before the wedding. Our honeymoon would be spent moving to Europe." She lifted her hands. "I guess there could be worse honeymoons."

"Wow." Despite the lump that settled deep in her stomach, Kiera pulled on her camera-ready face. Eyebrows relaxed, eyes bright. Smile. "What an opportunity for him. For both of you. What will you do with the townhouse?"

"Probably sell it. Unless you want it?"

"No, you sell it. Who knows where I'll be next April."

Terese frowned. "Not still here?"

Studying her half-empty mug, a burst of humiliation clogged Kiera's throat and she closed her eyes.

"Hon, you're scaring me. What's wrong?"

A deep sigh lowered her shoulders as she whispered, "They fired me."

Kiera stood on the front step of her childhood home, her finger hovering over the doorbell. She fought the urge to hide in the old treehouse like she had when she'd accidentally broken her father's new lure. And after getting detention for skipping class. Like she'd wanted to the day the police stopped by their lunch table and arrested Thomas.

She closed her eyes, rummaging through her chaotic emotions for courage. After her father's cancer scare two years ago, they'd been closer than ever, but she'd rather rip her acrylic nails off than see his disappointment.

Pulling in a sharp breath, she pushed her shoulders back and let her finger touch the bell. In the silence that followed, she tugged on her model smile.

The door swung open and she set her hands on her hips. "Surprise!"

Buck Simmons' green eyes went wide as a smile filled his pale face. "Well, look what blew in from the East Coast."

Tears sprang up as his arms wrapped around her. He felt thinner than when he'd visited New York just a month ago. She stepped back, laughing as she brushed at her wet cheeks. "Boy, I guess it's been awhile since I've been home."

"Far too long. Come in, come in. Don't know why you rang the bell in the first place."

Settling in the living room, the tears stayed just below the surface. Every inch of the room was familiar, from her mother's teacup collection in the hutch to the shelves lined with his award-winning woodcarvings, photos, and items she'd sent back from her travels. The house even smelled the same—coffee and burnt toast.

They chatted about the neighborhood, what her cousins were up to, and his latest woodworking designs. His words seemed stilted, his energy forced. He deflected most of her questions, asking his own that she deflected back.

Her wandering gaze landed on the white folder on the table beside him. She remembered that folder. She'd hated everything it stood for. Why would he have dug out that old information? Unless… She looked at his hands, bony and calloused. The telltale signs of needle marks sent the room into a hazy spin. *No. He would have said something.* "Dad."

He paused mid-sentence, eyebrows raised, then folded his hands and looked away.

"Are you—is it…?" She couldn't say the word. "Why didn't you tell me?"

Picking at his worn sweatpants, he sighed. "You've been so busy, Kiki, and so stressed about what happened with Thomas. I didn't want to burden you."

"Burden me! You could never be a burden to me." They hadn't defeated the lung cancer after all—they'd only pushed it to the background. Tears seared her throat.

"Honey, you don't need to be worrying about me in the middle of your busy life. I'm handling it just fine."

"That's not fair. Maybe I want to handle it with you." She tried to blink sense into the turmoil in her brain.

After a pained silence, he nodded. "You're right. I should have told you. But Mark's been a big help—"

"Mark? You told Mark but not me?" His guilty expression sent her to her feet. It was *her* job to look after her father. "How long have you known?"

"Ten, twelve days."

The truth was like a slap to the head. And heart. "You weren't going to tell me."

"Of course I was." The grim line of his mouth made him look far older than sixty-two. "Soon. I just didn't want you to worry."

"Let *me* decide if I'm going to worry." She whirled and yanked open the window, then released a slow breath to loosen the clench of her jaw. Two boys rode by on bikes, popsicles in hand. An older woman walked a tiny white poodle with a red bow at its ear. The world outside enjoyed a normal afternoon while her life continued to fall apart.

Since her mother's death twenty years ago, they'd been a family of two.

She couldn't imagine life without him. She wouldn't. She wrestled the anger and hurt down, turning her focus toward action. "Okay, so tell me the plan."

"We started chemo this past Tuesday. Doc hopes we can knock the cancer down until I can get into a study at the university. There's a new drug he thinks would work, but my counts have to be right before I can get in."

Crossing the room on wooden legs, she knelt beside his chair and rested her hands on his arm. "We beat it once, Dad. We can do it again." Despite the tumult in her chest, she kept her tone matter-of-fact. "We know what to expect this time."

He nodded, covering her hand with his. "The good and the bad."

"Well, the bad won't take us by surprise this time. We'll stay on top of it. I'll make the banana bread you like, and we'll have lots of ice cream on hand in case you don't feel good."

The corners of his mouth lifted and the old chair creaked as he leaned forward to press a kiss to her forehead. The familiar scratch of his whiskers calmed her rising fear. He smelled of wood and aftershave and life. "Your mother would be proud of you, Kiki. You've got her heart."

"And your stubbornness. This cancer isn't getting the best of you. I won't let it."

He chuckled. "I like the way you think. Between you and God, I'm in good hands." He squeezed her fingers, rested his head back and closed his eyes. "God is good, isn't He?"

Her normal response of "all the time" wouldn't come. God didn't seem to care that her life was falling apart one piece at a time. But what did she expect after ignoring Him for the past few years? The ring of her cell phone cut off her retort.

She patted his arm and stood, pulling the phone from her pocket. "It's Christine, my agent when I worked at Glitz. I'll take it outside, and then I'll make some fresh coffee."

"Sounds good, Honey."

Passing through the kitchen toward the back door, she answered the call. "Hello and why are you calling me back on your honeymoon?"

There was a pause before the familiar voice crackled to life. "Hi, sweetie.

Don't worry…more honeymo…than work."

"I should hope so. You got my voice mail?" She closed the screen door gently behind her.

"I…"

"What? I didn't catch that." The connection between this wooded backyard in Minneapolis and an island off the coast of Italy was sketchy.

"…voice mail. Kiera…not good…I wish you had called…"

"I know, but she was pushing me to sign it, and at that point I just needed to get out of there." The shaggy grass tickled the sides of her sandaled feet as she paced. "If they think so little of me because of Thomas's behavior, I don't want to work for them. Anyway, we can talk about it once the honeymoon is over."

"…understand. But Kiera…non-compete…"

She stopped. The hairs on her arms stood upright. "What?"

"…non-compete agreement…You can't speak…competitors…a year."

The world that had tilted at the firing now stopped with the screech of rusty brakes. She'd signed a non-compete agreement?

"Kiera?"

"I'm here. I can't—" She squeezed the bridge of her nose. "Does that mean I can't model either?"

"Not necessar…I'll look into…Hon, we'll talk when I get back… Don't panic."

Easy to say while honeymooning with a man worth ten million dollars. "Okay. Go have fun." *While I sit here trying to figure out why God pulled the plug on my life.*

Clicking off the call, she stood very still, waiting. For a message from heaven. A phone call saying Margaret had changed her mind. Her father to say it was all a joke.

Birds twittered overhead. A plane droned in the distance. The normally sweet smell of fresh-cut grass churned her stomach. As she sank onto the picnic table, the tightness in her throat seeped down into her chest. *Where are you, God? Why is this happening?*

A disorienting sense of panic sucked the breath from her. No job. No career. Soon no best friend. And now her father…

She dropped her face into her hands. *Help me help him. I don't know what to do.*

No answer. No promise of healing, no overwhelming sense of peace. Nothing. She pulled in a shaky breath, wiped away the tears, and straightened her spine. Okay then. With no divine message from heaven, she'd just get on with what needed to be done. Maybe God would have something wise and comforting to say later. Not that she deserved it, but her father did.

– 4 –

Peter finished the exit process in record time. This stint on the *Royale* was another rung on his ladder to success, according to Bill. Another step closer to his dream of stardom. But one more week in that cramped room would have sent him over the railing.

He dodged passengers ambling down the ramp and scanned the waiting vehicles for Bill's silver Mercedes. Spotting the convertible outside the wrought-iron fence, he jogged over and tossed his duffel bags into the open trunk, slammed it shut and slid into the passenger seat. "Hey, Bill. Thanks for picking me up."

"Welcome to dry land." Bill pulled away from the curb and headed toward his townhouse in Miami Beach. "How'd it go?"

"Good. Interesting experience." He glanced sideways. Bill's white sunglasses reflected palm trees and office buildings as he maneuvered through the busy city. "But it's not something I'd want to do again."

"I can understand that."

"You can?" He'd prepared for an unpleasant reaction. Bill didn't appreciate dissension in his ranks.

Bill's chuckle seemed genuine. "After your email last month, I was afraid you'd throw yourself overboard before finishing the assignment."

"Another week and I might have." He settled back in the seat. "Ships are a little too confining for this Iowa boy."

"That's what gin and tonic is for." Bill shot him a wink. "Might be a good thing for you to try once in a while, just to loosen up."

Peter managed a weak smile and closed his eyes. He'd seen what drinking had done to his grandfather. He wasn't about to follow that path, no matter how many times Bill suggested it.

To be under the management of William Djerf III was an honor, not to mention an impressive detail to wave in front of those who said he'd never make it. With over two decades in the music industry, there wasn't a better manager in the business. Or one with a bigger ego or shorter fuse.

Even if he didn't make it big, this opportunity was something he'd never forget. Bill wouldn't let him.

"Anyway," Bill said, "I've got you set up for a new gig starting a week from tomorrow."

"What?" Peter sat up. "I just finished a long gig stuck on a boat. I need a break."

"Peter, Peter." Bill ran a hand through his thick blond hair, sunshine glinting off the rings that crowded his fingers. "Building a career is hard work. You don't have the luxury of time off right now. This isn't high school sports. You're about to hit the big leagues."

Every inch of his body ached with exhaustion. "Even major leaguers get a break once in a while."

"This gig is Las Vegas, baby. Believe me, you don't want to pass that up."

"I do if the choice is recording a CD instead." He shifted in his seat. "Did you get my voice mails? I tried calling from our last port in St. Thomas. I met Mark Simmons last week and he offered to produce my first CD!"

The car lurched to a stop at the red light and Bill's head turned sharply. "You met Mark Simmons?"

"You know him?"

"We've tried to work together a few times."

"Tried?" Peter's stomach twisted. He'd assumed Bill would be thrilled.

"Let's just say we operate on different wavelengths. But the man cranks out number one albums, I'll give him that. I've never understood why he operates so far from the action. I mean, Minnesota? Give me a break."

Peter's excitement blew out of the car as they accelerated past a truck. It had seemed like a good omen to make his first CD so close to his happiest memories. "I want to work with him."

"After Las Vegas."

Peter pulled an image of Gram to mind. "Instead of Las Vegas."

The muscles in Bill's jaw worked as he weaved sharply through traffic. Peter resisted the urge to rub the bridge of his nose. Bill had ordered him to drop the nervous habit.

"I'm not Vegas material, Bill. I wouldn't fit there." He didn't fit in much of anywhere but definitely not in Vegas.

The convertible rolled through a stop sign. A van to the left screeched to a stop and honked. Bill gestured. Peter slid down in his seat.

"Mark Simmons is not my first choice," Bill said through clenched teeth.

"But he's got a great track record." He'd never argued with Bill, but this was worth fighting for. He'd tackle heaven and earth—and Bill—to keep Gram's memory alive. This CD would do just that. His heart took up a disjointed pounding. "He said I've got great potential. And he *offered* to produce my first album."

Bill's silence stretched for two blocks. "Fine. Since he offered, I guess we'd better grab the opportunity." There wasn't a trace of excitement in his voice. "*If* I can get you out of the gig in Vegas."

The car zipped past the last of the downtown buildings into blinding sunshine. Peter squinted, a thrill nearly lifting him out of his seat. He'd dreamed of being a singer since his voice changed in eighth grade. Now, at twenty-five, he was ready to take on the world. Or at least a crowd bigger than the lounge on the *Royale*.

A week later, he followed Bill through glass doors and into the opportunity he'd been impatiently waiting for. *Let the journey begin.*

"Welcome to Simmons Music Production, gentlemen." The middle-aged woman behind the front desk stood and held out a hand, her smile warm. "I'm Mary. You must be Peter."

He nodded as he shook her hand. "Peter Theisen. Nice to meet you."

She turned her smile to Bill. "And Mr. Djerf, we've met before. It's nice to see you again."

He gave a curt nod. "Mary."

Apparently Bill planned to punish everyone through this whole project. Peter smiled at the woman. "We're a little early. We weren't sure what traffic would be like."

"I'm glad you made it here safely. Mark is finishing up a meeting so it will be just a few minutes." She gestured toward the corner counter stocked with a coffee machine and small refrigerator. "Would you like coffee or a cold beverage?"

"I'll get a water, thanks." Peter headed toward the corner.

"How about a Bloody Mary, Mary?" Bill's question held only a partial note of humor.

"I'm afraid we don't have that, Mr. Djerf," she said pleasantly. "Perhaps a strong cup of black coffee will do instead?"

Peter bit back a chuckle and focused on opening the bottled water. He liked Mary already. He took a long swig, studying the reception area of the place that would be home for the next few months. The comfortable leather furniture, oak tables, and recessed lighting made the room welcoming, almost homey.

Mark's success and reputation could mean a high-gloss setting, but this seemed to reflect what Peter had experienced with him. Relaxed, down-to-earth, a regular guy. Who cranked out megahit albums.

Settling into a chair, he picked up a *People* magazine and turned to the cover article. He studied the actor's clothing, the relaxed way he wore a T-shirt and jeans in one photo, then in a tux with a gorgeous brunette beside him in another. The guy looked every bit the star Peter planned to become.

The front door swung open and he glanced up, then stared. A tall redhead strode into the studio, headed toward the front counter. Dressed in a light green jacket, skinny jeans and short boots, she was a magazine ad come alive.

"Kiera!" Mary hurried around the counter to hug her. "We didn't expect you until July."

"I'm surprising everyone. It's good to see you, Mary." Her voice was warm, deeper than Peter expected. "Is Mark in? I need to talk to him about something. Then I'd love to catch up."

"They've just finished up in the edit suite. You can wait in his office, if you'd like."

Peter watched the young woman move around the counter, long hair gleaming under the lights, and disappear down the hall.

Bill nudged his foot. "You can close your mouth now, Theisen."

He snapped his mouth shut, straightened in the chair, and shrugged. "You don't see women like her every day."

"You'll have your pick once you're on tour." Bill popped a blue pill into his mouth and took a swig of soda. "Speaking of which, you know I had other studios in mind for your CD. Simmons will have to do some fancy talking to make me change my mind."

Peter pushed to his feet and muttered he needed the bathroom. Mary pointed him down the hall in the direction the redhead had gone. He wandered the carpeted hallway, admiring the framed albums lining the paneled walls. Photos of the artist and Mark, and apparently the studio staff, were posted beside each record.

The studio was larger than it looked from the outside: one long main hallway with several shorter ones breaking off. Peter discovered four practice rooms, each with a baby grand piano. Farther down, a staff lunchroom, and double doors marked Rehearsal Room. After locating the bathroom, he meandered back toward the lobby, in no hurry to listen to Bill's sniping.

"Are you kidding?" An angry female voice in a room just ahead made him pause midstride. "How about my father not telling me the cancer was back? Or him calling you instead of me? Or maybe when *you* decided not to tell me."

"Oh, that," a man answered.

"Oh, that?" Her voice rose. "*That* is my father, Mark. It's my place to be with him during this, not left out because I was in New York."

"Let's sit down and—"

"I don't want to sit down! I want you to explain yourself. This was the lowest," her voice cracked, "most hurtful thing you could have done to me."

"I know. I'm sorry."

In the silence that followed, Peter wavered. Sneak by and hope to go unnoticed? Stay put?

"Why didn't you tell me?" Her words were a strangled whisper.

A heavy sigh followed. "He asked me not to, kid. I should have, but he was adamant about not telling you until you came home in July. Why are you so early, anyway?"

"Don't change the subject."

Whoever Mark was arguing with wasn't going to be distracted from her mission. Time to make a break past the door.

"Look, I've got a new client here," Mark said, "so how about you wait in my office for a bit."

"Fine, but we aren't—"

Peter was almost past the door when he collided with the redhead as she stormed from the room. She stopped short and caught her balance, fiery green eyes turning on him. "Do you mind? This is a private conversation."

"Sorry." He took a few steps back. "I just went…I was going…"

"Peter!" Mark threw a dark glance at Kiera before smiling at him, hand extended in greeting. "Good to see you. We're just finishing up here so go on in and have a seat. I'll be right back." He took her elbow and directed her down the hall. "Be as mad as you want at me," he said sternly as they walked away, "but don't use that New York attitude in this office."

Her reply was inaudible. Peter went into the room and sat at the midpoint of the long meeting table. When those green eyes had locked on him, his heart had tried to leap out of his chest.

He swiveled back and forth in the chair. If he met someone like her on tour, he'd be so tongue-tied he wouldn't be able to speak. A corner of his mouth twitched. And having heard her arguing skills, he wouldn't last one round with her. She'd make a good lawyer. Just showing up and turning that blazing look on the jury would win the case.

He shook his head and grunted. Even if his album made it big, he'd still be the Iowa boy stumbling his way through life, trying to prove he belonged in the big leagues. And keeping his distance from women like—

"Hi." The greeting held an apologetic tone.

He swung around, then scrambled to his feet. His chair crashed into the wall behind him.

The redhead had returned.

– 5 –

She waited in the doorway, hands clasped before her. Tall and slender, she stood just shy of his six foot one with her high-heeled boots. His pulse ticked wildly in his throat as they faced each other. With flawless skin and a dusting of freckles across her nose, she was amazing up close. Her posture and expensive clothes gave an aura of significance.

"Hi." Like an awestruck thirteen-year-old, he folded his arms across his chest and rubbed the bridge of his nose then stopped. He shoved his hands into his pockets.

"I wanted to say…" Her hesitant words were several decibels lower than moments earlier. She pulled in a short breath and stepped into the room. "I'm sorry for being rude. I have no excuse for blasting you like that." Her shy smile revealed a dimple in her chin. "I hope you won't think poorly of Mark."

"Of course not. I'd been to the…I was heading back…" He rolled his eyes. "Sorry I almost knocked you down."

"No harm done." Her brow relaxed as she held out her hand. "I'm Kiera Simmons."

"Peter Theisen." He released her warm fingers reluctantly. "Nice to meet you."

"You too."

"So." He cleared his throat. "How long have you and Mark been married?"

An unladylike snort erupted and she pressed her fingertips to her mouth.

Idiot! Why not just ask her age and weight? "Sorry. I shouldn't have asked that."

She lowered her hand, a smile playing at the corners of her lips. "He's my cousin. My much older cousin. I think he and Bethany have been married about eighteen years."

"Oh. Wow." He wiped the sweat from his upper lip. "Stupid question."

"Since we have the same last name, it makes sense." The dimple deepened in her chin. "Especially since I was in here yelling at him."

"Yeah, well…" It was amazing how many feet he could stuff in his mouth. "Okay, how about this. Do you live around here?"

She smiled, a real smile that reached her incredible green eyes. His heart ramped back up.

"Just moved home from New York City. How about you?"

"Myrtle, Iowa."

"I've been through there. It's nice."

In a small town sort of way. "I like it better here. My family has a cabin in Nisswa. I loved spending the summers up there with my grandparents."

Leaning lightly against the table, she crossed one ankle over the other. The anger gone, she was relaxed, poised. Gorgeous. "Isn't Nisswa a pretty area? My dad and I did a lot of camping up there. And our favorite little resort is there too."

"It's my favorite place in the world. It's where I learned to play piano and camp in the woods and water ski and…" He bit his lip to stop the flood of words. He *sounded* like a thirteen-year-old.

"It's a wonderful place." She tilted her head. "So you're a musician?"

"Mainly I sing. I met Mark on the cruise ship where I performed, and he offered to produce my CD." No need to mention it was his first.

An odd shadow flickered across her face. "You're a client?"

"Here you are." Bill's voice cut between them as he and Mark entered the conference room, his cologne reaching them before he did. "Doesn't surprise me you have a fan already."

Instant heat in his face, Peter glanced at Kiera.

Mark stopped beside her. "Bill, I'd like you to meet my cousin, Kiera Simmons. Kiera, this is Bill Djerf, Peter's manager."

She smiled as they shook hands. "Welcome to SMP, Mr. Djerf."

"Thank you, little lady. I feel right at home being welcomed by such a pretty gal. Mark sure knows how to decorate." He towered over her, a leer on his tan face. Then his eyes narrowed. "Wait, weren't you…"

Her smile froze as she tried to withdraw her hand.

He nodded emphatically. "That's right. You're the gal in the news. The big blowup with the financial—"

"Old news, Bill." Mark turned toward Peter. "Did you two get a chance to introduce yourselves?"

Peter met Kiera's shuttered gaze, wanting to leap into an apology for whatever Bill had done. He winked and received a faint smile in response. "We have a shared interest in Nisswa."

"Great. Kiera will be working with us this summer so she can answer any questions you have about getting around town. She's worked here off and on for years."

Her eyes, remarkably similar to Mark's, widened and jumped to her cousin. That seemed to be news to her.

"Kiera, can I see you in my office?" Mark said. "Gentlemen, if you don't mind, there are just a few things I need to cover with Kiera before we get started. Please make yourselves comfortable. I'll be back shortly."

Peter watched them leave the room. Shoulders back, chin up, her easy stride emanated confidence. He wanted that style.

"Okay." Bill pulled out a chair at the head of the table. "Let's talk strategy before Simmons comes back. We need a plan if we decide to go forward with this."

If? Peter retrieved his chair and sat, making a fist to recapture the feel of Kiera Simmons' firm grip. She was the prettiest girl he'd seen in a long time. Ah, who was he kidding? She was gorgeous. And out of his league. *Classy girls like her aren't interested in nerds like you, Theisen. Even nerds who can sing.*

Kiera walked beside Mark, teeth clenched. Once again she'd been recognized because of the overhyped scandal. At least Peter hadn't seemed to know her.

A tiny smile unlocked her jaw. Calling him cute was an understatement. Thick curly hair, brown eyes that crinkled at the corners when he smiled, dimples at either side of his mouth, and a bashfulness she rarely saw anymore. The combination would have women chasing him in no time, if they weren't already.

She released a silent breath. But if Peter was Mark's client, it meant one thing—he wanted his share of fame, fortune, and bright lights. She'd spent years around self-important people clawing their way to the top, trampling everyone in their way. How long had she been one of them?

"So now you've met the famous Bill Djerf." Mark's voice broke the silence as they reached his office. He motioned to a chair beside his desk.

"He's famous?" She wrinkled her nose. "For what?"

"For what you just saw." He swiveled his chair to face her. "He has an ego the size of Texas, even though he's from Kentucky. And a way of talking down to people he's just met. He makes things happen for his clients, but he's not someone to tangle with."

"Some people just like to hear themselves talk."

"Well, I don't want him talking about you so I'll be watching him while they're here."

A smile touched her heart. The oldest of her three cousins, Mark was her lifelong protector and defender. "So what's this about me working here?"

His eyebrows lifted. "Anything you want to tell me about New York?"

"Why?" She barked the word, then pulled on a calm expression despite the quiver in her chest. News had spread already?

"I called Buck when you went back to apologize. He told me you're here for the summer." He folded his hands and leaned forward on his desk. "I'm all ears."

She looked past him to the spring-green leaves fluttering outside his window. "I'm here to spend the summer with Dad."

After a loud silence, he shook his head. "Kiera, you've never been good at lying. You can't even look me in the eye."

She met his gaze directly. "No comment."

He threw his head back with a laugh. "Okay, I get it. We'll talk when you're ready."

Shifting in the chair, she looked away. She wasn't ready to broadcast her failure.

"Well, regardless of why you're here," he continued, "your timing is perfect. Mary wants to take the summer off to babysit her grandkids, but my production assistant ran off to L.A. with one of my clients last month. Mary deserves the time off but I'm too swamped to train in a temp. You've done just about every job around here over the years so you know how things work. It's a God-thing you showed up when you did. So how about helping me out?"

She let his request sink in as her gaze roamed the familiar office. Trophies were crammed on corner shelves. Papers and CDs covered the round meeting table, an Arby's bag on its side atop the mess. On the wall behind him hung artwork by his two preteen daughters beside a photo of him and Bethany at an awards banquet.

Comfortable clutter welcoming her home from a world that allowed no imperfection, no disorder. No forgiveness. But trying to fill in for Mary would be impossible. She'd been Mark's right hand from the day the studio opened.

"I would have no clue how to do Mary's job. You're safer with a temp."

"You know the staff," he countered, "and how the studio runs."

"And I can make copies and pour coffee, but that doesn't make me qualified to run the front desk."

"Can you operate a computer?"

"Very funny."

"And I know you can answer the phone. Can you take a message?"

She folded her arms, as much in fear as annoyance. "Mark, I'm not even slightly quali—"

"Any modeling jobs on the schedule?"

"No, but—"

"You're hired." Grinning, he leaned back in his chair. "You can start on

Wednesday. Mary will get you trained in before she leaves."

Heart fluttering against her ribs, she frowned. She'd just endured months of public humiliation. Did she really need to do it again? *I know nothing about running an office. Or anything else that doesn't require makeup, hairstyling, and clothes.*

"Kiera, if I didn't think you could handle it, I wouldn't ask. I'm not a glutton for punishment."

Her frown wavered as she studied him. His goatee sported a few more gray hairs, and his hairline continued its march toward the back of his head. But he was the same guy who'd been encouraging her, cheering for her since she could walk.

Maybe if she could avoid Bill Djerf, this might be a safe place to regroup. "Dad would be indebted to you for keeping me out of what little hair he has left."

"And I'll be indebted to you for helping me keep my head above water."

"I like it when you're in my debt."

He chuckled then grew serious. "There is one stipulation, however."

She waited.

"You aren't allowed to wear full combat makeup when you're in the office."

She rolled her eyes. Never one to appreciate her professional look, he'd called it full combat since she started modeling. "Hmm. That could be a deal breaker." She was only half-kidding.

"I'm serious, kid. I miss the real Kiera."

Was she brave enough to do it? Anna and her friends leaped to mind. It was time to put her own words into action. It was time to get real. She nodded. "It's a deal."

With a rumbling laugh, he came around the desk and swept her into a hug. His were the best, even when they squeezed the very air from her lungs. She offered a silent prayer of thanks. Maybe God hadn't totally abandoned her.

– 6 –

Kiera settled in the back corner of the spacious rehearsal room, eager to soak in the growing energy from the group that had gathered. She'd gotten to know many of the musicians and all of the staff over the years. It was like being back among family now.

She studied the familiar faces as they greeted each other and waved at her. There was James at the piano, running through one of the songs. Alonzo, amazing on the synthesizer. Jeff, the drummer Mark had specifically chosen for this CD. And Martha, violinist extraordinaire.

Peter stood at the front of the room looking through a handful of papers. Deep-set eyes and the shadow of a beard, jeans and a light green T-shirt—the perfect look for a CD cover. Yet his striking looks were a contrast to his sometimes awkward demeanor, especially around her.

Several times over the past few days, when he'd paused at the front desk, he'd stumbled for words. Color filled his face as he rubbed his nose or folded and unfolded his arms. He couldn't seem to get away from her fast enough. She was intrigued. Not interested, of course, but intrigued.

He set the papers on the music stand and lifted his head. Their eyes met and held, a smile tugging at his mouth. Warmth slid up her neck and she forced her attention away, resisting the urge to fan her cheeks. The rehearsal room was stuffy this morning.

Scanning the crowd, she encountered Bill's narrowed gaze. She'd found those ice-blue eyes locked on her several times since their introduction. He looked from her to Peter then said something to Mark. She crossed her arms and lifted her chin. He had nothing to worry about. She would be the only woman in America *not* chasing Peter Theisen.

"Okay, let's get this ball rolling." Mark's voice quieted the room. "Peter, we'll run through all of the pieces today to get a feel for what we'll be working on. Right now we just want an overall sense of the songs. It's what we call a scratch recording, to be used for future reference. Ready?"

Peter nodded and moved closer to the microphone as James started the intro. From the first note, Peter's smooth baritone flowed over the room, raising tiny bumps on Kiera's skin. He sang with little effort, eyes closed, his voice a blend of emotion and control. Power emanated from him, wrapping around her, sweeping her into the song. She wrapped her arms around herself, unable to look away from his expressive face.

Part of her wanted to run from the room and never look back. Another part was tempted to throw herself into his unsuspecting arms. The last part wanted to slap the first two into reality. She sat motionless in her corner and hoped the song would never end.

"Yes, I can wait." Kiera propped the phone against her shoulder as she typed. She was learning to multitask while on hold with the doctor's office. And the cancer center. And the pharmacy.

A week into the job without Mary, she felt more comfortable each day. She could transfer calls, write a decent business letter, and had even improved her typing skills. Simple as her accomplishments were, she was pleased that she'd caught on so quickly. Who knew the red-headed mannequin could run the front desk of a busy studio?

"Kiera, can you fax this over to Bob for me?" Mark asked.

"Sure." Without turning, she reached a hand up for the paper he held out over the counter. "Can it wait a few minutes?"

"Oh, sorry. Didn't see you're on the phone. It definitely can wait."

She swung the chair to look up at him with a quirk to her brow. "Are you sure you won't reconsider going into the Muzak business? I suspect it's pretty lucrative."

He leaned against the counter. "On hold again?"

"I don't know why it's so hard to reach a live per—" She held up a finger as the music cut off. "Yes, I'm here."

Mark walked away with a sympathetic shake of his head.

"I'm sorry, ma'am," the stilted female voice said. "I don't see the signed form you're referring to."

Kiera's pulse thumped in her ears. *Not again.* "We faxed it to you last week. It's the form your office sent for my dad to sign, which he did. We immediately faxed it back."

"Without it in his file, I can't give you the information you're looking for. That can only be released to the patient or his medical power of attorney."

"That's me. I'm his daughter."

"Would you like me to send the form again?"

"I'd like you to give me the information I asked for!" The sharp words slipped out before she could censor them. It wasn't this lady's fault. Or maybe it was. Blood pulsed through her fingers gripping the phone.

"I understand, ma'am, but without the form—"

"I know. I *know.*" Kiera pulled in a breath and released it. Couldn't she get her questions answered just once without the runaround? "Yes, please fax the form to me again. I'll have my father sign it and I'll hand deliver it to your office."

"That would be best. What number shall I fax it to?"

Kiera rattled off the number, matching the woman's clipped tone as she thanked her for her "help" and forced herself not to slam the receiver down. For a long moment she sat quietly, eyes closed, massaging her temples.

She would do whatever was necessary to get her father into the new drug study, but hitting yet another roadblock tied her nerves in knots. It didn't help that the multitude of forms they'd signed often seemed to get misplaced.

When had the world become so complicated? Her assistant had always told her when and where to show up for meetings, photo shoots, even doctor appointments. She hated fumbling for information. It made her feel inept, helpless. Frightened.

She slapped away the wave of self-pity and opened a new spreadsheet. It wasn't about her. The focus had to be on her father. It was all about him right now.

That evening under fading sunlight, Kiera sat nestled on the townhouse patio, her mind overflowing with ideas that filled page after page on her notepad. She sat back and breathed in the warmth of the evening.

"How about a refill?" Terese stood nearby, coffee carafe in hand.

"Sure. Thanks."

She filled Kiera's cup and set the carafe on the table. "What are you working on so diligently?"

Kiera took a careful sip of the steaming brew. "Just getting thoughts on paper."

"Those are some major thoughts, girlfriend." She settled opposite Kiera. "Care to share what you're working on?"

Kiera looked down at the legal pad that was nearly full. "Well…only if you promise not to laugh."

Terese frowned. "You really think I'd laugh at you?"

"You might, once you hear my idea." Kiera leaned back, rolling the pen between her fingers. "What would you think of a presentation for teens about self-image? Mainly on the difference between who God says they are and who society says they should be."

"I'd think I want to know more."

Flipping to the first page of notes, Kiera pulled in a deep breath and let the ideas fly. "I'd want it to be an interactive program, not just me droning on. I'd give a short presentation about the fashion industry, how marketing works, stuff like that. Then we'd talk about the issues they're dealing with. I want them to understand how unique they are, who they are to God and why that matters. I was thinking of calling it something like "One of Me," because there really is only one of each of us."

She pushed out of her chair and paced the square patio, ideas spilling into the warm air. "It would be aimed at boys and girls, since I think the guys face enormous pressure about their looks too. The steroid use I've heard about is really scary. So I'd want to include info that they can all relate to.

"I'd want to talk about things besides just how they dress and what makeup they wear. Eating disorders are a huge issue now, as is underage drinking. The pressure to have sex is insane for kids, which makes the issue of teen pregnancy a growing problem."

"That's tackling some heavy issues."

Kiera nodded. Was she crazy to think she could do this? The flood of ideas had yet to stop. "I know. And I want to be sure they don't think I'm some expert on all that. Ooo. Maybe I could have an expert come along and answer questions sometimes. Kids are in so many high-pressure situations now, it's unbelievable."

Terese tilted her head, her hair draping over the chair arm. "Where is all this coming from?"

"Even before everything blew up with Thomas, I'd been wrestling with who I was outside of modeling, outside of being a fashion statement. Thomas wanted me picture-perfect every minute." Her cheeks warmed and she looked away. "I felt like a mirage."

"But you always seemed happy with your life."

"I'd convinced myself I was. I mean, who wouldn't be happy living a jet-set life? But something has felt off for a long time. And now that I'm away from it…" She met Terese's gaze. "I feel like I've been given a second chance, Tess. To make a positive difference in the world."

"Wow. I had no idea you felt like this."

Kiera shrugged, clicking her pen. "I've had time to think lately. It's been hard looking at what my life had become. But I think God is calling me to something completely different. Something I can believe in."

Terese glanced at the legal pad. "So this is what you've been working on since you came home."

"Yes." Her heart fluttered. "Do you think a former model would be taken seriously if she gave talks to teens on how valuable they are just the way God made them? I want them to *think*. I want to make a differ—"

"Girlfriend, take a breath! Do you want to know what I think?"

She cringed. "Maybe?"

Terese laughed. "This whole idea is amazing."

"Really?" The tension tumbled from her shoulders, crashing into pieces at her feet. "People won't think it's stupid?"

"It's a fabulous idea." Terese scooted her chair closer. "I want to see every detail."

– 7 –

"Kiera, I have a new assignment for you." Mark stood at the counter.

She looked up from the computer, eyebrows raised.

"We have a couple hours this afternoon where James will be laying down some of the melody lines. How about giving Peter a quick tour of the cities?"

She forced a pleasant smile to her face. "I haven't done the two-city tour with a client for quite a while." She didn't want to be alone with Peter. She had too much to do. And his songs were clinging to her heart in the most disturbing way.

"I didn't think you'd mind."

She spun her chair to face him. Back straight, fists clenched in her lap. "Mark Simmons, don't you dare."

"What?" His wide-eyed expression lacked true innocence.

She lowered her voice and her brow followed suit. "I have no intention of dating anyone in the spotlight ever again. And with Dad's cancer back, I'm not interested in even thinking about a relationship."

"Did I say anything about that?"

"You didn't have to. I know you'd like to see me married off, but it's not going to happen any time soon so give it up." She softened her words. "I appreciate your concern, Mark, but I need to focus on Dad right now."

He held her gaze for a moment before nodding, a wry smile lifting his mouth. "I wasn't trying to set you up, even though I think Peter's a great guy." He lifted both hands to ward off her protest. "I've got the message loud and clear. No matchmaking. Honest."

"Good. I'm holding you to it. I'd be happy to show him around for an hour but if he wants an actual date, you'll have to point him elsewhere." She turned back to the computer. "I'm sure you'll find a hundred takers on this block alone."

Fingers poised over the keyboard, she stared blindly at the monitor, jaw set. Mark's sigh lingered as his footsteps faded. She glanced over her shoulder then dropped her hands to her lap and sagged against the chair. Hearing Peter sing put her strangely off balance. It didn't help that he seemed to be such a nice guy. But then, how people seemed wasn't always who they truly were. She'd learned that the hard way.

For Mark's sake and the sake of the CD, she would be the consummate professional. She started typing again. Even if spending time alone with Peter messed with her head.

Peter left the rehearsal room, hands in his pockets, and strolled into the reception area. Hopefully he hadn't agreed too quickly to Mark's suggestion that he get out of the studio. "Hey, Kiera."

She looked up with a polite smile. The kind he got from a teller at the bank. "Hi. How's rehearsal going?"

He dropped into the chair beside her desk and rested an ankle across his knee. "Seems to be going well. I haven't messed anything up yet anyway. They're being patient with me."

"You seem like a quick study so I doubt there's much patience involved on their part."

In what seemed the norm when he was near her, his heart stumbled around in his chest. "I'm pretty hard on myself when I'm learning new stuff. Well, not my own songs, of course, but studio stuff. Like recording and all that." *Shut up, Theisen.* "So anyway, I have to remember to just chill, soak in all the experience around me and do the best I can."

"Good advice for all of us. I hear you have an hour or so free. Would you like a whirlwind tour of Minneapolis and St. Paul, or is there something in particular you want to see?"

"I guess I'd be up for whatever you have in mind." If she stayed this formal and he kept acting like a moron, it would be a long hour for both of them.

She pulled her purse out of the bottom desk drawer and stood. "Okay, we'll just wing it. I'm ready to get out into the sunshine."

They drove past the State Capitol in St. Paul and through the downtown area, then returned to Minneapolis to park along the Mississippi River. Strolling the walkway shaded by tall ash trees, they chatted about the songs on the album, the music he liked to sing and what she liked to listen to.

On the Stone Arch Bridge that spanned the river, they stopped to watch the water crashing over St. Anthony Falls. Kiera explained how the locks and dams along the river allowed for the passage of commercial barges.

"When boats or barges are going downriver, they enter the lock when it's filled with water, then wait while the water is released." She gestured toward water gushing from the side of the concrete structure, swirls of yellowish foam joining the swiftly flowing current. "Once the water level in the lock reaches the level of the lower part of the river, the doors open and the boats can continue on down to the next lock."

She pointed toward the massive steel doors as they inched open. "Now we get to see what's been waiting inside."

A barge motored quietly through the doors to pass below them. A bargeman stood at the stern juggling oranges. The small crowd gathered on the pedestrian bridge overhead burst into applause, and he bowed as the boat disappeared beneath them.

"This whole thing is really cool," Peter said.

They crossed to the other side of the bridge and leaned against the railing, watching the barge move toward the next lock. Peter struggled to focus on the river, the barge, the birds trailing behind it—anything to keep from staring at the young woman beside him.

Kiera's wavy red hair, tossed by the summer breeze, shone in the sunlight. Large sunglasses gave her the air of being incognito. She was beautiful and trendy and smart. He was so…not.

He propped his elbows on the metal railing, watching the barge glide away. Even after the long months performing on the cruise ship, his high school nickname, "the singing nerd," still fit. He could learn to be cool before heading out on the CD tour Bill was planning. Couldn't he?

Two young women approached hesitantly, asking if she was Kiera Simmons. He looked from their hopeful faces to Kiera's passive expression. Why were they asking for her autograph? Who *was* she?

Kiera slid her sunglasses to the top of her head and greeted them with a warm smile. She chatted cheerfully, signing their scraps of paper with practiced ease. When one of them pulled a phone from a purse with *Paisley* in scrawling script along the side, Kiera asked Peter to take their picture.

He accepted the phone, relieved that his mouth had closed at some point. "Wow. This could be an ad in a magazine." Snapping several photos, his bumbling remarks were met with laughter. He winked in response to Kiera's grateful smile.

The girls hurried away, flushed and smiling, and he and Kiera resumed their positions at the railing. Sunglasses back in place, her slender hands formed a white-knuckled knot. He wavered between acting like he'd known who she was all along and pretending the whole thing never happened.

In the stilted silence, he ran a hand through his hair and released a short breath. "Okay, I'm an idiot. I should know who you are but…" He looked at her pensive profile. "Who are you?"

"Kiera Simmons."

"Well, I'm Peter Theisen, but nobody came asking for my autograph."

A long sigh relaxed her shoulders. "I've modeled long enough that I think people are used to seeing my face."

"I'll bet there are thousands of models out there who don't get asked for autographs."

She glanced at him. "The last three years I was the spokesperson for *Paisley*, which is a fashion line. That's all."

That's all? Man, he was blind as well as stupid. She'd probably done commercials and everything. "Wow. Sorry I didn't recognize you."

Facing him, she folded her arms, a deep frown on her face. "Why would you? It's clothing and accessories for young women."

"I'm sure everyone else in America knows who you are." *You're making it worse.*

She held his gaze. "I wouldn't expect you to know what I did before working at the studio, Peter. I'm glad you didn't."

They studied each other in silence. *Leave it alone, Theisen.* "Okay. Well, how about finding some place to eat? I'm starving."

The crease between her eyebrows eased. "There's a fun little restaurant right across the river."

Crossing the bridge, he was dimly aware of her pointing out several landmarks. When people started asking for his autograph, he would be as professional as she'd been. Friendly, approachable. There was so much to learn before hitting the circuit in September.

They stopped at the end of the bridge to admire the artwork of a man painting the Minneapolis skyline. Peter bought a small watercolor of the Mississippi after asking him to add two figures to the shoreline. Kiera giggled at the auburn hair of one, then pointed at a bird flying over the head of the other. He glanced upward before giving her a playful shove.

Down another block, they settled under a colorful umbrella on the restaurant patio, ordered raspberry iced tea and sweet potato fries, and sat back to enjoy people-watching in the sunshine.

Peter stretched his legs out and looked over at her. Sunglasses perched on her head, she was relaxed and smiling. This was the Kiera he wanted to know. "So tell me about life as a model."

"I started modeling for fun when I was in high school. It was an amazing time, at least in the beginning." She popped a fry into her mouth. "Mmm. I haven't had fries in forever. Anyway, I met great people and got paid a lot of money to travel and wear fabulous clothes."

"Was it fun?"

"It was. At least for a while." She looked out at the river, biting her lip. "My dad went to New York with me and traveled with me on shoots when I was young. Eventually he let me go on my own, but he made sure there were people always watching out for me. After I'd been modeling a few years, it wasn't as fun. It's a lot harder than it looks."

He raised an eyebrow. "How hard can it be?"

"Try holding the same pose for thirty minutes. Or looking genuinely happy in shorts and a T-shirt when it's fifty degrees and everyone behind the camera is wearing a jacket."

"Guess I never thought about that. Everyone always looks like they're having such a great time."

"It's acting. We just don't have any lines to say." She sipped her iced tea. "The long days can be brutal—hours of makeup and wardrobe, people putting clothes on you, doing and redoing your hair. Someone is always touching you. I know how a mannequin feels."

"Mannequins have feelings?" He cringed. *Stupid joke.*

Kiera laughed. "Yes, we do. We just can't show them until the lights go off."

He studied her for a moment, glad for this behind-the-scenes look into the world of a famous model. Except she didn't seemed famous. In the studio, she was just part of the team. "So why are you working at the studio?"

"My dad's battling cancer again. I need to be here for him now."

"Wow. That's rough. I bet he's glad you're here."

She smiled fondly. "I think he is. It's been interesting for both of us, getting used to me being here all the time. I've been in and out for the last few years, usually just for short visits, but now I pop in on him every day. I'm not so sure he likes that but it makes me feel better seeing him eating healthy and taking his meds. And I'm glad I can help Mark out too."

"Will you go back to modeling once your dad's well?"

"I don't know." She slid the sunglasses back in place. "Living in the spotlight makes you see yourself...differently. Being away from it has made me see things more clearly, including myself."

He loved imagining what he'd be like once he was famous. Smooth. Funny. No longer the guy from Iowa who never fit in.

"We're all just plain people," she added quietly, "but fame has a way of putting a person behind a rose-tinted camera lens so the rest of the world thinks they're perfect." She poked at the ice in her glass with a straw. "They're not. Sometimes they're far from it."

The last was spoken so softly he almost missed it. Staring toward the river, her usual composure slid away, the corners of her mouth tugging down. She looked sad. Ashamed.

Peter clutched his glass to keep from reaching for her hand. "Do you know what else you'd like to do?"

She was silent a moment. "I have a chance now to rethink my priorities, figure out what legacy I want to leave beyond photographs and ad work. Maybe I can undo some of the damage I've done."

"Damage?"

"Modeling itself isn't a bad thing, but..." She paused, looking out at the river. "Over the past year I've become more aware of how marketing impacts teens, how it skews their idea of what's important, of who they should be. I'm working on something that might counteract that."

His eyebrows lifted. "Sounds interesting. What is it?"

She started to speak, then stopped. "I'll tell you more once I've got a better handle on it." Pink stole into her cheeks and she glanced at him. "Sorry. That sounds more mysterious than it is. I'm just not ready to talk about it yet. Anyway, that's enough of me. Let's talk about something else."

An hour later, as they finished a second round of appetizers, her phone rang. She apologized for the interruption and answered. Eyes widening, she looked at her watch. "Really? I had no idea. I'm sorry, Mark. No, that's fine. We'll head back now. What's that? Okay, we'll be back by then."

She turned away and lowered her voice. "Yes, I'm sure you are. Just remember what I told you earlier. Good. We'll see you in a bit. Right. Bye."

Peter frowned at the heightened color in her face. "Everything okay?"

"Yes." She put her phone away before looking at him. "We've just been gone a lot longer than he expected."

He glanced at his watch. Three hours? It felt like three minutes. He raised his eyebrows in mock horror. "Oops." For a moment, they grinned at each other like naughty children. "Do we have to go back or are we free for the rest of the day?"

"Sorry. I said I'd bring you back."

"Maybe we could say we got lost?" The afternoon couldn't end yet.

She pushed to her feet. "I think they'd see through that. But he did say they were ordering pizza so we don't have to rush."

"Good." He tossed cash on the table before falling into step beside her as they retraced their path.

After a comfortable silence she prompted, "So tell me about some of your performances."

He sorted through memories of the last few busy years. The early events made him cringe, his inexperience obvious in his many missteps. "Okay. If you promise not to repeat this to anyone until the CD is done, I'll tell you my most embarrassing moment."

"It's that bad?"

"Promise?" He tried to look stern.

"Fine." She stopped to face him, holding up three fingers in a pledge. The corners of her mouth twitched. "On my honor, I promise not to repeat a word of this to anyone ever in my lifetime. Or at least not before the CD is done."

As they walked, he paused several times to position her just so to replay the events that led to his falling off the stage. She was the stage manager, then the orchestra director, then a member of the audience.

She stood over where he'd flopped onto the grass, hands on her hips, a sparkling laugh filling the air, and his heart did a crazy flip. He jumped to his feet and brushed off his shorts, then stood still as she brushed the back of his shirt, his skin tingling beneath her light touch.

When they arrived at her car, he followed her to the driver side. She lifted those green eyes and he swallowed. She had amazingly long lashes.

"Kiera, I just…thanks. I know you didn't volunteer for this but I had a blast."

Pink touched her cheeks. "I did too." She slid into the car. "But they're not going to let us out of the studio again if we don't get back there pretty soon."

"Good point." He shut the door and went around to the passenger side, fighting the grin that threatened to take over his face. *A pretty girl smiles at you and you turn into a bumbling idiot. What a nerd, Theisen.*

– 8 –

At the small table in his hotel room, Peter flipped another playing card and put it in place, humming his newest melody. There was something soothing and mindless about the game Kiera taught him during lunch a few days ago. It seemed to let his creative juices flow unhindered. When something clicked, a melody or lyric he was struggling with, he scribbled it in his ever-present notebook.

"Don't you have a song to finish?"

Bill's irritated words pulled him from the rhythm his toes were tapping and he looked up. "I finished one and I'm almost done with another."

With a practiced move, Bill tossed two white pills into his mouth and washed them down with a swig of beer. There was a pasty hue to his tan face. "Then how about cutting out the cards and finishing it?"

"I am. Kiera taught me this game. It's a great way to let my mind work on the song without creating my own writer's block."

Bill snorted. "That makes no sense."

Peter held up the notepad scribbled with words and musical notes. "Finishing song number two, even while I play cards."

"I think the air in this God-forsaken place is getting to you."

God-forsaken? "It's getting to me in a good way. I've worked the kinks out of 'Autumn Leaves,' and I'm just about done with 'Heartland.' He flipped another card. "Seems Minnesota air fuels my creativity. And this version of solitaire helps."

In the silence, he looked across the room. Bill stared out the window, frowning over fingertips tapping a slow beat. "Bill?"

The blue eyes that turned toward him were slow to focus. "What?"

"Something on your mind?"

Bill rubbed the back of his neck, eyes closed. "Nothing new. Just getting tired of the same old issues with the same old people."

"I think today's recording session went well."

Now he smiled. "You've done a good job learning the ropes. That will help us stay on schedule."

"I feel like I've run a marathon already, just trying to understand everything. Mark's staff is great."

The smile disappeared. "Remember our deal. Nothing gets in the way of finishing this album perfectly."

In the studio fourteen hours nearly every day, when would there be time? "Nothing has." The silence pulsed with an undercurrent he couldn't identify. "You think differently?"

"I've wondered if a certain redhead isn't trying to catch your attention."

His mouth dropped open. "Kiera? Are you kidding?" That was the most bizarre statement he'd ever heard.

"No, I'm not kidding. I've seen her making goo-goo eyes at you when you're singing. And while that's exactly the reaction we want from your audience, I don't want you falling for her now and getting off track."

"Bill, that's so ridiculous I could laugh. In fact, I will." He threw his head back and faked a bittersweet laugh. "Kiera Simmons does not make goo-goo eyes at me, and she never will. Girls like her aren't interested in guys like me."

"Meaning what?"

Pushing away from the table, Peter moved to the window. The absurdity of Bill's statement blurred the amazing view of the Mississippi ten stories below. He'd stood here after spending the afternoon with her, wondering what it would be like to have her beside him. *With* him. He blinked and crammed his fists into his pockets. *Dream on, pal.*

"Meaning she's a top fashion model. And a spokesman. Woman. Person."

He released a short breath. "She's used to big bucks and having her pick of any hotshot in the world. I'm just a guy from Iowa making my first album."

"She strikes me as a bright girl who knows talent when she sees it. I wouldn't put it past her to be planning to ride your coattails as you hit the big time. And you will soon."

Those words, which usually made Peter's heart dance in wild anticipation, fell flat. Anyone would be happy to have her hitch a ride. He'd be thrilled.

He folded his arms and leaned back against the windowsill. "Don't worry, Bill. Kiera Simmons isn't going to ride my coattails anywhere. There are much bigger fish in the sea for her."

An old memory flitted past from his middle school years. He'd been laughed out of the audition for the school musical *You're a Good Man, Charlie Brown.* And the girl he'd secretly liked had laughed along with everyone else.

He hadn't gotten the red-haired girl then, and he wasn't going to get her now. "Trust me," he added. "This CD is the only thing on my to-do list."

Bill studied him for a moment then nodded, apparently satisfied. "Good. This record is your girlfriend for now. Once you get out on tour, you'll have your pick. And Kiera Simmons will be eating her heart out."

Well, one of them would be.

When her phone rang, Kiera finished drying the bowl and set the kitchen towel aside. "Hey, Chris. Does the honeymoon seem ages ago?"

Christine's hearty laugh was tinged with melancholy. "It sure does. How are you? Hanging in there?"

"I'm fine." *Surprisingly so.* "I'm filling in at Mark's studio, which has turned out to be a great way to keep myself occupied." As was creating *One of Me.*

"Well, I'm working on getting you back out here. Your lovely face needs to be in front of the camera."

Christine's emphatic words sent a chill through Kiera. It was good to be home with Dad, among real friends. A world away from cameras and modeling and city lights. "Actually, Christine, I've really enjoyed being in the studio. Mark's team is great, there's a ton of work to do, and no one is taking my picture."

"What?" She squeaked like she'd been pinched. "I've never known anyone who responds to the camera like you, my dear. It would be a travesty to keep that face hidden. I just wanted to let you know I haven't forgotten you. Oh, there is one thing I wanted you to hear from me first."

Kiera held her breath.

"Paisley has put out a statement about the new spokesmodel—why you're gone, who the replacement is. All the sordid details. From what I hear, it will be on tomorrow's *Entertainment Tonight*."

Kiera sank into the kitchen chair, rubbing her temple. "Why can't they leave me out of it?"

Christine gave a brittle laugh. "You've forgotten what a big deal it was when you were hired. They need the publicity of promoting your replacement."

Kiera flinched. *Fiona.*

"I tried to convince Margaret to bring you back on," Christine continued. "You were by far their biggest revenue source. But she's got a bee in her bonnet and just didn't buy it."

No doubt Thomas was the bee.

"So," Christine said, "we'll build a new empire. Part of that empire is my big news. I've been promoted to art director at Glitz."

"Chris, that's fabulous!" Kiera had signed on with Glitz when Christine was new to the agency. In a sense, they'd grown up together.

"One of the things on my new to-do list is get you lined up for even more exposure than you got through Paisley."

The words should have thrilled her; she could prove to the fashion world she wasn't a has-been. But life had settled into a routine where her work mattered, not the camera angle. She was happier than she'd been in a long time. "I don't want anything high profile again, Christine."

"Oh, that will pass, sweet girl. Once the frenzy of the news dies down, you'll be able to go back out there and remind them who you are."

Of course. The fashion world loved nothing better than drama. An ache filled her chest. She had to tell her father before he heard it from someone else. She'd have to tell all of them. She just wanted the whole thing to be over. "I have to go, Christine. Thanks for the call. And congratulations."

"I'll keep you posted as I get things worked out. Keep your head down and it will all blow over soon."

After the call disconnected, Kiera stared out the window, a hand at her throat. Would her poor choices haunt her forever?

No. She set her jaw. She'd own up to the truth and go forward with this new life. She was so done with the old one.

– 9 –

"Peter?"

"Hey, Kiera." He shifted on the piano bench, mentally slapping his heart back to a normal rhythm.

She stood in the doorway of the practice room, looking anywhere but at him. He stood. "What's up?"

"Well, I… There's something I need to tell you."

"Okay." His heart sank. She was going back to New York just as they were getting to know each other.

She stepped into the room and perched on a chair. He settled back on the bench, facing her. The freckles sprinkled across her nose stood out against her pale skin. Her discomfort made him squirm. "Are you okay?"

Green eyes lifted to his briefly and she managed a crooked smile. "Sure. I'm fine. I just…" She studied her clasped hands. "I want to share something before you hear it on the news."

"You robbed a bank?" *Smooth, Theisen.*

Her pinched expression relaxed. "Not quite. More like on the so-called entertainment news."

"Ah." He leaned back, his elbows creating a clashing chord. "You're actually a man pretending to be a beautiful model."

"Nope."

It was fun making her smile. "I give up. Lay it on me."

"Okay. Well, you know I worked for Paisley as a spokesmodel for the past three years. And I worked for an agency called Glitz before that."

"Got it."

"But maybe you didn't know I dated a guy for about a year who was running for the Senate in Minnesota."

"Didn't know that." Of course. She certainly wouldn't be dating a guy from...Iowa.

"His name was Thomas Ramsey."

"Was?" Ridiculous hope flamed in his chest.

"Well, it still is. Anyway, it was more of a celebrity relationship than a serious one, if that makes any sense."

"It doesn't, but I doubt that's what's going to be on the entertainment news."

She rubbed her nose and he hid a smile. He wasn't the only one with that habit.

"This past January, he was arrested for embezzling funds from his campaign. There've been some other charges as well and probably more to come. When he was arrested in New York, he threw my name into the mix, but the only connection they found was me being stupid enough to date him. So with a black mark on my name, Paisley fired me."

"Bummer."

She frowned at him as if waiting for something more.

After a long pause, he raised an eyebrow. "Is that the news?"

"Well...yes." Her brow crinkled. "I just thought you should know the whole story from me instead of hearing it on television. They don't always tell the story accurately."

He grinned. "Does anybody think they do?" She'd have to come up with something better than that to change his growing appreciation of her. "Thanks for telling me. I'm sorry you went through that. It sounds rough."

Her mouth opened then closed and she got to her feet. "Okay. Well, I'll let you get back to work."

He stood, watching her move quietly across the room. "For what it's worth, that guy is a jerk, and Parsley or whatever made a big mistake letting you go. But I'm glad you're here."

She paused at the door. He thought her chin trembled but then she gave a short nod. "Thank you," came the whispered reply before she closed the door behind her.

He turned back to the piano, shaking his head. Were they crazy? Why fire someone like Kiera Simmons because of something an idiot did? A grin threatened as he settled on the bench. He was glad the guy was in jail. He deserved it.

"Well, this is a nice surprise." Buck greeted her from his rocking chair on the front porch, an ever-present block of wood and carving knife in hand.

Kiera smiled as she climbed the steps and plopped beside him in the matching wicker rocker. "I haven't been by for a few days so I figured I'd better make sure you're staying out of trouble."

He chuckled. "What did I do before you came home to keep me on the straight and narrow?"

"Good question." She leaned closer to inspect his project. "That doesn't look much like a lure."

He held up the partially carved block. "Thought I'd try my hand at garden gnomes."

"Eww." She leaned away, nose wrinkled. "Not those creepy looking ones, right?"

"Nah. More like a leprechaun than a gnome."

"With curly-toed shoes?"

"You know better than to believe that blarney, Little Missy." He winked. "Leprechauns don't have curly toes. They have pointy ears."

"Oh, that's right. Silly me." She settled back in the chair, smiling. "Never could keep your nonsense straight."

Rocking in comfortable silence, she breathed in the familiar aroma of fresh-cut wood, content to watch the easy way he handled the knife. She'd never tire of the magic he performed on a simple piece of sandalwood. "Why didn't I inherit any of your artistic genes?"

"You got your mother's looks instead, for which you should thank the good Lord. Those looks have made a comfortable life for you. You wouldn't have gotten two cents if you looked like me."

She rested her head back with a sigh and looked out at the yard. Financially, she'd done well but the lifestyle had taken its toll. She was tired.

Her father focused on carving a corner of the block into a softly rounded tip, then his gaze lifted to meet hers, the laughter gone. "Want to tell me the real reason for this visit?"

"Keeping you out of trouble isn't enough?"

"It would be if you weren't doing that little twitch thing. It's a dead giveaway."

"What twitch thing?"

The corners of his eyes crinkled. "You tap out certain rhythms when you're working up the courage to tell me something."

"I do not!" She looked at her fingers resting on the chair arms and realized they'd been drumming. She started rocking again, hands clasped in her lap.

"So?" he prodded.

She drew in a quick, silent breath and focused on the maple tree across the street. "Well, now that you mention it." It had been humiliating explaining it to Mark and then Peter, but to tell her father how she'd failed...

She tried twice before words formed. "I was fired."

He didn't miss a beat as he rocked and carved. "Figured as much."

Her gaze swung to his. "Why would that even cross your mind? I've never been fired from anything in my life." She rocked harder. "I was doing a great job at Paisley. They said my revenue share was the highest in ten years. The newest campaign was done and ready to go. Even Margaret loved it. But she said—"

Buck's hand stopped the vigorous rocking of her chair. "Kiki, it's okay. I figured it was fallout from Ramsey. Right?"

She nodded, blinking hard.

"I hope he rots in prison for a long time," he added.

Her eyebrows shot up. Strong words like that were a rarity from her father. A tiny smile touched her mouth. "I hope so, too."

He resumed rocking and carving. “So, are you planning to stay around here for a while?”

She matched his gentle rhythm. “How about permanently?”

“Sounds good to me, if you don’t think you’ll be bored to the teeth away from all the action.”

“Nope.” She sighed and closed her eyes. “This is exactly where I belong.”

– 10 –

The restaurant was crowded, the hum of voices, laughter and music deafening when Kiera arrived to join the studio staff for Friday evening happy hour. The hostess pointed her toward the back corner where she slid onto the only open stool, next to Peter. The boisterous greeting from the group made her laugh.

After several productive weeks of rehearsal and recording, they were in high spirits. Jokes flew across the table, good-natured teasing bounced between Jeff and James. Peter ducked as a wadded napkin grazed his head.

"Are they always like this?" His question was shouted into her ear.

"When they've worked as hard as you guys have, they get pretty crazy."

He grinned and her stomach flipped over. She reached for the last chicken finger and turned her attention away from him.

Conversation moved to baseball, and she smiled when Peter rattled off the current stats for the Minnesota Twins. He'd done his homework on the local team and was rewarded with slaps on the back and cheers.

Her phone vibrated on the table but she ignored it, sure she wouldn't be able to hear Terese over the noise. When it rang again a minute later, concern made her pick it up. Plugging one ear tightly, she strained to hear her roommate's voice.

"Kiera? Buck's…Fairview Hospi… Can you…"

"What? I can't hear you. Hold on." She hurried through the restaurant and stopped just outside the front door. "What did you say about Dad?"

"Jason and I just brought him to Fairview. He called saying he was having trouble breathing."

She swayed, clutching the phone with both hands. "Why can't he breathe? What's wrong? Why didn't he call me?"

"I think he tried but you didn't answer. It sounds like maybe a reaction to a new med. They aren't acting like it's life threatening. He's going to be okay, Kiera."

"I'll be there in fifteen. Tell him I'm coming." She hung up and leaned against the rough brick of the building, trembling. *He'll be okay. God, be with him.*

Dodging waiters balancing enormous serving trays, she raced through the restaurant to grab her purse.

Peter caught her wrist before she could step away. "What's wrong?"

"My dad's at the hospital. I have to go."

He kept hold of her. "I'll go with you. Hang on." He said something to Jeff then put his hand to her back, propelling her out of the restaurant.

Outside in the quiet evening air, she paused to look up at him. "Peter, you don't have to come. I'm sure he's fine." Her bravado was shaky at best.

"Give me your keys. I'll drive, you pray." His firm directive made her blink, her chin quivering. After a heartbeat's hesitation, she dropped the keys into his outstretched hand and led him to her car.

Except for an occasional direction, the ride was silent. Within minutes he'd parked in the ramp. The emergency room receptionist directed them to Buck's cubicle.

Terese greeted her with a warm hug and quick assurance that the last report said Buck was doing fine, breathing on his own. They had just taken him down the hall for some tests.

Kiera turned to hug Jason. "Thanks for getting him here, you guys. What would I do without you?"

Her roommate offered a reassuring smile. "I'm just glad he called me when he couldn't reach you."

Kiera went out to the large desk in the center of the busy ER, letting the threesome introduce themselves. A young nurse led her around the corner to a room where they were monitoring his breathing.

Drawing a steadying breath, Kiera pushed open the door. Her father lay very still on the gurney, a plastic mask covering his nose and mouth. Several monitors beeped and whooshed with his breathing.

The male nurse standing across the bed looked up with a smile. "Ahh. You must be the daughter we were hearing about."

"I'm Kiera." She stopped beside the bed, willing her heart to slow as she looked at her father's ashen face. His eyes were closed, his hands limp at his sides. "How is he?"

"Doing well. He's a bit woozy right now from what we gave him to open his airways and calm his breathing, but everything is looking good." He set a hand on her father's arm and leaned down. "Mr. Simmons? Your daughter is here looking very worried. Can you wake up a bit for her?"

Kiera took his hand. "Dad?" *Please wake up. Please.*

His eyelids fluttered open slowly.

"Hey." She smiled. "What are you doing hanging around the hospital on a Friday night? No card games going on?"

His mouth curved upward at the corners. The squeeze of his fingers was pathetically weak.

"We'll be keeping him overnight," the nurse said, "to make sure he has a restful night."

"Good. That's good." She looked down at her father again. "I'm going to let Terese and Jason know and then I'll be back, okay? Don't give the nurse a hard time."

He nodded and closed his eyes. She kept hold of his hand, trying to form a prayer. *Thank you* was all she could whisper.

Assuring Terese and Jason that Buck was doing well and she'd be fine staying with him, she shooed them out the door to the party they were headed to when Buck called. After they left, she stood in the middle of the small room, staring at her father's jacket on the hook.

What if Terese hadn't been home? She wrapped her arms around herself. *No what ifs. We agreed the first time around we'd never go there.*

"How're you doing?" Peter's arm came around her shoulders and she jumped.

Clutching her last shred of control, she gave a stiff nod. "I'm okay, thanks." With a sharp breath, she stepped out of his embrace and faced him. "I hate hospitals."

"Me too. But it sounds like he's in good hands here." His smile was gentle.

"It's a good place. The staff is exceptional." She rubbed her arms. "But I still hate being here. Why don't you take my car and head home? It could be awhile before he's admitted and there's no point in you hanging around until then. I'll sleep on a cot in his room."

He returned to the chair he'd occupied since their arrival. "I'll wait until you're sure everything's all right. Being here by yourself would stink."

"I'm used to it. It's okay." But it would be nice to have someone here to talk to.

He held her gaze calmly. "Go find your dad. I'll just hang out here reading…" He pulled a battered magazine from the Plexiglas holder on the wall behind him. "*Field and Stream.*"

Kiera raised an eyebrow. He didn't seem the fishing type. Catching trout—probably not. Catching the attention of every female in America? Definitely. "Do you fish?"

"I loved fishing up at the cabin, but I haven't had a chance in years." He studied the cover. "I'm sure there's a lot I could learn."

The nonchalant answer pulled a smile out of her. "Good to know. Buck can talk fishing and bait and rods and reels for hours on end. And if you want to make serious points with him, ask to see his lure collection."

Dark eyes lifted to hers. "He collects lures?"

"Makes them. He's a woodcarver. He's made probably a thousand lures so far and won tons of awards. He's even had famous people buy them. It was a hobby that turned into a living."

"I'd like to see them."

"You'll be buddies for life."

His laugh followed her into the hall. It was comforting that someone had her back, at least for tonight. And it was extra nice that it was Peter.

She turned into her father's room as a female nurse finished adjusting his oxygen mask. She smiled warmly at Kiera. “This is just a precaution, hon. He’s breathing fine on his own but we want to bring his oxygen level back up.”

Kiera stood at the bedside, relieved to find him looking up at her with clear eyes. “You are determined to give me a heart attack, aren’t you?”

His answering grunt was muffled behind the mask. When he started to sit up, several monitors beeped a warning.

“Mr. Simmons,” the nurse scolded cheerfully, glancing up from her laptop. “You’re setting off enough bells to wake the dead. I’ll be happy to show you how to work the bed in just a moment.”

Wrinkling his nose at her, he settled back against the pillows.

Kiera laughed, shaking her head. “You’re the worst patient, you know that? And it’s not like you haven’t had lots of practice.”

The nurse silenced the monitors, then showed him how to use the bed control.

Kiera shook a finger at him. “Now behave yourself or they’ll bill you for breaking the bed.”

His chuckle released the last of the tension that had gripped her shoulders since Terese’s call. Despite an allergic reaction to his newest med, he was still Buck, the father she adored, and still fighting the good fight.

He’s going to be just fine. Right, Lord?

Just after midnight, Kiera and Peter sat in her car in an empty McDonald’s parking lot, coffee in hand. Windows open to welcome the gentle breeze, Kiera studied him in the glow of the street lights. He’d spent the entire evening waiting patiently for her. Thomas would never have done that.

“So tell me about your family,” she said.

“I’m the third of three. An older sister and brother. I was a definite surprise since Sarah is eight years older and Andrew is ten. My dad’s a surgeon and my mom’s a… Well, she keeps busy with lots of social stuff. My brother is a resident at Johns Hopkins. My sister’s a lawyer in Chicago.”

"Are they excited about the album?"

"I suppose so." He offered a crooked smile. "My parents don't have much time for creativity. As a way to make a living, anyway. And my siblings are busy with their careers. I spent most of every summer at my Gram's cabin in Nisswa. Growing up, I was free to chase whatever dream I wanted, but I was sort of lonely."

Her heart squeezed. It was the opposite of how she and Buck had lived the last twenty years. "I'm sorry. When you make it big, I'm sure they'll be excited."

"We'll see." He shifted to face her. "Okay, your turn."

"It's been just me and Buck since my mom died in a car accident when I was six. Terese has been my best friend since third grade. She bought a townhouse a few years ago and we've been roommates ever since. Well, at least half-time. Bouncing between here and New York, I was grateful she didn't mind a part-time roomie. Did they tell you they're getting married in April?"

"They mentioned it while we were waiting for you. Those are some nice friends."

"They're the best. And then there are my Simmons cousins who've been my big brother and sisters all my life. Mark is the oldest, then Jen and Emily."

"If the girls are at all like Mark, they must be great."

"They are. But the most important person in my life is Buck. He's the best dad."

His brow lifted. "I've heard Mark refer to him as Buck, but you do too, sometimes. Have you always called him that?"

"Since I was about ten." She grinned. "I just thought it was cool. And nobody I knew got to call their dad by his first name."

"His given name is Buck?"

"William. Can't remember how he got the nickname, but everyone's called him that all my life." A sigh slipped out. "I've been so fortunate to have such an amazing dad. I've always hated letting him down. I felt like I did with the whole Thomas mess."

"I can't imagine he'd blame you for any of it."

"I should have known better. Dad never liked him. Said he was too slick. He was right." She frowned out the front window. "The worst part was I let myself drift away from my faith during that time. Thomas said he was a believer but…"

She looked at Peter. "A solid faith was the best gift my dad gave me. Now that I'm home, I'm trying to make it a priority. I'm so glad to finally be back at my home church. Do you have a home church in Iowa?"

"I was active in the youth group in junior and senior high. We did a lot of great stuff, and I really enjoyed it. Then I started singing on weekends. I've been on the road most of the last two years so I've kinda grown away from it."

She nodded. It wasn't the answer she'd hoped for but she understood it. "I let my life dictate my faith but that was backwards. I didn't realize how much my faith needs to dictate my life until I let it fall to the side. I really missed going to church."

Peter settled back against the driver's door with a thoughtful frown. "But can't you believe without going to church all the time?"

"Sure, but I think it grows deeper around other believers." Being away from her Faith Community Church family had clearly impacted her decision-making on the road. "To try to go it alone…it didn't work for me. And I don't believe it works for most people."

"This is pretty important to you."

"Without it, life is just…black and white." She paused, searching for a way to describe it. "This will sound crazy, but you know the movie *The Wizard of Oz*?"

He nodded, a corner of his mouth lifting.

"It's the difference between the black and white of Kansas and the brilliant color of Oz. I can't imagine settling for Kansas when there's a world of color and adventure to be shared with other believers. That's why I love going to church, having that time to worship and learn and be with other people." Her cheeks warmed under his thoughtful gaze, and she focused on finishing her coffee.

Peter was silent for a long moment. "I've been so busy building my career,

I haven't had time for church." He looked at her, an eyebrow raised. "Could I maybe go with you some time? I think I'd like to see your Land of Oz."

Her eyes widened. "Of course! But Peter, I don't want it to sound like it's some magical place where people's feet don't touch the ground. It's a church of real people. Sometimes we act stupid, feelings get hurt. But we love God and we try hard to follow in Jesus' footsteps."

"I'm not expecting Oz, but I would like to visit when you wouldn't mind a tagalong."

"Pick a Sunday and we'll go."

"Great. How about the Sunday after next? Unless that's too short notice for you."

She hoped her eyebrows hadn't shot right off her forehead. "No, that's not short notice. That would be fine." *Get a grip on yourself. It's an hour of worship, not a date.*

He grinned. "Then it's a date."

– 11 –

Peter leaned over the front counter to see what Kiera was giggling about, and chuckled at the YouTube puppy video. When it ended, she swung her chair to face him as their laughter died down.

"Nothing like starting the week with a good laugh," he said, then lifted his eyebrows. "So, how's your dad?"

"Doing great. They let him go home Saturday afternoon. And being the over-protective daughter that I am, I stayed at his house that night." She grinned. "He made a fuss about it but he was happy I took him out for a big breakfast after church."

"Peter, we're waiting for you." Bill's voice sliced between them.

Peter straightened, shooting a wink at Kiera. "Duty calls."

She watched him head toward the recording studio, then turned back to the computer, humming softly. A moment later, a shadow fell across her desk. Bill had replaced Peter at the counter, his expression stony.

"Hi, Bill. How was your weekend?"

"Good, thank you. Very productive. Peter and I got a lot of planning done for the tour."

"That's great." Her insides chilled under his serious expression.

"You and Peter seem to have hit it off."

"He's a nice guy." She smiled. "I think he'll do great on tour."

"He will if he stays focused. You understand the need to help him concentrate on the opportunity at hand."

It wasn't a question. She nodded, leaning back in the chair.

"And if he gets distracted, it could cause problems for more than just him. The early venues have signed contracts and are ready to print tickets. The tour is in motion."

She nodded again. This felt like a warning. "Mark says you're an expert at launching careers. Peter is fortunate to have you on his team."

"As I am to have him on mine. I'm glad you understand the importance of not letting anything or any*one* distract him from the job before him. We all saw what happened when you lost your focus."

The dig went deep, knocking the air from her lungs. Though the fallout from the recent entertainment show's story had put her back in the news, it had been mercifully brief. She lifted her chin, refusing to respond or let him bully her.

A faint smile flitted across his smug face. "I'm glad we understand each other, Miss Simmons." He turned and left the reception area, his lingering cologne clogging her throat.

Heat blasted through her. How dare he? On her feet, she closed her eyes and clenched her fists, wobbling as she wrestled her raging emotions back into place. The need for fresh air, and to be far from the high and mighty Bill Djerf, sent her out the front door. In the blinding sunshine, she stalked down the sidewalk toward the corner.

She no more wanted to date someone launching into the spotlight than she wanted to throw herself in front of the oncoming truck. Actually, she'd prefer the truck. One failed public relationship was enough. Her next one would be with someone grounded. Humble. Genuine.

Reaching the coffee shop, she flung open the door then flinched when it slammed against the wall. How dare he think she needed to be warned away from his precious client! Maybe he should warn Peter about being too friendly with the help. *He* was the one who stopped by the front desk to greet her every morning. *He* shared his lunch with her when she was too busy to take a break. She was simply being polite in return. Bill Djerf couldn't pay her to date his prized commodity.

"Hi. What can I get you this morning?"

Kiera dragged her attention to the girl behind the counter and forced a smile. "I'll have a peach black tea. Large. Extra ice." Which she could throw at Bill if he came near her again.

"Sounds perfect on this beautiful morning. Anything else?"

"No. Thanks."

"Okay. That will be three sixty-five."

Kiera looked down at her empty hands. She'd stormed out of the office without her purse, and there were no pockets in her skirt hiding a few bills. Warmth crept up her neck as she lifted her gaze to the girl's.

"I forgot my purse. Sorry. Cancel the order and I'll be back in a bit. With money."

She left the shop shaking her head. Why was she letting Bill get to her like this? It didn't matter what he thought. She wished Peter well. And she'd be praying for him. He was going to need it.

On Wednesday, Kiera stood beside her father in the studio reception area. "Dad, this is Peter Theisen. Peter, my dad, Buck Simmons."

"So you're the young man who stayed with my daughter at the hospital last Friday."

Peter had looked forward to this meeting all morning, since Kiera mentioned her father would be stopping by. "I was happy to do it, Mr. Simmons. And I'm glad to see you doing better now." Exchanging a hearty handshake, he was drawn to the older man's friendly face and warm grasp.

"My friends call me Buck. I hear you were the calm amidst the storm." His fingers tightened around Peter's hand, and he leaned forward to whisper loudly, "I sure appreciate that. When she gets wound up, I end up pulling my hair out."

Kiera gave him a pointed look. "You don't have any."

Running a hand over his bald head, he sighed. "True. But if I had some—"

"You'd be giving me grief about *something* just to have an excuse to pull it out."

Peter chuckled. The resemblance between father and daughter was amazing. Tall and thin, matching dimpled chins. His green eyes were identical to Kiera's, but without the tinge of caution that often flickered in hers.

"So, Peter, how's the recording going?"

"Just fine, sir. It's been a great learning experience. Even though I don't know what I'm doing, they're still game to finish the album."

Buck patted Peter's shoulder. "That nephew of mine must think you're worth the effort. I hear he's pretty selective about who he works with. Let's sit down and you can tell me all the details. Kiera never does."

She rolled her eyes and headed toward the recording studio. "I'll let you know when they need you back in there, Peter."

"Tell me how you and Mark got connected," Buck said as they settled into chairs in the reception area.

Peter told him about signing on with Bill, learning the ins and outs of being a performer, and his gig on the cruise ship where he'd met Mark. Buck listened intently, seeming interested in all of it. When he folded his arms and nodded, a slight tilt to his head, Peter saw Kiera reflected in the gestures.

"How was it raising a daughter on your own?" Peter asked.

"Rough at first," Buck admitted, shifting on the padded chair. "Marion was a natural mother. The two of them had great times together. When she died, I had to just muddle through. Maybe I'd have done better with a boy, but I think she turned out okay despite having me for a dad."

"She thinks you're the best."

"Good to hear." His eyes crinkled at the corners. "She sets some pretty high standards, so I'm glad to hear I measure up,"

Peter laughed.

"I'll tell you, when that girl sets her sights on something, she gets it done no matter what. She's not good at asking for help either. Seems to prefer just powering through. I 'spose that comes from being on her own so much."

"She's been great at helping me get the hang of things around here," Peter said.

Buck nodded. "She might not like asking for help, but if someone else needs it, she's right there."

Peter tucked that insight away as the conversation turned toward fishing. When Kiera reappeared, he glanced at the clock, surprised an hour had passed. Buck was a great guy—funny, intelligent, and full of stories about his only child. He suspected she wouldn't take kindly to the telling, but he now saw her in a new light. She was as much brains as beauty, strong willed, with a fierce love for family and friends. And Buck Simmons adored her.

"You're off the hook," she told him. "They're breaking for lunch. Dad, we're ordering in subs. Do you have time for a sandwich?"

Peter saw him wince as he unfolded his lanky frame and got to his feet before turning a smile toward his daughter. "Not today, Honey. Defending my horseshoe title against Gustafson at one-thirty. Do you have plans for dinner?"

"Nope. Do you?" She lifted a hopeful eyebrow. "Got a date?"

"Yes. With my beautiful daughter and this nice young man. I'll put some steaks on the grill and you two can show up at seven. Bring a salad. Odds are Mrs. O'Connell will provide us with dessert. Think you'll be done for the day by then, Peter?"

Kiera stared at her father, and Peter couldn't decide if he should laugh or bow out of the invitation to save her the discomfort. Mark entered the reception area and made the decision for him.

"We'll make sure we're done by then." Mark crossed the room and threw his arms around his uncle. "Buck, how are ya, you old coot?"

"Let's put it this way, Marky. Don't put your tap shoes on just yet. You won't be dancing on my grave anytime soon."

The men laughed.

Kiera gasped. "Dad, that's an awful thing to say!"

He shrugged. "It's the truth." He looked over at Peter. "Kiera can give you directions to my house. I'll see you at seven o'clock."

Peter shook his hand and nodded. It was a directive. He would be having dinner with Kiera and Buck Simmons. He couldn't think of anything he'd rather do.

"Why is this such a big deal, Kiki?" Buck asked from where he stood cutting up vegetables.

Kiera splashed water across the counter as she scrubbed furiously at a potato. "How was he supposed to say no? You didn't ask him, you just assumed he'd want to. I don't like having guests come under duress."

"He's not capable of saying no?"

"Peter's a nice guy. He'll come because it's the polite thing to do."

"And if he's miserable, he can make a polite excuse and leave early. My cooking's not that bad, is it?"

"Of course not." She scrubbed harder, ignoring his perusal.

"Are we having mashed potatoes?"

"No. Why?"

"You're scrubbin' the skin right off that thar tater," he drawled.

She stopped to look at it, then set the half-skinned potato in the sink and picked up another one, scrubbing more gently.

"Do you want to tell me what the real issue is?"

She shrugged.

"You and Peter seem to have hit it off."

She stabbed the potato with a fork. "I can't imagine anyone not hitting it off with him." Another stab. "But he's so focused on his career he hasn't gone to church in years."

"He's going with you on Sunday."

Her head lifted. "How do you know that?"

"He told me. He said he's very interested in looking at faith from an adult perspective."

"Looking at faith." She slapped aluminum foil around each potato. "What does that mean anyway? It's not a science experiment."

"For some people, it's not something they're willing to rush into. I think Peter is open to renewing his faith, but he's not taking the idea lightly. If he makes that commitment, he'll do it wholeheartedly. I see that as a healthy, intelligent way to consider living a life for God."

"Thomas supposedly had a strong faith and look where that got him. And me."

"Peter is not Thomas. You have to let that go."

"I *have* let it go. I wish him a very happy life. In jail." She turned and leaned against the counter, arms folded. "Dad, there's no way I'm going to have another relationship that starts and ends in the spotlight. I learned that lesson the hard way."

Buck met her gaze calmly although she thought his mouth twitched. "Peter's just coming for dinner, Honey. He's not moving in."

She looked back at him for a moment, then turned abruptly and reached into the cupboard for a plate. "Well, that's a good thing."

"Knock, knock."

Peter stood at the screen door with a sheepish expression. "Sorry for coming in the back way. I was admiring the sidewalk pavers and ended up back here."

Kiera pushed the turmoil in her mind aside and attempted a smile that felt more like a grimace. "Front, back. Doesn't matter to us. Come on in."

Buck accepted the bottle of red wine Peter handed him while Kiera finished cleaning the counter, praying for a calm spirit. By the time they sat down to Buck's steak dinner, she was able to laugh and chat freely. After enjoying the neighbor lady's lemon meringue pie, Buck suggested a few rounds of cribbage. Peter admitted he'd never played but picked it up fast enough to beat Kiera in the fourth round.

When she carried their empty dessert plates to the kitchen, she looked twice at the clock. Eleven already? Peter was good company and it was evident her father enjoyed talking with him. Hearing them agree to meet for another round of cribbage, she knew Peter would now be "part of the family" while he was in Minnesota. She would just stay scarce when the two men got together. She didn't need another lecture from Bill.

Buck declared it time to turn in, and the men shared a warm hug. Peter thanked him for the meal, encouraging him to stop by the studio anytime he was in the neighborhood. Promising to lock up on their way out, Kiera pressed a kiss to her father's cheek before he went upstairs.

Peter followed her into the kitchen and began rinsing dishes as she filled the dishwasher. They cleaned in companionable silence, and Kiera felt another chunk drop away from her frozen heart. He was so easy to be around.

They turned off the lights and locked the door, then strolled out to their cars parked side by side in the driveway. She pulled in the sweet night air and sighed with delight.

"Thanks for a great evening," he said as they faced each other. His shy smile was lit by moonlight. "I know you got drafted into this event too. Sorry that I keep getting pushed on you."

He was apologizing? "Peter, I don't get drafted into anything. I'm known for being pretty stubborn and opinionated, so don't think I couldn't have come up with a sudden bout of flu if I didn't want to be here."

He chuckled. "Good to know. I enjoyed talking with your dad. He's a great guy."

"Isn't he? I know he enjoyed talking sports and guy stuff with you. No matter how hard I try, I make a poor son."

He offered a crooked smile. "But you make the best daughter."

Her chin quivered at his gentle words and she pulled her car door open. "Well, I'll see you Sunday night at 6:45. I'll email you directions to the church. It's easy to find from your hotel. Have a good weekend."

As she drove off, she wiped impatiently at her wet cheeks. "Peter is a new friend," she said aloud. "You can never have too many of those, so thank God for his friendship and get over yourself."

The problem was, none of her friends made her heart dance when they smiled or stirred her to tears and delight when they sang.

– 12 –

Sunday evening, Peter stood beside Kiera in the crowded Faith Community Church sanctuary, stuffing his inner thirteen-year-old under the pew. The weekend had dragged by as he waited for this evening to arrive.

"Hey, everybody!" The worship leader's voice rang through the spacious room. "Welcome to Faith. Take a minute to greet someone near you."

Kiera turned and held out her hand. "Hi. I'm Kiera. Welcome to Faith."

"I'm Peter. Nice to meet you." He hoped his polite nod hid the goofy way his heart was jumping around. "I'm happy to be here."

The people in front of them turned to say hello and she pulled her hand from his. He greeted the people to his left, their names barely registering. He was asking for his heart to get stomped on when Kiera made it clear she wasn't interested. Not to mention incurring the wrath of Bill if he so much as asked her out for coffee. He hadn't mentioned this outing. Or dinner at Buck's.

The band started another song, and the room filled with clapping and voices raised in worship. The simple, heartfelt words that flashed on the large screens touched a chord deep inside him. It was a genre of music he'd never experienced in a worship service, with an energy that surprised him. It was fun and heartwarming.

As they settled on the cushioned pews, a man with shaggy dark hair and a light beard, in jeans and a striped shirt, strode to the front of the stage. "God is good," he declared and the crowd called back, "All the time."

"All the time," he said and they responded with "God is good."

"Do you believe it?" he demanded with a smile.

Laughter rang out. "Absolutely!"

"Amen! Man, have we got energy going in here tonight or what? I think the Holy Spirit is up to something good, don't you?"

Whistles, clapping, stomping feet. Peter glanced at Kiera who was laughing and nodding.

"Welcome to Faith Church, everybody. For those of you who are visiting or just haven't been paying attention lately, I'm Joel Barten, one of the pastors here. And I am glad you listened to the urging God put on your heart to be here tonight. Let's get started."

He slid on a pair of glasses and opened his Bible. "We're going to continue our walk through the book of Colossians. Chapter three, starting at verse twelve."

Kiera held her Bible so Peter could see. He leaned closer, their shoulders touched and for a moment he lost his focus. *Pay attention, Theisen.*

As Joel worked his way through the passage, something stirred deep in Peter's heart. He soaked in the pastor's passionate words. Chosen by God. Forgiveness. Peace of Christ. Friendship with God.

He blinked. Friendship with God? How could he have a friendship with someone who ran the universe? Wasn't that like trying to be buddies with the CEO of the largest company in the world? God should have more important things to do than spend time caring about a struggling singer in Minnesota.

"God loves you." Joel pointed at someone near the front. "And you." He pointed to the left. "You. And you." He seemed to be pointing directly at Peter.

He'd known as a child that God loved him. Gram had made sure of that. But the world was bigger and meaner now. It wasn't as easy to believe it anymore.

"It isn't complicated," Joel said. "There aren't hundreds of rules to follow or hoops to jump through. You don't have to meet certain criteria. You just need to believe what the Bible tells us plainly. By His choice, Jesus died for us. All of us. It was His choice, people. So for us to respond with anything other than joyful gratitude and humble acceptance is to ignore the eternal significance of His sacrifice."

Joel closed his Bible and stood quietly a moment. "Yet sometimes it can be the hardest thing to do. We're on a journey, my friends, to discover who God is and who we are. Let's do it together. And we can start right here with prayer."

As the pastor prayed, Peter sat with eyes closed, absorbing the reassurance that blanketed his heart and calmed his mind. The simple prayer for clarity and an open mind to hear God's voice resonated like a beautiful chord within him.

I want that. I want to hear your voice, God. I want to know you. But...how?

Wrapping the prayer with an energetic "amen," Joel said, "Before our last song, I want to remind you that the Alpha class is coming up. It's a great place to come with questions, wrestle with doubts and have a few laughs while you're at it."

Peter glanced at Kiera. Maybe she'd consider going to that class with him. He had doubts. He had questions. He needed to wrestle with this whole thing. And he liked this pastor. He had a feeling they'd have some good discussion.

Joel seemed to be looking at Peter again. "It's open to everyone—just let us know you're coming so we have enough food. Now let's take some time to worship this great God of ours. C'mon, everybody. On your feet. Lift your hands and praise God Almighty."

The crowd stood as the electric guitarist started a lively riff. Peter studied the musicians. The bass player wore sneakers. The drummer had blonde dreadlocks. That they were excellent musicians was obvious in the tight performance. The music filled him with a sudden, strange joy, and unleashed a longing for more of...something.

As the song ended, Kiera smiled up at him, her expression peaceful. He smiled back, glad he'd come tonight, especially with *her*. He'd enjoyed her Oz far more than he'd anticipated.

A few minutes later, standing at the edge of the crowd milling in the foyer,

Peter watched Kiera greet one person after another, each having some story to share or question to ask. She'd introduced him to the first few but as people gathered around her, he stepped out of the way, content to watch.

"Welcome to Faith Community Church."

He turned to find the pastor smiling at him, hand outstretched.

"I'm Joel Barten."

"Peter Theisen."

"Your first visit here?"

"It is. That was a thought-provoking message you had."

Joel was slightly shorter than Peter and not as young up close. "What thoughts did it provoke?"

"I grew up in a family of doctors and lawyers. Church wasn't on the radar for them. I was involved in youth group, but I've gotten away from it in recent years. After what you said about having a relationship with God, I'm curious to hear more as an adult."

"Then you should consider coming to the Alpha class. I have to warn you though—few people make it through the whole ten weeks without some major changes in thought patterns."

Peter chuckled at the good-natured warning. "I'm open to change. Do you lead it?"

"Only the large group time. We also spend time in small groups."

Kiera appeared at Peter's side and smiled warmly at the pastor. "Hey, Joel. Great message."

"Thanks, Kiera. You know this young man?"

"I do." She looked at Peter. "Sorry to keep you waiting around for me."

He smiled and put a casual arm around her shoulders in a gesture that felt natural and easy. "Didn't mind at all. Do you know everyone here?"

She shook her head, remaining within his embrace. "It's been growing so fast and I've been in and out the past few years. But we've attended here my whole life so I guess I do know quite a few."

"Kiera is going to be one of our small group leaders for Alpha this summer," Joel said.

She turned to Peter. "Want to come to the class with me on Wednesday?"

Hopefully the jolt of surprise that ricocheted off his ribs didn't show on his face. "Sure. Sounds interesting."

Kiera and Joel chatted about his visit with Buck earlier that week and the prayer shawl the knitting group planned to bring him on an upcoming visit. Watching their easy exchange, the earlier longing intensified. To be part of a place where people cared about him and his life…

He sighed quietly. With the tour looming, he'd continue to be a nomad for a while longer. Maybe Faith Church could be his home base while he was gone, a sort of home away from home.

Leaving the building, Kiera looked up at the sprinkling of stars overhead. "It's been amazing to watch God work through this church and especially through Joel. He's a remarkable man."

"He seems like a great guy. I had this weird feeling when he was up front that he was talking right to me."

"Maybe he was." She turned a smile on him. "Or maybe it was God."

"Yeah." A shiver rippled down his back. "Maybe it was God."

– 13 –

Peter hooked his fingers and stretched his arms overhead, leaning back on the piano bench. Working alone in the studio on a quiet Saturday afternoon after a busy week was perfect. The new melody line was almost right.

He arranged the sheet music on the ledge and started from the beginning. *Yeah, this works. Nice bridge. And now the last—* He dropped his hands on the keys. *No. That's not right. It needs...it needs...something better. Think!*

A knock at the practice room door interrupted his irritated erasing and he looked up. Dressed in khaki shorts and a bright turquoise tank top, hair loose around her shoulders, Kiera looked more casual than he'd ever seen her. And gorgeous, but that was nothing new. "Hey, Kiera!"

"Oh, I'm sorry. I thought you were James. Sorry for interrupting."

"Wait," he called when she started to pull the door shut. "Come in. I need an opinion."

"You're sure? I didn't mean to interrupt."

He motioned her into the room. "You're just the person who can help me. Would you listen to this and tell me what's wrong?"

She approached slowly, her lopsided smile tinged with skepticism. "You want *me* to help you with a song? Prepare to be underwhelmed."

He laughed and slid over on the bench. "I bet you'll be surprised. Okay, so I've got this melody line going, and I know how I want it to end, but I'm stuck on this one part. Tell me where you think it should go."

She perched beside him, hands clasped, back straight. He started the song, a bit louder than necessary. When he got to the trouble spot, she winced and shook her head. "You're right. That's not it."

"So what is? That's where I'm stuck."

"Well…" She bit her lip. "Keep in mind that even after hanging around the studio most of my life, my music vocabulary is pretty limited. I'm thinking it should go up instead of down."

He considered her idea and turned back to the keys. "Okay. How about something like…" He played a simple line. *Better.*

"Yes, but maybe have it go more like—" She waved her hands. "I can't sing but if it went hm-*hm*-hm," she used her index finger to indicate the notes, "then it could go back down."

Smiling at her shy hum, he tried again and a grin broke across his face. He snatched up the pencil and jotted a note. "That's it! Why didn't I think of that?"

She stood with a laugh and brushed her palms together. "Well then, my work here is done. I'll let you get back to the song."

"So what are you doing in here on a Saturday?"

Arms folded, she cocked an eyebrow at him. "I could ask you the same thing."

"I needed to get this song out of my head. What's your excuse?"

"Just checking on a couple of faxes." She leaned against the side of the piano. "Terese and I were going canoeing but her allergies kicked in so I'm short one paddle. I'm walking over to Lake Calhoun to cancel our reservation."

He liked the idea of being out on the water, away from the studio. With her. "I haven't canoed in years but I'd be happy to fill in if you still want to go."

Her face lit up. "Really?"

"Really." He slid the lid closed and got to his feet. "I may be an embarrassment to be seen with, but what I lack in style I'll make up for in entertainment."

She laughed. "It's not like we're canoeing the rapids. It's just around three lakes."

"Three lakes? How many days are we going to be out there?"

"Try a couple of hours. The lakes are all connected. You'll see."

Thirty minutes later, settled in the rental canoe, Kiera pushed them away from the cement landing. "No backing out now," she said.

He shot her a grin from his perch in front. "I could always paddle backwards and stop any forward progress."

"You could." She steered them under the bridge toward the adjacent Lake of the Isles. "But I know how to dump you out without getting myself wet."

He twisted on the seat. "Buck taught you that?"

Her smile sparkled with mischief. "I taught him. Now start paddling."

They followed the winding shoreline, commenting on the beautiful, multimillion-dollar homes with perfectly manicured lawns. The wide array of walkers, bikers, inline skaters and runners moved faster than their meandering pace. Gliding through a narrow channel leading to the next lake, they slowed to chat with people sitting in the yards that lined the water.

"Beautiful day," Peter called, as they exchanged waves with an older couple.

"And beautiful girlfriend you have there," the man called back. His wife swatted his arm.

Peter glanced back at Kiera and gave an exaggerated nod. "She gives this perfect weather some stiff competition, doesn't she?"

Cheeks pink, Kiera splashed him while the man laughed and waved farewell. Their leisurely pace along the edge of Cedar Lake led them to what she called Brownie Lake. Tucked away in its own private world, the secluded haven was lined with evergreens, graceful willows, and waving wildflowers.

Alone on the tiny lake, they drifted in the peacefulness, bare feet dangled over opposite sides of the canoe. Peter lifted his face to the sun peeking out from behind a cloud, closed his eyes and filled his lungs with the familiar scent of pine and lake water. Ignoring the distant hum of cars, he imagined he was at the cabin. Gram's face floated to mind—white hair pulled back in a braid, her softly wrinkled cheeks lifting in a smile.

"Peter, you have a gift," she'd said often when they sat together on the deck at night looking at the stars. "To waste that gift is to turn your back on the One who gave it to you."

"And that's God, right, Gram?"

She'd smoothed his unruly hair with a gentle touch and nodded. "That's right. And I hope you'll never forget that."

"I won't, Gram. I promise."

The conversation had filled him with yearning, a feeling that had stayed with him through the years, intensifying since her death last year. To do something special, share his love of music with whoever would listen.

This album had to fly. He had a promise to keep.

Kiera glanced at Peter as they floated on the glassy water. In tan shorts and a red T-shirt, dark hair tousled in the breeze and his nose pink from the sun, he was as handsome as any of the male models she knew. And far nicer than most.

She cleared her throat. "So what made you decide on a singing career?"

"I just love to sing. A career where I get to travel around and sing for people sounded pretty darn good. Anything to get out of Iowa."

"You didn't like it there?"

He lifted a shoulder and looked out across the lake. "I just… There's something bigger out there for me. Some place where I can make my own mark in the world."

She studied his pensive profile. They were on such different paths. "You're going out into the world to find your place and I've come home to find mine."

Their eyes met across the length of the canoe. "You didn't find it in modeling?"

"No. Not for lack of trying either. At first I was like you, thinking there was something out there in the great big world calling my name." She dropped her gaze and trailed her fingers in the cool water. "But it was home that was calling. The bright lights and the attention were a smokescreen, keeping me from seeing what I'm being called to do."

"Which is?"

"Helping kids discover who God created them to be."

"Is that what you mentioned before? The secret project?"

She nodded. "I'm calling it *One of Me*. It's a program I want to take into the community to talk with kids about self-image and who they are in God's eyes."

"That sounds great, Kiera."

"Thanks. We'll see what kind of reception it gets."

His dark eyes narrowed. "I admire that," he said.

"That I can climb on a soapbox with little provocation?"

He chuckled. "That you're so sure about what you're supposed to do and you're going after it."

Warmth inched up her neck. "Thanks."

The gentle breeze of earlier now swooped around them and she glanced up at the approaching clouds. "We'd better hurry. The last place we want to be in a thunderstorm is on the water in an aluminum canoe."

They paddled quickly toward their starting point but the storm was faster. By the time they passed under the last bridge, the clouds had opened.

Kiera watched Peter lean into the wind, paddling hard. Her heart ached for him, for the journey he was on. *Please God, surround him with people who will help him make the best choices. And keep him close to you.*

A tiny smile touched her mouth. It had been an amazing afternoon. She hadn't enjoyed herself this much since…since maybe ever. Bill's voice resonated with the distant thunder, reminding her she had no place in Peter's life beyond the studio, and the smile washed away. If he found out they'd spent the afternoon together, he'd be in her face again.

The young man who had sent them off hours earlier squatted at the edge of the landing, face scrunched against the blowing rain as he grabbed the end of their canoe. Peter climbed out, then reached down to help Kiera. He pulled her toward the concession building at a run, dodging raindrops as big as gumballs. Beneath the overhang, they sagged against the stucco wall, breathless. The sky rumbled, lightning reflected in the shiny black asphalt.

Soaking wet, hair plastered to her face, water squishing in her shoes, Kiera had never felt so unglamorous. Or so happy.

"Want to run for the car?" His voice came close to her ear.

She turned her head to find him smiling down at her, inches of warm, humid air between them. "No way. This is the best view in the place."

'That's what I think." His voice was low and teasing.

It was a long moment before she pulled her gaze away to watch the rain dance across the lake. Something in those brown eyes put her off-balance. The erratic rhythm of her heart matched the rolling thunder.

She hated to see him change from this sweet, unassuming man into someone who believed their own hype. A sigh slipped out. But it seemed inevitable. She'd pray for him to come through it unscathed. It seemed a useless prayer.

– 14 –

"I am so sorry, Kiera. If I didn't think my sneezing and coughing would disrupt the program, you know I'd be there." With wadded tissues littering the floor beside the couch, Terese apologized yet again as Kiera stood ready to head to Faith Church Wednesday evening.

Of course Terese needed to stay home. And of course Kiera would be just fine. Giving her first *One of Me* presentation. Alone. In front of teenagers. *Why did I ever think this was a good idea?*

"It's okay, Tess. Stop apologizing, for Pete's sake."

"I will since 'Pete' is going in my place." Even with puffy, red-rimmed eyes, Terese's knowing expression was clear.

"Very funny. Pray for me, please. If nothing else, that the kids aren't bored out of their minds."

"I will and they won't be. Have fun, girlfriend. You're doing exactly what God has called you to do. You rock!"

With Terese's words ringing in her head, Kiera headed out to her car where Peter waited. *Lord, give me the right words tonight. And maybe help me forget Peter is there?*

The ride to church was far too quick. Within minutes they'd finished carrying her totes into the youth room. She stood at the front, looking over the empty chairs. This was where she would launch her dream. Here, in this beloved building among people she knew.

But if it flops, the whole church will know. Why didn't I pick a place where

I don't know anyone? At least then it wouldn't be another public failure.

"So how can I help?" Peter stood beside her, hands on his hips.

His words sliced into her spiraling thoughts. "Actually, I'm okay. You can go out for coffee or head back to the hotel." She raised an eyebrow, praying he'd take the hint. "It will be a couple hours at least."

"And miss your first presentation? No way."

They looked at each other for a moment, then he lifted his hands with a sigh. "Okay, okay. I'll go sit in the back of the room."

"And you won't try to make me laugh?"

"Well..." His mouth lifted at the corners. "I'll try not to."

As he walked away, she shook her head and opened the first tote. When *didn't* she laugh when he was around?

Teens and their mentors trickled into the large room and she bantered with them as she finished setting up, the nerves that had kept her awake last night fading. When Pastor Joel joined her at the front for the introduction, she acknowledged Peter's thumbs-up with a nod.

You've called me to this, Lord. I know it. I'll do my best but I'd sure appreciate some help staying focused.

She took a sip from her water bottle, flashed a warm smile, and *One of Me* was launched. It was a lively group, evenly mixed with girls and boys. During the first half hour, she shared her modeling journey, including both funny stories and those that had made her question the industry and her role in it. She talked about marketing and the billions of dollars poured into advertising products from dog food to clothing to vacation spots.

She showed commercial clips with messages about the "right" diapers for babies, the "best" place to eat, and "the" clothes and accessories every teen should have, explaining how advertising manipulated emotions and self-esteem, all to get their money.

Throughout the presentation the group had been attentive but quiet. When she opened it up for questions or comments, the silence was deafening. Either it had been so good they didn't have a single question, or... She reached for her water bottle.

A hand slowly went up. "But what if," the heavyset girl said, "boys are only interested in girls that look like the magazines? We'd never get a date if we didn't look like that."

Girls around her nodded while the boys snickered. It was an objection Kiera had expected.

"Great question." She clicked from the Q&A slide to a picture of a current teen actor heartthrob. The girls released an audible sigh before giggling.

"Cute?" Kiera asked.

"Hot," came the swift reply, followed by another burst of giggles.

"Okay, hot. Girls, how many of you think he's hot? About half. How about this guy?" She flipped through several more photos. Each time, she asked for a show of hands and then encouraged them to look around at the response.

"So some of you liked hottie number one, but not all. Some liked number two. Not as many liked number three, but a few did. Okay, guys. Your turn."

After the same routine with famous young women, she settled back onto her stool. "Ladies, if you try to fit the images of the girls we just saw, only *some* of the guys will think you're cute. And if there's a particular guy you like, he might not be at all impressed with the image you *think* you should have. Then what? Do you change your looks just for him? What if, after a date or two, you decide he's actually a jerk and you don't even like him? Then what do you do with your look?"

"Guys, listen up." She waited until she had their complete attention. "You can take steroids to buff up and try to look like a pro football player, but what if the girl you've got your eye on thinks big muscles are creepy? What if you can't develop muscles like that so you decide to drink to look cool? But then it turns out the girl you like is turned off by drinking. What then?"

The room had quieted as she posed the questions. "When I was modeling, I got to change my look with every shoot. Trying on different images was fun at first, but you know what? When I went home at the end of the day, this was reality."

The slide showed her without makeup, hair down around her shoulders in no particular style, wearing jeans and a T-shirt. Not played down, just who she was naturally. "Not the air-brushed girl in the magazine who looks like she's having fun because she's wearing the right clothes and has perfect hair. Just me. Bad hair days, zits, spinach in my teeth and all."

She paused while their giggling subsided. "I've never been any more special than my roommate, my friends, or the girl working hard at McDonalds. No *more* special but still *as* special because there's only one of me—regardless of what disguise I wear."

She reached for her Bible atop the podium. "There's no place in the Bible that talks about how driving the right car, wearing the right makeup, or buying expensive clothes will make you a better person. But it does talk about the true source of beauty. 1 Peter 3:4 says, 'It should be that of your inner self, the unfading beauty of a gentle and quiet spirit, which is of great worth in God's sight.'"

Leaning back on the stool, a smile touched her mouth. "Isn't that amazing? Who we are on the inside, our inner self, is of great worth to God. So while it's not bad to be fashionable, to wear clothes you like and feel good in, that's not what will make you truly attractive. I think that's way cool. But it's so not what the fashion industry wants you to know. They want to tell you what to wear, how to act to fit in, even how to think."

Most of the teens and mentors sat quietly looking at her with thoughtful frowns. A few in the back were intent on their iPhones and another pair to the right whispered and giggled.

"So with media embedded in our lives 24/7, is it even possible to make our own decisions? Be our own selves? What do you think?"

There was a brief silence before the discussion morphed from challenging resistance to honest discussion. Conversation flowed among them as they raised questions, offered solutions, and shared laughter.

Kiera lifted her gaze and encountered Peter's smiling wink. Pushing back tears, praise lifted from her heart. *Thank you, Lord. For the privilege of being here. For booting me out of modeling to this amazing night. For calling me to just be me.*

An hour later, Kiera settled back against the passenger seat and released a long, contented sigh. While the presentation had gone better than she'd dared dream possible, she felt like she'd run a marathon. She looked sideways at Peter. "Thanks for coming." Surprisingly, she meant it.

"I'm glad I got to see it. That was great, Kiera."

"It was a pretty incredible group of kids."

"But the way you handled their questions and their skepticism, and how you countered it with your experience and what the Bible says about who they are..." He shook his head as he stopped at a red light and shifted to look at her. "You surprise me every day with another part of you that's just...wow."

"Thank you." She bit her lip to stop the sudden quiver in her chin, unable to look away from him. "That's the nicest thing I've heard in a very long time."

A car horn tooted. Peter winked at her and turned his attention back to the road. "Only the truth, pretty lady. Only the truth."

She released the breath that had stuck in her throat and hid a smile.

"Kiera! Kiera Simmons!" The shout came from across the street.

She paused beside Peter and turned, then sucked in a sharp breath. Her plastic glass hit the sidewalk, showering their legs with iced tea. A blonde woman in a bright red suit hurried toward them, a news cameraman in tow.

Kiera turned a panicked gaze to Peter. "Let's go."

"Okay." He took her hand and pulled her along. "We're almost to the studio."

"Kiera! Jan Nelson from Channel 43. Can I ask you a few questions?" The thump of running feet grew louder. "What do you think of the new charges being brought against Thomas Ramsey?"

Slowing to a stop, Kiera drew a deep, steadying breath before turning to face the woman. "I'm sorry. What was the question?" The words were stiffly polite.

She leaned against Peter and he squeezed her fingers, inching slightly in front of her. Whatever was going on, the woman would have to get past him.

The blonde smoothed her straw-colored hair, huffing from her dash across the street. "Have you heard about the new charges being brought against your boyfriend?"

"No, I haven't."

The woman's shrewd gaze moved to Peter for a moment. He returned her perusal. The urge to shove the camera away from the shaking girl beside him curled his hand into a fist.

Her attention jumped back to Kiera. "No one notified you?"

"Why would they?"

"How does that make you feel?"

"That no one told me? It doesn't affect me at all."

Peter chuckled quietly. She sounded cool and disinterested.

"The charges could send your boyfriend away for a long time. Apparently his financial dealings have affected a large number of people. And my sources tell me your name has come up again as a person of interest, especially as it pertains to the fraud charges. Surely this is of concern to you?"

Kiera swayed against him, her freckles standing out against her pale face. He put his arm around her shoulders. *God? We could use some help here.*

"First, he's not my boyfriend. And I was never involved with Mr. Ramsey's financial dealings so, no, I'm not concerned."

"Are you expecting him to contact you?"

"Not at all. We haven't been in contact since his arrest and I don't imagine that will change. Thank you for asking." She turned and walked away.

"But Kiera—"

"She has nothing more to say," Peter said over his shoulder. Grasping Kiera's fingers in a solid, reassuring grip, he kept her close against his side.

"Who are you? Is this another boyfriend, Kiera? You must have a reaction to the charges against Thomas Ramsey."

Peter swung open the door of the studio and ushered Kiera in, then pulled it closed behind them. She moved to her desk out of view of the street and sank down on the chair, a trembling hand at her forehead.

"Hey." He squatted before her. "It's over. You handled it perfectly."

Her teary gaze latched onto his. He reached up to brush his fingers against her warm cheek, smiling. "You did great."

Tears spilled over and she threw her arms around his neck. "Thank you for staying by me."

Peter held her securely, jaw clenched. He would do whatever it took to protect her. When she sat back in the chair, he reached up on the counter for a tissue. She accepted it with a wobbly smile. "Thanks. Sorry about the meltdown."

"Nothing like being chased by a reporter on your coffee break. Or iced tea break, in this case."

She blew her nose then looked at him through wet lashes, giving her a childlike appearance. His heart squeezed. She was even beautiful when she cried.

"Seeing her brought it all back—weeks of reporters following me everywhere. I couldn't go anywhere without someone sticking a microphone in my face. It was awful."

"You turned white when you saw her. What was she talking about?"

"I got a letter last week saying there's a new investigation and that I'd be notified of any pending action that might involve me. I tossed it."

"Involve you how?"

She shrugged, her mouth still tugging down at the corners. "I don't know. He tried to pin some of it on me right away but the investigators couldn't find anything, of course. It's one thing to be in front of a camera when it's a job. It's so different when they're after you personally. I can't imagine going through that again."

With a sharp breath, she lifted her chin and squared her shoulders. Her professional look slid back into place. "So I'm going to focus on the here and now and not worry about it." She offered a lopsided smile. "Thanks for the iced tea. Sorry it got all over your jeans."

"We'll go back for another one soon."

"Okay."

Her smile made his heart do its funny little dance. *Man, Theisen.*

– 15 –

Prepared to park behind the studio to avoid the small but relentless knot of paparazzi, Kiera swung past the front to see if they'd given up on her yet. Bill stood on the sidewalk by the front door, talking with the blonde reporter.

Why in the world…? A loud honk yanked her attention back to the road and she stomped the brake to keep from hitting the oncoming car. The man drove around her, mouthing something undoubtedly unpleasant.

She turned left and pulled into the private lot, where she sat unmoving. Bill wouldn't use this opportunity to say something about her. No, that was ridiculous. He'd barely spoken to her since his warning, busy traveling or cracking the whip over the SMP team.

Forcing the foreboding to the back of her mind, she went inside and headed toward the front desk. He had to be promoting Peter and the upcoming tour. He lived and breathed marketing and PR. He was very, very good. Obnoxious but good.

"So get over yourself," she said aloud. She settled at her desk and powered up the computer. "It's not about you all the time."

"So who's it about?"

She spun around, hand at her throat. Peter was standing in the doorway, an eyebrow raised. "You said it's not all about you so I'm wondering if it's about me?" The eyebrow wiggled.

"Around here, yes, it's all about you, Mr. Theisen," she said, smiling. You're the rising star. I believe Bill is outside right now talking you up to the local news."

Both eyebrows jumped up. "He is?"

"Yup. You should wander your way out there and make a cameo."

"Nah." Color rose in his face. "I'll leave that to Bill. I'm the singer. He's the PR guy."

He was afraid of being on camera? "You're going to have to talk to the paparazzi eventually, you know."

"I know. And I can do it. I just don't like it."

"Maybe I should follow you around with a video camera so you can get used to it before the tour starts."

He laughed. "That's an idea, but it's a bad one."

"Fine. Don't say I didn't try to help." She turned to her computer with a toss of her head, enjoying his chuckle. "Now, don't you have work to do?"

Midway through the six o'clock news, Kiera stared at the television, a glass of milk almost to her mouth. She was wrong. Bill had plenty to say about her, all with a smile on his smug face.

"That's true. Miss Simmons does bring some glamour to SMP. But the focus here is on creating great music, not on the theatrics of her celebrity life. Mark Simmons is one of the best in the business. He knows the music industry and delivers top-rated albums. It was kind of him to give his cousin a temporary job after she was fired."

His brow creased as if he were truly concerned. "We certainly hope that her implication in the fraudulent activities of her boyfriend won't in any way be associated with my client, Peter Theisen."

He went on to discuss Peter's new CD and upcoming tour. She glared at his face filling the screen as his voice reverberated in her head. What right did he have to spread lies about her? The news program cut to a commercial. Swallowing against the burn rising in her throat, she stood and pointed at the offending television. "You are the most pompous, arrogant, evil—"

The ring of her cell phone cut into the tirade. She struggled to wrestle her fury down before glancing at the caller ID. It was Peter. "Hello."

There was a pause on his end. "Oh. You saw the news?"

"Yes." It was difficult to speak through clenched teeth.

He sighed. "I'm sorry, Kiera. You were right. I should have gone out there when you mentioned it. Maybe I could have stopped him."

"I'm sure the damage was done by then. Forget it."

"I can't forget it. That was a lousy thing for him to do. Could I...how about I come over. So we can talk."

"There's nothing to talk about." She rubbed her temple. "Besides, it would just put more fuel on his fire. Please don't make it worse."

He was silent.

"Peter, I don't blame you for Bill's behavior, so we're good. Honest. I'll see you at the studio tomorrow, okay?"

"But..." He gave a noisy breath. "Okay. Call me if you need anything."

She hung up and flung the phone at the chair. Fists clenched at her side, she prayed her father hadn't seen the news. *Lord, why didn't you stop this?*

"What's wrong?"

She jerked around at Terese's voice. "Nothing. Just...Bill being Bill."

Terese approached cautiously. "It's more than Bill being Bill. What happened?"

Kiera shut her eyes briefly to keep from blasting Terese with her hurt. "He took the opportunity for free PR and talked to the reporter that's been hounding me."

"About?"

"About my implication in my *boyfriend's* illegal activities. And the fact that Mark had to give me a job because I was fired." She met Terese's stunned gaze and forced a brittle smile. "But he did say I bring glamour to SMP."

"Oh, Kiera. I'm sorry." Terese gave her a long hug.

"Apparently this is how it works in Bill Djerf's kingdom. Any potential threat is dealt with by public lynching." She blinked hard. She would not cry. He wasn't worth it.

Her phone rang. Terese retrieved it and held it out. "It's Mark."

Kiera tried to sound normal over the knot in her throat. "Hi, Mark."

"Hey, kid. You watch the news?"

"Yeah. Sorry for the negative publicity."

He snorted. She could picture him rubbing his face, glasses askew. "The only negative publicity was Bill looking like a total jerk. I wish I'd known he planned to talk to the reporter. I'd have told him it's not allowed on my front porch."

"It's not your fault. It's mine." He'd always been her champion and now she was causing trouble for him and the studio. "I guess it's what I get for being stupid."

"This has nothing to do with you and everything to do with him. I'll be talking to him tonight."

"Please don't." The thought of another confrontation with the pompous man set her skin crawling. "Let's just let it blow over. I don't want it to affect your relationship with him."

Her doorbell rang as Mark grunted. "I appreciate that, Kiera, but I'm still going to tell him that's not how we do business at SMP. I expect him to show you the same respect he shows all of the staff."

Her anger softened. "Well, I'm tougher than I look. He doesn't scare me." Hearing Terese approach, she turned and started. Peter stood next to her roommate, his dark eyebrows pinched upward. "I need to go. Peter just stopped by."

"Did he?" He made it sound like an everyday occurrence. "Okay, then I'll leave you in very capable hands. See you tomorrow, kid."

"Thanks, Big Cuz." She clicked off the call and lifted her gaze to Peter's as Terese slipped from the room. "For someone who wasn't supposed to come over, you got here awfully fast."

"Hi to you, too."

She folded her arms. "This isn't necessary, Peter. I'm fine. I'm just sorry that my past is reflecting poorly on the studio."

"It's not. Let's go for a walk."

It was a directive and she hesitated, weighing the pros and cons according to Bill. He couldn't be any more unpleasant than he'd already been.

They walked in silence the first block. With each step, Kiera's shoulders relaxed and the knots in her neck loosened. It was easy being with Peter, even now when she should have sent him on his way.

"Knock, knock."

Her head lifted. "What?"

"That's not how knock-knock jokes work." He gave a huff. "C'mon, work with me here. Knock, knock."

She stopped to look up at him, hands on her hips. He looked back at her and waited.

"Fine." A smile tugged at the corners of her mouth. "Who's there?"

"Wendy."

"Wendy who?"

"Wendy wind blows, de cradle will rock."

A laughing snort escaped despite her attempt to squash it. "I shouldn't laugh. It just encourages you."

"And I appreciate the encouragement." He started walking. "Wanna hear another one?"

"One's my limit."

He chuckled and slid his hands into his pockets. The cheerful swagger in his step sent a smile through her heart. They turned at the corner and walked another block in silence.

"Thanks." How had he made her smile in such a short time?

He gave her a gentle bump with his shoulder. "Anytime. Well, look at that. An ice cream store just ahead. I'm thinking you're a mint chocolate chip kind of girl, am I right? I'm more butter brickle myself." He continued the chatter, steering her to the end of the line in the crowded shop. "I don't like cherry, but I love anything with strawberry in it. I might try—"

"Hey, that's Kiera Simmons! Jess, look. It's Kiera Simmons. The Paisley girl."

The girls' excited voices shattered the pleasant moment. The buzz of conversation lowered to a hush as all eyes turned toward her. Kiera couldn't pretend she didn't hear them so she gave the room a quick smile before turning back toward Peter, praying no one would comment on the news segment.

He draped an arm around her shoulders and pulled her close as he pointed up at the chalkboard that listed twenty flavors. "I know I said I wanted butter brickle, but now I'm thinking Rocky Trail. Or maybe Gone Marbles. You don't have to get the green stuff just because I said so."

"That's very big of you." The crowd chatter resumed and she leaned against him, feigning interest in the flavor listing while her heart fluttered crazily. "I think I'm going to have raspberry sherbet with a few chocolate chips thrown on for fun."

"Wow. Living large, I see. Hey, what did you think of the song we finished this week?"

Under the security of his arm, she let him direct the conversation. An hour ago she'd been steaming mad at the world. Now she stood snuggled against the man who threw her insides into a tizzy. Life was strange.

Wandering back toward the house, they devoured their treat, enjoying the warm evening air and conversation punctuated with laughter. When his arm brushed hers, she savored the tingle that danced across her skin, not bothering to scold her heart for its response. She'd do it later.

Settled on the front step, they played cribbage until Terese brought out lemonade and a plate of cookies. She joined the conversation for a bit then went back inside, throwing a sparkling wink at Kiera, who focused on draining her glass. It would all look different in the morning light, but for now she would simply enjoy the moment.

After the sun had set and the mosquitoes descended, Peter declared it Kiera's bedtime, making her laugh. They stood and stretched.

"Okay, just so you know," he said, as they strolled toward his car, "I plan on winning every game going forward. I was just being nice to you tonight because of Bill."

"You think so, hmm? Well, not only will I win every game, I'll double skunk you."

"Yeah, right. Big talk."

They faced each other at the curb and she linked her fingers together, looking at her feet. "Thanks for coming even though I told you not to." She lifted her gaze and admitted softly, "I'm glad you did."

He grinned and tucked her hair behind her ear with a gentle touch. "My pleasure. Thanks for sharing some of your sherbet with me."

"I don't think sharing is the right word," she corrected.

"Okay, thanks for not putting up a fight when I stole some." He rested his forearms on her shoulders, his smile fading as he looked down at her. "Tomorrow will be okay, Kiera."

She nodded, unable to agree but grateful for his assurance. The skip to her heartbeat was probably from the thought of facing Bill. "We'll deal with it when it gets here."

"Good plan." They looked at each other in the quiet of the evening, Peter's arms keeping her in place, his gaze drifting over her flushed face. When it paused on her mouth, she held her breath, wanting him to, afraid he would.

"Goodnight, pretty lady." He brushed a kiss to her forehead then pulled her into his arms like it was the most natural thing in the world.

She rested there, arms around him, soaking in his kindness, his friendship, and his cologne. Much as Bill would squawk if he knew, she was far too content to move.

"I'll be praying that God takes your hurt away," he said softly.

She leaned closer and his arms tightened in response.

Returning to the house, she closed the door behind her, and leaned back against it with a sigh. Eyes closed, she smiled as her heart finally slowed. When she straightened, Terese's amused gaze was waiting from where she sat on the couch, a large bowl of popcorn in her lap.

"What?" Kiera felt silly. And weirdly elated. And scared to death. And—

"You like him, hmm?"

She wanted to protest but a long breath escaped instead. "I like him." She crossed the room and flopped onto the couch. "I like him a lot."

"Hon, it's about time you let your guard down. And I can't imagine a nicer guy to let past the sentry than Peter."

Wrapping her arms around a throw pillow, Kiera rested her chin on it. "But it's such a bad idea, Tess. I'm going to end up with a broken heart."

Terese frowned. "He doesn't strike me as the kind of guy who plays around. It's easy to see he's pretty head over heels for you."

Warmth swept through her. He did seem happy to be with her. But then, so had Thomas. "In September he'll leave for good. He's building a career that will take him around the world. And he's that good. He's going to be famous, Terese. I can feel it."

"So?" Terese cocked her head. "If things progress, you can go with him."

"There's no way I'd follow him around like a groupie. I'm building my life here. My friends and family are here. Besides, I'd never leave Dad while he's dealing with the cancer."

Terese shrugged and turned her attention to the popcorn, picking between the white kernels. "Well, maybe you could just let the relationship unfold before you turn down his as-yet-nonexistent marriage proposal."

Kiera relaxed into a rueful smile and nodded. "Good point. Now pass that bowl over here, please."

Bill gestured Peter into his hotel room as he rolled his eyes at the cell phone at his ear. "Right. That's what I was thinking…No, let's not do it that way…Because it won't work…Because I've done it before, Rob, and I know it won't be any different this time…"

Peter moved silently across the carpet to stand at the window, staring out at the city lights. Knowing God stood with him stilled the shaking in his legs.

Bill muttered a few coarse words, hung up and sent the phone spinning across the table with an oath. "Some people are determined to live life stupid."

Peter remained silent at the window, sweat trickling down his back. Since leaving Kiera, he'd prayed for self-control and the right words. The hurt he'd seen on her face bolstered his confidence and he turned.

"So, Peter. What brings you by so late? As if I don't know." He lowered into a chair, set one ankle across the other knee, and looked up expectantly.

"Why did you do that?"

"Do what?"

"C'mon, Bill. We're way past playing games about this. What was the point of slamming Kiera like that?"

Bill raised an eyebrow, his expression relaxed except for the set to his jaw. "Slamming her? I don't understand. I was giving an interview about you and your tour."

Peter strode closer and settled into a firm stance, arms folded. "Don't mess with me on this. She's been a good friend while I've been here, making sure everything runs smoothly, bending over backwards for both of us, and you know it."

Bill snorted. "Oh, take off the rose-colored glasses, Theisen. That's her job. She's the office help."

She was far more than office help. "So why not leave her alone and let her do her job?"

He shook his blond head slowly, his smile irritatingly arrogant. "Peter, Peter, Peter. If you're going to get so caught up over the first little gal you come across, it's going to be very hard to meet the other hundred thousand out there waiting for you."

"I'm not 'caught up.' I'm asking you to be respectful."

His smile stiffened at the edges. "I'm your manager, Peter. You hired me to jump-start your career, which is what I'm doing. You, on the other hand, seem intent on derailing it before it gets started."

"What does lying about Kiera have to do with my career?"

"She has nothing to do with your career. That's the point. She's a washed-up glamour girl looking for her next free ride. My job is to make sure you're not it." He tapped his fingertips together, holding Peter's gaze. "How 'bout this? You keep your focus on the album and the tour prep, and I'll keep my focus on the trajectory for your career. If we work together, you'll be a star within the year. Deal?"

Peter shook his head. He wasn't leaving until they understood each other. "My focus has been and continues to be on singing, but that doesn't mean I'm going to let you slam one of my friends, especially on camera. Leave her alone and we've got a deal."

Their gazes locked and Peter pressed his lips together to keep from saying more. Bill continued tapping his fingers as he released an exaggerated breath. "I will not say another word about her on camera. Once you leave Minnesota, I guarantee she'll become a distant memory." He held up a hand when Peter started to speak. "Until then, I will give her all the respect the front office staff deserves."

"And plenty more, Bill." He let the warning sharpen his tone.

Bill's nod spoke more of condescension than acquiescence, but Peter accepted it as the peace offering it was. Striding down the quiet hall toward his room, he shook his head. "Thanks for keeping me calm, Lord. I hope Bill got the message."

That beautiful redhead wouldn't go through this again on his watch.

– 16 –

Early the next morning, Kiera settled at her desk, grateful for the overflowing In basket. She rubbed gritty eyes, took another sip of coffee, and pulled up the spreadsheet Mark needed for his meeting. It should keep her busy most of the morning.

She glanced up when Peter arrived, unable to stop the tiny smile that answered his wink. Mark joined her to check her progress on the spreadsheet and compare notes on several ongoing projects. His firm hand on her shoulder warmed her heart.

Throughout the morning, each member of the studio staff meandered through the reception area with a pleasant greeting or silly joke. Their encouragement brought tears to her eyes more than once.

Though she heard Bill's deep twang from the back of the studio, by mid-morning she had yet to see him and prayed that would hold for the day. When her cell phone rang, she welcomed the distraction of talking to her father.

"Good morning, Kiki," he said cheerfully. "How's the day going for you so far?"

"Great, thanks." He never called to ask how her day was going. Obviously he'd seen the news yesterday. "It's a beautiful, sunny day. Who could have an issue with a morning like this?"

"Good point. Glad to hear it's going well."

In the awkward pause that followed, she gave a tiny sigh. "Dad, I'm okay.

Thanks for checking on me but everything's fine here. Another day or two and it will be back to normal." If there was such a thing with Bill in the studio.

"Do you have to work closely with him? I don't trust him."

Did anyone? "I know, but it's just for the time being. And to answer your question, no, I really don't." She straightened and put a smile in her voice. "It's all good. Honest."

"You'll tell me if it's not?"

"Of course, but I expect it all to be fine. So, is today your golf league day?"

After chatting for a few minutes, he extracted another promise to keep him informed. Clicking off the call, she sat quietly, holding the phone between her hands. His concern, however poorly masked at first, warmed her heart.

She swung her chair back toward the desk and the warmth cooled. Bill stood at the front counter. She set the cell phone down and greeted him with a polite nod. "Good morning, Mr. Djerf."

"Miss Simmons."

They remained looking at each other in stilted silence until she lifted her eyebrows. "Can I help you with something?"

He cleared his throat, his ice-blue eyes moving past her as he pursed his lips. "I wanted to…apologize if my remarks on the news clip yesterday painted you in a bad light."

If? Her eyes narrowed as she lifted her chin and waited.

"That was not my intent, of course. I was happy to use that opportunity to get some press for Peter's album, but…apparently…my comments were misconstrued." He turned his gaze back to hers. The only sincerity she could detect was in his discomfort in speaking to her. "I will certainly be more careful in my choice of words going forward."

"I would appreciate that. Thank you."

He gave a nod and returned to the recording studio. Kiera sat still a moment. That was probably as close to an apology as he could manage. It did nothing to soothe the hurt that still edged her heart but she would accept it for what it was and move on.

The memory of Peter gently tucking her hair behind her ear sent a delighted tingle through her, and she returned to work with a smile. She could ignore Bill. Peter, on the other hand…

Relaxing in his hotel room a few evenings later, Peter glanced over at Bill. "I've decided to head up north for the long weekend."

There'd been no chance to share his plans for the approaching four-day break since the idea formed after Bill's interview fiasco.

"That sounds good." Bill didn't look up from the entertainment section of the newspaper.

"What are you going to do?" Peter asked.

The paper rustled as he turned the page. "I'll be in L.A. Friday through Tuesday. I have back-to-back meetings to see if we can't get Cliff Hanger out of the mess he made for himself yet again."

Peter grinned at the nickname Bill had given the client who seemed to move from one self-made crisis to another. "What did he do this time?"

Bill looked over the top of the paper. "His third DUI this year, for starters. That boy is going to bury himself in the hole he's digging." He dropped his arms, the newspaper crunching into his lap. "Maybe you can explain it to me. Why work so hard to attain your dream only to throw it away? How do people get so sidetracked?"

Before Peter could reply, Bill continued. "I get the whole celebrity thing. I understand wanting to have some fun. But this new generation of artists is so self-absorbed, I don't know how to respond. I'm all for work hard, play hard. But I don't get work hard, then play so hard you throw it all out the window."

Peter swallowed with difficulty, his stomach churning while his foot tapped a quiet rhythm on the carpet.

Bill's tirade slowed. "Okay, enough of that. At least I can count on you to make the right choices." He returned his focus to the newspaper. "So what are your plans? Going up to the cabin?"

"Mm-hmm. I haven't been there since last fall. I thought it would be a nice change of scenery. A chance to revisit some old haunts." In the ensuing silence, heat rose slowly up his neck, sweat forming along his hairline. The conversation was about to take a nasty turn.

"Tell me you aren't taking her." Bill's quiet words sucked the air from the room.

Peter set his jaw and looked at his manager. What was he afraid of? He could do what he wanted in his free time. "Her and Buck."

Bill's silence was worse than if he'd resumed his earlier tirade.

"We're leaving Friday before lunch and we'll be back Monday afternoon."

Bill got up from the couch and strode across the room to stare out the window, hands clasped behind his broad back. Peter's heart hammered against his ribs. Maybe if he explained his feelings for Kiera, the fun they had together. And the difference renewing his faith had already made in his life.

He shook his head slowly. Bill cared about one thing—Peter's career. He cared about that too, but he also cared about Kiera and Buck and God, and being happy in life beyond the microphone. After years working with single-minded focus, the world had exploded with possibilities.

He opened his mouth but the sharp motion of Bill's hand stopped him. "Don't. Don't tell me how wonderful she is and how she's the one. Do not tell me that you can travel the country building your career and maintain a relationship with an out-of-work ex-model in Minnesota. Do not tell me that having a girlfriend will make your singing better. And whatever you were about to say, I hope it wasn't that believing in God has made you a better person."

He stood ramrod straight, shoulders set. While his tone remained calm, it was impossible to mistake the warning in his words. "Because if you were to say any of that, I would have to leave this room and drop you as a client. We've worked too long and too hard for me to stand by and watch you throw it all away. I have enough clients who aren't focused on their careers. I don't need to add one more to the kindergarten I seem to be running."

He turned and pinned Peter with a penetrating gaze. "You can have your tryst up north, with or without her ailing father. But understand one thing,

Theisen. There are a thousand people just as talented lined up behind you. I took you on because I thought I saw a work ethic and a passion that's hard to come by nowadays. If you can be sidelined by the first girl who wiggles her hips at you, you don't have what it takes."

Peter stood as his manager approached. Bill had several inches on him and at least fifty pounds. His large body resonated with power and anger. It was a good thing they weren't in a dark alley somewhere.

Bill stopped in front of him, breathing heavily though his expression remained calm. "Your job is to provide the fantasy material for women across the world. To sell records, you have to sell yourself." He pointed a finger at Peter's chest. "To make millions, you have to work harder than you ever thought you could and provide what your audience wants—*you*. But if you're pining away for some little gal in Minnesota rather than focusing on the millions in front of you, your career is dead in the water. And I won't waste any more of my time on you."

He walked stiffly to the door, then paused. "Think about that while you're sitting by the lake with Miss Simmons. And when she bats her big green eyes at you, think about all the other women who would like the same opportunity. When you come back, you let me know if I should bother returning to Minneapolis."

Even the quiet click of the closing door held a threatening note.

Peter took Bill's place at the window. The lights of the city gleamed under the black sky. He turned his gaze in the direction of Buck's house, hidden behind a mass of thick trees.

Talk to me.

He blinked and glanced around as the words covered his troubled heart. "I want it all. I want Kiera and I want success and I want to make a boatload of money to take care of her and Buck. I want to show everyone who said I wouldn't amount to anything just how wrong they were."

The taunts were as clear as if it had been yesterday. "Hey, skinny boy. Don't you ever eat? You got arms like a girl. I can count your ribs." Laughter at his very first audition. Name-calling. Bird legs. Babyface. Stick neck.

A slow breath left his lungs. But he'd hated the silence of being ignored even more. His siblings had gotten all the attention. He'd been average. Less than average. He pushed his shoulders back. He wasn't average anymore. Bill had been right to take him on for his work ethic.

"I'll make this the best album ever," he told his reflection. "And I'll have Kiera Simmons too. I can have it all, right, Lord? As long as I'm walking with you, and I'm faithful to Kiera, I know you'll bless it all. She showed me where it says in the Bible I just have to ask and I'll receive. So I'm asking you to make me famous so I can show everybody just how wrong they were, including Bill. And I can prove to the world why someone like Kiera would pick me."

The resounding silence was deafening.

Mid-morning on Friday, the front door of the studio opened and Buck wrestled Kiera's large red suitcase through the doorway, his black duffel on top. Once inside, he stood looking at her with an exhausted smile, sweat beading on his forehead. "Ready?"

Kiera stared over the front counter. Either he'd lost his mind or she'd forgotten he was taking a trip. "Um. Are you going somewhere?"

"Aren't you?"

"Not that I know of. Where are you going?"

"The same place you're going."

She stood and put her hands on her hips. "Buck Simmons, I think you've finally lost it. What are you talking about?"

"Didn't Peter tell you?"

"Why don't you fill me in?"

"Nope." He moved his duffel to the floor and settled on the suitcase, pulled out a hanky and mopped his face.

She spun around and strode down the hall, her father's chuckle following on her heels. Peter and Mark were in the conference room, talking over papers spread across the long rectangular table. Their conversation halted when she stopped in the doorway.

Mark lifted an eyebrow. "What's up?"

"Buck's in the front office. I think he's lost his mind."

The men exchanged a glance before Peter came around the table. "I guess I forgot to tell you what's happening."

"You guess?"

He turned her around and put his hands on her shoulders, steering her out of the conference room. "Let's go see if he brought what I asked."

"Have fun, kids," Mark called.

"Peter, what's—"

He squeezed her shoulders but kept her moving forward. "You aren't very good at rolling with things, are you?"

"You're just figuring that out?"

"Trust me on this."

Buck was still sitting on her suitcase, chatting with Jeff.

"Thanks for bringing the stuff, Buck." Peter glanced at his watch. "Wayne should have pulled the car out back. Let's get the luggage in and start rolling."

Kiera stamped her foot. "I'm not moving until someone tells me what's going on!"

Telltale creases at the corners of his eyes, Buck collected the duffel and rolled the suitcase past his daughter, following a grinning Jeff toward the back of the studio.

Peter stood before Kiera and met her gaze. She folded her arms. Why did people insist on keeping secrets?

"I'd like to spend some time at Gram's cabin. And I thought it would do you and Buck good to come along. You know, change the scenery? It's been a rough couple of weeks."

As she stared at him blankly, a shadow dimmed the hope in his eyes, and a rush of words spilled out. "We have Mark's blessing to take a break for four days. And you saw that Buck's packed and ready to go. He's waiting in the car. So…would you come with me—with us—for the long weekend?"

Go away with him? "*This* weekend?"

He nodded. "Right now."

An unexpected yearning filled her chest. "But…I have to pack. I need clothes and—"

"Terese took care of everything. Clothes, makeup, and all the other girl stuff."

"That's what's in my suitcase?" He'd planned this for her? A tiny song played in her heart. She beat back the voice of control that screamed an objection and managed a shaky laugh. "Then how can I say no?"

He chuckled. "You can't, so let's go. A weekend up north awaits."

– 17 –

Driving slowly along the wooded lane leading to the cabin, Peter pointed out neighbors' cabins he remembered from years ago. "Aubie and Bette lived in that one. They were ancient when I was a kid. I can't imagine they're still around. And this was the McDonoughs'. Ian McDonough was as Irish as a Minnesotan can be. And here's ours."

Steering the car off the road, they followed a narrow dirt driveway until a log cabin came into view. Kiera pulled off her sunglasses as they approached. "Peter, it's lovely." Exactly what a log cabin should look like, from the expanse of windows looking out at the lake to the wraparound deck and window boxes filled with geraniums, coleus, and petunias.

"It's home to me." He glanced at her, then at Buck in the backseat. "I'm glad my folks didn't sell it when Gram died. Come on. Let's get unloaded so I can show you around."

The reserve she'd clung to on the ride up slipped away as they followed Peter through the house. That he loved this place, and his grandmother, was evident. Her heart warmed at the emotion in his voice when he talked about his beloved Gram.

He pointed up the stairs. "The three of us kids slept in the loft up there. But when I was the only one here, I got to sleep in the bedroom next to hers."

Kiera and Buck followed him through the homey family room. Family photos lined the mantle of a stone fireplace, a colorful afghan was draped over the back of the couch. The island in the kitchen was covered with ceramic tiles of soft nature hues. Three mismatched mugs stood beside a coffeemaker.

"Mmm." She inhaled the enticing aroma. "The coffee smells wonderful."

"Courtesy of the property managers," Peter said, stopping to fill each mug. "I gave them a heads-up that we were coming."

She accepted his offering with a smile. "You're already quite the host."

"I would be too," Buck said, sipping from his mug, "if I had a property manager."

"You do," came her retort. "Me. But you can make your own coffee."

Peter led them down the hall and gestured toward the bedroom on the right. "Buck, why don't you take this room, and Kiera can have the other one. I'm going to sleep in the loft and pretend I'm ten again."

Kiera stepped past him into the larger of the bedrooms. A queen bed with a headboard of gleaming oak was covered by a beautiful, hand-sewn quilt. "Did your grandmother make this?"

"She made all the quilts in the cabin." Pride tinged his words. "She always won the sewing events at the local fair with her quilts and doilies and stuff. I didn't appreciate it much when I was young."

"But now you have such wonderful, tangible ways to remember her. She sounds like the perfect grandma. I never knew any of my grandparents."

"I was really lucky to get to spend my summers up here with her." His smile was shy. "I'm glad you're getting to know her a little by being here."

"Me too." Her heart somersaulted. "Thanks for inviting me. Us."

He nodded and stepped backwards toward the door. "Well, you go ahead and unpack and I'll get some lunch ready."

"Thanks, Peter." Flipping open her suitcase, she smiled at the clothing choices Terese had made, comfortable favorites she'd have chosen herself. On a slip of paper tucked inside the cosmetics bag, *Have fun!* was scrawled in Terese's loopy handwriting.

Kiera lifted her head and looked at her reflection in the bathroom mirror. Being here, caring about Peter as more than a friend and colleague, would leave her more battered than the fiasco with Thomas had. It had been more show than substance with Thomas. Her friendship with Peter already went far deeper.

Eyes closed, she listened to the cadence of the men's voices down the hall, muted words interrupted by laughter. *Enjoy the moment. In less than two months he'll be gone and this will be a pleasant memory.* A sigh escaped as she set the empty suitcase in the corner and left the cozy room. They had this weekend to relax and play. She was going to enjoy every minute.

An hour later, as Peter prepared hamburgers for the grill and Buck sliced vegetables, Kiera watched them share a laugh. Her father already looked better—color in his face, his eyes bright. He loved nothing more than talking about the "big ones" that always seemed to get away when he was fishing alone. He could entertain crowds for hours with funny stories and poignant insights on living life well. She never tired of listening to him.

Banned from helping with this first meal, she wandered down the gentle slope to the dock. Sunshine glittered off the water. A boat sped by, pulling two skiers who waved as they bumped along. She waved back.

Settling on the edge of the dock, she pulled in a deep breath of fresh summer air and slipped off her sandals. She dangled her feet in the cool water, circling her toes and watching ripples spread. A growing restfulness muted the barrage of thoughts banging against her temples. She lay back, melting into the warmth of the wood. Another boat hummed over the water. Children splashed and played somewhere nearby.

The heat from the deck loosened her shoulders, inviting her to let her concerns slide away. A long breath escaped as she folded her hands on her stomach. This was heavenly. The peaceful solitude of the moment released a collage of images as she closed her eyes. The strength of Peter's handshake at their first meeting. Peter smiling as he sang so effortlessly. Playing cribbage with him on the front porch swing and his gentle goodnight kiss.

She brushed at a fly on her arm, refusing to be roused from memories that made her smile. Peter's teasing while they canoed the lakes. Sharing a laugh with the SMP team. A knock-knock joke in the midst of her angst.

The fly became more persistent, touching one forearm, then the other. Irritated, she lifted her head. Peter crouched beside her, a long piece of grass in hand and a grin lighting his handsome face. She grunted and dropped her head back down, closing her eyes and scolding her heart for its silly leap. "Go away. I was happily dreaming."

"I could tell by your smile. Don't let me stop you."

It was impossible to relax with him there, especially when the light touch continued on her arms, her hands. When it touched her nose, she raised up on her elbows with a snort. "You are a pest, Peter Theisen. Is this how the weekend is going to go?"

"Maybe." He got to his feet and held out a hand. "Come on, lunch is ready."

"I'm so comfortable here in the sun, would you bring me a plate?" She offered her prettiest smile. "Please?"

"Uh-uh. No princess behavior at Gram's cabin. Hurry up or we'll eat without you."

Releasing an exaggerated sigh, she picked up her sandals and let him pull her to her feet. He led her off the dock, then steadied her while she slid her shoes on.

He lifted an eyebrow. "Think you can beat me up the hill wearing those?"

She met his challenge with a demure bat of the eyes. "Oh, I don't think so." She bolted for the cabin, a laugh drifting behind her. "I know so!" She reached the deck two steps ahead of him and did a teasing victory dance. "Modeling isn't just standing around looking pretty, you know. We have to stay in shape. I happen to like to run."

Peter followed her onto the deck. "You could have warned me, Buck."

"Leave me out of whatever your issue is," came the retort. "Let's eat, Kiki. The burgers are gettin' cold."

"Wait—Kiki?" Peter looked from Buck to Kiera, eyebrows lifted.

She turned away. "He's called me that as long as I can remember."

"I like it. It's cute."

"Figures. Now quit chatting and let's eat."

Settled at the patio table, they joined hands and Buck asked a blessing on their simple meal. Animated conversation was punctuated with teasing as they passed the food. The contentment of the warm dock lingered, lighting a smile in her heart. She might regret it when she had to face Bill on Tuesday, but she was glad she'd come.

Saturday afternoon, Kiera's phone rang as she sat on the dock reading a book, occasionally watching her father and Peter fish. "Hey, Christine."

"Hello, darling girl. How are you?"

"I'm wonderful. How are things on the East Coast?"

"Busy, busy, busy. I'm calling with a fabulous idea that I want you to sign off on."

The words sent a chill across Kiera's sun-warmed skin. "Okaaay."

"I think we've found a way around the non-compete issue. While you can't speak for a competitor, that doesn't mean you can't be the face of, say, a different type of company."

Kiera didn't want to be anyone's face.

"So here's what we're think—"

"Wait." Once Christine got started, it was impossible to stop her. "I don't want to come back right now." Or ever.

"Kiera, I promise this is all above board. We're not doing anything that would get any of us in trouble."

"I'm not worried about that." Maybe she should be, but that wasn't the issue. She pushed out of the chair and walked down the steps to the sand. "I'm happy doing what I'm doing now. I don't want to start modeling again."

"My dear girl, that's just nerves talking. It's hard to get fired, I realize that, but nobody has a bad word to say about you."

"It's not about being fired, Chris. It's about doing what I enjoy, and working with Mark and the staff at SMP is what I enjoy now."

Christine released an expletive. "You can't possibly hide that face in an office somewhere in Minnesota. It was created for everyone to enjoy."

Kiera rolled her eyes. Christine was prone to exaggerate when it suited her. "I'm tired of being a prop used to sell things, being manipulated to look the way someone else wants me to look."

She lifted her head and found Buck and Peter turned in their chairs, watching her. She looked away and dug her toes into the warm sand. "I just want to be me now."

"A little more time away and you'll realize how much you miss it."

"I don't miss it, that's the point. I'm really happy doing what I'm doing, being with the people I'm with." And creating *One of Me*, a program Chris would strongly disapprove of. "Thank you for thinking of me. Really. It was wonderful starting out with you and Richard and the Glitz team, and then getting the Paisley job, but…I just don't want to do it anymore."

The silence on the other end made her smile. Christine was never speechless. Maybe she'd hung up.

"Well, let's not make anything final over the phone." There was an edge to Christine's clipped tone. "I'm not going to push you right now but Glitz needs you, and I think eventually you'll realize you need us."

As she hung up, Kiera shook off the uneasiness at the back of her mind. She'd never need modeling again. She had everything she needed or wanted right here. She looked back and met Peter's smiling gaze.

Peter built a bonfire that evening in the fire pit on the beach. They made s'mores and chatted, the growing darkness muting their conversation. An hour later, Buck yawned for the third time and pushed slowly from his chair. "A day in the sun sure does me in. Goodnight, you two. I'll see you in the morning."

"'Night, Dad. Sleep well."

"Goodnight, Buck."

In the silence that followed, Kiera settled deep into her chair and rested a contented gaze on the fire. Peter forced himself to look past her peaceful face toward the lake. Lightning danced in the approaching clouds. Rain would arrive soon, bringing an early end to their evening.

"Tell me about Gram." Her quiet request startled him.

His eyes jumped to hers and he smiled. Where to start? "Gram was Evelyn Marie Theisen."

"That's my middle name too."

"I knew there had to be a connection. You remind me of her."

"She was a tall redhead with a temper?"

"Not the redhead part. Or the tall part. Or the temper either, I guess." *What a nerd.*

Kiera smiled.

"You have a similar sense of humor. And she was feisty like you." At her indignant harrumph, he chuckled. "She was my dad's mom, and definitely my favorite grandparent. I was her favorite too, or so she told me. She probably said the same thing to all the grandkids, but I knew it was true for me."

Kiera's giggle danced through the fire and tickled his heart. He cleared his throat. "She got me started on piano. I'd sit on the bench beside her for as long as she wanted to play."

"I didn't see a piano in the cabin."

"After she died, I had it shipped home. It's being stored at my folks' while I'm on the road, but once I settle somewhere, I'll get it back. Then I can pretend we're playing together again."

"That's sweet, Peter."

He shrugged. The thirteen-year-old tried to tie his tongue but he forced the words out. "Well, it's the most tangible way to remember her. I loved spending summers here. Since my dad rarely stepped foot outside the operating room, he'd drive us up and stay for a few days, fly home and then back a week later to drive my mom home. I'd stay until school started."

Memories paraded through the firelight. "We'd fish and boat and build forts in the woods. All the stuff kids do when they're let loose in a place like this. Even my brother, who always had his nose in a book, would lighten up and ride bikes and stuff with me."

"It sounds fun. I can see why you love it here."

He stood and dropped another log on the fire, poking at the glowing embers with a stick. Then he turned and looked up the hill at the cabin. The only light came from Buck's room. "When it was just the two of us, we'd sit in her big deck chair at night, wrapped in blankets. She'd tell me about the constellations, what all the scary noises were in the woods, and what song she'd teach me to play next. Those were my favorite times.

"She was my greatest cheerleader when I started singing professionally.

She'd call before every performance to remind me that God would be there on stage with me."

He folded his arms and blinked quickly. "I'd tell her about all the plans I had for my future." He sighed. "I wish she was around to help me navigate life now."

In the silence that followed, he swallowed against a sting of loneliness. It was nearly a year since her death. It seemed like only days.

"More than following a plan," Kiera said softly, standing beside him, "I think Gram would tell you to follow your heart."

He faced her and studied her upturned face, the sudden hammering in his chest making it difficult to breathe. "What if…" He paused, then brushed his knuckles lightly against her cheek. "What if my heart led me to a beautiful redhead who makes me laugh and act stupid and work harder than I ever thought possible? What would she say then?"

Their gazes held and she bit her lip. "She'd tell you to follow your heart."

He took her face in shaking hands, rubbing his thumbs against her cheekbones. *This is such a bad idea.* When she remained steadily looking up at him, he lowered his head and kissed her. Her lips were soft and sweet, beyond anything he could have dreamed. She slid her arms around him, returning his kiss with matching eagerness.

He was sure his heart would batter its way right past his ribs and fling itself off the dock. He'd never felt joy like this. Unexpected, crazy joy.

Lightning flickered overhead, thunder rumbled gently as the storm moved closer. The sticky sweet air pulsed with warmth. Finally, needing to find his equilibrium, Peter drew back to rest his forehead against hers, releasing a shaky breath. "Wow."

"Yeah." The simple word was barely audible.

He lifted his head to smile down at her. "I think we'll always associate thunder and lightning with that."

Her answering smile glowed in the firelight. "I've always liked storms."

They looked at each other in silence. She was the most beautiful girl he'd ever known, and she was wrapped securely in his arms. *His* arms. *If this is from you, God, thanks.*

Buck had called a second time before Kiera emerged from her room for breakfast, showered and dressed. Shuffling toward the kitchen, she debated returning to bed. She'd barely slept after an amazing evening sitting on the patio below the deck, watching the storm roll in and talking until two in the morning.

Lying in bed, staring into the darkness, Peter's handsome face had danced through her mind; closing her eyes, she'd tasted his kiss, felt the warmth and security of his arms, heard the rumble of thunder. And while it sent her heart into crazy spins, it put a tremor in her legs now that made it hard to walk the short distance to the kitchen.

What had she been thinking to let herself fall for him? *You knew you shouldn't have come up here. But nooo, you were so sure you could handle it. Now look at the mess—*

"Good morning, sleepyhead," Buck said from his post at the stove. "Thank you for gracing us with your presence this morning."

"You're welcome." The words were clipped. Keeping her gaze from where Peter sat at the table, she poured a glass of juice and drained it.

"Wow, this lake air must be life-altering." Buck's words held laughter. "I didn't know you drank anything but coffee first thing in the morning."

"I was thirsty." She forced a glance in Peter's direction. "Good morning, Peter."

"Morning, Kiki."

Buck laughed. Kiera rolled her eyes. "Sounds like the name of a dancing poodle."

"Well, someone sure got up on the wrong side of the bed." Buck put two large pancakes and sausage links on a plate, then held tight when she reached for it. His green eyes smiled encouragement at her. "Maybe you should start with coffee?"

She flushed and pulled the plate away. Starting with coffee would be a good idea, followed by a quick escape back to the city. She devoured her breakfast in silence while the men chatted.

Afraid to look at Peter and determined to put some distance between them, she cleared her place then pulled on a light jacket. "I'm going for a walk. Leave everything and I'll clean up when I get back." She was out the door before either could reply.

Striding down the dirt road, she kicked at a rock. She should have known better than to let him kiss her. But she'd practically thrown herself at him so what did she expect? Then snuggling up to him to watch the storm? Another kick. *Handing him your heart like that, you might as well have included a machete so he could hack it to pieces.*

But…he was so sweet. So unassuming. He'd looked as stunned as she felt after that first heart-stopping kiss—eyes unfocused, a goofy smile on his adorable face.

She slapped the memories aside and continued along the winding lane, locked in battle with her thoughts, until she reached the main road. For a long minute, she stood at the crossroad.

Looking up at the cloudless sky, she raised her hands. "You had to put him in my life now? You couldn't have waited a few years until he got the fame thing out of his system?"

Tears filled her eyes and she lowered her arms, face still lifted toward the sun. "I don't want to care about him. I don't want to go through that again." She dropped her head and whispered, "I'm afraid."

She stood in the silence, tears sliding off her cheeks onto the dirt. Then she drew a shaky breath and pulled up all the resolve she could find. She didn't have to let things go any further. She couldn't undo the events of last night, but she could stop any forward progression before she got even more attached.

Bill was right. Peter needed to focus on the career mapped out for him. She'd remind him that he didn't have time for a relationship. Wiping her face, she set her shoulders and turned back toward the cabin. She would just keep Bill's face in front of her. He could make things difficult for everyone, including Mark, if she didn't watch her step. She wouldn't give him another reason to humiliate her.

Seeing Peter's long frame propped against the elm at the end of the driveway put a brief hitch in her stride. He pushed away from the tree and met her in the road, his expression serious. "Up for a little more walking? I want to show you one of my favorite places."

"Sure." She forced cheerfulness into the single word. It had been easy to resolve to be detached when she was alone.

They veered off the road into the woods past the cabin. Peter seemed to be following a memorized path as there was nothing guiding them. He remained silent, jaw set, gaze focused ahead. When they started up a steep hill, he reached a hand back to her. A pang went through her when their fingers connected. She would have pulled away if his grasp hadn't tightened.

As they crested the hill and started down, he released her hand and slowed his pace, pulling in a deep breath. She did the same. Fresh pine and wildflowers. How often she'd enjoyed a setting just like this camping with Buck.

A moment later they stood in a clearing beside a creek winding toward a large pond. The private area was guarded by stately pines and spindly birch, carpeted by white and purple clover.

"Wow." The serenity calmed her fluttering heart.

"My sister and I found it. The three of us would bring books and camp here all day, reading and just hanging out. Gram would even pack a picnic for us." He put his hands on his hips and looked around. "It hasn't changed except it's even more private since the trees have grown."

Kiera watched him lift his face to the sun and smile. Then the smile faded as his gaze turned to hers. She looked away. *Remember Bill. Remember the goal.*

"There's a log over there." He pointed. "Let's sit for a minute."

They settled several feet apart, silent. Kiera swallowed back the knot tightening her throat. This was why she should have kept her distance last night. There'd be no going back to the way things had been before.

"I'm sorry, Kiera."

Her gaze swung to his. "For what?"

His shadowed eyes were so different from last night. "For making you uncomfortable. I didn't..." He got to his feet and moved a few steps away, folding his arms as he watched a hawk circle lazily overhead. "I crossed the line and put you in an awkward position. I'm sorry."

She stared at him. He was apologizing for kissing her?

"After everything you went through with Ramsey, the last thing you needed was for one of Mark's clients to hit on you." He dug the toe of his shoe into the clover. "I wasn't doing that. Well, I was, but not that way. Okay, it was sort of like that but I don't want you to think… Man, what an idiot!"

Color flooding his face, he spun away and refolded his arms. Tears burned her eyes. He was so sweet, so *different*.

Silence stretched between them until he swung back, frowning determination on his face. "Okay. It's like this. I'm not great with women. In fact, I'm a pretty big idiot. And around you I'm an idiot times ten. But that's because…I like you. I like being with you. But I got carried away last night."

He sighed. "It's obvious you're uncomfortable now, and I'm sorry about that. You don't have to worry about me trying it again. I promise I'll keep my distance." He turned back to the pond and stuffed his hands in his pockets, shoulders slumped.

His words filled her with healing warmth. *Face it, Kiera. You came up here for exactly this reason. He's not like the other guys.*

She enjoyed being with him more than she feared the potential for another broken heart. The thought of losing his friendship pushed her to her feet and she moved to stand beside him. "Please don't."

He looked sideways at her. "Don't what?"

She held his serious gaze. "Don't keep your distance."

He turned to face her and waited.

"Your apology means the world to me, Peter. But I'm the one who should apologize. For being such a nutcase around you."

When he remained silent, she pulled in a breath. *Time to be honest with both of us.* "After the fiasco, I promised myself I'd never have my private life splashed across the news again." She looked up at him, the earlier reserve crumbling around her feet. "But I don't want to lose your friendship. I came this weekend because…I wanted to spend time with you. Away from the studio.

"I was glad you kissed me last night," she admitted shyly. Heat bloomed on her cheeks but she pushed on. "And sitting there through the rain, talking so long—it was amazing. But then I got scared. I don't do scared well."

He reached for her hands. "Neither do I."

"There's a lot working against us already. Bill will flip out. You've got a CD to finish and a tour to prepare for. I'm getting *One of Me* off the ground and there's Dad's cancer to—"

He put a finger to her lips. "Life is full of stuff, Kiera. If it isn't those issues, it'll be something else. How about we focus on today and let tomorrow worry about itself?"

The gentle words washed her fear away. He was right. All they really had was the moment in front of them. With a nod, she stepped closer and slid her arms around him. His racing heartbeat matched hers. "Good idea."

– 18 –

As the boat motored along the Lake Minnetonka shoreline, Peter glanced sideways at Kiera where she sat with her eyes closed, smiling into the sunlight. She hadn't seemed to stop smiling since their time at the cabin two weeks ago. He certainly hadn't.

He put his hand up to shield his eyes from the afternoon sun and heard the click of the camera. He grinned over his shoulder at Will, the photographer Bill had hired for the CD cover shoot. "That's a picture? Me squinting into the sun?"

Will nodded. "That symbolized you looking into the future, and with the lake in the background it was perfect."

"Well, then." Peter shot Kiera a wink. "Let's call it a day now that you've got the perfect picture, along with a thousand that apparently weren't so perfect."

"Nice try," Will said, chuckling. "I have one more place that I think will be perfect for the back cover. We're almost there."

The boat picked up speed and Peter grasped the sidebar, studying Kiera's profile. He could never have imagined how his life would change when he reached Minnesota. If anyone had told him he'd be dating a spokesmodel, he'd have laughed himself stupid. He'd simply hoped to find someone, someday, who might think his being a singer was pretty cool. Kiera had looked past that immediately, focusing instead on the man he hadn't known he could be.

This amazing redhead had crept into every inch of his being, from encouraging his faith to bolstering his confidence, making him sing with more assurance than ever before. And then there was his heart.

There was so little time left before the tour. With only one song to finish, the CD was going into edit and his days would be spent meeting with Bill and the tour manager, while her evenings were filled with *One of Me* presentations. Every moment they had together was precious.

They slowed to a stop beside a dock, and the driver quickly anchored the boat. Peter helped Kiera climb out, keeping hold of her hand as they made their way to the shore. He couldn't keep his eyes off her—the wind playing with her hair, her smiling face flushed from the sun.

"Okay, Peter." Will's voice startled him. "Get yourself settled in the middle of those rocks, facing the lake."

Peter climbed over the boulders and settled atop the flattest one. Will followed to adjust his jacket and explain where to put his feet and hands. "Perfect. Hold that and I'll be ready in a second."

He returned to the shore and got situated with his cameras. The clicking began. "Okay, a little smile. Good. Now look past the camera at Kiera but keep it serious. Whoa, great look." The camera clicked repeatedly. "Okay, now you can smile at her. Maybe not that big. Love it. Kiera, can you go sit next to Peter? I want to get a few pictures of the two of you, if you don't mind."

"I don't mind at all." She climbed over the rounded boulders to settle beside him, offering an impish grin. "Excuse me, sir. Is this rock taken?"

"It is now." He pulled her into a warm hug. "Now *this* will make for worthwhile pictures."

Will snapped photos, adjusted the lens, turned the camera sideways. "Kiera, turn towards me and lean back against Peter. Perfect. Peter, put your left arm around her and rest your right arm on your knee. Good. Kiera, look up at Peter. Don't turn quite so much. Perfect. Both of you look to your right, across the bay. Now try it without smiling."

Peter laughed. "That's impossible when she's around."

"Well, think of something serious for a minute."

An image of leaving on tour sobered him quickly.

Kiera rested her head against him and sighed. "I'd rather be laughing. I can't think about sad things when I'm with you."

He pressed a kiss to her temple and tightened his arm. "Me neither." He couldn't think straight when she was around. He'd never have believed he'd be so happy being a babbling idiot around someone. The thought made him smile and the camera clicked again.

"Hey, Kiera!"

Heading for The Java Depot to meet Peter, Kiera looked toward the voice that called from across the street. A man stood on the opposite curb, camera pointed her way. Without breaking stride, she continued toward the shop, jaw clenched.

Sitting at a small table in the back, Peter had an iced tea waiting for her. His welcoming smile disappeared when their eyes met. "What's wrong?"

"Nothing." She took a long sip of the peach tea. "Mmm. That's good."

"Hey." He set his hand over hers. "Don't shut me out."

The irritation faded as she looked into concerned brown eyes. "Sorry. It was just a guy with a camera. He yelled my name then took pictures. It just...bugged me." She squeezed his fingers and smiled. "So why the clandestine meeting a whole block from the studio?"

He grinned. "I just wanted some alone time with you and I didn't want to wait until after the business dinner tonight."

"That's sweet. You know Bill will drag the meeting out as long as he can."

"Sad but true." He sighed, rubbing his thumbs over her skin. His smile returned when he lifted his gaze to hers. "However, he's underestimating me. He can stretch the meeting to midnight if he wants. Afterwards, I'll just prop a ladder against the townhouse and climb up to steal a kiss from Sleeping Beauty."

She was unsuccessful at keeping the blush from her cheeks. "You saw me at the cabin first thing in the morning, Mr. Theisen. Sleeping Beauty I'm not."

He winked. "A matter of opinion. Anyway, I have some news. Ready?"

"Ready." The shine in his eyes made her heart spin faster. "I think."

"I talked to my folks the other night. Once I've got some money saved from the tour, I'm going to buy the cabin from them."

"Peter, that's wonderful!"

"After spending the weekend there with you and Buck, I realized it's the perfect place to decompress from touring and recording. You think it's a good idea?"

"It's a great idea. You'll love having your own private getaway."

He studied their clasped hands, then looked at her from under his brow. "I'm hoping you liked it enough to want to go back."

Liked it? She'd never forget it. Or their first kiss. "I loved it." The words wobbled out and she cleared her throat. "I'll be thrilled to go back whenever you invite me."

"Consider it an open invitation." His smile warmed. "When I'm there, I want you there with me."

When they stepped out of the coffee shop twenty minutes later, reporters with cameras and microphones swarmed around them, shouting questions and jostling for position.

"Peter! Are you looking forward to the tour?"

"Kiera, how does it feel to be dating the next big superstar?"

"Peter, over here. How about a shot of you alone?"

After the initial shock, Kiera pulled on her professional face, smiling calmly at each camera despite the pounding against her ribs. It was too familiar—the chaos, the shouting. She glanced at Peter. The alarm in his eyes offset his confused smile. He looked from person to person, trying to answer the questions raining over them.

After another agonizing minute, Kiera started them moving again, desperate for the quiet of the studio. Peter followed her lead, an arm wrapped securely around her shoulders.

The chaos continued as they headed toward the studio. Kiera stopped smiling but kept her modeling persona in place until the door closed behind them. In the welcome silence, they faced each other.

He set his hands on her shoulders. "Are you okay? I have no idea what that was about."

She opened her mouth to reassure him but Bill's voice interrupted.

"That," he said, "was all about you." He crossed the reception area to join them, ignoring Kiera as he clapped a hand on Peter's shoulder. The weight of his grip forced Peter to release her. "Welcome to the world of fame, Peter."

Kiera turned quickly and stepped around the counter to settle at the front desk, lips pressed in a hard line. The paparazzi had sent a rush of nausea through her that had made her knees weak and now made her want to cry. He'd done that on purpose.

"I don't get it. Did you set that up?" Anger edged Peter's question.

Kiera stared blindly at the papers she'd picked up. Even a glance at Bill would shred the trembling control she clung to. What was she thinking? This was what she'd been desperate to escape. And what Peter was heading into. She blinked hard against the sudden burn in her eyes.

"I just happened to tip a few people off as to where you could be found," Bill was saying. "And with whom. For now we'll capitalize on what's left of Kiera's name recognition to get you some early publicity. Once the tour starts, you'll be generating your own."

Unable to breathe, she swung her chair to the computer and typed random words on whatever the document was that she couldn't see through her tears. She would *not* give Bill the satisfaction of seeing the pain his callous words caused.

"Why would you want our pictures out there now?"

"That's what celebrity is all about. Hype is essential to ticket sales. No hype, no interest in your shows. I'm assuming you *do* want people to see your show?"

"Of course but—"

"It's all about exposure, Peter. The women need to see you now so they'll want to see you in concert and afterwards."

"Afterwards?"

"At the meet 'n greets, remember?" Bill's sigh held an exaggerated note of patience. "Get used to the attention, my inexperienced friend. Once the tour starts, your life will never be the same."

Kiera kept her attention glued to the screen as their voices faded from the reception area. Bill was right. This was just a taste of what Peter's life would be like in the coming months. And hers. The dreaded paparazzi everywhere, all the time. Determined to make "news" where there wasn't any, in the name of entertainment.

"Lord," she whispered against the heaviness in her chest, "I can't do this again. I can't."

The phone rang and she jumped, shoving the emotions down before picking up the receiver. "Simmons Music Productions. How may I help you?"

What she needed to know was who would help her.

Kiera strode through the hotel ballroom one last time to triple-check the event details, then returned to the suite where she and Buck were encamped for the busy weekend. The invitation-only reception, set to start in two hours, would introduce Peter to the media. The public CD release party that followed would promote the tour. It was a celebration of months of hard work. She dreaded all of it.

Dressed and waiting for Peter a half hour later, she stood at the expanse of windows and stared unseeing at the cloudless sky. As often as she'd prayed for someone to share her life with, she hadn't truly believed she would meet someone like him. In three short months she'd found a love she hadn't dared dream possible. And now she had to let it go.

Lord, help me do this. I don't want to let him go. She brushed at the tear that slipped out. *But he's not mine. He's yours. Keep him close to you on this tour. And maybe...he could come back to me someday?*

A knock at the door startled her, and she pulled in a steadying breath as she crossed the large room, her evening gown swirling around her legs.

"Kiera Simmons?" inquired a young man's voice from behind the bouquet of crimson roses.

"Yes. Oh, my." The aroma of fresh flowers spilled into the room. "They're beautiful."

"Sign here. please."

She set the overflowing vase on the glass end table, signed her name, and thanked him. As the door closed she smiled, bending to take a deeper breath. A card was wedged among the flowers.

> To the most beautiful and amazing woman in the universe,
>
> I can't find the words to tell you how you've rocked my world. This album is better than I ever dreamed it could be, and I know it's because of your influence, support and love. You are and always will be in my heart. God sure knew what He was doing when He called me to Minnesota.
>
> Yours forever and for always,
> Peter

Clutching the card to her chest, she sank down on the couch in a rustle of taffeta and silk. Slowly she shook her head, eyes closed. *I can't let him go. We need more time.* There were so many more memories to make.

"You okay, Kiki?" Her father's concerned words floated into her pain and she opened her eyes. He stood in his bedroom doorway, frowning across the room at her as he fumbled with his tie.

"Yes, just tired." A corner of her mouth lifted. He'd never been good at ties. She pushed the melancholy away and moved closer to help him. It was a ritual she cherished. "There." She stepped back and perused his attire. The suit coat seemed roomier than the last time he'd worn it. "Very handsome."

"I'd return the compliment but I think it would be an insult." He smiled and tipped her chin up. "I think there's someone else you'd rather hear it from anyway."

"I've always loved compliments from you." A knock at the door made her heart jump. "But they're nice from him too."

Buck stepped past her and opened the door. "It's the star of the hour. Come in, come in. You clean up pretty good there, Mr. Theisen."

Peter stepped into the room, tugging at the collar of his tuxedo shirt. "Thanks. You're lookin' pretty good yourself. I still don't know why we couldn't wear jeans to this." He set a white box on the table beside the roses.

Buck excused himself. "I want to polish my shoes before we head down."

As Buck went into his room, Peter approached her slowly, his dark eyes focused intently on her. No one had ever looked at her the way he did every day—with such warmth and longing, and even a hint of surprise.

"Wow." He stopped before her. "You look amazing."

She managed a shaky smile. The shimmering hunter green made her feel truly beautiful, not just camera-pretty. She wanted him to be proud of her. "I have the most handsome date in Minnesota. I have to look the best I can."

The corners of his eyes crinkled. "I'll have to fight the guys off with a bat." He tapped her nose. "Don't forget who you came with."

She giggled. "Never."

He drew her into his arms and lifted a hopeful eyebrow. "We still have time to make a break for it. We could jump back into our jeans and head for the cabin."

"And leave your new fans without their star? Not hardly. Although," she added with a sigh, "it's awfully tempting."

"It sure is. Hey, I brought you something." He released her and retrieved the box. "Now we'll both have one."

Tears stung again as she lifted out a gleaming silver picture frame. "Oh…" She ran her fingers across the glass over a photo of the two of them from the CD cover shoot. It had been a glorious day—she could still hear the cry of the gulls and crash of water against the rocks, feel the warm breeze where they'd sat beside the lake, Peter's arms wrapped securely around her. It had been magical.

"We look so happy," she whispered.

"Because we are." He set the frame down and gathered her back into his arms. "Kiera Simmons, I am the happiest man in the world when I'm with you. Never in a million years would I have thought I could feel like this about someone."

He traced a finger along her eyebrow then down across her cheekbone. "This picture will travel everywhere with me. It'll keep me going, knowing you're here cheering me on, praying for me." Color rose in his cheeks as he gave a crooked smile. "And loving me no matter where I am."

Her breath caught at his shy words.

He cupped her face with cool hands. "I love you, Kiera. With every inch of my being. And I thank God for the gift of sharing this journey with you."

Warmth blazed through her. His were not the same words Thomas had uttered because he was not the same man. And she was not the same woman. "I love you, Peter. Forever and for always."

The joy that lit his face set her heart flying.

– 19 –

Kiera let her gaze run around the theater, hands clenched in her lap. The release party had been a huge success. Weeks of rehearsal were behind him. The magical summer was over and Peter's first concert would start in just minutes.

She'd been praying for him to stay calm and focused. Maybe she needed to add a prayer for herself to keep breathing so she wouldn't pass out and miss everything. He'd seemed relaxed and comfortable in the days leading up to this kickoff concert. When she'd left him backstage moments ago with a kiss and hug, he'd been chatting with the band. Didn't he have enough sense to be nervous?

Buck's hand covered hers. "Holding up, Kiki?"

She nodded. "I've been praying nothing goes wrong and that he stays calm. And especially that it's fun. I can't imagine getting up in front of all these people."

"You did when you were modeling and speaking."

"That was different. On the runway, it was a grown-up version of dress-up. They were looking at the clothes, not me. And I didn't speak in this kind of setting, This…" She waved her free hand around the theater that was nearly full. "This is all about Peter. For two whole hours."

"And it's his dream come true."

She nodded and settled back against her seat, glancing to the left. Terese and Jason were deep in whispered conversation. Kiera drew a deep breath and closed her eyes. There seemed to be no doubt God was calling Peter to this career. And if He was calling him, He would provide everything he needed. *Right, Lord?*

The house lights dimmed, drawing a cheer from the crowd. A moment of darkness, then the stage lights came on to reveal the musicians in their places—Jeff settled at the drums above and behind the piano, Martha and four other string musicians seated to his right, Alonzo at the left beside a bass guitar player. Cheryl Lee, the backup singer, fiddled with her earpiece. The piano sat empty in the middle of the stage.

"Ladies and gentlemen." Bill's voice filled the theater from somewhere offstage. "Welcome to the State Theatre in downtown Minneapolis. Please remember no flash photography is allowed during the performance. Please silence your cell phones and pagers. Thank you."

The theater went dark again. An electric hush fell over the crowd. Kiera leaned forward in her front row seat. *Please let it go well.*

"And now, in his inaugural concert of the *Road to Love* tour, please welcome...Peter Theisen!"

A spotlight illuminated the piano where Peter now sat, handsome and smiling in jeans, a white shirt and tan jacket. "Hello, Twin Cities!"

On the edge of her seat, Kiera clapped so hard her hands stung as she watched him take in his surroundings with childlike excitement. His gaze swung down to hers and he gave a nod then started the first song of his first concert of his first tour.

Her heart swelled as he slid easily into this new role. After the first song, she relaxed into her seat. As it always did, his voice lifted her into another world, inviting her into the music, wrapping her in warmth. Two hours later, she couldn't believe it was over.

He thanked his wildly appreciative audience and said goodnight, then followed the band offstage. The crowd was on its feet, a thundering ovation demanding his return to the spotlight. He reemerged with a self-conscious wave; it took another minute before quiet had been restored.

"Wow, you guys are amazing."

"We love you, Peter!" shouted a chorus of female voices from the balcony.

He laughed. Kiera flinched.

"Not half as much as I love you all for being here. Thanks for spending the evening with me and forgiving me when I forgot the words." Laughter rolled through the theater. "I'm thinking a teleprompter is a good idea. Anyway, thanks again for coming. And tell your friends about the tour. We're heading out next week and we'd love to see them at our upcoming concerts. Check out the *Road to Love* website for details.

"Okay, enough of the commercial. Here's my favorite song. Unfortunately it didn't make it on this record. I wrote it for my lovely lady, Kiera. The official title is 'Hearts Entwined.'" He looked down at her, a grin stealing across his face. "I call it 'Kiera's Song.' I hope you like it."

What? Kiera pressed trembling fingers to her mouth. He'd written a song for her? The familiar melody that she'd helped him with that long-ago Saturday brought a rush of tears. Joyful memories spilled over, filled with love and laughter. The final notes rang out and he shot her a wink then stood to thank the crowd one more time.

When the house lights came on, Kiera hugged Buck, then Terese and Jason. He'd received a standing ovation at his very first concert. She was thrilled for him. And just the tiniest bit jealous.

Peter's last few days in Minnesota passed in a blur of final rehearsals, dinner with friends they'd made in the Alpha class, a barbeque with Buck, Terese, and Jason, and a farewell party at the studio. Then it was Friday night. Their last night alone together before his life took on a new focus. And hers was left with a Peter-sized hole in it.

After a quiet dinner at their favorite restaurant where they'd only pushed the food around their plates, they returned to the townhouse. Peter turned off the car then shifted to face her. His dark eyes were sad as he slid a hand behind her neck to pull her close. The kiss was gentle and sweet, tinged with desperation. She leaned into it, trying to memorize the feel of his lips, the reassurance of his familiar cologne, the strength in his touch. When he leaned back, she was slow to open her eyes.

"I love you." His voice was hoarse.

She nodded. "I know."

"Don't forget me."

"How could I? You're the smile in my day." She lifted her hand to his face, running her fingers along his jaw. "I never dreamed I could feel this way about someone, loving them with my whole being. Now I know it's just part of who I am. I could never, ever forget you, Peter."

He reached up and captured her hand, pressing a kiss to the back of it. "Let's go inside."

Kiera turned on a light jazz station and lit several candles, then they snuggled together on the couch, feet propped on the ottoman. Conversation came in bursts followed by pained silence.

She rested her head against his shoulder and closed her eyes, searing the moment into her mind. The steadiness of his heartbeat. The gentle warmth of his fingers wrapped around hers, his thumb rubbing the back of her hand. "Thank you."

"For what?"

"For this. For making life simple and wonderful and fun. For loving me for who I am."

"That's easy to do." There was a smile in the words.

"It means more to me than I can say." She looked up. "It's been easier getting to know myself outside of modeling than I thought it would be, and that's because of you."

He dropped a kiss on her nose. "Then you're welcome. I can say the same to you. This summer has been all about getting to know each other and ourselves in the process." He grinned. "With you, it was a lot less painful than it would have been on my own. Now wait here. I'll be right back."

He went into the kitchen, returning with two white boxes.

She frowned. "Whose are those?"

He set them on the coffee table and settled next to her. "Yours."

"What were they doing in my kitchen?"

"Waiting for you." He pointed at the bottom box. "Open the big one first."

She perched on the edge of the couch, a smile dancing in her chest, and slid the red satin bow off the box. Inside were a dozen of the most beautiful yellow roses she'd ever seen, a pair of red roses nestled in the center. The buds were ready to burst into bloom.

"Oh, Peter. They're so beautiful! And my favorite color. I've never seen roses this big. Where did you find them?"

"The Potter's Bench in Uptown." His smile widened. "They're pretty cool."

She lifted one out, admiring the satiny yellow petals edged with deep peach, and inhaled deeply. "Thank you."

"You're welcome. Okay, now this one." He handed her the smaller, unadorned square box.

She lifted off the cover and removed the cotton. "Oh…" Tears stung her eyes as she held up a delicate silver chain with a crystal teardrop. "Oh…"

Cradling it in her hand, she touched the sparkling diamond in the center with shaking fingers. How did he know her so well in such a short time? Thomas would have chosen something large and extravagant that screamed money. This whispered a promise of love.

She pulled him close for a kiss. "It's perfect. Thank you."

"I wasn't even sure what I was looking for until I saw it."

"I'll wear it forever," she declared, blushing as she always did under his admiration. "Will you put it on me?"

He fumbled with the clasp for a moment, then sat back, his chest puffed a little. "I knew it would look beautiful on you."

She touched it with gentle fingers, then gave an apologetic smile. "My gift for you isn't nearly as wonderful." She retrieved an envelope from her purse and handed it to him as she settled beside him. "I wish it were fancier."

"I don't care what it is. It's from you and that's enough." He slid out the card and DVD, reading the heartfelt words she'd written before lifting his gaze. "You made a DVD for me?"

"It's pretty simple." She held back an apology. "Pictures of us from the past months. Things to remind you of what we've shared."

"Can we watch it now?"

"If you want."

He moved quickly to put it in the DVD player and returned to the couch, tucking her under his arm.

The songs she'd selected were some of his favorites, playing behind pictures of the two of them, photos of favorite spots in Minneapolis and the cabin. Hiking, laughing, hanging out at Faith, in-studio rehearsals. The final song was "Hearts Entwined." As it faded, the last photo stayed on the screen—the two of them sitting on the rocks during his photo shoot, wrapped in a kiss.

When he sat silent and still, Kiera squirmed. He was too nice to say he hated it.

He looked down at her and she saw the tears on his cheeks. "You..." He paused, swallowed hard and drew a deep breath. "You couldn't have bought anything that would mean half as much as this."

Relief released the breath she'd been holding. "Really?"

"This is exactly what I need to be able to leave you. I haven't wanted to think about what my days will be like without you, but now I'll have something to go back to each night after the show."

She smiled. "I made a copy for myself. I'll watch it every night too."

They were silent for a long moment, studying each other.

"I still don't know how I'm going to leave you," he said in a husky tone. Behind them, the desk clock counted off the minutes until his plane left in the morning.

"Remember, we won't say goodbye." The words squeezed past the knot in her throat.

He shook his head. "I wouldn't leave if I thought it was goodbye. You know I love you more than life itself. I can't imagine living an hour without you."

"I know." She forced a smile. The searing pain in her chest felt like he was tearing her heart in two. "I love you."

"I'll call you every night after the show so we can get caught up on the day's news. And when we have a break in two weeks, I'll be back."

"You'd better be or I'll come looking for you."

He grinned. "I like that idea. I'll be hiding in plain sight, the guy on the corner wearing a sandwich board that says 'Waiting for Kiera Simmons.'"

She burrowed against him, warm within his embrace. "You say the nicest things."

"Only the truth, pretty lady. Only the truth."

– 20 –

With the *Road to Love* CD released and Peter and Bill now on tour, SMP moved on to other clients. Kiera met with Mark the following Friday.

"I can't thank you enough for taking over Mary's job this summer." His eyes twinkled. "I have to admit, I wasn't sure how you'd do taking orders from me, but you were quite the professional."

She lifted her chin. "I'm glad I surprised you. But then I surprised myself. Thanks for giving me a safe place to land and get my life back in order."

"Nice how God worked everything out, isn't it? Even," he added with a widening grin, "getting you and Peter together."

She rolled her eyes. "Go ahead. Say it."

"I told you it was a good idea."

"I know you've been trying hard not to gloat."

His smile faded. "I'm just glad you didn't shut him out, Kiera. Ramsey gave you a rough ride and I'm thankful you've gotten to see what a relationship should be like."

"He's pretty amazing." She bit her lip as a now-familiar longing swept through her. "It was so much fun working with him on the CD. With all of you. You've put together an amazing team, Mark."

"You're sure I can't talk you into staying on as my production assistant? You're as much a part of the team as anyone now." He wiggled his eyebrows. "And we work well together."

She'd wrestled with the decision for the last week. The studio was so quiet now without Peter's cheerful presence; her life was quiet. "I've been praying about it, and it feels like my focus needs to be on *One of Me*. The presentations have gone well so I think it's ready for a full rollout."

"With all the work you've put into it, it'll do great. I'm impressed, kid."

Her heart swelled under his praise.

"Just know, Kiera, you're always welcome here. And if you need any kind of reference, I'm all over it."

Leaving his office a few minutes later, she paused to wipe her eyes. She'd been blessed in so many ways since the fiasco. While she'd come to SMP with her tail between her legs, she would leave with her chin up, ready for the next adventure.

When her phone rang that evening, Kiera snatched it up after the first ring. Terese left the room with a laugh and Kiera wrinkled her nose at her disappearing friend. Since sending Peter off on tour a week ago, his nightly calls were the highlight of every day.

"Hey, Beautiful."

"Hey." Her heart did its happy dance at the sound of his voice. "How are you?"

"Good." He sighed. "Tired. Exhausted, actually. You?"

"I'm good now that I'm talking to you. It's been a long week."

"Has it ever. I don't like not seeing your beautiful face every day. How about we Skype instead of just talking?"

"I'd love that. Let me get to my computer." She retrieved her laptop from the dresser and climbed back onto the bed. "You're in Indianapolis now, right?"

"Got in about an hour ago. Everybody is crashed in their hotel room. Nobody even wanted dinner."

"Was it a long drive from Chicago?"

"Not bad but for some reason we're all wiped out. Tell me about your day. I want to hear about something normal."

Her finger paused over the Skype icon. Was that what he thought her life was? Just normal? And probably boring now that he was on tour.

"Kiera?"

"Sorry. I'm getting onto Skype now." She hit the button and waited as the program rang him. A moment later, his face filled the screen and she caught her breath. He was more handsome every time she saw him. "Hi."

"Hi. Wow, it's good to see you." He settled back against the headboard. "Okay, tell me about your day."

"Let's see… Oh! The big news is that Terese and Jason aren't moving to Germany. They decided it was just too much with the wedding and starting married life in a foreign country. I guess he was nervous about declining the promotion but they said they understood and they'd keep him mind for the next opening."

"That's great. I'll bet you're glad about that."

"Thrilled. I've really needed some good news lately. Your turn. What's happening out there on the Road to Love?"

"The real road to love leads me right back to Minnesota," he said with a wink. "Hey, I heard a new joke from Cheryl Lee."

After an hour of laughter-filled conversation, they prayed briefly together before hanging up. Kiera sat looking at their photo atop the dresser. She hadn't thought of her life as dull; she was still building her new career, albeit in fits and starts. But now, compared to his, it certainly seemed that way.

"You okay?"

She looked up at Terese's voice. "Sure. Why?"

Terese plopped down next to her. "Usually you hang up with a dreamy smile on your face. Tonight you're frowning at the picture."

"I'm fine."

"You're the worst liar." Terese got to her feet. "You know where to find me." She was almost out the door when Kiera spoke.

"I'm normal."

Terese turned back, dark hair swinging. "That's a good thing, isn't it?"

"It is." Kiera pulled at an errant thread on her bedspread. What was wrong with her? "It's also boring and dull and…" She shrugged and fell silent.

The bed jostled as Terese resumed her spot. She squeezed Kiera's arm. "Don't go there, Kier. You know that life isn't what it looks like. Right?"

She loved the kids she was meeting through *One of Me*. She loved her dad and her life in Minnesota. It hadn't been lacking before now.

Terese's fingers tightened. "Right?"

"Right." She forced the word out and met Terese's frown. Of course she was right. "Been there, done that." She wouldn't want that life even if he asked her to join him. And he hadn't.

Later, alone in the dark silence of her room, Kiera stared at the ceiling. She had three presentations lined up this week and two for next—several church youth groups and one at the YMCA. She'd been thrilled about it. Before the phone call.

She turned on her side and closed her eyes. A lone tear slid over the bridge of her nose. Tomorrow was just another normal, ordinary, lonely day.

Flopped on his back in the bland hotel room, Peter propped his hands behind his head and studied the water stains on the ceiling. Conversations with Kiera usually left him jazzed for another day on the circuit, not drained.

What is wrong with you, Theisen? You're living the dream. Three shows this first week and each one was better than the last. The record was already starting to sell thanks to Bill's relentless marketing. Women were cuddling up to him for photo ops when he went out to sign CDs after the show. One had even pinched his rear last night.

"What's missing, Lord? I should be dancing on the ceiling instead of staring at it." A sigh escaped into the silence. "I just miss Kiera so much it hurts. I miss my life in Minnesota and hanging out with Buck. Don't take this wrong, but I thought it would be more exciting on the road."

He sat up and stared out at the darkening sky. He enjoyed his bandmates. Jeff could now challenge him in cribbage. Cheryl Lee had taught him backgammon and how to drawl like a true Kentuckian. Alonzo was teaching him Spanish. But even with a great team, he was still lonely.

Hearing about Kiera's day makes me feel left out. Like she's moving on without me. It makes me wonder what I'm doing out here by myself.

His gaze landed on his Bible on the nightstand. After the Alpha study, he'd known he wanted—needed—to follow God, so when Pastor Joel had suggested they do an online study together, he'd jumped at the idea. He'd been surprised at how much he loved digging into Scripture, responding to Joel's direct and often challenging questions. Asking his own questions and sharing his doubts with Joel resulted in lively discussions as he struggled with how to live a life of faith while chasing his dream of stardom.

He reached for the Bible and flipped it open to where they'd left off at Ephesians 3:20. "Okay, Lord. I'm ready. What have you got for me tonight?"

– 21 –

Kiera sank onto the kitchen chair and reread the letter. Printed on stiff white paper with an official-looking logo, the words had an ominous tone. As the investigation into Thomas Ramsey's financial activities was ongoing, her investments were temporarily frozen.

She closed her eyes and pulled in a steadying breath. When she'd invested large amounts with Thomas and his partner, they'd repeatedly assured her that everything was legitimate and aboveboard. *Lord, what does this mean? I need that money to help Dad pay his bills. Let it be unfrozen soon.*

Reading the letter a third time gave no extra clues. Further information would be available in the coming weeks.

Talk to Peter.

She rolled her eyes at the thought. Peter had enough going on in his life. He didn't need to hear about her ex-boyfriend's financial investigation. Anyway, once they released her money, there'd be nothing to tell.

The directive niggled at her as she slid the paper back into the envelope. For now it was just an investigation. She would tell him if there was an actual problem.

Later that evening she pulled up her online accounts, satisfied to see all was well. What she'd saved was taking a hit from Buck's medical expenses but they had time before her savings dried up. By then the investigation would be over and she could draw on her investments.

Releasing a deep sigh, she logged off. *The last thing Dad needs is to worry about finances. He needs to focus on getting stronger. I'll take care of the rest.*

Intent on her conversation with the girls who'd approached her after the *One of Me* presentation, Kiera ignored her cell phone vibrating in her pocket.

"That part where you talked about it being okay to like fashion but not letting it define us sorta makes sense," the tall girl said, "but it's still a little confusing."

"Here's a way to look at it," Kiera responded. "First we have to understand what *does* define us. Maybe it's our friends, or wanting to be the best at something, or our need to fit in. But what if it were actually our relationship with God? How would that change how we see ourselves?"

"So, like instead of trying to fit in and please our friends, we try to please God?" the second girl said.

"But how do we know if He's happy with us or not?" the third asked.

"That's where digging into the Bible will help." Kiera pulled hers out of her shoulder bag and turned to a passage she kept marked. "This is a verse that I go back to all the time. It's from the second chapter of Ephesians. 'For we are God's workmanship, created in Christ Jesus to do good works, which God prepared in advance for us to do.'"

She pressed the book to her chest. "Isn't that amazing? God didn't just slap us together. We're His workmanship. He's an artist who designed us in different shapes and sizes and colors. So if He took the time to make each one of us as unique beings and has good things planned for us, I think it's safe to say He loves us. Even when we don't always make good choices."

"That's a relief." The girls laughed.

Kiera turned to another verse. The exchange continued until a father stood in the doorway, gesturing at them. As they gathered their backpacks, Kiera handed each of them her card.

"Email me any questions you have," she said, "or if you just want to talk you can call me. I'll be praying for you."

She finished packing up, a song in her heart. What a joy it was to be involved in this ministry—seeing God at work in these kids, watching their eyes light up when they understood their significance to Him. And what an honor to get to share focused time with them.

Before leaving the church she remembered the earlier call and retrieved her cell phone, hoping Peter had left a message.

"Kiera?" Buck's weak voice stopped her heart. "Honey, I'm not... feeling well. I thought you...could come—" The message ended abruptly and she stood paralyzed for a second. *Oh, God. Help.*

She dashed to her car and jabbed several times before the key went into the ignition. Pushing the tears down, she focused on dodging cars, barely slowing at stop signs. Why wasn't there a direct route between the church and her dad's? She continued to press redial on her phone. No answer. Squealing around a corner with only three blocks to go, flashing lights lit up her back window.

"No! Not now!" The siren gave a short wail so she signaled and pulled to a stop, curling shaking fingers around the steering wheel.

As soon as the officer got close to her open window, her fear tumbled out. "I'm sorry. I know I was speeding but my dad called and he's sick. He has cancer and he sounded awful but then he hung up or passed out or something. I need—"

"Slow down, ma'am. What did you say?" His voice was firm but not unkind.

She forced herself to draw a breath over her pounding heart. "My dad has cancer. He left a voice mail saying he was sick but then the phone went dead. I've been trying to call him but he doesn't answer." Tears flooded down her face. "Please let me go. It's just up here three blocks. Once I know he's okay, you can arrest me or take me to jail or whatever, but please let me go!"

"I'll follow you there, ma'am. What's the address of the house?"

"3934... No, wait. 3943 Humboldt. It's a two-story brown house."

"Be careful."

"Thank you. Thank you."

The policeman followed close behind the final few blocks. Kiera was out of the car stumbling up the porch steps before the squad car finished moving. She rang the bell and pounded on the door while fumbling for her key. "Dad? Daddy, open the door. It's Kiera."

"Let me have the keys, ma'am."

She held them out and pounded again. "Dad?"

"What's your father's name?" He stepped in first.

"Buck Simmons. His real name is William but nobody calls him that. Dad?"

"Mr. Simmons? Minneapolis Police."

Only the kitchen light at the back of the house was lit. Kiera dashed across the living room into the kitchen. "Dad!"

He was face down on the floor, the phone under the table. She dropped beside him and put her hand on his back. *Thank you, God, he's breathing.*

"Don't move him, ma'am." From behind her, she heard the officer calling for an ambulance. Then he knelt on the other side of Buck and placed two fingers under his chin. "His pulse is strong. You said he has cancer?"

"Lung cancer. For the second time. They just increased his chemo, I think. Or was that last month?" She put a trembling hand to her forehead, trying to make sense of her jumbled thoughts. "I can't remember."

"Dad?" She leaned over him. "It's Kiera. There's a policeman here too. We're going to get you to the hospital."

With a groan, Buck opened his eyes and blinked slowly. When he made a move to push up, the officer set a hand on his shoulder. "Mr. Simmons, just stay where you are until the paramedics get here. We want them to check you out before you move."

"I'm not…hurt. Must have…passed out. I need to turn over."

Kiera managed to smile at the officer. "He's a stubborn old Irishman."

"Who you calling old?" With a grunt, he rolled onto his back and sighed. "That's better."

"Your nose is bleeding." She jumped up to get a washrag, her legs wobbling as she stood at the sink.

When she held the cloth to his nose, he took hold of it. "I've got it." The words were muffled. His green eyes looked up into hers and clouded with concern. "You look awful."

She dropped onto her rear with a "hmpf," pushing her hair from her face. "At least I wasn't flat on my face in the kitchen."

The officer chuckled as he stood. "I hate to leave you alone with her, Mr. Simmons, but I hear the ambulance. Do you think you'll be safe?"

Kiera opened her mouth then clamped it shut when she met the man's smiling wink.

"Eh. Her bark is worse than her bite." The teasing words were spoken with less than his usual energy.

She blinked quickly. This second cancer journey had so many more bumps and detours than the first. He needed a break. They both did.

A sudden bustle of activity brought two paramedics into the room wearing starched white shirts and serious expressions. They set to work, treating him with efficient kindness. Despite his protests, Kiera insisted he go to the hospital. Arms folded, she didn't waver even when he gave her his best stink eye. Under other circumstances, it would have made her laugh. But she wasn't laughing tonight. She was very, very thankful.

She let herself quietly into the townhouse after midnight and tiptoed to her room. A moment later, Terese had her wrapped in a long, comforting hug.

"How is our favorite fisherman? And just what kind of a stunt was that, anyway?"

Kiera laughed and wiped her face. Good heavens, but she had turned into a crybaby this past month. "He'll be fine. He was super dehydrated so they'll keep him through tomorrow and get him juiced back up. He said he 'forgot' he's supposed to be drinking lots of water. That man doesn't forget anything. Usually."

Terese sank onto the edge of the bed, dark hair tousled. "He sure likes to keep things exciting."

"I could do with a little less excitement, thank you."

"Peter called here when you didn't answer your cell. Did you talk to him?"

"Just before I left the hospital. He wanted to get on a plane tonight."

"Is he coming back early?"

"He can't cancel a show just to sit and look at Dad, who's going to be fine."

Terese studied her fingernails. Her mouth twitched. "Can you imagine Bill's face if Peter said he was canceling to come back here?"

They looked at each other before bursting into laughter, flopping onto the bed next to each other. "I'll bet his face would turn purple."

"He'd end up in the room next to Buck's at the hospital."

They laughed harder as they exchanged a few more comments, then slowly quieted, heads together as they caught their breath.

"Thanks, Tess," Kiera said.

Terese bumped her head against Kiera's. "We needed a good laugh." She rolled off the bed. "Go to bed, kid. You need it."

"Goodnight."

"Glad Buck's okay." Terese's voice floated behind her as she left the room.

"Yeah. Me too." Kiera climbed under her blanket still fully dressed and snapped off the bedside lamp. "Me too," she whispered.

– 22 –

Only eighteen more hours. If she could hold on until tomorrow, Peter would be home and all would be right with the world. In the meantime, there were financial decisions to make. Kiera forced her attention back to the bank statements and medical bills spread across the dining room table.

The doorbell rang and Terese breezed past. "I'll get it. It's the package I've been waiting for."

Kiera sifted through the bills, copying amounts and due dates onto a spreadsheet. It was frightening to watch the total in the expense column rise while the savings column dwindled. This new chemo was even more expensive than the last. His insurance covered very little.

God? We could use some help here. And Dad needs your healing peace right now. The treatments have been so hard. Seeing Peter is going to be good for him. For both of us.

She lifted her head and straightened in the chair, enveloped by the same feeling she had when Peter looked at her with a particularly intense expression. It was the craziest, most wonderful— Her heart picked up speed as she turned slowly.

When their eyes met, the world burst into color. She leaped out of the chair with a happy cry and threw herself into his waiting arms.

After a long moment, Peter leaned back to look down at her, running his fingers across her forehead and down her flushed cheek in a gesture so familiar it made her heart ache.

"Hi," came his strangled greeting.

"Hi," she whispered. Then his kiss took her breath away, turning her legs to jelly.

He finally loosened his arms and tucked a few stray hairs behind her ear, pained joy on his face. "God only knows how much I've missed you. My heart has hurt without you."

"Sometimes so much it's hard to breathe." Her eyebrows rose. "But you're a day early. How did you make that happen?"

"I couldn't wait." His sheepish grin was endearing. "We had a few things we were going to work on today but everyone needed a break. Bill chartered a plane to fly to Los Angeles and they took a detour to drop me in Minneapolis on the way."

"I'll have to remember to thank Bill the next time I see him."

Peter laughed, pulling her back into a hug where he cradled her for a long, quiet moment. "So what did you have planned for tonight?"

"Washing my hair."

"You spend an evening doing that?"

She tilted her head to look up at him. "Only when I'm trying to fill the time."

He pressed a kiss lightly against her smiling mouth then to her forehead. Her arms tightened around his neck.

"Hey." His whisper was hoarse.

She was slow to open her eyes. It had to be just a beautiful dream. "Hmm?"

"Do you have any idea how much I love you? How often I dream about you?"

Her toes curled. "I dream about you every night," she said, "about things we've done, things we're going to do." Her smile faded. "But sometimes it's not a good dream and you're walking away from me and I can't get you to come back. Sometimes I get afraid because I'm so happy with you I figure it can't last."

He pulled her close. "I know. I've thought the same thing, but then I remind myself to give it to God." His breath was warm against her forehead.

"I figure He wouldn't bring us together just to tear us apart. We have to enjoy every minute we're together." He leaned back and grinned. "So what should we do tonight?"

"Could we just keep it low key? Maybe order pizza or something?"

"How about seeing your dad? And we have to make time to hang out with Terese and Jason this weekend."

"Let's go find her to see what they've got planned. Hey!" She put her hands on her hips. "Are you the package?"

"What?"

"Terese knew you were coming early, didn't she? That's why she raced past me when the doorbell rang."

He lifted a shoulder.

She laughed. "You two are so sneaky."

He wrapped his arms tight around her. "Man, it's good to be home."

Home. Her heart spun with delight. He'd called this home.

Kiera stuck her head into the kitchen. "Are you decent?"

"Depends on who's asking." Seated at the table reading the newspaper, Buck looked thin and tired, but his eyes smiled at her over glasses perched on his nose.

"Me." Peter stepped around her.

Her father's mouth fell open and he blinked several times. Kiera laughed. "Wow. Buck Simmons, speechless. That will never happen again."

He pushed to his feet and he and Peter exchanged a long, backslapping guy hug. Kiera was sure she would burst with joy. She'd been living for this.

"I knew you couldn't stay away for long," Buck said.

"That's for sure. Two weeks is going to be my max."

At his declaration, Kiera slipped her arms around him. "Sounds good to me."

"Any plans for dinner, Buck? I'd be happy to go get something or we could order in."

Buck waved a hand and trudged to the refrigerator. "I'm sure there's something in here we can eat. Kiera made a great meatloaf last night."

The men made sandwiches standing side by side. Kiera watched them, smiling. He'd missed Peter as much as she had. Spending time with Peter over the weekend would be great medicine.

With little coaxing, Peter agreed to stay with Buck, quick to admit he hated the lonely hotel rooms. Taking his carry-on upstairs after dinner, he admired Kiera's childhood bedroom. Posters still lined the walls, stuffed animals crowded the shelves, pictures of friends were everywhere.

He studied the prom pictures. "Hmm. Couldn't settle on just one boyfriend, I see."

"Never had a boyfriend in high school. I started modeling during my junior year, and I just wasn't around enough. Terese kept trying to set me up but it never worked out. They wanted a girlfriend they could actually take out once in a while. Go figure."

He wrapped an arm around her shoulders. "I can relate, although it's my schedule causing problems now."

Resting her head against him, she sighed. "We'll figure it out. Thanks for staying here this weekend. Dad is thrilled."

"He looks tired. Is he still doing chemo?"

"He started another round with a different drug last week. It's wiping him out." She looked up. "I don't think it's working and that scares me."

"Me too. I pray for him every night, Kiera, that God will heal him."

She faced him. "What if He doesn't?"

They looked at each other in pained silence before Peter shook his head. "We can't go there. We just have to keep putting it before God."

"I do. Every minute."

Monday arrived far too quickly. It seemed he'd just arrived and was holding his beautiful lady in his arms yet now he'd landed in Newark, New Jersey. With the third week of the tour looming ahead, he ran through a mental to-do list as he followed people off the plane.

Check with Jeff on the transition from "La Bambina" to "History Repeats Itself." It felt choppy on Thursday. Run through vocals with Cheryl Lee this afternoon. Call Buck to say thanks for letting him stay over. Call Kiera every couple of hours to tell her what a great time he'd had.

The ring of his cell phone made him smile as he fished it out of his pocket. Maybe she had telepathy and knew—oh. "Hey, Bill."

"Have you landed?"

"Getting off right now. Where are you?"

"Still in L.A. My plane leaves in thirty minutes. I wanted to give you the latest sales. How do you feel about being number forty-five on the list?"

Peter stopped and a woman bumped into him. With a quick apology, he stepped to the side of the jetway. "Seriously? Forty-five?"

"And climbing."

He started walking again, sure his feet weren't touching the floor. If he had to be away from Kiera, this was the only thing that would make it okay. "Man, I'm… Wow. It's all thanks to your hard work."

"I may be running the promos, but you're the one doing a great job on stage. How are you feeling about tonight?"

"Good. I was just thinking about what we need to cover in rehearsal."

"I should get into Newark before the sound check. I need to be in Nashville tomorrow and Wednesday, but I'll meet up with you again in Jersey City for Thursday's show. Oh, and you have a couple more radio interviews on the schedule this week. And there's a photo op tomorrow night at an event in Paterson."

"This is amazing." Peter stepped onto the down escalator. "How do you keep it all straight?"

"Thank God for modern technology. But I'm thinking about hiring an assistant if this keeps up. Okay, time to board. I'll catch up with you at the theater."

Peter whistled his way through the terminal. Sometimes it felt like he was just along for the ride. All he had to do was his favorite thing—sing. Bill did the real work. They made a good team.

"Honey, you are even more gorgeous up close." The words reeked of stale smoke.

Warmth rushed into his face. "Thanks." Peter scribbled his name on the CD liner. It was the fourth show of the week, this one in Atlantic City. He needed sleep. "Did you enjoy the show?"

The woman beamed a toothy grin at him, her ratted hair piled on top of her head. *Like yellow straw.* The thought made him smile, then he realized his mistake as she moved closer.

"I'd have enjoyed it more like this. Do you do private parties?"

"Sorry, no." He took a step back and held out the CD for her, keeping a pleasant expression plastered to his face. "I don't have much free time."

"We wouldn't need much time. Here, hon." The woman thrust her camera at the teenage girl behind her and glued herself to Peter's side, snaking her arm around his waist.

He tried not to grimace. This was just not how he'd pictured the celebrity life.

"I'm available for short parties between shows," she whispered.

"Thanks for coming by." He tried not to jump when she pinched his behind. She collected her camera, shot him another meaningful smile, and strolled away.

He released a quick breath, wiping his hands on his jeans, and turned to the teenager. "Hi. How are you?"

She glanced up with a shy smile then dropped her eyes to the CD clutched in her shaking hands. "Fine."

His shoulders relaxed. *This* he could handle. "Did you enjoy the show?"

"It was my first concert and it was really cool."

"Wow. Your first? I hope it lived up to your expectations."

"I loved it. I can't wait to play this in the car."

"Thanks for buying it." He scribbled his name on the liner, then handed it back and shook her hand. "And thanks for coming tonight. I really appreciate it."

Dragging back to the hotel room, Peter could barely keep his eyes open. He stretched across the bed and reached for his cell phone. Maybe if he closed his eyes for just a minute, he'd find enough energy to have a coherent conversation with Kiera…

When the phone rang, still in his hand, he opened one eye. Good. She was calling him first. The nap seemed to have revived him. "Hello?"

"Did you forget our breakfast meeting?"

Both eyes flew open as Bill's voice jarred him into consciousness. Sunlight streamed through the window and he blinked.

"Peter?"

"Sorry. I'm a little…what time is it?"

"Nine."

He pushed up on his elbows and rubbed his face. "In the morning?"

Bill chuckled. "What'd you do, tie one on last night?"

"No, I just lay down for a minute and now it's morning."

"Concert tours can be killers." Bill's voice held a rare note of sympathy. "At least until you get used to it. I'll order breakfast for you. Get down here as soon as you can. I've got news you're going to like."

In the shower, Peter let the hot water stream over his head. It was the first night he hadn't called Kiera since their weekend at the cabin. He calculated the time difference. Minnesota was an hour behind so she'd be at church. Unless it was Saturday? No, yesterday was Saturday.

He dressed quickly and dialed her number on the way to the elevator. It went to voice mail. "Hey, Sweetheart. Good morning. I can't believe we didn't talk last night. I am so sorry. I got back to the room after the concert and lay down for a minute before calling you. I woke up when Bill called half an hour ago, still flat on my face with the phone in my hand."

He stepped into the elevator, nodding at the older couple inside. "I sure hate that I missed you. I feel sort of…off this morning." The line went dead as the doors closed and he released a short breath, jamming the phone into his pocket.

"Sounds like someone has some apologizing to do," the gentleman commented with a grin. The woman elbowed him but Peter smiled.

"I'm hoping my girlfriend's not mad at me."

"How about sending flowers?" the woman suggested.

He brightened. "That's a great idea. Thank you." He looked at the man as the doors opened. "You have a very smart and lovely wife, sir."

"And she reminds me of that often."

Peter walked into the restaurant still chuckling. Hopefully he and Kiera would have a relationship like that when they'd been married decades and raised a bunch of kids.

"Well, you're looking better."

He slid into the booth. "Just got a glimpse of what Kiera and I will be like when we get old."

Bill looked toward the empty doorway, then back at Peter. The waitress appeared with plates laden with eggs, bacon, toast, and fruit. Peter pulled in a deep breath and directed a happy smile at her. "This smells great. Thanks."

She blushed. "You gentlemen let me know if you need anything else." She glanced again at Peter before moving away.

"Now you're even getting the waitresses in a tizzy with that Peter Theisen smile."

He squirmed and turned his attention to his food. "So what's your news?"

"How would you like to sing a duet with Tony Bennett?"

Peter stared at him, a bite of egg caught in his throat. "What?"

"Tony Bennett. I believe he's on your bucket list? He's doing a holiday special, and he liked your record so much he's invited you onto his show."

"When did he hear my record?"

"I sent it to him hot off the press."

"You sent my record to Tony Bennett?"

Faces turned toward them and Bill gave a friendly nod before leaning toward Peter. "You seem to be forgetting the part that he liked it and has invited you on his show."

"I'm having trouble with the whole idea." He picked up a slice of toast then set it back down. "Whoa."

"I told you things would start happening once you got out on the road. It's a matter of getting your music in front of the right people. Now that it is, life is going to change big-time. This is just the first of many offers."

The waitress returned to refill their coffee cups, leaving the table with another shining smile at Peter. He returned it automatically. Bill sipped his coffee and smirked.

– 23 –

Kiera stared at the invoice. She'd finally convinced Buck to let her take over the bill paying while he was in treatment. How could anyone pay these astronomical amounts? Chemo, blood work, overnights at the hospital, doctor visits, equipment … Each procedure seemed to be more expensive than the last.

She dropped her head back against the chair. *God? There are so many bills I don't know what's been paid and what hasn't. We could use some help.*

God is our refuge and strength, an ever-present help in trouble.

The familiar verse spilled over the tumult in her mind and she drew a calming breath before studying the bill again. He'd had more lab work done which meant another bill would be coming. By Christmas they'd be about a hundred thousand behind.

Panic built like a balloon inside her chest. Her fingers tightened on the pen. "Get a grip on yourself. There's a way to handle this."

The bills now came with warnings at the bottom, highlighted in neon yellow. "Payment expected upon receipt or further action will be taken."

"Can't get blood out of a turnip," she muttered. Her savings would be wiped out soon, but at least there were the investments to fall back on.

When the phone rang an hour later, she'd managed to chase the circling blackbirds of fear to the back of her mind. "Hello?"

"Hey, Sweetheart."

"Hi!" A smile filled her heart. When he hadn't called last night, she'd gone to bed feeling forgotten, but his voice mail had sounded genuinely remorseful.

"Did you get my message this morning?"

"I did. It was a funny visual of you sleeping all night with a phone in your hand."

His laugh held relief. "I didn't move at all. I was still on my stomach, the lights were on, and I was still in my concert wardrobe."

"What's your concert wardrobe?"

"Jeans, a T-shirt, and a jacket."

She laughed. "I see."

"I love your laugh."

"No way. I sound like a cartoon character."

"Which one?"

"Woody Woodpecker comes to mind."

The conversation veered toward cartoons they'd watched as children, their favorite TV shows, and movies they wanted to see the next time Peter was home, which was yet to be squeezed into his brimming calendar.

"Hey, before we hang up, I've got to tell you my news."

She smiled at the excitement in his voice. "It sounds like good news."

"Very. I'm going to sing with Tony Bennett on his holiday show."

"What? With the real Tony Bennett? This year?"

"The one and only. And yes, this year. I couldn't believe it when Bill told me at breakfast this morning. Isn't it amazing? Me and Tony Bennett."

Excitement tinged with jealousy crawled along her skin. What was wrong with her? "Peter, I'm thrilled for you. And I'm so proud of the great work you're doing."

"Thanks. I wish you were here so we could celebrate together."

"Me too." But there were plenty of other women who were. Pictures of him had popped up on an entertainment show just last night in a short clip about rising stars. The same night he hadn't called.

"Well, I'd better finish paying the bills. I'm so glad you called to share your news."

"You're the first person I think of when something comes up." His voice quieted. "It's lonely out here without you."

The pictures on television didn't exactly shout lonely. She gave herself a mental slap. "It's lonely here too."

"I'll call you after the show tomorrow night, okay? You gonna be around?"

"Yup. I'm working on a few tweaks to *One of Me* so I'll be home all evening."

"Cool. I'll want a full report on how it goes."

She laughed. "Yes, sir. We'll share reports tomorrow night."

He paused. "I love you, Kiki."

"I love you too." Tears burned behind her eyes.

"I'm going to turn on the DVD now. It's how I go to sleep, looking at you."

"You're so sweet. I'll turn it on too. Sleep well."

Kiera sat still, cradling the phone in her hands. She'd turn on the DVD once she climbed into bed. Maybe. It had gotten hard to watch. Too often she ended up in tears, fighting off the dread that hung over her in the dark, whispering about how their lives were growing apart. But perhaps seeing the photos of them together, happy and in love, was just what she needed tonight.

When she answered the doorbell the next afternoon, a man in a black suit greeted her formally, showing her a badge as he introduced himself. Kevin Mahoney, Federal Bureau of Investigation. "May I come in? We have something to discuss."

"What about?"

"Thomas Ramsey."

Her heart skipped a beat as she stepped back and motioned toward the living room. She closed the door against the cold November air and went to perch on the edge of the armchair.

Seated on the couch, he pulled a manila folder from his black leather bag.

"You're familiar with Thomas Ramsey?" The straightforward gaze he leveled on her stopped the snort that threatened.

"Yes."

"Have you been in contact with him recently?"

"Not since January." Her attorney's advice when the investigation first launched leaped to mind. No extraneous details. Just the facts.

"Are you aware of the latest charges against him?"

"Yes. Well, from a few months ago." She accepted the stapled packet he offered. The flash of sympathy in his eyes made her pause.

"Thomas Ramsey has been indicted on counts of money laundering, tax evasion, and securities fraud. Also conspiracy and mail fraud."

She looked down at the papers. Formal statements in block letters stared back at her. "What does this have to do with me, Mr. Mahoney? I never had anything to do with his financial dealings."

"I'm not here about that part of the investigation. We're contacting everyone who has invested any amount of money with Mr. Ramsey or the two people charged with him. This was quite an elaborate Ponzi scheme, ma'am."

Her breath caught. Ponzi schemes meant lots of people lost lots of money. She tried to blink sense into the abrupt chaos in her brain. "I checked on my investments last week. I don't think my money was involved in whatever he was doing." *Please, God.*

He hesitated then reached toward her and flipped over a few of the papers she held loosely. "This fourth page will show you the investments he had listed for you, Miss Simmons. Ponzi schemes give the illusion that all is well with the contributors' investments. The truth is, these accounts don't exist."

Yes, they do. They have to. Spine stiffening, she studied the familiar account names. She'd checked them weekly, sometimes daily, as her savings dwindled. "But these amounts have fluctuated over time. If they were fake, wouldn't they just stay the same?" She lifted her gaze to his, beating back the rising hysteria. Her own voice sounded far away. "How would the numbers change if it's not real?"

"There are computer programs that can make things look legitimate." His stoic expression softened and he reached forward again to flip to the next page.

Kiera looked down in slow motion. Next to each account number were bold red letters: NONEXISTENT. Over and over, all down the page. Beside the ugly words were a dollar sign and a zero. A dollar sign and a zero. Every single account she'd thought safely held her money didn't exist.

The ink blurred as her breathing turned sharp and shallow. No. He was scum and he'd done despicable things, but he wouldn't have ripped her off. Not her and Buck.

Meeting his gaze, she willed herself to hold it together. The pity on his face sent pinpricks along her arms. "I know he wouldn't do this. He knew my dad had been sick. I was so careful with my savings, and he promised—"

She closed her shaking fist around the papers and pushed to her feet, wobbling to the front window. The silence in the room pounded at her. There was only enough money left to cover the mortgage for another month or so. What would happen to Buck's treatment?

"So where is my money, Mr. Mahoney?" She faced him. "How do I get it back?"

"We were able to recover very little of the investors' money. These men created an elaborate process that allowed them to move the money to accounts that can't be traced. Out of the country."

Bile snaked up her throat. "How can I verify this? I'm not just going to take your word for it."

"I understand. I would do the same." He wrote on the back of his card and held it out to her. When she didn't reach for it, he set it on the coffee table. "You can call the number on the card or stop by the FBI office and speak with one of the supervisors. There are two of us working the case here in Minnesota. The main investigation is in New York. We won't have a finished report for a while, but you're welcome to contact any of us at any time if you have questions."

Of course she had questions. Everything she'd worked for was falling apart because she'd trusted Thomas Ramsey. "Here's one for you. How do people like him sleep at night, knowing they've destroyed people's lives?"

A frown creased his forehead. "I don't know, ma'am. But I can tell you that he'll be sleeping in a jail cell for a very long time. The evidence keeps growing against these men, and with statements from you and the other victims, we'll be able to put him away for many years."

Victim. The word left a metallic taste in her mouth. She had plenty of statements to give them about Thomas Ramsey, none of them printable. Rage pulsed through her veins. She turned away. "I'll stop by the office," she said through clenched teeth.

"I'm sorry, Miss Simmons. I know it doesn't help, but I'm truly sorry this is happening to you." A moment later she heard the front door close.

She wrapped her arms around herself to hold in the growing scream. Thomas had twisted the knife one more time. She swayed on her feet and blinked hard. *Don't you dare faint.* Instead, she bolted for the bathroom.

Through the evening fear wrestled with blinding anger. Then despair washed over both. She paced her room, clutching her Bible to her chest, repeating the promises she'd memorized.

So do not fear, for I am with you; do not be dismayed, for I am your God. I will strengthen you and help you; I will uphold you with my righteous right hand.

She sank down on the edge of her bed. "I'm so afraid, Lord. I don't know what to do. Keep me strong for Dad."

Trust in the Lord with all your heart and lean not on your own understanding.

Tears slid down her cheeks as she dropped her head. *I have no understanding of any of this. I need to trust you. Show me how.*

In the morning, she called Mark. It was the answer she'd woken with after a fitful sleep. He'd know what to do. And he'd help with a few of the bills too.

Mary said he was in meetings with a new client but promised he'd call her back after lunch. Kiera paced the house, dusted haphazardly, washed a few dishes, and paced some more, glad Terese was at work.

Straightening the bills and paperwork on the dining room table, Agent Mahoney's business card fluttered to the floor. She looked down at it for a long moment.

"If you have any questions," he'd said. She was a quivering mess of questions. She stuffed the card in her jeans pocket and pulled her jacket from the closet. Rather than wait for Mark to call, she'd get her questions answered first. Then she wouldn't have to bother him.

Making the short drive, she sat in her car, staring at the glass-paneled building. There had to be a mistake. The information couldn't be right. The woman at the front desk led her to a windowless office, leaving her with a glass of water. Kiera sat stiffly at the square table, temples pounding. *Please, God. Make it all right.*

Agent Mahoney joined her a minute later, accompanied by a heavyset man. "Miss Simmons, this is my supervisor, Agent Frank Lindholm."

The man's thick hand grasped hers firmly. "I'm sorry to meet you under these circumstances, Miss Simmons." He lowered into the chair across from her and opened the file he'd brought. "Agent Mahoney told me about his visit with you. I'm glad you felt comfortable enough to come in."

She lifted her chin. "I believe my involvement is a mistake, Mr. Lindholm. I'm finding it impossible to believe Thomas would have done this to my father and me, so I would appreciate it if you would review my information."

"I understand your concern. Let's look at the information that's been gathered so far."

He showed her the same papers Agent Mahoney had given her, along with several others where people's names had been hidden. Agent Mahoney interjected a few comments but otherwise sat quietly as his supervisor methodically snuffed out her last hope.

Half an hour later, Kiera stumbled outside into the cold air. She gulped in several large breaths, eyes closed as she leaned against the building. It was all true. He'd taken everything, every last cent. The shaking that had started in the sterile office intensified and she wobbled toward her car like a drunken sailor.

What do I do now? God, help us!

Her shaking finger missed the unlock button on her fob and set off the car alarm. Startled, she dropped the key ring. With the horn blaring, she fumbled around for the keys, unable to see through her tears.

Finally settled in the silence of the car, she rested her head against the steering wheel. "Lord, where are you? Dad needs that money."

Her purse vibrated and she groped inside for her phone. Mark's name glowed on the ID. *Thank you, God.* "Hi, Mark."

"Hey, kid. Sorry for the delay getting back to you." His words were hard to hear against the background noise.

"Where are you?"

"Hold on." The noise dwindled to quiet. "Better? I had the window open. I'm running over to pick up Elise for her ortho appointment. Sounds like she has to go another year with the braces." He snorted. "Poor kid. But there's no price for my daughter's perfect smile, is there?"

Kiera struggled to focus as his words raced past her. She cleared her throat. "Right."

"After that Bethany and I are meeting with a couple of sales guys. The furnace went out last night, but it's limping along for now. That means a new air conditioner too, since they're both as old as the house."

"Wow. Expensive."

"Yup. The worse part, though? She just found out she's being laid off at the end of the month. At least she got some notice, but she loves that job. I can't believe people are still getting laid off. I thought the economy was on the upswing."

A jolt cut through the fog in Kiera's mind. Mark had his own life, his own problems. He didn't need to add hers to the mix. She could ask him later for help with the bills, once the money ran out.

"I'm sorry about Bethany's job." The words sounded stiff.

"Thanks. So what are you up to?"

"Leaving an appointment." Her fingers trembled around the phone. "I'll let you go get Elise. We can talk later."

"Did you call for something specific?"

A life raft. "Just to say hi. Give Bethany and the girls a hug for me."

She hung up, set her phone aside and started the car. She'd left home with a sliver of hope. She was returning with none.

– 24 –

Peter sat in his dark hotel room and watched snowflakes dance outside his window. He'd been on the road for five weeks, performed twenty-some shows in a bunch of cities, and lost ten pounds. At this rate, he'd be down fifty when the tour ended in May.

Feet propped on the windowsill, he folded his hands behind his head. Tonight's show had been one of his best so far. Maybe it was the unexpected snow here in…wherever he was. Pittsburgh. The crowd's energy level had soared from the start, pulling him along.

Standing alone at the mic felt normal now, his band filling the stage behind him. It was fun throwing out jokes and making conversation with several thousand people and talking with them afterwards at the meet 'n greet. He'd even seen a few clips of himself on *Entertainment Tonight*, surrounded by fans. That had been a rush.

Glancing at his watch, he hit the speed dial number for Kiera. She hadn't answered earlier. Again, the call went straight to voice mail.

"Hi, Beautiful. You must be having quite the evening. Or maybe your cell phone needs charging. Anyway, I miss you. I wish things weren't scheduled so tight. I need to get home to see you.

"The show went great tonight. They're getting a surprise snowfall here so I think that's why everyone was so jazzed. It was fun. I almost called you from the stage but I'd left my phone in the hotel room. You wouldn't have thought it was funny, but I would've loved it. Hey, speaking of funny, did you get the email I sent you? It came from Jeff. I thought the punch line was hilarious. Well, call me whenever you get in. I'll be up late watching the DVD. I love you, Kiera."

He tossed the phone onto the bed, then turned on a light, slid his Bible aside and opened his laptop. There were only a few nights he hadn't gone to sleep watching their DVD. As the pictures flashed across the screen, he tried to shake off the shadow hovering at the edge of his thoughts.

Kiera had seemed distant the past few conversations. He tried to include her in all of his news, but she seemed less interested now. While she was quick to say she loved him, he had the distinct sense that something—or maybe someone—was pulling her away.

Pausing the slideshow on a close-up of them, he studied their profiles. Something was wrong, but if he couldn't get her to tell him what it was, he couldn't fix it. He went to stand at the window, frowning at the peaceful winter scene, then turned to pace the room. Would she tell him if she found someone else? Could he blame her? He was out here playing rock star while she was home caring for Buck.

And just what are you going to do about it, Theisen? It's your choice to be out on tour.

He turned to look at their picture on the screen again. None of the women he'd met in city after city could hold a candle to her beautiful smile, her spark, her sense of humor. She loved him; he knew it in his bones. But he'd better not think that was enough. He'd send flowers once they got to Philly. That would remind her how he felt. He couldn't let her slip away.

"Hey!" Peter's heart somersaulted when he heard Kiera's voice the next day. It had been a long, silent night. "Wow, is it good to hear your voice. I've been missing you big-time."

"Me too."

"So tell me everything that's been going on. I know it's only been a few days but it feels like we haven't talked in a month."

"It does feel like that, doesn't it?"

Her sigh reached across the miles and wiped the smile from his face. "You okay, Sweetheart?"

"Just…stuff going on. Tell me what's happening out there first. How've the shows gone?"

He rattled off several funny stories from the last few performances and meet 'n greets. Her laughter seemed forced. "How's Buck?" he asked. "Everything going okay with him? I talked to him yesterday, but he was meeting his friends for coffee so it was brief. He sounded okay."

"He's tired all the time. The chemo's been much harder on him this time around." There was a pause. Was she crying? "And he worries about me and money and paying bills. The usual dad stuff."

"I could send a check to help with whatever you need. The tour has already been good for my bank account." There was a knock at his door. "Hey, can you wait a sec? Someone's at the door."

Bill waited in the hall, eyebrows raised. "Ready?"

In his excitement at connecting with Kiera, Peter had forgotten their lunch meeting. He held up a finger. "Almost."

The larger man frowned at the phone in Peter's hand. "Lobby. In five."

Letting the door shut, Peter went to the closet for a sport coat, phone propped against his ear. "Kiera? Sorry about that. I forgot we're having lunch with some radio station people. Can I call you back?"

"I've got a lot going on today so I won't be able to talk much. Why don't we just catch each other tomorrow sometime?"

"But we were just getting started." He shrugged into the jacket. "I hate it when we get interrupted like this."

"Me too. But that's the celebrity life." She cleared her throat. "Well, have fun with Bill and the radio people. I'll talk to you tomorrow."

"Kiera—"

"Have a good day, Peter. Love you." The call disconnected.

Call her back. Now.

The thought was immediate and urgent. He paused, then grabbed his room key. If he didn't get downstairs right away, he'd hear about it from Bill.

Even with things going better than they'd planned, Bill still drove the show hard. He'd call her as soon as he got back.

The down arrow lit and the doors opened. Two young women in the elevator squealed. Kiera was right. The celebrity life never stopped. He stepped in with a smile.

Kiera read the email for the third time. Who was Kyle Matthews? Did Christine put him up to this? Already running late to pick up Buck for a doctor appointment, she closed her laptop. She'd delete it when she got back.

Late that afternoon she read the note again, her finger hovering over Delete. It was definitely the Glitz logo. After a decade as part of the New York agency, she could draw that familiar design in her sleep.

She pushed away from the table and paced the room. Going back into that lifestyle frightened her more than the financial mess she was in. She stared down at the computer screen for a long moment. They so desperately needed the money, but was she strong enough not to slide back into the craziness?

"Hellooo?"

Terese's voice made her jump and she spun around. "What?"

"Dinner's ready."

"Be right there." She slammed the laptop shut and headed into the kitchen.

Hours later she returned to her desk, determined to delete the troublesome email. After reading it one last time, she was surprised to find herself typing a brief reply. She hit Send before she could reconsider, then stared out the window, hands clenched in her lap. What had she done?

With a Bible study at Faith the next morning followed by lunch and shopping with her girl cousins, Kiera had little time to think about the strange email. When she checked her inbox that evening, hoping for something from Peter, her breath caught.

Kiera,

Thanks for your reply. I'm glad you're open to talking about some opportunities that have come up. I'm going to be in Minneapolis in a few weeks and would like to meet you. We could meet at a coffee shop or restaurant. Let me know what's best for your schedule and I'll make it work in mine.

All the best,
Kyle Matthews

She stared at the screen, shaking her head. *God, you wouldn't want me to go back on the road after bringing me home. I can't leave Dad.*

Her cell phone rang and she looked at Peter's name for a long moment before answering. "Hello?"

"Hey, Kiera."

"Hi." The delightful tingle that usually ran through her at Peter's familiar voice was squashed by a sudden desire to hide. She put a smile on her face. "How are you?"

"Good, but I sure miss you."

The reproach in his voice stung.

"I miss you, too. We've both been so busy lately. But right now I'm all yours." She settled cross-legged in the middle of her bed. "Where are you, by the way?"

"Beats me. Let me check…Harrisburg, Pennsylvania. We head to Hilton Head tomorrow where we'll do two shows."

"I can't believe all the extra shows you've added. Are the second ones selling out too?"

"Not quite, but sales are good. Did you hear that Bill's promoting a third single from the album now?"

"Which one?"

"'Autumn Leaves.'"

"Oh, I like that one. But then, I like all of them," she added. "Hey, yesterday I was in a store and I heard 'Winter Song.' It was so cool I burst into tears. The clerk thought I was nuts. She didn't believe me when I said you're my boyfriend. When I showed her pictures on my phone, I thought she was going to faint. It was pretty funny."

His deep laugh brought out the tingle and she smiled, relieved. She pulled the comforter over her legs. "So tell me what you did today."

When they hung up an hour later, she sat quietly, eyes closed, smiling.

"Now that's the expression I like to see after you've talked to Peter." Terese's voice from the doorway didn't disturb the peaceful feeling.

"It was a good call." She released a sigh. "I sure miss him."

Terese perched on the edge of the bed, eyebrows raised. "Is he coming home soon? It's been over three weeks."

The peacefulness waned as she shook her head. "Bill is keeping him busy every free minute. Tons of publicity and new shows."

"He needs to come home. You don't want to forget what each other looks like."

Kiera managed a smile at her teasing, but the familiar ache filled her heart. "Oh, I won't forget. He's popping up on the entertainment shows a lot now. He'll forget me first."

"Hardly." Terese patted Kiera's leg and stood. "That man is too in love with you for that to ever happen. See you in the morning."

"G'night." Kiera stretched out on the bed and turned on her side, propping her head on her hand. She reached toward the photo of the two of them and ran her finger gently across his smiling face.

– 25 –

Kiera sank down on a chair in The Java Depot and wrapped her fingers around the steaming cup. *This is just a business meeting. Stop acting like you're sneaking around behind Peter's back.* She took a sip, letting the warm liquid calm her. *Kyle is probably old, bald, and married, with hair coming out of his ears and—*

She smiled just as the door opened. A tall blond man entered, wearing an expensive wool coat, a red scarf tucked at the collar. Their eyes met and he smiled broadly. *So much for old.* She watched him order a drink and chat with the server who blushed and giggled in reply. Obviously he was used to schmoozing his way through life.

He paused to slip a holder onto his cup before approaching her table. "Kiera Simmons?"

She extended her hand. "And you would be Kyle Matthews."

His hand, warm from the coffee cup, engulfed hers. "Guilty as charged." He slid out of his coat and draped it over a nearby chair before settling across from her. "I'm glad we could meet this weekend. I've heard so much about you, curiosity has been eating me alive."

She gave him a professional smile. *Nice opening line.* "They must have been quite the stories."

"All good, I assure you. You left an excellent reputation behind."

"Nice to know, thanks."

They studied each other a moment before he gave a sheepish smile.

"Sorry. It's rude to stare but you're more beautiful in person than your amazing photographs."

"Thank you." He hadn't looked like the gushing type. She waited for him to continue, surprised to see pink steal into his face.

He cleared his throat and straightened. "So, let me tell you a little about me and then we'll get to why I sent the email. I've been with Glitz for about seven months now. Worked independently for most of my agent career but got an offer I couldn't refuse." He grinned. "Working with Richard has been a great education."

"Dear Richard. He was my dad away from home when I started modeling." Why did she just say that? "How is he?"

"Doing great. He sends his greetings. I've known him for a number of years and he wore me down. When Christine got her promotion, they slipped me into her spot. So like I said, I've heard quite a bit about you." He raised an eyebrow. "Christine told me your dad is ill?"

"His cancer returned last spring. We're praying for another remission."

"My dad died last spring, right before I started at Glitz." His handsome face clouded. "I miss him a lot. He was a great guy. Anyway, I'll be praying for your dad, that he comes through this okay."

Her eyebrows lifted. "Thank you. I'd appreciate that."

"I got a call from a client you worked with before Paisley, asking if you're still modeling. I told them I would find out. And here I am." The smile returned, bringing a sparkle to his blue eyes.

Her mouth twitched in response.

"Tell me what you've been up to since leaving Paisley."

At least he had enough class not to mention the firing. "I've been busy with a curriculum I developed to show kids how important they are just the way God made them, without the makeup and trendy clothes and the airbrushed life. It's been a great experience already. The kids seem to really enjoy it."

"Sounds interesting."

"I've had so much fun meeting kids from all over the metro, sharing stories, hearing about their lives." She swirled the coffee in her cup. "It's been great."

"Christine said you weren't interested in getting back in the business, so I'm curious why you agreed to meet today."

That was a good question. Heat slid up her neck, closing her throat. She'd been clear with Christine. She didn't want to return. *So what am I doing here?*

She stood abruptly. "Actually, you're right. I'm not interested. It was nice meeting you. Give my best to Richard and Christine. Goodbye."

The brisk November air burned her eyes as she burst from the coffee shop and hurried toward her car. What was she thinking? She couldn't go back. She wouldn't.

"Kiera, wait!"

Fumbling in her purse for her keys, she blinked against the tears. What did she think would happen, meeting him like this? She wanted nothing to do with that life.

He stopped beside her, putting a hand to her elbow. "Kiera, I didn't mean to offend you. Don't run off. I'd like to talk some more."

She shook her head, still digging through her purse. *Where are they?* "You didn't offend me. I'm sorry I wasted your time." She squinted through the window.

"Are you looking for these?" Her key ring dangled from his long finger.

She stopped. "How did you get those?"

He handed them to her. "You left them on the table. Look, we don't have to talk about Glitz or modeling or anything like that. Since I'm here, I'd just like to get to know you."

Kiera hesitated, the keys digging into her palm. "Contrary to what you're thinking right now, I am not a nutcase."

The grin that filled his face pulled a smile from her. "I didn't think you were. How about we take a walk and you can tell me about your dad? He must be quite the guy to keep you away from such an amazing career."

He'd pushed the right button; she was a sucker for talking about Buck. And that would keep them from any talk about modeling. "Okay."

An hour later they'd covered six blocks and returned to warm up in the coffee shop, a fresh cup in hand. Kyle was relaxed, friendly, and curious.

With genuine interest, he asked questions about Buck, about working with teens, and especially about her curriculum.

He answered her questions with an easy charm that melted some of her reserve. He was the fourth of five, all girls but him. He loved football, hated soccer. Life at Glitz was fast-paced and energizing. He looked up to Richard, and trusted his judgment and counsel. It had been a good decision, joining the company.

"Can I tell you about the job you've been requested for?"

She nodded and sipped her coffee. The job he described sounded ideal—a two-day project in Chicago working with people she'd known well and enjoyed. When he mentioned the price they were willing to pay, she bit her lip. It would pay off a good piece of debt. Maybe then she could breathe again.

What are you thinking? This isn't something you just do once and then skip off to the bank. They'll want more and more of your time. You can't leave Buck alone for that long.

"Your reputation is different than most." Kyle's voice broke through the chaos in her head. "You're a hard worker, conscientious, and very professional. That's why this company asked specifically for you. They're willing to pay to get you on board."

"Even with my tarnished reputation?"

He shook his head. "Paisley's reputation suffered, not yours."

The kind words wrapped warmth around her heart. "Will you lose the job if I say no?"

His expression remained calm. "No. Since they asked for you, I wanted to give you a chance to consider it, but I'll fill the job if you say no." He raised an eyebrow. "I'll still be able to put food on my table."

His Dolce & Gabbana suit was perfectly tailored, the Magnanni oxfords gleamed in the light. The Burberry wool coat he'd set aside was immaculate. He definitely didn't look as if he needed the commission he'd get from signing her.

He leaned back, an arm resting over the chair next to him. "If you don't want to do it, that's fine, Kiera. I'm just glad I got to meet you. Both Richard and Christine told me I'd be impressed. They were right."

She methodically shredded the sleeve of the cup. *God? Where are you? I don't know what to do.* All was quiet.

When she lifted her gaze, Kyle was waiting. Despite her resolve, she liked him. He wasn't hard sell. There was a genuine air about him that had put her at ease. Her defenses dropped away and the whole money story came out. He listened, nodding in sympathy, asking an occasional question. Instead of feeling humiliated with her life spewed across the table like this, she just wanted to cry. This was the conversation she so desperately needed to have with Peter. Face to face, wrapped in his arms, not on the phone across thousands of miles.

"Your dad is lucky to have you as his watchdog and champion."

She smiled at the image. "Thanks. He's a great guy. I'll do anything to make sure he gets the best care possible."

"Why don't you take a few days to pray about it? If you decide to accept this assignment, I'll make it as easy as possible for you."

They looked at each other for a moment. He seemed more like a friend than an agent. A handsome new friend who hadn't batted an eye when she revealed her messy life. "Thank you. I'll do that. Can I send you an email when I've decided?"

"Sure. Shoot me an answer by Monday so I can make sure the job is covered."

They strolled out to her car and faced each other as she pulled her keys from her coat pocket.

His smile was warm. "It was a pleasure meeting you, Kiera Simmons. You're as remarkable in person as the stories led me to believe."

Warmth touched her cheeks under his appreciative gaze. "Thank you. It was nice meeting you too. I'll be in touch."

She pulled out into traffic, her heart fluttering strangely. She had no clue what the right decision was. Either way, life was going to get even more complicated.

Leaving the hotel elevator, Peter glanced at his watch. He'd just closed his eyes for a short nap. Two hours later, he had ten minutes to get to the theater. He could already hear Bill's rant about being on time.

"Well, it's not like they can start without me," he muttered, swinging through the revolving door into the cool afternoon air.

"There he is! Peter!"

The high-pitched voices startled him and he stopped. Four young women surrounded him, talking at once, leaning in close, a feminine hand at his back.

"We loved your concert last night. Can you sign this, please? The line was so long. We heard you were staying here."

"Hi, ladies. Wow, this is a surprise. Sure, I can sign that. Thanks for buying the CD. You want me to sign your shirt? No, I don't think I'll write that." He fended off the raucous comments and signed his name across the brunette's shoulders. "I'm glad you liked the concert."

"We're coming again tonight. And we've already formed a Peter Theisen Fan Club on Facebook."

He looked up at the blonde's announcement. He'd seen a few fan clubs pop up online, but this was the first time he'd met one. "You started a fan club? That's great!"

She beamed under his attention, clinging to his arm. "We're the first members but we know there will be about a hundred after tonight's concert."

"Can I be a member? I'd like to be able to chat with everyone." A couple of the girls squealed, bouncing on their toes, and he laughed. "Unless it's a bad idea to join my own fan club?"

"It's a great idea." She batted her eyes at him.

He looked at his watch. "Ladies, I have to get ready for the show. Stop by and say hello afterwards, okay? Then I can get your names and find out about the club."

The girl squeezed his arm, blonde curls bouncing as she nodded. "Okay. I'm Bree. I'll bring information for you. And we'll scream really loud for you tonight."

He pulled open the back door of the cab. "Sounds great!"

As they pulled away from the curb, he looked back. The girls were huddled together, squealing and jumping up and down. He settled against the seat and crossed his arms, nodding. *The Peter Theisen Fan Club. This feels pretty darn good.*

Even Bill's dark frown couldn't dampen his spirits as they ran the sound check and a short rehearsal. He had fan clubs. Every time the thought surfaced, he smiled. And during the show, when he thanked Bree and his newest fan club, their answering screams made him laugh. Yup. Amazing.

When he called Kiera that night, Peter bubbled over with the news about his new fan club. She asked a few questions, told him how excited she was for him, then fell silent.

"So tell me what's happening there. What's new with Buck?"

A deep sigh floated between them. "I'm worried about him, Peter. He's so much weaker. He hasn't done much carving the past few weeks. And he sleeps a lot."

The tears in her voice squeezed his heart. He needed to be there—holding her, sharing her fear. "I wish I could be there to help, Sweetheart."

"Me, too. But the bigger issue is what I found out about my invest—"

A loud banging at his hotel room door startled him out of his chair.

"Theisen, open up. We're starving out here."

"Kiera, hold on. I've got to let Jeff in before he breaks the door down." He unlocked the door and stumbled backwards as Jeff, Cheryl Lee, and the band barged in. Several carried pizza boxes. Others had bottles of champagne. "What in the world?"

"It's party time, Theisen. Your CD hit the top twenty today. Number nineteen."

He stared at Jeff, mouth open. "Are you serious? Nineteen?"

"Top ten isn't far off," Cheryl Lee piped up.

"Woo hoo!" Peter danced around the room, pounding people on the back, getting pounded in return. Then he realized he was still holding the phone. "Kiera? Did you hear the news? The CD is at number nineteen."

"And still climbing," Jeff called from across the room. "Hi, Kiera."

"Jeff says hi."

"Hi back. Peter, that's so exciting. Congratulations." It was difficult to hear her over the hum of voices filling the room.

"Thanks."

"I'd better let you go so you can party."

He turned away from the noise and plugged his ear. "Already? But you were starting to say something."

"It's nothing. I'm tired and it sounds like you have a room full of people waiting for you to celebrate. I'm glad I could be there, at least virtually, when you found out."

"Me too. I'll call you tomorrow, okay?"

"Sure."

It sounded like there were tears in her voice again. He moved toward the window. "Are you okay, Kiki?"

"I'm fine. You go celebrate. We'll talk tomorrow."

It would be impossible to have a conversation amidst the celebratory chaos. "Well… okay. Give Buck a slap on the back for me. I'll talk to you both tomorrow. I love you."

"I'll tell him you'll be calling. Goodnight, Peter." And the line went dead.

The phone still at his ear, he frowned. She hadn't said she loved him. He started to dial her number again but Jeff thrust a glass of champagne in front of him.

"Theisen, we can't do a toast without you so get over here, will ya? Kiera will be there in the morning."

Call her.

He hesitated then slid the phone into his pocket and accepted the glass. Jeff was right. Kiera would be there in the morning.

Jeff held his glass high. "Here's to *Road to Love* on its way to the top ten."

The crowded room erupted in cheers and Peter hoisted his glass, trying to smile. It was great news and these were great friends. He was on his way to the top. So why wasn't his heart rejoicing, too?

– 26 –

It used to be that a good cry would solve everything. Now after several of them, Kiera had a pounding headache, burning eyes, and a stinging pain in her heart. Never had she felt this alone, this forgotten.

Buck was not getting better. Bills continued to mount. Her hard-earned investments were gone. Terese would soon start her new life with Jason. And Peter was celebrating his rise to stardom. Any one of those alone would be tough to handle. All happening together sucked the air from her life.

"Hello, Kiera Simmons."

She blinked and looked up. "What?"

Terese stood frowning at her across the kitchen table. "What is with you, girlfriend?"

Kiera shrugged and looked down at the stack of bills she had unconsciously covered with her hands. "Nothing. Just a lot on my mind."

Dropping into a chair, Terese propped her chin in her hand, dark eyes fixed on Kiera. "I hate to say this, but you look terrible. Care to fill me in?"

"It's just…stuff. Nothing big." She shuffled the papers and prayed Jason would call to distract her friend.

"Oh, it's big. Is it Peter?"

When isn't it Peter? "No."

"Buck?"

"No." *Of course it's about Buck.*

"Is there a problem with the presentations?"

"No." *That's the only reason I smile lately.*

"Gee, this is fun."

Kiera tried to force a response but the words stayed lodged in her throat.

"You know, Kier, we've been friends for a long time and gone through plenty of stuff together. It still amazes me sometimes because we're such opposites. This is one of the more obvious differences. Something is very wrong, but instead of letting me carry some of the burden, you clam up and suffer in silence. I can't help if I don't know what the problem is. It kills me to see you hurting like this."

Kiera cringed at the hurt on Terese's face. "I'm not trying to shut you out. Not on purpose, anyway. You know how hard it is for me to share my problems."

"Yes, I know." Terese rolled her eyes. "The old Simmons curse, blah blah blah. It's not easy for me either, but I do it because that's what friends do. They share life—the good and the bad."

"I know. But…this isn't something you can do anything about."

She crossed her arms. "Try me."

Their gazes locked in the silence. Kiera looked away first and released a heavy sigh. She tapped a finger on the papers. "These are Dad's medical bills. The chemo is costing a fortune." Icy tentacles tightened around her heart. "A few weeks ago, a guy came from the FBI to tell me…to say that…all my investments are gone."

"Gone where?"

"Gone. Away. Thomas was running a Ponzi scheme and took all of it."

Terese's mouth dropped open. "What?"

"Since Dad's insurance doesn't cover much, we've blown through most of my savings. I don't make enough from *One of Me* to keep up with the bills so we've gotten behind. I'm doing the best I can but they're starting to make noise about calling a collection agency. And…" Her chin quivered. "I don't know how I'm going to pay you next month's rent."

Terese's arms came around her. "Hon, I don't care about the rent. Why didn't you tell me earlier?" She held tight a moment longer then squatted before the chair. "They're sure it's all gone?"

Kiera nodded. "I guess it's payback for getting involved with him in the first place."

"This has nothing to do with you." The response was swift and sharp. "You're the victim here."

"I hate that word."

"I know. Okay, let's figure out how to get those bills paid. How about a fundraiser? You know, like a spaghetti dinner. Oh, I know! Peter could do a benefit concert. That'd be great."

"No." Kiera shook her head. "Dad would hate the attention. I would too. He's working hard enough to fight this thing. He wouldn't want people feeling sorry for him. That Irish blood of his is way too proud to ask for help."

"Well, you're only half Irish so you can be half as proud."

"I couldn't do it to him, Tess. He'd hate it."

"Okay, we won't call it a benefit. Peter would be happy to do a concert and give—"

"No."

"Kier, Buck wouldn't have to know it's a concert for him."

"I'm not going to tell Peter about this."

Terese dropped back on her rear, staring up at Kiera like she'd grown another head. "Why not?"

"He's got enough to worry about without adding the expense of flying home to squeeze in a concert he won't get paid for."

"He *loves* Buck! This wouldn't be an imposition."

"It would be to Bill, and he'd make Peter's life miserable." She bit her lip and played with a paper clip. Finally she shrugged. "Anyway, he's too busy. I've tried to tell him but we're not on his radar like we used to be."

"That doesn't mean he doesn't love you and Buck. He'd expect to help."

"He doesn't take time out of his busy life to even call Dad now." She lifted her chin. "If he can't do that simple thing, I'm not about to ask him for money. And I don't want you going behind my back and asking him, Terese. I mean it."

"Kiera—"

"Promise me you won't say a word to him. I'm dead serious. I don't want him involved."

Terese opened her mouth, then snapped it shut and shrugged. "Fine, but I can't imagine keeping something like this from Jason. I *wouldn't.*"

"Well, you and Jason are planning a future." The bitter words stung. "We aren't."

"What about Mark? You know he'll help."

"I know he'd help in a second but I just can't add to the other stuff he's dealing with. Anyway, Dad would be humiliated."

"It's just help paying the bills, Kier. Nobody's going to take out a billboard announcing that Buck Simmons can't pay his bills."

"I have an idea that should solve this and won't involve anyone else's help."

"That figures. What is it?"

Kiera pulled in a breath and set her shoulders. "You're not going to like it, but I want you to hear me out before you say anything. Okay?"

Terese frowned. "Okaaay."

Shifting in the chair, Kiera rubbed her nose. "One of my old clients requested me for a specific shoot coming up. A new agent at Glitz came out for a visit yesterday to tell me about it."

"Kiera!"

She held up a hand. "We talked for quite a while. He's a nice guy, Tess. You'll like him. He seems to have a strong faith. But most importantly, he understands my predicament and that I'm not about to go back to modeling full time. So…I have a two-day job coming up in Chicago." There. She'd made her decision. A sense of relief should be coming anytime now. "It's a one-time thing to help pay off a chunk of debt. And then maybe I won't feel like I'm suffocating."

"I thought the non-compete agreement said you couldn't work for a year?"

"I can't be a spokesmodel anywhere for a year, representing a specific line. Modeling is okay."

"Does Buck know any of this?"

Kiera pursed her lips, silent.

"He doesn't know about his own bills?"

She shot to her feet. The chair crashed against the wall. "What would you rather I do, Tess? Tell him everything? By the way, Dad. I know you're sick but we're drowning in debt from all the chemo that doesn't seem to be working. Thomas stole everything I worked years for, so I'm going back to modeling to pay off the bills just to watch them pile up again."

Terese sat wide-eyed.

Tears spilled over as Kiera flung her arms out. "I don't want to do this any more than you want me to. But I won't have to go begging to Peter or Mark, and Dad won't have any more stress added to his life. It's modeling, Tess, not bank robbery."

She whirled around and stood at the kitchen sink, fingers curling around the edge of the porcelain. "I'm doing the best I can and I may lose him anyway. But he's going to have every treatment possible, and money is *not* getting in the way. He would do the same for me. And so much more." Pain clawed up her throat. "This is all I can do for him. I'm trying so hard...but it's not enough."

She sank down to the tiled floor, buried her face in her hands and sobbed.

Terese dropped beside her and wrapped her in a warm hug, making comforting sounds as they rocked. "It's okay, Kiera. You're doing a great job. Shh. It's going to be okay."

Resting in her dearest friend's arms, Kiera clung to the words of assurance. She couldn't consider the alternative.

That evening she sent Kyle the response he wanted, a determined clench to her jaw. She followed it with an email to Pastor Joel asking for prayer. His immediate "of course" calmed the turmoil in her heart. She could do this—for her father.

– 27 –

Kyle was right on many counts. The Chicago studio welcomed Kiera with everything but blaring trumpets. Wide smiles and welcoming hugs were exchanged as she reconnected with staff she'd worked closely with in her previous life. She felt an unexpected excitement as she and the producer looked over the storyboard. It was all so familiar.

An hour later she sat in styling. She'd always enjoyed the chatter that went along with the pampering. The makeup woman was cheerful and efficient in her work. They formed an instant connection as they traded stories about their fishing-obsessed fathers. The young man who styled her hair regaled her with stories of some of the famous people he'd worked with.

When he turned her chair to face the mirror, her eyes widened. She'd forgotten how easily she could be transformed through the magic of makeup, a curling iron, and lots of hair spray. Red hair pulled up and back, curls everywhere. Makeup playing up her green eyes in shimmering shades of brown and playing down the dark circles beneath.

Her own words echoed in her head. *Be yourself. You don't need the extras to be you. God made one of you so celebrate it.*

"Incredible." Kyle's voice came from behind and their eyes met in the mirror. The glowing approval she saw brought warmth to her cheeks, and she smiled weakly and looked away. It was all fake.

"Kiera," a woman called, "they're ready for you in wardrobe."

A flurry of activity followed and then she stood in the middle of the room in a wedding dress of shimmering ivory, a romantic silk satin gown with dropped waist and lace detail that shouted expense in the most elegant tone.

Her eyes burned. During a few lonely nights, she'd let herself picture this look with Peter beside her, dark eyes crinkling as he gave that smile that made her heart dance. As they exchanged vows and rings and—

"Ready?"

She blinked and nodded. "I am. What a beautiful dress. I feel like a princess."

Once under the lights, it all flooded back. How to move, where to look, what to do with her eyes and mouth and hands. She listened to the photographer's patter and did as she was told, closing off the emotions lurking at the edge of the set. And through it all, she thought she heard the shattering of her heart.

Kyle insisted on taking her to dinner at a restaurant high above the city. After ordering for them, he told entertaining stories of his career, his strong faith apparent in how he lived his daily life.

Propping her chin in her hand, Kiera asked, "You're not married?"

His smile faded. "I was married to my high school sweetheart for ten years, but my travel schedule did our marriage in, and she found someone else."

"I'm sorry."

"Yeah. I was too. But she's happily married with two great kids. I'm glad for her. It wasn't realistic to ask her to wait for me while I traveled all over the world. I was sad but not surprised. It all comes down to choices."

"Do you like your life?"

He finished the last of his wine. "Yes and no. I love what I do. But I want a family and I know that won't happen while I have this job." His blue eyes met hers, filled with an intensity that sent tiny bumps along her skin. "When I find the right woman, I'll make the change."

She moved her gaze past him to the city lights glittering far below. Was that what would happen to Peter? He'd find the right woman who could draw him from the stage?

"Sorry. That was a downer. How about you? Anyone special in your life?"

Even as her heart ached, envisioning Peter's face pulled out a smile. "Yes. He's on tour right now so he's away for a few more months."

"He's in the military?"

"No, a concert tour. He's a singer. Peter Theisen?"

He nodded thoughtfully. "I've heard of him. New on the music scene, if I'm thinking of the right guy. Quite the rising star."

"That's him." Rising right out of her orbit.

They were quiet a moment before Kyle cleared his throat and set his white cloth napkin by the plate. "I'd better get you back to your hotel. We have an early day tomorrow."

He left her at the hotel room door with a gentle squeeze of her hand and a warm smile. It was several hours before she relaxed enough to doze off, a photo of Peter in hand.

Late the next afternoon, Kiera's plane pointed its nose toward Minnesota. Seated in first class, she looked at the check in her hand. Though nowhere near her Paisley salary, it was more money than she'd made the past six months from both Mark and *One of Me*. So where was the thrill of victory?

She looked out at the blue sky. Kyle was a nice man. Hopefully God would direct him to the right woman soon. And maybe, while He was at it, He could mend her own broken heart.

Tucking the check back in her purse, she rested her head against the seat and closed her eyes, anxious to see her father. He'd assured her over the phone he was fine, especially after beating Terese and Jason at five games of cribbage, but she needed to see for herself.

It was no surprise to find an email from Kyle the next morning, but learning another client had requested her for their upcoming shoot tightened her throat.

Why not? a dark voice whispered to her heart. *It's easy money. A few more jobs and you'll be ahead of the bills. It's what's best for your father.*

A gentler voice countered. ***You're safe in My hands. All will be well.***

She went on to check other emails, hoping for one from Peter. With a deep sigh, she closed down her computer. Thanksgiving was just days away. With *One of Me* presentations and holiday prep, there was hardly enough time to fit in another job anyway.

When her cell phone rang that afternoon, her heart jumped at Peter's name. "Hi!"

"Hi. I've got some downtime, so I thought I'd see if I could catch you. Is this a bad time?"

"It's never a bad time for you."

"I can't believe we haven't been able to catch each other."

Guilt poked at her. "I know. It's been busy."

"So what have you been up to?"

He wasn't going to like it, but then why did that matter? He wasn't the one trying to pay off thousands of dollars of medical bills. "Actually…I was in Chicago for a couple days."

"You were?" He paused. "What were you doing there?"

"Oh, just helping a friend. They needed some shots for an ad so I said I'd be happy to do it. An easy way to make a few extra dollars. It was a quick shoot. In and out."

Peter's silence was like a physical slap in the face, and she stood to roam through the townhouse.

"Oh. What friend?"

"A guy from Glitz. His name is Kyle."

"I don't remember you mentioning him before."

"I just met him recently." She kept her voice upbeat. "Richard and Christine told him to call me. Anyway, it was a fun change of pace, a short walk down memory lane, but now it's back to the real world." In the stilted silence she pointed the conversation back to him. "What have you been doing? You've had at least one show this week, right?"

"Two. They went great. I did some photo work too. It would have been fun to do it together."

"It would have. Photo work for what?"

"The fundraiser concert that's coming up. They wanted to have new stills from everyone."

"What fundraiser?" It was like making small talk with a stranger.

"Fiji's hurricane relief."

"Oh, that's right. How cool that you got invited to be part of that."

"I'm excited to be involved. And then the week after Thanksgiving we film the holiday special with Tony."

Tony. He was now on a first-name basis with music icons. "That should be fun. Are you nervous?"

"Sort of. I'm trying not to think about it. Hey," his voice rose with energy, "how about you meet me there?"

"At the filming?"

"Yeah! That would be great. It's in L.A. You could come out that Wednesday, be there for my part of the recording on Thursday, and then we'd have all day Friday before I have to be back in Virginia."

"It sounds wonderful, Peter." Temptation and longing seared through her. "But I don't think I should leave Dad again so soon."

"Not even for a couple of days?"

She frowned. Had he forgotten what real life was like already? A ticket to Los Angeles at this late notice would be eight hundred dollars or more.

"Couldn't we at least pull off two days?"

The accusation in his tone stung. She was desperate to see him, feel his arms around her. She needed to remember what they'd built over the summer that now seemed so far away. But in Buck's weakened state, it had been hard enough being gone over the weekend.

"Kiera?"

"I love the idea but it just won't work." The chill in her voice matched the ice forming around her heart. "I have a couple of presentations scheduled those days, and with the holidays coming up, there's so much to do. Maybe I can catch the next one. I'm sure this is just the start of your appearances."

He was quiet for a moment. "Yeah, I guess it's hard to get away on short notice."

She rolled her eyes, irritation flattening the longing. "You're coming home for Thanksgiving, aren't you?"

"Of course."

In the silence, tears rose in the back of her throat. How had they come to this already?

"I have to pick up Dad for a massage appointment in twenty minutes. Do you have a show tonight?"

"Yes." More accusation.

She cringed. She hadn't looked at his performance schedule for a few days. "Oh, that's right. I forgot what day it is." It was shocking how easily the lie rolled off her tongue. "Well, break a leg. Sell a bunch of CDs."

"I hope we will. I'll call you later, okay?"

"I'd like that."

"I miss you, Kiki." His words were quiet.

Her fingers tightened around the phone. She missed their old life, the easy way they talked and laughed. "I miss you too." So much it hurt.

Heading out to the car, she brushed away a stray tear. It didn't always have to be about her. *I'll do better, starting tonight. He needs my support, instead of listening to me whine about how difficult life is. The tour won't last forever. He'll be home in May.*

May. Only a lifetime away.

– 28 –

"Why are exam rooms always so cold?" Buck shifted on the table, his paper gown rustling. "They make you take your clothes off, give you a tissue to cover up with, and then turn the thermostat down."

Kiera grinned at Mark, seated beside her in the molded plastic chairs. "Hmm. I always get the cloth kind, don't you?"

He nodded. "I think they save the paper ones for the *old* folks."

"Who invited you here anyway?" Buck grumbled, adjusting the back of his gown.

"Your daughter. She said you've been a little unruly lately."

"That's Buck Simmons," she laughed. "Uncontrollable. Downright scary sometimes."

Her father's mouth twitched.

Mark went to the sink and filled a paper cup with water, offering one to Buck who declined. "So have you seen that new rod and reel that just came out at Cabela's?"

Kiera leaned her head back against the wall and watched them chat and kid with each other. When the doctor had asked her to bring Buck in for a few more tests, and to discuss those from last week, his subdued tone set her warning bells ringing. Mark had cleared his afternoon to be here with her.

The door opened and the doctor entered, his smile more muted than normal. Kiera sat up straight and glanced at her father.

"Mr. Simmons," he said as they shook hands. He turned to greet Mark and then Kiera, giving her what felt like an extra squeeze before settling on his stool. He swiveled to face them, and Kiera knew. *No. Oh God, no.*

The fight was over. They'd run out of options and she was going to lose her dad. Amazingly, as the doctor confirmed the dread in her heart, she sat dry-eyed and upright.

"There's one more treatment we could try," he said, focused intently on her father, "but it's still new enough that we can't be sure of the outcome. It's definitely worth a shot, but you need to know up front that it's a complex treatment that may affect your quality of life."

Kiera wobbled out of the chair and stood next to Buck, putting an arm around his bony shoulders. He reached up to grasp her fingers as he shook his head. "I'm tired, Doc. This old body can't handle any more. It's time to just let things run their course."

The world stopped for a moment. She couldn't breathe. *Jesus, help us.* Her gaze met Mark's. Tears in his eyes, he gave a firm nod. She pulled a thread of courage from him and squeezed her father's shoulders.

"We'll do whatever you want, Dad." The words stumbled over the knot in her throat.

"Thanks, Kiki."

They said goodbye to Mark in the parking lot, then drove home with only talk radio making conversation in the car. She glanced several times in his direction, unable to speak, not surprised by his calm expression.

She made soup and sandwiches while he dozed in the chair. After supper, she settled on the couch with a crossword puzzle while he whittled slowly.

"I don't think I'm strong enough to go to Mark's for Thanksgiving this year, honey."

"Okay. Then we won't go." She kept her eyes on the paper, grasping the pencil like a lifeline. *But it's our last Thanksgiving with all of them.*

Buck sighed from his recliner. "It's not fair for you to miss the big dinner. You go ahead and just bring me back some turkey."

"Oh, like that's going to happen. I'm happy staying right here with you. We'll have our own little Thanksgiving. And next year it will be our turn to host so we'll enjoy the break this year."

His gaze reached across to her. “Kiera, honey, just because I’m not up to it doesn’t mean you have to sit here with me.”

She lifted her eyes to meet his. “Give it up, Dad. You’re stuck with me.”

The clash of Simmons stubbornness was almost audible. Buck grunted. “Fine. Sit here looking at your old man, if you want.”

“I want. And I also want to move home for the holidays.” When his mouth opened, she held up a hand. “Don’t even bother. This isn’t up for discussion. I’m moving my stuff in tomorrow.”

“Kiera, I—”

“I said don’t bother, Dad.” She set the newspaper aside and stood to stretch. “I’m going to make a fresh pot. You want some?”

He looked at her, brow drawn down. Then he sighed and nodded. “Sure. Thanks, Kiki.”

She’d won this battle but it was little consolation. She started the coffee then stood at the sink praying for strength. “Peter, I need you here,” she whispered. “*We* need you.”

Blinking hard against the tears, she filled two mugs with the steaming brew and returned to the living room. It would be a quiet Thanksgiving, but she would enjoy every minute of it with her dad.

She stopped beside his chair. “Ready for me to beat you in a couple games?”

His grin warmed her heart as he accepted the mug. “You never learn.”

“Oh, but I have. I learned how to blow smoke from the master.”

He chuckled and reached for the cards. “Touché.”

Peter let the door slam behind him as he stepped into his hotel room. After a less-than-stellar show, Bill had reamed him out in the car ride back to the hotel. Like he didn’t know it had stunk. Several times Cheryl Lee had raised an eyebrow at him when he missed his cue. He was experienced enough now to cover it, but he’d mouthed “sorry” at her when the song was over.

Yanking off his jacket, he threw it across the room and flung himself on the bed. The conversation with Kiera still gnawed at him. Clearly she had little interest in what he was doing on the road. Out of sight shouldn't mean out of mind.

Who was this Kyle guy, anyway? She'd never mentioned anyone from Glitz. She'd been adamant that that part of her life was over. Or so she'd said. Why hadn't she mentioned it?

He stared up at the ceiling, questions and images knotted in his aching head. He'd been on the road ten weeks now, although tonight it felt like twenty. Ten wasn't all that long. He'd made it back to Minnesota once and they'd had a great time. Well, he had. Maybe she hadn't.

With a huff, he rolled off the bed and booted up his laptop. The best way to get answers was to check the Glitz site. Fifteen minutes later he straightened and pinched the bridge of his nose. The guy was legit, which was good in a lousy way. He had a solid reputation, he was single, and he was way better looking than Peter.

If he's after Kiera, I'm toast.

He still wanted the dream, but he also wanted Kiera. Those months in Minnesota had changed him. While he met women day after day, some pretty and some over-the-top with come-ons, not one caught his attention like the red-haired girl back home. She made him laugh and cry and want to be a better person. He'd fallen hard.

He grabbed his cell phone and dialed. It went to voice mail. "Hey, Bill. It's me. We've been so busy we haven't talked about Thanksgiving. I'm thinking you've got our flights home arranged, right? I know there's a show that Sunday in Arlington, so I assume I'll return either Saturday night or early Sunday. Let me know the details."

Thirty minutes later there was a triple knock at the door. Bill waited in the hallway, tie askew and hair mussed.

Peter stepped back to let him in. "I'm surprised you're still up."

"I was downstairs having a late-night cocktail with a lady friend when I got your message."

"You have a lady friend in Richmond?"

Bill flopped into a chair at the small table. "A lady friend in every city, if

I can swing it."

Peter held back a grimace. "You left her to come talk to me?"

"The evening wasn't going anywhere. So tell me again what you said about Thanksgiving?"

Peter sat on the edge of the bed and repeated his message.

Bill was shaking his head before he finished. "Not going to happen."

"What's not?"

"You going home. Or me for that matter."

Peter's heart hit warp speed. He had to go home. It wasn't a matter of *if*, just when. "Why not?"

"You've got rehearsals scheduled for Wednesday, Friday, and Saturday."

"For what?"

"The military show that goes live Saturday night, remember?"

"No. Oh, wait. Yeah, I guess I forgot it was on Saturday." This wasn't happening. A chill settled over him. "Why on Wednesday?"

"Because you've got two songs plus a show number and you have to be in top shape."

"I know my songs. It doesn't require extra rehearsal."

"It does according to the producer. So you and I will be spending Thanksgiving in New York, my friend."

"Oh no, I'm not." Peter was on his feet, shaking his head. "I'm going home. I *need* to go home. If I have to fly in Thursday morning and out that night, I'm going home, Bill."

His manager shrugged. "Check the flights. I doubt there's a seat to be had at any price."

Peter whirled around and pounded out an airline address on the keyboard. His heart rattled against his ribs while he waited. Airline after airline showed every flight booked. He typed in one last address with trembling fingers. No flights to Minneapolis/St. Paul at all that day or the night before.

Nauseous, he slumped into the chair. *Idiot! Why didn't you think of this before?* He'd figured Bill had it all lined up.

"Sorry."

"No, you're not. You're determined to keep me away from Kiera, but I'm warning you, Bill." He stood and jabbed a finger toward him. "If I don't get some time to see her over the holiday, I'll cancel out of the military show."

Bill rose and casually crossed the room to stand toe-to-toe with him. His eyes, clear and laser-focused, were like looking down the barrel of a shotgun.

"You don't warn me about anything, Theisen. I made you and I can unmake you just as fast. This show isn't something you cancel out of unless you intend to commit professional suicide." With a snort, he turned away. "And I'm not trying to keep you away from anyone. I told you not to get involved with her. This is what tours do to relationships."

Peter's fists clenched as he felt Kiera slipping away from him.

Bill went to the counter and filled a glass with ice, then pulled a soda from the mini-fridge. "She'll have to admire you from afar because you're going places, Theisen. I've never seen anyone hit the circuit and get a response like you have."

He raised his glass. "So here's to an amazing career that you're willing to flush over an ex-model who's got her sights set on another man."

The callous words squeezed Peter's heart. "What?"

There was a slight lift to Bill's blond eyebrows. "I have it on good report that she and the gentleman were high atop Chicago having a romantic dinner."

"How do you know she was in Chicago?" Sweat formed under his collar.

"How do you think I got where I am today?" Bill winked. "I know things. I have eyes everywhere. I can make and break careers, marriages, and futures with very little effort."

Silence pounded in Peter's ears as he watched Bill drain the glass and head for the door.

"I'm sorry to say, Theisen, I'm your date for Thanksgiving. We'll see what we can work out for Christmas. Oh, by the way, I've hired an assistant to start next Monday. Madelyn Birning. You'll like her."

The click of the closing door hit like a punch to his stomach, forcing Peter down on the chair. He stared blankly across the room. Bill's spiteful words were tossed out just to prove his control over Peter's career, and his life.

Kiera hadn't mentioned having dinner with her "friend." But then, she hadn't said much of anything. He dropped his head into his hands, fingernails digging into his scalp. *Was* she moving on? Didn't she have the guts to tell him?

"God, you brought her into my life so I know you can fix this. I can't lose her."

He pushed to his feet to pace the room. He wasn't going to listen to Bill's words. He was going to believe in what they'd built together, believe in her promises. In his feelings for her that ran deep and strong in his soul.

Yanking his phone from his pocket, he dialed her number, needing to hear her voice now more than on any other night of the tour. When the call went to voice mail, Bill's words came back in a rush. He cut off the call, turned out the light, and stretched across the bed, burying his face in the crook of his arm. And he let the fear and sadness out.

– 29 –

Kiera was in the kitchen early Thanksgiving Day putting the turkey in the roaster. She hummed along to the music playing from her iPad, enjoying the peaceful morning. It was going to be a good day.

After their meal, she planned to pull out the Christmas decorations and get started. This would be a holiday to remember. She wanted every day to be special for him. Ideas had churned in her mind last night as she drifted off. She would pull out all the stops.

Her phone vibrated on the counter and she smiled at the name. "Happy Thanksgiving."

"And Happy Thanksgiving to you, my beautiful lady. What are you up to?"

"I'm working on a pie crust. What are you doing? It sounds like you're walking."

"I am." A paper bag rustled in the background. "Hey, I could use some help."

"Okay. I'll do what I can. What do you need?"

"I need help with the door."

She paused, rolling pin in hand. "What?"

"I don't have a free hand. Would you open the door?"

"Peter, what are you—"

He chuckled. "Turn around, Sweetheart."

She turned in slow motion. His handsome, smiling face was framed in the back door window. For a moment she could only stare, the phone still at her ear. His eyebrows rose and he nodded encouragement. As if in a dream, she set the phone and the rolling pin on the pie crust, and moved toward the door. Her eyes locked on his, the pounding of her heart stole her breath.

A burst of cold air swirled around her when he stepped into the kitchen and set the grocery bags on the table. Then he opened his arms. "No Thanksgiving hug?"

With a sob, she threw herself against him, his leather jacket cold against her cheek. She pressed closer. Perhaps it was a dream but she was going to enjoy every amazingly real sensation. His cologne, his embrace, the warm aroma of cooking mixed with the scent of the pumpkin spice candle on the counter.

"Happy Thanksgiving," he whispered. Arms tight around her, he kissed her forehead.

Finally she drew back enough to look up at him. "But you said you had rehearsals this week."

"I do so it's only for the day." His eyebrows pinched together. "I found a ride on a private charter. I have to be back at the airport by ten o'clock tonight. I'm sorry. I wanted it to be longer."

She traced his jaw with trembling fingers. "But you're here."

"Nothing and no one was going to keep me away." He leaned in for a kiss, its sweet gentleness engulfing her.

"Well, look what happens when I sleep in." Buck's voice was filled with joy.

Tears continued to drip down Kiera's face as she smiled at her favorite men. All was right with her world. At least for today.

"Good to see you, Buck," Peter said as they hugged. There was far less to hug than there had been a month ago. Swallowing against a sudden rush of fear, Peter released him and swung Kiera back into his arms. "I can't tell you how good it is to be home."

"Almost as good as it is to have you home," she grinned.

They stood still, arms around each other. He ran a finger across her cheek, his heart catching at the softness, and she pressed closer, smiling up at him.

"I love you," he whispered.

"I love you back. Forever and for always."

If only he could store those words deep inside, to be pulled out whenever he was missing her.

She rose up on her bare feet and pressed a kiss to his cheek, then stepped back. "Okay, there's work to be done if we want to eat sometime today. Hang up your coat and let's get busy."

"Yes, ma'am."

She was the most beautiful drill sergeant he'd ever encountered. He chopped and diced, set the table, swept the floor, and then paused to shine her shoes that were sitting by the back door. Her laughter filled every inch of him with crazy joy.

They talked nonstop as they worked side by side, filling in the holes from being apart too long. Whenever they took a break, he pulled her into his arms, ignoring Buck's teasing and her laughing protests. He had ten hours in which to cram weeks of living. He couldn't possibly get enough of her.

Settled around the table, Buck's thin hand grasped his in a firm grip as they bowed their heads for a blessing. Kiera's hand snuggled into his on the other side and he grinned, closing his eyes.

"Lord God," Buck said, "thank you for the amazing food before us. Today, like every other, we have so much to be thankful for. We don't deserve your kindness and mercy, but we accept them with humble joy in our hearts. Lord, I ask your blessing on these young people. I've thanked you often for bringing Peter into our family. Continue to bless his music, give him the stamina and wisdom he needs to do his job well. Keep him close to you, and bring him home often.

"And as always, I'm grateful for my wonderful daughter. What great joy Kiki has brought to my life."

She sniffed. Peter's eyes stung.

"Give her strength for the journey ahead of us. Keep her close to you, as well. And maybe, Lord, you could teach her to make stronger coffee? We pray all this in the name of our blessed Jesus. Amen."

Tears still sparkling, Kiera tried to look offended. "What's wrong with my coffee?"

"Not a thing." Buck helped himself to a slab of turkey. "I just like it stronger. I think living in New York watered down your taste buds."

"I think I learned to enjoy the nuance of real coffee flavor more than drinking mud."

Peter soaked in the teasing banter, lobbing a comment into the fray on occasion then retreating when they ganged up on him.

After the meal, Buck settled into his recliner "for some football" and promptly started snoring. Peter and Kiera cleaned up the turkey meal mess in comfortable silence.

"He's not fighting it anymore," she said eventually, her hands in soapy water.

"The cancer?" Peter's heart clenched as he looked over at her solemn profile.

Her shoulders wilted. A tear slipped down her cheek and dropped into the bubbles. "He said he's tired." She turned her head to look at him, chin quivering, eyebrows pinched upward. "I don't know how to let him go."

He crossed the room in two steps and gathered her in his arms, soap dripping off her hands. She cried quietly against him, and he blinked against his own tears.

Losing the battle for Buck's life was going to devastate the young woman he held close. And himself as well. *God, help us through this.*

– 30 –

With Thanksgiving behind them and the holiday season in full swing, Kiera was stretched thin. Kyle worked several new jobs around her *One of Me* schedule and time with Buck. Cost was no issue as he flew her around the country, often in and out in a day. While she had to force herself to get on the plane each time, she was relieved to watch the medical bills dwindle. The hospice care they'd set up last week had no fees, but the gentle warmth of the volunteers and aides was priceless.

Kyle got acquainted with Buck as he flew in to go over upcoming jobs, his visit relieving the monotony for Buck of being homebound. Kiera watched them joke together, glad for her father yet protective about Peter's place in their lives. But Peter wasn't here.

Terese was an invaluable source of laughter and teasing during her frequent visits. Kiera would be forever grateful. She told her so one evening as they chatted on the phone.

"Oh, Kier," she replied. "It's like visiting my own dad, you know that. I'd be over there whether you were working or not."

Kiera sighed, propping the phone against her shoulder as she placed chicken breasts in the roasting pan. She missed sitting with Terese sharing a laugh over coffee. "I know. Being out of state on a job, even for a day, scares me. I feel a lot better knowing you're stopping by."

Terese was silent for a moment. "Are you sure you need to keep modeling?"

"I'm catching up with the bills so I'll be done soon. It's a godsend these jobs came along when they did. At least I'm not having a heart attack when the mail comes now."

"What does Peter think?"

Kiera busily washed her hands.

"Kiera!"

"I'll tell him when he's home for Christmas. We've hardly talked since Thanksgiving. He's so busy we only catch each other every few days."

The silence was pointed. Kiera rolled her eyes. "I promise I'll tell him. It doesn't affect our relationship either way, you know."

"It's something you're keeping from him. That totally affects your relationship."

When they hung up, Kiera pushed the guilt to its relegated corner of her mind and slid the pan into the oven. Of course she would tell him…soon.

Settled before the TV with a light dinner on their laps, Kiera looked away from the evening entertainment news show and picked at her food. Once again photos of Peter were "news." Arm in arm with singers and actresses, mobbed by fans. When did he find time to perform?

Buck turned the television off and she looked over at him. "Are you feeling okay? Do you need anything?"

"I'm fine." His gaze rested on her and she turned her focus on her salad. "The question is, are *you* okay?"

"Eating like a horse." She brandished a fork crowded with spinach leaves. He must have noticed she'd lost a few more pounds. Her clothes hung on her.

"I'm not talking about your appetite, Kiki. I'm talking about your heart."

The spinach nearly choked her as she forced it down. "My heart is sad, but that's nothing new. I'm okay, Dad." The clicking of the oxygen tank created a strangely comforting sound.

"When did you hear from Peter last?"

"A few days ago. I'm sure we'll talk tonight." She wasn't sure about anything anymore. Every day seemed blurry at the edges.

He continued to study her. "You know better than to believe these so-called news shows."

"I do." Although pictures rarely lied. "But it still hurts."

"I'm sure it does. That's why we aren't going to watch them anymore." He rested his head back, adjusted the oxygen tube, and closed his eyes.

"Do you need pain meds?"

"Just catching my breath."

In the quiet, she wrestled the television images from her mind.

"Peter loves you, Kiera. More than Kyle ever could."

Her eyebrows shot up. "What does Kyle have to do with this?"

"I've watched him when he comes to visit. He has feelings for you."

"Dad, we have a nice working relationship." She ignored the warmth in her cheeks. "There's nothing beyond that. He knows I have a boyfriend."

He frowned. "It's not that simple, honey. With Peter on the fringes of your life right now, you're in a vulnerable place. I just want you to be careful not to lead him on." He lifted a hand when she opened her mouth. "Unintentionally, of course."

She looked back at him, lips pursed, then allowed a smile to soften her face. "Vulnerable has never been a word associated with me. But I understand what you're saying. It's just…" She waved the thought away. "I can't imagine Kyle thinking there'll be something between us. I like him. I appreciate his faith. He's funny and we have good conversations. But I don't look at him as more than a friend. I'll be careful," she added with a nod, "not to lead him on."

"Good. Now I can sleep at night."

She laughed. "If that's keeping you up, we need to get you a good book or something worthwhile to think about."

"Nothing is more worthwhile than you, Kiera Marie."

A crash brought Kiera racing out of her bedroom early the next morning. Buck sat at the bottom of the stairs, rubbing his elbow.

"Dad!" She slipped on a step in her haste, catching herself on the railing, then squatted beside him. "What happened? Are you okay?"

"Of course," he said, then muttered, "That's the third time this week."

"You've fallen three times?" She slipped her arm under his and helped him slowly to his feet. She had to weigh more than he did now, which didn't say much for either of them. "Why didn't you tell me?"

Grimacing, he limped to his rocker and settled in with a sigh. "Because you'd fuss, like you are now. I just missed the last few steps. Got a little light-headed, I guess."

"I'll get you some ibuprofen and—"

"Just coffee. Black." He brushed her hand from his shoulder. "I'm fine, Kiki."

She set off for the kitchen, grumbling loudly. "Fine, schmine. Falling down the stairs isn't fine."

When Nan, the hospice nurse, arrived that afternoon, Kiera briefed her on his falls and his lack of appetite while he pouted in his easy chair. The nurse nodded and made notes in his file.

After taking his vitals, she sat back and studied him with a kind but serious expression. "Mr. Simmons, I'm glad to see those falls haven't hurt you in a serious way yet, but you do realize that a broken hip will land you in the hospital? Perhaps for good?"

Kiera's heart skipped a beat.

Nan continued, "I know you don't want that, nor does your daughter. Nor do we. I would like to suggest we order a hospital bed for this lower level."

He snorted. "That's ridiculous. Where would I sleep? In the kitchen?"

"Dad—"

Nan put a gentle hand on Kiera's arm and smiled at Buck. "That would certainly be handy for a midnight snack, but I think right over there in the corner would be a better spot. You'd have privacy from the front door and windows, and you'd be able to use the bathroom and get to the kitchen with no more stairs. And it's close to your favorite chair and the television."

"I'm not an invalid," he declared, green eyes blazing at her and Kiera, "and I won't be treated like one. I'm not dead yet."

"And I'd like to keep you that way," Kiera shot back. "Dad, I want you home, not in the hospital with a broken hip or a cracked head."

"I already have one of those," he grumbled, turning his glare toward the living room.

"It's just something to think about, Mr. Simmons," Nan said. "It's your decision. Now, I need to move on to the next client." She put her equipment in her bag, gave his arm a gentle squeeze and stood. "It's always a pleasure to see you two. I'll be back next week."

When Buck remained silent, Kiera rose and walked her to the front door. "Thanks for coming. We'll let you know about the bed."

She nodded. "It's a process, Kiera. Let him think on it for a bit. We'll talk soon."

Kiera closed the door against the frigid air and collected the coffee mugs. Buck's petulant expression would have made her laugh if her heart wasn't breaking. A hospital bed. The beginning of the end.

By the end of the week, he had reluctantly agreed that getting up the flight of stairs was more work than he could handle. Kiera nodded and quietly called Nan.

The large mechanical bed arrived ten days before Christmas. Kiera busied herself rearranging furniture in an effort to keep the tears at bay. Buck napped in his chair.

Standing in the kitchen waiting for the water to boil for tea, she called Peter. It went to voice mail. "Hi. I just…thought I'd say hi." She released a jagged breath and sagged back against the counter.

"Dad's hospital bed came today. It feels so final. I know where this is heading but still… It feels awful and sad and scary." She reached deep for control. "Well, that's all. Just thought if you weren't busy, you might pick up. But I guess it's silly to think you have any time to yourself with all the concerts and interviews."

She sighed again. "Anyway, call when you get the chance. It feels like forever since we've talked. I miss you."

Holding the phone against her heart, she stood still, the whistle of the tea kettle rising in pitch. She couldn't stand the sadness in her life one more minute.

"Kiera?"

Susan, Buck's favorite hospice aide, stood in the doorway looking at her with concern on her brown face. "You okay, hon?"

Kiera meant to nod but her head wagged slowly back and forth. Susan offered a sad smile. "I know. This is such a hard time. You sit yourself down there at the table and I'll bring you the tea."

"I can get it."

"I know you can, but I'm here to make things a little easier for both of you."

Kiera did as she was told, grateful for the older woman's bustling activity. Watching the aides and volunteers provide warm, wonderful care to her father often brought her to tears. They were such a blessing.

Susan set the cup of tea in front of her, then pulled out her own tea bag and made herself a cup as well. Settled across the table, she set her hand over Kiera's and closed her eyes. "Father, thank you for this lovely young woman who cares so deeply for her father. Give her the strength and courage she needs that can only come from you. I'm thankful for the blessing of being here with her and her delightful father. Amen."

Kiera soaked in the calm that draped over her. "Thank you."

Susan smiled as she dunked her tea bag. "The Lord will heal even the saddest hearts. He knows your pain, Kiera. You're not alone."

Kiera stirred the tea slowly. When had she last spent time in her Bible or in a prayer lasting longer than ten seconds? "It sure feels like it sometimes."

"Walk by faith, hon. Remember that what you know is more important than how you feel."

They chatted about the weather, the Christmas gifts Kiera had for Buck, what Susan had planned for the holiday. The desperation that dogged her every day faded just a bit. She wasn't alone. Though Peter was miles away, God had provided these wonderful people to walk this journey beside her. She would be forever grateful.

Tears burned behind Peter's eyes as he listened to Kiera's message. Her normally strong, confident voice was barely audible. The pain in her words stabbed him. He should be there with them, not standing alone onstage after rehearsal, fifteen hundred miles away.

"Theisen! Let's go!"

An hour and a half until showtime—he'd call her once he was dressed. He had to connect with her, talk with Buck. They needed to know how often he thought of them and how much he cared.

But ninety minutes later he was jogging up the steps to the stage, having never had a free moment to call. Maddie, the new assistant, had kept him tied up with scheduling questions and details he couldn't have cared less about. As he strode onstage, he lifted a fist in the air. *This one's for you, Kiera.*

After the show, Cheryl Lee stopped him on his way to the meet 'n greet, a magazine in hand. "Peter, look at this." She flipped it open and held it so he could see. "Isn't that Kiera?"

Peter took it and stared at the two-page spread. It was Kiera, all right. In amazing living color, looking perfect and confident and every bit the fashion model she said she wasn't.

"It *is* her, right?"

Maddie joined them, peering around Cheryl Lee. "Wow. She's pretty. Who is that?"

Cheryl Lee's gaze stayed on Peter a moment longer before she answered. "Peter's girlfriend, Kiera Simmons."

"That's your girlfriend?" Her brown eyes were wide. "She's gorgeous."

"Yeah." He studied Kiera's glowing face. "She is."

Cheryl Lee frowned. "I thought you said she wasn't modeling anymore."

"She isn't. Well, she wasn't. She's just done a little bit lately."

"She'd have to define a little bit. I've seen her in several ads."

He looked up. "You have? Which ones?"

"Well…" She tapped her chin. "There might have been a TV spot for something. And I'm pretty sure she was in *Women's Weekly.*"

Peter blinked. "So it was for the same product?"

"Heavens, no. It was all different. She's so gorgeous with that red hair, it's impossible to mistake her."

"Theisen, let's go. Your adoring fans are waiting." Bill's command carried down the hall.

Peter looked at Cheryl Lee. "Can I keep this?"

"Sure. Maybe you can get her to sign it for you," she teased, starting toward Bill. "You'll both have adoring fans chasing you down the street."

"Yeah." *Imagine that.* He followed her and Maddie, who carried her ever-present portfolio containing Peter's life in minute detail.

His stomach hurt, like someone had sucker punched him. Making his way into the crowded foyer, he squinted against the spotlights. Screams swirled around him and he kicked into celebrity mode, smiling, waving. He signed autographs and posed for pictures, chatted with fans and let women hug him, all without conscious thought.

Why was she modeling again? Why hadn't she told him? How could she do that and take care of Buck? His heart flipped over when he realized who was behind the assignments. Whatshisname—the guy who was after his girlfriend.

But the question that nagged him late into the sleepless night was simply "why?" Why hadn't she told him? Why was she keeping it a secret? He needed answers.

– 31 –

Christmas morning dawned cloudy and crisp, with a fresh dusting of powdery snow. The aroma of coffee, cinnamon, and pastry greeted Kiera in the kitchen along with Buck's smile.

"Merry Christmas, Kiki."

She gave him a hug and kissed his cheek. "Merry Christmas, Dad. You're up early."

"It's Christmas Day. I'm not about to lay in bed all morning. I have cinnamon rolls in the oven and the coffee's ready."

"Why don't you sit down and I'll—"

"No, you sit down. It's my turn to treat you."

She hesitated before following orders. Concern urged her to make him sit, but he hadn't looked this happy in a long time. He moved deliberately as he got plates from the cupboard, set forks and napkins on top and carried them to the table, pulling the oxygen tank with him. Then he retrieved two mugs. Finally he pulled the baking pan from the oven. The sweet aroma made Kiera's mouth water.

While he set the pan on a trivet in the middle of the table, she retrieved the coffeepot. He dropped into the chair, breathing heavily but smiling. "Phew. This baking is hard work."

They exchanged smiles, then he cut two large rolls from the dozen in the pan.

"Dad, these are perfect. Boy, we haven't had cinnamon rolls in forever."

"You haven't had *mine* since last Christmas," he said. "Wasn't about to let this Christmas go by without them."

She licked the icing from her fingers and forced a grin. "Thanks. It's the perfect way to start the day."

After a leisurely chat, they moved to the living room to exchange gifts. A cheerful fire warmed the room; the tree sparkled in the corner. It was familiar and homey. Kiera gave him a photo album that started with pictures from his childhood all the way up to Thanksgiving Day with Peter. He cried as he looked through it.

She settled beside him on the wide bed, her arm across his shoulders. They paged through it a second time together, sharing memories, laughing over many.

Buck pulled a box from his bedside table and handed it to her with a proud smile. Savoring the special moment, she opened the long, narrow jeweler's box slowly. Her eyes went wide when she lifted the cover.

"Dad, they're beautiful." Tears spilled over as she put a gentle finger to the double string of pearls nestled in white cotton. With the faintest pink blush, they were exquisite.

"Your mother wore them on our wedding day," he said. "I was going to give them to you when you got married, but since you don't seem to be in a hurry, I thought I'd give them to you now."

"Will you fasten it for me?" She held up her hair as he hooked the necklace, then she stood and faced him.

He reached for her hand, approval sparkling in his eyes. "As beautiful as your mother," he declared.

Kiera vaguely remembered her, but from pictures she knew that was truly a compliment. She hugged him hard. "Thank you," she whispered. "I have to find a mirror."

In the bathroom, she stared at her reflection. Buck had given her the pearls because he wouldn't be alive when—if—she finally married. She sank to her knees beside the vanity, arms folded against the pain that doubled her over, a fist stifling her sobs. It was a long moment before she could draw a breath.

"Pull it together," she whispered fiercely. "He's waiting for you. Come on, get up." Coaching herself to her feet, she splashed cold water on her face, then drew a slow, deliberate breath and faced herself again. "You can do this. You *have* to do this."

When she returned to the living room, she went to the tree to collect the rest of the gifts stashed underneath. And throughout the day, she gently touched the pearls at her throat. Her mother's pearls.

Kiera was in her room the next morning when the doorbell rang. A tremor of excitement and apprehension made her pause. There had been little conversation with Peter over the last week. When they'd discussed plans for his visit, he was quieter than normal, not bubbling over with his usual stories and news.

She moved down the stairs quietly, listening to the two men talk and laugh with Susan, then stopped on the second step. Peter carried himself with confidence now. This tall, handsome celebrity had replaced the shy, uncertain man who'd stolen her heart.

When Buck glanced past him, Peter turned and her heart did a two-step. He still stole her breath. He approached, holding her gaze, and she came down the last step and went into his arms. The foreboding of earlier was pushed aside by the joyful relief that flooded through her as he wrapped her in familiar warmth.

"Merry Christmas, Kiera."

"Merry Christmas, Peter. Welcome home." She lifted her head to smile up at him and was drawn into a kiss that made her knees weak.

"Susan, it looks like we need to go into the kitchen and leave our lovebirds alone."

Kiera pulled away from Peter with a breathless laugh. "You do not. We'll behave."

"Well, we'll try, anyway." He grinned and tightened his arm around her shoulders. "Right?"

"Right. We'll try."

With the luxury of four whole days off, Peter was determined to enjoy every minute. They spent an evening with Terese and Jason and had dinner with Mark and the studio team. Long walks with Kiera and an ongoing cribbage tournament with Buck filled the remaining hours. He needed to find the right time—and the courage—to talk about Kyle and her secret modeling life.

With Buck's blessing, he invited her out to dinner on his last night home. Hearing her come down the stairs, he looked up and stared. Her hair was pulled up and back in a mass of soft curls. The dark brown dress accented her long, slim frame, dancing around her knees as she descended. A shimmering pearl necklace circled her slender neck. But it was the glow on her face that caught his breath. With love like that in her eyes, she couldn't possibly be seeing someone else.

He moved toward the stairs and held out a hand. "Whoa. Kiera…" He shook his head. Words wouldn't do this justice.

She placed her hand in his, cheeks flushed, and bit her lip. "Thank you. You look amazing yourself. I have the most handsome date ever."

Buck wobbled into the living room from the kitchen, leaning heavily on his walker, Susan at his side pulling the oxygen tank. His gaunt face lit up at the sight of his daughter. "Kiera Marie, you are the spitting image of your mother."

She smiled. "Thanks, Dad."

"Did her mother have red hair too?" Susan asked.

"Nope. All the redheaded stubbornness comes from me. The rest of her comes from Marion." Making his way toward the hospital bed, he slapped Peter on the back. "Peter, you are one lucky man."

"I know it, Buck." He squeezed her fingers. "I totally know it. Ready, pretty lady?"

"Ready."

Susan helped Buck swing his legs into bed. "You kids have fun," she said. "Buck is going to beat me at Go Fish."

"I'm sure he will." Kiera shot a mock frown at her father. "Behave yourself or Susan will quit."

"Bah." He waved a gnarled hand at her, huffing from the short walk. "She loves me too much."

On the ride to the restaurant, Kiera shared details about her recent *One of Me* presentations and peppered him with questions about the tour. Over a three-course meal, they talked nonstop. When the band started playing, Peter stood and extended his hand. "May I have this dance?"

"I didn't know you danced."

Her wide-eyed look made him chuckle. "I may not be the best, but I think you're safe from me stepping on your toes." He led her onto the parquet floor and swept her into his arms.

As they danced, her warm smile filled with delight. "Wow. I'm impressed."

He laughed. "Me too." How he managed to stay on tour and not just throw it away to stay here in Minnesota astounded him. He may have already reached the success he'd dreamed of, but now he wanted this beautiful woman to share it with. He wanted it all.

They danced, returned to their table to chat and rest, then went back to the dance floor. He kept her laughing and talking, drinking in the glow in her eyes, committing the magical evening to memory. The tour would quickly suck these memories dry. For these last few hours there was no Whatshisname, no tour and no runway. Just the two of them, exactly the way it should be.

After midnight they strolled with reluctant steps to the parking lot, arm in arm. Stars sparkled in the black sky, the crisp air turning their noses pink. Settled in the car, they chatted about the amazing food, the wonderful music, and how much they didn't want any of it to end. Finally Peter started the car and pointed it toward home. And with her hand tucked in his, he took a deep breath.

It was time to talk.

– 32 –

Kiera rested her head against the seat, the happiest she'd been in months. Dancing the night away, the sole focus of Peter's attention despite the women who stayed at a barely discreet distance—life couldn't be any better than it was at that moment.

"Kiera?"

She turned a smile toward him. "Hmm?"

"I've been wondering about something."

The peacefulness evaporated. "Okay."

When he was quiet, warning bells chimed and she straightened in the passenger seat.

"So about a week ago, right after we finished a show, Cheryl Lee showed me a magazine she'd been reading."

The bells changed to a blaring foghorn. She should have told him.

Stopping at the red light, he looked at her, frowning. "How much are you modeling now?"

"I'm still doing *One of Me* presentations, if that's what you mean."

He pulled his hand away and turned left. "What I mean is how often are you modeling?"

She swallowed hard. "A couple times a week."

The car swerved abruptly to the curb and lurched to a stop. He swung to face her, eyes wide. "A couple times a *week*? What happened to one gig for a friend?"

"It started out as just a one-time job." Her pounding heart reverberated through her body. "Then a few of my old clients heard about it and started requesting me. It's not a big deal, Peter."

"Then why didn't you tell me?"

She dropped her gaze and clutched her trembling hands together. Terese had warned her. So had Buck. "I didn't tell you because...because you're so busy it just never came up."

"Oh, no. Don't blame this on me. We've had a million conversations when you could have said something."

"I know. I just... It's not that big of a deal to me." *Only enough to make me nauseated every time I board a plane.*

"I don't believe that for a minute. You started *One of Me* because of what you thought commercialism does to people, especially kids. Are you still out there teaching it?"

"Yes, but—"

"How can you do that with a straight face? Isn't that talking out of both sides of your mouth?"

She lifted her chin, pushing back against the heat that rose in her chest. "My message to the kids hasn't changed. I believe everything I say in that program."

"Yeah," he snorted, "and then you make money doing exactly what you're preaching against."

"I don't preach against modeling. I just want kids to recognize who they are without all the other stuff." She blinked against the force of his disdain. "Why do you care what I do back here, anyway? I can't just sit around waiting for you to make time for me."

"This isn't about whether I'm here or not. This is about you keeping secrets. I even had to hear from someone else that you're out having dinner with the joker who dragged you back into modeling. Did you bother telling him you have a boyfriend?"

"Of course! And you should hardly point a finger at me. I have to watch you parade around with women falling at your feet for all the world to see. Do you ever tell them you have a girlfriend?"

"Whenever I get the chance."

"Right. I'll bet that chance presents itself, oh…never. You act all high and mighty about me doing some modeling like it's a crime, while you spend your days flirting with women all across the country. I think there's something wrong with that picture, Peter." She stared out the front window, blinking rapidly.

Peter took a deep breath and released it slowly. "So tell me about Whatshisname." Resentment colored the restrained words.

"He's an agent at Glitz."

"And?"

"And, like I told you before, he sent an email one day asking if I would consider doing the one job."

"Out of the blue."

"Yes, out of the blue. I didn't go looking for this, Peter. Richard gave him my email after the client requested me."

"Why didn't you say no?"

She pressed her lips together. He didn't need to know they'd been drowning in medical bills while he raked in thousands. She didn't want his money. She just wanted him. "It didn't sound like a big deal at the time. Just a two-day shoot in Chicago. I didn't plan on doing any more than that."

"Why didn't you tell me you had dinner with him?" The hurt in his question pierced her heart.

She turned toward him, wanting to reach for his hand. Her fingers knotted together. "Because it was a business dinner. That's all, I promise. It wasn't a date, Peter. It was just dinner after a long work day. I flew in that morning and out the next afternoon. That's all it was. And I *did* tell him about you."

He looked at her, jaw clenched, then blinked and looked away. "I still don't understand why you haven't told me. How hard is it to say, 'Hey, I'm doing some modeling'? What did you think I was going to say?"

"It just…I didn't expect to keep doing it so it didn't seem like a big deal."

"Keeping secrets is a big deal, Kiera. It's hard enough for us to keep this relationship afloat when we're apart so much. If you can't tell me the truth, we're dead in the water."

Anger started to boil again. This wasn't just about her. "So I'm supposed to tell you what I'm doing, but you don't have to tell me what you're doing?"

His eyebrows lifted. "I tell you all the time."

"You tell me about the shows and the traveling, but you forget to mention the women you're seeing."

"I'm not seeing any women."

"There are tons of photos of you and all sorts of beautiful women in the news. But I'm not supposed to mind that your face shows up on TV with them hanging on you."

"Your face is plastered in more places than mine. Cheryl Lee said she's seen pictures of you everywhere."

"Me. Not me with men hanging on me. Just me playing dress-up."

"Looking gorgeous and provocative and—"

"What? It's an ad, Peter. Just a stupid ad for products no one needs. And I'm fully dressed, unlike half the women you're photographed with."

"And then you run out and stand before a bunch of kids, telling them to do as you say, not as you do."

His words were like a slap in the face. Despite her clenched jaw, tears welled in her eyes. He reached for her hand but she pulled away and shook her head, folding her arms. Angry words echoed in the silence.

He sighed. "Kiera, I love being on tour. This is important for my career. But I love you just as much. When I saw your pictures and heard about Kyle taking you to dinner—"

"You felt a little bit of what I feel every day," she finished for him. The words tasted like metal. "You don't like the fact that I went to dinner *once* with Kyle, but I'm not supposed to mind seeing pictures of you and that girl, your 'assistant.'"

"Maddie."

"Whatever. You seem to be joined at the hip."

"She's Bill's assistant too. She just keeps track of our schedules."

"Like Kyle keeps track of mine. But we don't have our picture taken because we don't do anything together outside of work."

They looked at each other in the dim light of the dashboard. The impasse seemed as wide as the miles that kept them apart. She needed to keep modeling to pay the bills, and he needed to be on the road to build his career.

She released a quiet breath. "I think we should call it a night before we get into it again. I'm really sorry I didn't tell you about the modeling." When he reached for her hand again, she didn't pull away.

"I'm sorry for being so jealous, Kiki. We need to make a better effort to connect with each other, no matter how busy we are."

"Okay." It sounded good but nothing would change. How could it?

Sliding a hand behind her neck, he pulled her gently toward him and rested his forehead against hers. His lingering kiss tasted of salty sadness. She wanted to throw herself into his arms and beg him not to leave, tell him how much she needed him. Instead, she put a hand to his cheek and managed a smile. "I love you."

He pressed a kiss to her palm. "I love you too. Forever and for always."

The ride home was quiet, as was the lingering hug and kiss at the bottom of the stairs. Kiera went up to her room and gently closed the door behind her. Then she lay across the bed and cried.

Buck's voice came from the darkness at the far end of the living room. "Did you sweep her off her feet?"

Peter trudged over and sank down on the foot of the bed. "I did. And then I dropped her."

Buck grunted as he shifted. The oxygen tank clicked evenly. "We're men. We do both really well. She's a feisty one, Peter. More complicated than her mother. She gets tangled in her own independence sometimes."

"I'd agree with that."

"After Thomas, I prayed a lot for God to send the right man to show her what real love is. You've done a great job."

"Yeah, well, I messed that up tonight."

Buck reached over in the moonlight and patted Peter's knee. "You'll make it up to her. She wants you to. Just don't leave her hanging. With you gone so much, she's pretty vulnerable. Especially to other men who might have their eye on her."

He nodded. "Whatshisname. Man, I hate being gone like this."

"It's just for a time. The tour won't last forever."

"Right now it feels like it will."

They were quiet for a moment. "Peter, I don't know how much she's told you, but I'm sure you can see I won't be here much longer. It's scaring her to death, even though she won't say so. I'll sure pass more easily if I know there's someone who'll be watching out for her."

"I'll be here for her." Tears clogged Peter's throat. "That's a promise."

"I hoped you planned to stick around."

"I plan to stick around forever. I love your daughter, Buck. If it's okay with you, I'll marry her once this tour is over. Even if she doesn't like the idea."

Buck's chuckle turned into a moment of wheezing. "It's more than okay with me. She loves you, Peter. She might lift that chin and act all hoity-toity, but she needs to know you're there for her."

"I'll be right here, and I'll make sure she knows it every day for the rest of her life. I think we'll name our first child after you."

"Better hope it's a boy."

Peter reached out to grasp his friend's frail hand. "You can rest easy, Buck. I'll take good care of her." The words barely made it past the knot in his throat.

Buck's hand tightened on his. "That does this tired old heart good. And I want you to know, you make a fine son. You have a good head on your shoulders and a good heart for others. I couldn't have picked anyone better for my Kiera."

"I wish you and I had had more time together."

"Me too. But what we've had was good. Now go get some sleep. You're back on the road tomorrow."

"Unfortunately I am. Goodnight, Buck."

"'Night, Peter. I'll be praying for you."

– 33 –

Kiera watched with a broken heart as her beloved father faded a little more each day. She rescheduled *One of Me* presentations for later in January, not wanting to be away from him for a minute. The hospice volunteers and paid caregivers were in attendance around the clock now, which offered a small amount of comfort. Their gentle care, frequent smiles, and warm hugs helped her through the long painful week after Christmas.

Terese and Jason came by in the evenings while the Simmons family alternated day visits. Kiera fielded calls from Buck's closest friends, scheduling short visits for them to say goodbye. It was an amazing time of heartfelt conversation, tears, and laughter as friends and family gathered around the hospital bed. Buck was alert much of the time, telling fishing stories and sharing memories.

Peter called to say he was unable to get away yet. After the New Year's concerts, he'd be free and on a flight home. Kiera took the news with calm acceptance. He had a job to do out there in the world and she had one to do here. Perhaps they could salvage some type of friendship in the end.

New Year's Day evening, Kiera sat at Buck's bedside reading as he napped. His stretches of sleep were longer and more frequent, but when he was awake his thoughts were clear, his humor intact. Their conversations were filled with gratitude for the life they'd had together. She couldn't be more thankful for this time with him.

Setting the book aside, she stood and stretched, then went to the kitchen to refill her coffee mug. Returning to her chair, she saw Buck's eyes open and focus on her. "Hi. How're you feeling?"

He shifted. "Lazy."

"That's what I've always said. Can't find anyone lazier than Buck Simmons."

He chuckled and reached a hand toward her which she took. "Kiki, I don't want you…to be alone." He tired so easily now he couldn't complete a sentence without needing an extra breath.

"I'm not alone. You know how many friends we have. And I have Terese and Jason and all the people at church. And of course there's Mark and Emily and Jen, and their families." How lucky they were to have so many people who cared about them.

"Kiera, look at me."

She met his gaze. "I'll be okay, Dad. Really." How was beyond her, but she would hold fast to God and hope that was enough.

He squeezed her fingers weakly. "That's not what I meant…young lady," he said, "and you know it."

"Do you think I'll be an old maid?" She tried to look indignant.

"Not if Peter…has anything to say about it."

She looked away and shrugged. "Peter has a very busy life. Hopefully when the tour ends he can come home for a while, but I'm not holding my breath anymore."

"That young man…will love you forever. Don't give up on him. He loves you…and you love him."

"I don't think it will be enough."

"It's enough." He rested a moment. "Don't let your pride get in the way."

"*My* pride? He's the one who got mad about my modeling. I'm just supposed to sit home twiddling my thumbs until he can fit me into his schedule?"

"He's a good man with big dreams…and a solid love for my stubborn… self-protecting daughter."

"Why shouldn't I be self-protecting?" She went to the window, staring into the blackness. "Our lives have gone different directions. I don't think there's a way to make this work. Especially," she added, arms folded tightly, "when one of us has a job that requires ongoing contact with women who throw themselves at him at every opportunity."

"There is if you love him."

"I do." *So very much.* "But I don't think I can wait for him to make room for me in his life. I want more than this. I want someone to share life with, not just give me a report at the end of the week. I want to be more important than his job." There. Her ugly, selfish thoughts were out in the open, but it didn't make her feel better. More like petty and childish.

"Come here, Honey."

Fighting back the ever-present tears, she settled beside him on the edge of the bed. He reached for her hand again.

"Kiera, I want what's best for you. I want you…to have a full life. I want you to be happy. And I believe that Peter…is what's best for you. But you have to figure that out…for yourself. You are too much like me," he added. "We're stubborn, independent people…that God has to sometimes…knock over the head to get us to listen to Him."

She clung to his hand, her heart aching that these conversations would soon be no longer. "I don't mean to be stubborn. I'm just afraid."

"I know. It's easy to fear…what we can't see. But I want you to remember that God sees. He loves you and Peter." Sweat beaded on his forehead. "You can trust Him…with your fear and your heart. He knows and…He'll work it out. If you let Him."

If I let Him. She looked at his beloved face, the gentle words poking at her.

"Peter has a heart for God…and for you. Let the tour finish up. Then spend time together. Don't make any decisions…you might regret. Promise?"

She wanted desperately to promise him the world. But who knew what decisions would be made in the coming days and weeks? Couldn't God give her a peek into the future to know for sure Peter would still love her when the tour was over?

Buck squeezed her hand, eyebrows raised, and she managed a smile.

"Promise."

He closed his eyes and sighed. "Good. I know…you don't go back on…your promises."

Holding his hand while he slept, she let her tears flow. She wanted to believe Peter was her future, that everything would work out like a fairy tale. But in the real world, the prince was busy with thousands of other women. She wasn't the only girl at the ball now.

The thought put another crack in her broken heart.

Peter studied his tuxedo-clad look in the hotel room mirror. An image of Kiera at the launch party flashed through his mind and he closed his eyes, trying to capture the memory—the amazing dress, the love in her eyes, her slender hand in his.

Even in jeans and a baseball cap, she was the most beautiful woman he knew. Just thinking that she was his made him grin like an idiot. He needed to hear her voice. Touching base with her would calm his nerves, which for some reason were jumpy about tonight's mystery event. The call went to her voice mail and he left a quick message. He'd try again later.

Bill waited in the lobby, looking relaxed and comfortable in his tux. Peter raised an eyebrow as they headed toward a black sedan with tinted windows and a chauffeur who was holding the back door open. "We have a driver for this event?"

Bill shrugged. "You're one of the main guests."

"I am? Are they hard up for guests?"

"You have got to get over this Midwest attitude that you aren't as important as other people. You're a star, so you have to act like one."

Bill was unusually quiet as they cruised through Garden City, Long Island. Peter eyed him warily, edgy in the silence. "Am I the only entertainment?"

"The only singer."

The response was too vague. "Okay, why don't you tell me what's really going on. You're acting weird."

Bill's chuckle sounded forced. "Nothing is 'going on,' Peter. This is a fundraiser for a friend of mine and you're the star attraction. There will be a lot of important people there tonight with connections vital to your career. Your job is to just be yourself and sing a few songs."

"What songs?"

"Whatever you'd like. I was thinking your single that's on the radio right now, and then maybe a couple other ones. That's up to you."

The car glided to a stop before the historic hotel. Peter turned a frown on his manager. Something wasn't right. "Give me more information or I'm not getting out of the car. What's really going on?"

Bill took his time releasing a noisy breath. "Okay. Here's the whole story. It's a fundraiser for an old friend of mine whose granddaughter has leukemia. The granddaughter heard your CD and wants to meet you, so they asked if you'd come perform after the dinner."

"Who's your friend?"

"Aaron Boswell."

"Do I know him?"

"I don't believe so."

He folded his arms and frowned. "So why the secrecy?"

Bill turned his eyes toward the front. "An auction will also be part of the entertainment."

"And?"

"You're one of the things they're auctioning."

"*What?*" An image of a side of beef with his face on it flashed through his mind.

"It's all in fun, Peter. A number of men are being auctioned to have a date with the young ladies who will be there tonight."

"Oh, no." He shook his head sharply. "This is so not happening. You can just forget it. Auction yourself."

"Sure. They'll raise a lot of money auctioning off dinner with a fifty-year-old man." He turned back toward Peter. "It's just to raise money so the little gal can get the treatment she needs. It's a lot like your friend Bart."

"This is *nothing* like Buck so don't try that angle. They wouldn't stoop this low." He sat silent, fuming. "Fine. I'll sing but I am not getting auctioned off to anyone."

"Peter, there's no funny business with this. It will just be dinner with someone who I'm sure is an attractive young woman with plenty of money. Who knows? Maybe you'll like her."

"I prefer my girlfriend." He glared at Bill. "I'm not doing it."

"You're on the program. This will be great for ticket sales and name recognition."

"Oh, right. Peter Theisen, a singing piece of meat to be auctioned at your fundraising event. That's the reputation I want."

"Try Peter Theisen, singing sensation and Good Samaritan. Willing to jump in and help whenever he can. This is why I didn't tell you earlier. I knew you'd blow it out of proportion."

The driver turned to look back at Bill. "I have to move the car so others can get in. Do you want me to drive around the block?"

"No. We're getting out." Bill opened the door then looked at Peter. "Give it a try, Theisen. If this doesn't boost sales, it won't happen again."

"I don't care if it boosts sales to the moon. You can bet it won't happen again." He swore under his breath and slammed his way out of the car. A warning pounded with the uneven rhythm of his heart. Nerves on alert, he had the distinct impression he wasn't supposed to enter the Garden City Hotel. The sensation became so intense he stopped on the sidewalk, staring at the entrance, unable to pull in a breath.

Go back now.

He blinked in surprise. The words rang through his head as clearly as if someone had spoken them aloud. He glanced sideways. It certainly hadn't been Bill.

"Peter." Bill's voice was calm. "It will be good publicity, you'll have a nice dinner date, and I'll owe you one."

His jaw clenched as a battle raged inside. It might sound harmless but Kiera wouldn't like it. *He* didn't like it. Yet here he stood, like a well-dressed puppet on Bill's strings.

"Okay," he ground out. "I want to fly back to Minnesota for a few days next week. That's the least you owe me."

"I can arrange that."

"Bill! Good to see you!" A white-haired gentleman strode through the large glass doors and approached with a wide smile. He extended a hand to Bill first, then introduced himself to Peter. "Thank you for coming to sing tonight. Leila is going to be thrilled to meet you."

He seemed genuinely thankful to have them there. Peter smiled woodenly. "I'm glad we could come."

Go back now.

"Come in and join the party. I want to introduce you to some people."

Propelled into the golden opulence of the Grand Ballroom, Peter was swept into the world of wealth and sophistication. The warning had stopped but the echoing silence was unnerving.

Leila was not the child he expected but a stunning young woman with long blonde hair and sparkling blue eyes. She was momentarily speechless when they were introduced, then blushed as they shook hands.

"I should be angry at you, Grandpa, for springing this on me," she scolded the older man with a smile.

"But you're not, so put that thought out of your pretty head. Why don't you introduce our guest to your friends?"

"I'll do that right now." She claimed Peter's hand and pulled him away from her grandfather and Bill. Peter heard their chuckles and shot Bill a warning glance.

Leila chattered about the event as she led him through a maze of linen-covered tables toward a gathering of young people. With a glass of champagne thrust into his hand, Peter lost track of names as he greeted one after another.

A volley of questions rained over him about the music industry, where he'd been on the tour, which celebrities he'd met. The lively conversation settled his nerves. If Kiera were beside him, it might even be fun.

Seated at the piano two hours later, he sang his first single to hit the airwaves. The crowd of over three hundred applauded enthusiastically. At their encouragement he sang two more before returning to his seat beside Leila amidst thunderous appreciation.

Her smile was radiant as she took his hand, gushing her thanks. He was glad he'd agreed to perform but he'd be happy to leave now. His nerves tingled a warning again.

"Oh, my." The female emcee, energetic and funny before Peter's performance, now fanned her face with both hands. "That was an amazing performance by a really hot performer. Thank you, Peter. That was wonderful."

He nodded, embarrassed by her actions but happy the crowd responded with whistles and cheers. It was nice to be appreciated. Maybe Bill was wrong—

"Okay, now for the next portion of the evening."

The whistles intensified. Peter winced. There was a rustle of activity as the older people headed toward an adjacent room. He watched them go, his feet itching to follow.

"Girls, get your checkbooks ready. Guys, we have a few surprises for you as well. We want to raise as much money as possible for the young adult wing of the cancer hospital, so loosen those purse strings."

Peter frowned and glanced at Leila. She looked awfully healthy for someone with leukemia, but what did he know? Maybe she was in the early stages. She beamed back at him and squeezed his hand. Unable to think of a polite way to untangle himself, he let her maintain her possessive grasp. It was a good thing Kiera couldn't see him.

"We all know how this auction works. Our handsome gentlemen will tell you what they have planned for the evening, and then the bidding begins. I think our volunteers have some wild and crazy things planned, so prepare yourselves, girls."

Planned? The lump in Peter's stomach grew through the first two men's sales pitches. Extensive planning had gone into their dates. Sweat formed along his hairline and he loosened his collar. He couldn't form a coherent thought let alone any grand ideas for a date with a stranger. What would he tell Kiera? *How* would he tell her?

"Hi. I'm Bob. I'm a firefighter." The third young man stood at the microphone bare-chested, red suspenders holding up his firefighter pants, a plastic hat on his curly blond hair. "What do firefighters know? We know what's hot, and I've got a *hot* date planned for one lucky lady." He proceeded to describe a night of dinner and dancing and...whatever followed. The catcalls were loud, the bidding wild.

Peter's stomach churned.

The young woman who "won" Bob hurried forward and clasped her hands around one of his impressive biceps, shrieking as she kicked up a stilettoed foot. Peter watched them leave the stage, unable to pull in a full breath.

Remember what matters.

The words were barely audible over the raucous commotion. He blinked them away but they returned louder, more insistent.

Remember what matters.

He took a quick inventory. *Kiera matters. Buck matters. My faith does too, of course.* He cringed. Had he ever answered Joel's last email from before Christmas? Obviously his career and image mattered or he wouldn't be here.

"And now we have the amazing Peter Theisen. Peter, come on up here."

Leila squeezed his hand again and then clapped excitedly. She hadn't bid on any of the other men and he suddenly understood why.

Mouth dry, hands clammy, he stood before the microphone and waited for the cheering to die down. Letting his gaze run over the crowd, chaos crowded his thoughts. *What do I do, Lord? I'm sorry. I should have listened to you.*

Leave now.

Right now? In front of all these people? But Bill said it would be a good thing to do. For the cancer wing. For my career.

His gaze moved to the back of the room where Bill stood, giving him a thumbs-up.

Peter opened his mouth, but for a moment nothing came out. "Well...my date will consist of..." His heart pounded so hard he was sure they could see it. He should leave. Now. "My date will start with a pre-concert lunch followed by a backstage tour. You'll get to meet the musicians, see how a concert is put together, and sit in on a rehearsal. Then you'll have a seat right on stage for the concert."

His heart slowed its frantic pace. That sounded pretty good. Kiera would be okay with that. He relaxed, getting into the moment as the girls shrieked. "After the concert, we'll have an evening of dinner and dancing which just might last through the night."

That could happen. If the concert ran late and they didn't get out to eat until after midnight, they might still be visiting into the wee hours. Some girls could talk forever. Hopefully he'd stay awake. "Then we'll wrap things up with breakfast and a limo will bring you home."

The bidding went crazy. As the numbers rose he smiled, pleased with the way he'd handled it. Someone would get to see behind the scenes of a concert, they'd have dinner and maybe go dancing, and then the limo—that Bill would pay for—would take her home. Sounded harmless, even fun.

The smile faded. So why did it feel like Bill had tightened the puppet strings?

– 34 –

Just after eight on Sunday morning, Buck's breathing slowed. He'd been restless through the night but now he was calm and quiet. Sitting on the edge of the bed, Kiera held his cold hand between hers. The time she'd dreaded and fought against was here. She had to let him go.

She stood and leaned down to press a kiss to his cool forehead. "It's okay, Dad," she whispered. "You can go to Mom." She ran her hand over his forehead.

"Tell her hi for me. Tell her I'm all grown up now," she added with a choked laugh. "Tell her you did a great job. She should be proud of the dad you were. The best in the whole world." She struggled to draw a breath. "Tell her…I'll be okay. I love you, Daddy," she whispered. "I love you."

There was another quiet breath and then nothing. In the silence, Kiera rested her forehead against his. He was gone. Her life with him was over.

"Oh, Dad." Strength drained from her legs and she lowered into the bedside chair. Pressing the back of his hand against her cheek, she cried as she rocked. The silence was overwhelming.

Then it seemed arms came around her, filling her with peaceful warmth. She lifted her head at the strange sensation and looked around. Susan had stepped into the kitchen to give them privacy. She was alone in the room but she was suddenly absolutely sure she wasn't. God was there, holding her, caring for her. She wasn't alone after all.

"Thank you, Lord," she whispered in awe, tears coursing down her cheeks. "Thank you for not forgetting me."

Still holding her father's hand, she cried, wrapped in joy-tinged sadness. He wasn't just gone. He was walking with God. The image was vivid—she could feel the warmth of the sun, smell the fresh air, see the joyful reunion between her parents, her father whole and healthy. She smiled at the vision. It was a holy moment as she released her father and mentally placed her hand in God's to start a life with only Him as her father and protector.

She had no idea how much time had passed before she felt a hand rest on her shoulder. She reached up to cover it with her own.

"You're not alone," Susan said in a hushed voice.

"God is here," Kiera agreed.

The woman moved around to stand at the other side of the bed, her brown eyes wide. "I felt it as soon as I walked into the room. I still feel it."

Kiera smiled through her tears. "God didn't leave me to grieve alone. He's here with me, yet I know He led Dad right to Mom."

Susan studied her for a moment. "In all my years in hospice, Kiera, I've never experienced anything quite like this."

"He's always been there. You just haven't noticed."

"Maybe that's true." She placed her hands on Buck's still legs, looked at his peaceful face and sighed. "Your father was truly a wonderful man. I will miss him very, very much."

Kiera turned her gaze back to her father and struggled to breathe. "Me too," she whispered.

Peter closed his portfolio and smiled at Maddie Birning as they sat in the hotel lobby after breakfast Monday morning. Skeptical about Bill's decision to hire an assistant, he was glad now for her thoughtful, organized presence. They'd worked together for a month and he felt more in control of his life.

"Thanks, Maddie. This has been a good meeting. You're going to get my flights set up for Minneapolis for next weekend, then?"

She nodded, gathering her notes. Her dark hair gleamed under the overhead lights. "I'll have that for you by tonight. Oh, we forgot to talk about what you want for dinner before the show tomorrow."

He grinned and leaned back, hooking his hands behind his head. "I think I could get used to this."

"You're supposed to." Her smile revealed perfect white teeth and a dimple at the corner of her mouth. "So what would you like?"

"What's everyone else having?"

"They aren't the star. You are. So you decide and that's what they'll get."

He frowned. "That sounds weird. I'm just one of the group."

"Peter, without you, they wouldn't have this job. You're in charge."

He hadn't thought of it that way. "Well, let's have…Chinese. Can you find a Chinese restaurant that will deliver?"

"If they don't, I'll go get it. Chinese it is."

"Great. Thanks, Maddie." He turned the volume up on his phone and noticed a missed call from yesterday when his battery had died. Getting to his feet, he smiled as the message started, then froze.

Kiera's tearful words tore into him and he sank back into the chair, stunned. Buck was gone. And he hadn't made time to go back like he promised. He hadn't been there for her. For either of them. His eyes burned as he replayed the message.

"Peter…it's Kiera. I wanted to let you know that…Dad died this morning." A pause as she sniffed. "I know your tour schedule was booked months ago so I don't expect you to rush home, of course. I just wanted you to know."

He waited, heart aching.

"He wasn't in any pain at the end. It was very peaceful. I can't believe he's gone… He loved you, Peter. He always asked about your tour, wanting to know what city you were in. I'm so thankful for the time you spent with him. It made him happy."

She cleared her throat. "So the reviewal and service will be Thursday afternoon at…the church. Can't even think of the name of my own church." She laughed shakily. "Sorry. At Faith, of course. Well, call if you get a chance."

"Peter?"

Maddie's voice broke through and he blinked. "What?"

"What's wrong? You look awful."

"Buck died." It felt surreal saying the words.

"Buck?"

"Kiera's dad. A good friend of mine."

She put a hand on his arm. "I'm so sorry. What can I do?"

What could anyone do? Buck was gone. Kiera was devastated. And he hadn't been there. "I need to get to Minnesota as soon as possible."

Flipping open her notebook, she nodded as she wrote. "I'll get the earliest flight possible on Sunday."

"No. She said the funeral is Thursday. I need to be there on Thursday."

Maddie lifted her head and frowned. "Peter, you have shows Wednesday, Friday, and Saturday."

"I don't care if I have shows scheduled until doomsday." He stood. "I will be in Minnesota on Thursday and Friday, at the very least."

"We should talk to Bill—"

"You talk to Bill. I need to call Kiera." He stalked away, dialing her number with a shaking hand. When it went to voice mail, he dialed Terese. She answered on the second ring. "Hey, Terese. It's Peter."

"Hi, Peter." She said his name with such emphasis, he knew Kiera was nearby.

"Can I talk to her?"

"Sure. Hold on."

Through the sound of the phone rubbing against clothing, he heard Terese's voice followed by Kiera's.

Terese came back on. "Peter? We're just leaving for the funeral home. We're supposed to be there in ten minutes. Can she call you back when we're done?"

"Let me talk to her for just a second. Please."

"Okay."

A moment later, Kiera's voice came on. "Hi."

"Honey, I just got your message now. I am so sorry about Buck."

“Thanks.” The defeat in that simple word wrenched his heart.

“How are you holding up?”

“Okay. There are so many things to do, I don’t have a lot of time to think.” Her words were slow and measured.

“I wish I’d been there with you. With him.”

“Yeah,” she sighed. “Me too.”

Her response stabbed like a knife. He should have been there to say goodbye. He should be there right now.

“I’m coming as soon as I can get a flight home. I’ll be there for sure on Thursday and Friday.”

“That would be nice, but I’ll understand—”

“I will be there,” he repeated firmly. “Go make your plans now and I’ll talk to you later, okay?”

“Okay. Thanks for calling.”

Thanks for calling. That’s what you said to an acquaintance. He closed his eyes and leaned against the wall next to the elevator. He was writing himself right out of her life.

He blindly poked at the elevator button, struggling to keep the tears back. Once he got to his room he could fall apart. It took forever for the doors to slide open. He punched the six and then folded his arms, keeping his head down to avoid eye contact with the others. Through the whispering in the back, he heard his name. Sixth floor couldn’t come fast enough.

An hour later there was a sharp rap at the door. Peter rolled off the bed, checked the peephole and barely had the handle turned before Bill pushed into the room.

“What do you think you’re doing, Theisen?”

Peter returned to his laptop propped on the bed. “Looking at pictures on my computer.” Kiera. Buck. Their time at the cabin. His real life.

“Funny. You are *not* cancelling any shows. This week or any other week.”

He didn’t look up. “Buck Simmons died. I’m going home for the funeral."

"Well, lucky for you it's on the one day you don't have anything scheduled. You can fly in and out the same day."

"I'm going home on a red-eye Wednesday evening. I can be back for the Saturday show if Kiera's doing okay."

"We aren't cancelling the Friday show. You can fly back Friday morning."

Peter met Bill's seething gaze, a strange peace keeping his response calm. "I'm flying back Saturday morning, Bill. I've already got the flights set."

"Theisen, you don't make those decisions. I do. When you signed the contract, you gave me control over your life. And we aren't cancelling the Friday show."

Peter shrugged and turned back to his laptop. His heartbeat ramped up but he kept his expression neutral. "Then I hope you know my songs well enough to go on stage. I'll be in Minneapolis, not Atlanta."

"You're quite the comedian."

"Do I look like I'm being funny? Dump me as a client, Bill. Or sue me for breach of contract. I don't care. But I'm going home Wednesday evening and I'll be back in time for Saturday's show."

The strained silence dragged on. "Fine," Bill said finally. "You can go and we'll see if we can postpone the show. But don't try pulling a stunt like this again. Understand?"

"It's not a stunt, Bill. It's family. I'm sorry Buck's death is an inconvenience for you."

Bill stormed from the room, leaving a trail of curses behind. Peter released the breath he didn't know he'd been holding.

– 35 –

Peter pulled up to the curb at the Simmons home. The sense of homecoming was muted by grief. He climbed out of the car and stood a moment, shivering in the cold as he studied the familiar house. Buck wouldn't be there to welcome him, to challenge him at cribbage, to swap fishing stories…to share his wit and wisdom.

Kiera's car was in the driveway, wedged in by several others. How many times had he parked beside her, starting with that first unexpected dinner? Now there were other cars surrounding hers, other people supporting her.

The promise he'd made Buck at Christmas weighed heavily on him as he headed to the front door. When he rang the doorbell, the door opened and Mark's face lit up. He ushered Peter in with a warm greeting and nodded toward the stairway. "She just went upstairs for something."

"Okay if I go up?"

"I think you should."

He took the stairs two at a time. Glancing into Kiera's empty bedroom, he continued down the hall. Buck's door was open and he paused in the doorway.

She stood at the foot of the bed, running her fingers along the oak footboard. Dressed in a black jacket and pants, she looked tall, slender, and lost. Her head turned and their tearful glances met. She pressed trembling fingertips to her lips, and Peter strode forward to wrap her tightly in his arms.

They stood in silence, sharing their pain. In just six months, he'd come to love Buck as a friend and a father. He wasn't prepared to lose him so quickly. He leaned back to look down at her, brushing the wetness from her cheeks with a shaking hand. "I'm so sorry I wasn't here with you."

"I told Terese it seemed fitting it was just the two of us."

"I still should have been here."

"How long can you stay?" There was no reproach in her voice.

"Until Saturday morning."

Her eyebrows rose. "Bill is letting you stay that long?"

Ouch. "I told Bill how long I'd be gone."

"But he didn't like it."

He shrugged. "I don't care if he liked it or not."

"Sorry to interrupt." They turned at Terese's voice. "We should head over, hon."

"We'll be right down," Peter told her then looked at Kiera. "Ready?"

"No." Her green eyes latched onto his. "Will you stay with me?"

"Every minute, Sweetheart. Whatever you need."

The strain eased between her eyes, the ghost of a smile lifting her lips. "Thank you."

When the line of cars pulled up in front of Faith Church, Peter couldn't believe the photographers huddled on the sidewalk. A cloud of cigarette smoke and frozen breath hovered over them. Bill gave out the details of the funeral?

"What in the world?" From her seat beside Jason, Terese looked back at Peter. "How did they find out where you were?"

"Bill. Or Maddie." He shook his head, releasing a sharp breath, then squeezed Kiera's hand. "I'm sorry."

She slid dark sunglasses on. "Let's go."

Jason pulled up to the back door to let them out. The photographers had followed the car at a run. When Peter stepped out and reached a hand back to Kiera, the cameras clicked like chattering teeth.

"Peter! Kiera! What can you tell us about Buck Simmons? Are they rescheduling your concert tomorrow night? How long have you two known each other?"

He wrapped an arm around her shoulders and glanced toward the cameras. It was the first time he'd felt real irritation at the paparazzi that trailed him. "Please, everyone. This isn't the time."

They fell silent but the cameras remained pointed toward them.

"We could use Maddie right about now," he grumbled, pulling the door open.

Inside, out of view of the cameras, Kiera stopped and pulled her sunglasses off. "Really."

The ice in her voice stopped him. "Only because she's great at running interference."

As she studied him, his defenses rose. Kiera couldn't understand how helpful Maddie was in his crazy world. She walked past him and started up the stairs, her silence screaming at him. Terese said she would wait for Jason, shooting Peter a glare before turning back to the door. After a moment's hesitation, he followed Kiera.

Pastor Joel met them in the large foyer. He hugged Kiera and they exchanged a few quiet words. Then he turned to welcome Peter with a hug as well. A short, round man in a navy suit approached Kiera, his expression solicitous. He asked a question and she looked over at Peter. He joined them and took her hand.

"Peter, this is Jerry from the funeral home."

They shook hands, then Jerry turned back to Kiera. "Why don't you follow me?" He led them toward the Fireside Room where the casket stood amidst a garden of flowers, fishing poles propped against the end of it. The fragrance of the bouquets was achingly sweet.

Kiera stopped in the doorway, her fingers resting on the pearl necklace.

Peter put his arm around her shoulders and whispered, "You don't have to do this right now. Do you want to wait a bit?"

She shook her head. "It won't be any easier later."

Approaching the casket, she wobbled and he tightened his arm. Tears dripped silently down her cheeks as she gazed at her father's passive face. Peter rested his head against hers.

"Oh, Dad," she sighed. "I don't know how to do this without you." She put a shaking hand over his and dropped her head.

Peter set his hand over hers and squeezed his burning eyes shut. His friend and mentor was gone, leaving this fragile young woman in his care. He'd let Buck down once; he wouldn't do it again.

"Come on, Sweetheart. Let's go sit down for a minute."

She nodded, head still bowed, and let him lead her from the room to a bench in the hallway.

Terese approached with a bottle of water, her face pale. "Here you go, Kier. You okay?"

Kiera nodded again, accepting the bottle. After a long drink, she lifted red-rimmed eyes and pulled in a deep breath. "This helps. Thanks."

"People are already arriving. Where do you want to stand? They can come to wherever you are."

Kiera looked back at the room where the casket was. "I'll stand in there with Dad."

Terese frowned. "Are you sure? Don't make this harder on yourself than it already is."

"That's where I want to be." She looked up at Peter. "It's where people will go anyway."

"Then that's where we'll stand," he agreed.

Within a few minutes, the foyer was crowded and a steady stream of people filed past the casket. Kiera greeted each person, thanking them for coming and for what they'd meant to Buck, then introduced them to Peter with a story about how they knew her father. She hugged and chatted, occasionally glancing over her shoulder at the casket.

During a brief lull, Peter pulled her close to share some of his energy with her, but it was her poise and determination to be strong that gave him strength instead. She was an amazing woman. No wonder he loved her.

Kiera soaked in Peter's presence. During those moments when he pulled her close, she relaxed into him to recharge. She needed his supportive arm to lean into, his solid shoulder to rest against. It gave her strength to greet the next person, to laugh at their stories.

"Thank you for coming, Barbara, and for the beautiful plant. I'm going to put it on the window ledge right by his favorite chair so I can enjoy it this winter."

She turned and caught her breath. "Kyle! What a surprise."

He gave her a long hug before answering. "Nothing could keep me away, Kiera. I'm so sorry about your dad."

"Thank you." She forced a smile. "Kyle, I want you to meet Peter Theisen. Peter, this is Kyle Matthews from Glitz."

The men shook hands, greetings stiff and polite. Her fingers went numb within Peter's possessive grasp.

"You're on tour out East, aren't you, Peter?"

"For now." He put an arm around Kiera's shoulder and smiled. "It's been a fantastic experience so far. Without Kiera's support, I'm not sure I'd be able to stay on the road. It's grueling."

She glanced up at him and bit her lip. Having screaming women throw themselves at him was grueling? There were other words that seemed more appropriate.

"How long have you been on the road?"

"About four months. We're heading south now, then the tour will wrap up on the West Coast."

Kyle glanced at Kiera. "That's a long time to be gone."

"I make it home as often as I can."

She looked back at Buck's placid face and knew he'd have a funny comment about the two roosters scratching the ground before her. Time to end the face-off. "Thanks so much for coming, Kyle."

He set his hand gently on her shoulder. "I had to be here for you, Kiera."

"I have good support. And people who bring me things to drink," she added as Terese appeared with another bottle of water.

Peter's eyebrows lifted when Terese greeted Kyle with a hug, and Kiera pushed down a warped sense of satisfaction. Perhaps if he saw she wasn't just pining away for him…

She turned abruptly to the elderly couple next in line. "Marv and Anita. Thank you so much for coming."

Finally Jerry ushered the last few people into the sanctuary. As the organ began playing, Kiera faced the casket. For a moment she couldn't breathe, and she pressed her fingers to her mouth to hold back the rising sob. Peter's arms came around her and she buried her face against him. She couldn't do this. *God, why?*

Jerry cleared his throat from somewhere behind her, and she straightened and wiped her face. This was her last moment with her father. It was his beloved face but without the spark that had made him such a wonderful man.

"Thank you, Daddy," she whispered. "It was a great life. You did good, kid," she added, repeating what he had said so often to her. She leaned down and kissed his cool forehead. "I love you."

She turned away and drew a deep breath, setting her shoulders. This was her chance to honor the man who had loved and cherished her all her life. She would do him proud.

– 36 –

Friday passed too quickly as Kiera and Peter opened hundreds of cards, reading the heartfelt words aloud, wiping tears from their faces. Food, flowers, and plants occupied every flat surface in the old house.

He made sandwiches for dinner and she dutifully took several bites. Her appetite had been gone for weeks, but she appreciated his doting and did as he ordered—a bite of sandwich, a few chips, a drink of milk. Repeat.

She refused to acknowledge the bitter thoughts niggling at the edge of her mind. He would leave in the morning and return to his happy life. She had Christmas decorations to put away, a house to sort, decisions to be made. And she would do it alone.

"Cribbage?" He held the board and Buck's favorite deck of cards.

As much as she'd like to play a game in his honor, she shook her head with a sigh. "I can't form a complete thought. There's no way I'd be any competition."

"So what's your point?"

It took a second for his joke to register and she smiled. "I don't think taking unfair advantage of your competition constitutes an ethical win."

"That might be true, but as Buck always said, a win is a win."

"Then you can pretend we played and you won. Happy?"

He dropped beside her on the couch and tucked her under his arm. "Now I am. Winning at cards doesn't come close to this."

She snuggled closer. "Thank you for being here. I know it caused problems with Bill."

"Bill who?" He turned on the television and the energized voice of a woman selling detergent filled the room. Kiera closed her eyes and relaxed against him, content to hear the strong beat of his heart over the muffled voices on TV. She floated in a comfortable quiet until his sharp breath made her lift her head.

"...and the surprise of having new heartthrob Peter Theisen being auctioned off set a new record for the charity—"

The channel changed abruptly and Kiera sat up. The wide-eyed expression on Peter's pale face made her heart stop. He'd been part of an auction? "Turn it back, please."

"It's just another stupid story."

"Then turning it back shouldn't matter." They stared at each other, then he pointed the remote at the TV.

"...already raised one hundred thousand dollars when Peter Theisen was put on the bidding block."

Kiera watched as his familiar voice described the date he was offering in smiling detail, right down to spending the night with the stranger who won. There was screaming and frantic bidding when he finished. Then a pretty, young blonde ran up on the stage and flung herself at him. He caught her with a surprised expression, allowing her to wrap her arms around him and plant a drawn-out kiss on his mouth.

The program moved on to another story and Peter shut the TV off. Silence pulsed. Neither moved. So while she'd been watching her father die, he'd been auctioning himself to the highest bidder. Promising an evening that should have been reserved for her once they married. All while going back on his promise to her. To Buck.

"Kiera—"

She lifted a hand to stop him and pushed to her feet. Wandering the living room on stiff legs, she touched familiar knickknacks and tried to form words, searching for emotion of some sort. Nothing. She was suddenly and completely tired of the whole mess.

"It's not what it looked like." There was little conviction in his words.

She looked across the room at him. "So what was it?"

He stood and faced her, frowning intensity on his face. The face that other women kissed and adored during long romantic evenings together. "Bill told me it was a fundraiser for a girl with leukemia."

"Ah." She nodded. "The girl who won."

"I thought he was talking about a kid." He rubbed his forehead. "He told me I was just doing a few songs. He never said anything about the auction."

"For not knowing about it, you described a lovely date in amazing detail."

"I made it up as I went along. I thought it would be okay to have someone tag along for the evening, see what goes into making a show. Then we'd have dinner and it would be over."

"Not without a romantic *breakfast*."

His expression altered, his face wore a greenish tint. She should be the one feeling sick. The warmth of the fire on her back was all she felt.

"It's not like I'm going to sleep with her."

"You'd pass up an opportunity with someone who looks like *that*?"

"She doesn't come close to you."

"Please." She rolled her eyes. "Where have I heard that before? Oh, that's right. Thomas said something like that when I found out *he* was sleeping around."

"I'm not sleeping around!"

She shrugged. "Not yet."

His mouth dropped open. "You think that little of me?"

"After that video, the *world* thinks you're sleeping around. Come on, Peter. You just offered yourself to the highest bidder."

"But you know better." His voice wavered.

She stared down at the flames. "I don't know anything anymore."

He grasped her shoulders, turning her to face him. The panic and pain in his dark eyes should have touched something in her.

"You know that I love you. You *know* it. And you know you can trust me not to be with anyone else. This whole tour is about appearances. I'll make sure she gets her money back and not have her come anywhere near the tour. I don't care about her or any other woman. I love *you*."

The words that had thrilled her these past months now stabbed her heart. "Do me a favor. Don't love me anymore. It's killing me."

His eyes widened and they stared at each other for a long, silent moment before he dropped his hands and stepped back.

"Peter, we both know this relationship isn't going anywhere. You need to be out there doing whatever Bill says you need to do to build your career. I'm tired of sitting back here watching it all. I'm sick of your celebrity life and your excuses."

His face darkened. "You're living your own celebrity life. Your face is on more ads and billboards than mine will ever be."

She shrugged. "They take my picture, I go home. End of my celebrity life. Your celebrity life involves women and parties. And auctions and dates with women you don't even know."

"So where does Whatshisname fit in your so-called non-celebrity life?"

"Kyle is my agent. But he doesn't control my life like Bill controls yours. If there's an assignment I don't like, I say no. Apparently you can't. Or you don't."

"I came here despite what he wanted."

"*After* my father died." Her chin quivered. "You promised both of us you'd come back in a week and you didn't. Now I doubt you had plans to."

He was silent before her accusation. The only sound was the gentle crackling of the fire. Tears filled his eyes. "Kiera, I can't lose you over this."

The long-forgotten free-fall sensation made her set her hand on the mantle. "It's not over this. It's over everything. Once you went on tour, it all changed. Our circumstances, what our relationship was built on. This is just the final straw."

"So this is it? After everything we've been through, we just call it quits?"

"What else can we do?"

He took her shoulders again, his fingers biting into her. "We can fight for it. We have something amazing. It's worth fighting for."

"How?" There wasn't an ounce of fight left in her. "Nothing will change. You'll be on the road for four more months. I have things to do here. You can't come back any more often and I can't follow you around the country.

How do we fight for it?"

Creases formed across his forehead as his eyes narrowed. "So you can just walk away from me, from what we have? Just like that? Because I know I can't."

Tears stung. "Not just like that. But when the choice is to continue letting my heart take a beating or try to salvage what's left and move forward, I'll move forward."

"Without me."

She nodded in slow motion. "Without us."

The shock on his face pierced through her. What was she doing? When had this decision been made? The breath ran out of her, a slow, painful leak. *When he didn't come back before Dad died. When I had to watch him parade his life and his women on national television.* When she thought the loneliness would shatter her into a million tiny pieces.

He'd chosen the other women over her. He'd chosen to auction himself to strangers. The stage was his real love, just as she'd known it would be.

He released her and shoved his hands into his pockets. "Wow. Okay. Well, I guess I'll just…go. I don't think there's anything I can say right now that will make you understand how I feel about you." Shoulders slumped, his mouth formed a pinched line. "I know this is the most awful time for you, and I thought I could help you through it, but…I'll give you some space—for now.

"I'm not giving you up, Kiera." He held her gaze. "I *love* you. I'll be back and we'll fix this. I have a lot to prove to you, and I have every intention of doing that. I owe it to you, and I owe it to Buck."

He took her face in his hands. "I will always love you. Forever and for always."

As he pressed a lingering kiss to her forehead, she leaned toward him, clenching her fists to keep from throwing herself against him. It was about self-preservation now, not feelings.

He looked at her in silence, eyes shiny with unshed tears. "Call me if you change your mind. I'll be there for you."

But I need you here.

He turned and trudged up the stairs, leaving her standing by the fireplace. Returning minutes later with his suitcase, he set it by the door and looked across the room at her. Frozen in place, arms folded tightly, she looked back at him.

Shaking his head, he grabbed his jacket off the coat rack and went out into the cold without looking back. A hand over the searing pain in her chest, she stared at the door and listened to the fading crunch of his footsteps in the snow until her legs buckled. She curled up in Buck's recliner, pulled his blanket over her and closed her eyes.

Now she was truly alone.

Ladies and gentlemen, the captain has turned off the safety belt sign."

Peter blinked. He didn't remember driving to the airport or going through security. Or even getting on this plane. He turned his gaze to the bumpy gray clouds below. What just happened? He'd flown into Minneapolis to be with the love of his life and was flying out two days later with a gaping hole in his heart.

He dropped his head back against the seat. *What kind of idiot am I? When Bill didn't tell me the details of the charity event, I should have known something was up. But no, I just went along, assuming everything would work out.*

He rubbed his temples to ease the ache that had taken over when he left Buck's house last night. Why didn't she understand it was all just for show? She'd been in the limelight enough to know how it worked. But he had to admit it didn't look good. He could have stopped the kiss. He'd been so caught up in the moment he just played along. Kiera had a right to be mad.

His eyes narrowed. She'd thrown in the towel so quickly, without giving him a chance to explain. She'd just walked away from what they had without a fight.

"Sir?"

He looked toward the voice.

"Would you like a beverage?" The redheaded flight attendant smiled.

"Juice, coffee, soda?"

"No. Thanks." He leaned his head against the wall. He just wanted Kiera. But apparently she didn't want him. *Wait. Is that what this is about?* No, that couldn't be it. But…the guy did give her several long hugs at the funeral, right in front of him. He'd even held her hand and kissed her cheek when he left. And she'd never pulled away or tried to stop him.

The air cut off in his throat. *You moron! You pretty much gift-wrapped her and handed her over to Mr. Glitz by not being there when Buck died.* And the auction video had to show up right after the funeral…

He should turn this plane around and head right back to Minnesota, make her understand what she meant to him. But the tour demanded his attention now. It had taken her place in his life, just as Bill had said all those months ago. His heart was still hers but his life—until May—was owned by Bill.

He tightened his arms and closed his eyes. She would get what she wanted—time with Mr. Glitz. And he would be left on the sidelines.

He was such an idiot.

– 37 –

Leaning back in the dining room chair, Kiera stretched her arms overhead, wiggling the cramp out of her right hand. The thank you notes provided an opportunity to linger over memories and be thankful for the wonderful people they'd known.

Terese emerged from the kitchen with two steaming mugs. "Here's a fresh cup."

Kiera's heart skipped as she accepted her father's "favorite mug"—a first grade art project. "Thanks. We're getting a lot done, don't you think?"

"I'd say we're about halfway through. And we're still able to move our fingers, so that's good." Terese had moved in with her for the week, making sure she ate and slept, helping her write thank you notes and make a list of what needed to get done.

Kiera glanced at her friend with a silent prayer of thanks. She couldn't have handled the silence alone. Would she ever be able to?

"So what do you hear from Peter?"

The innocent question pushed the air from Kiera's lungs. It had been a week since the funeral. Seven days and nights of deafening silence since she'd lost both of the men she loved. The silent phone screamed at her the loudest. He hadn't called even once. "Not much."

"This tour is keeping him busy."

"Mm-hmm."

They worked in silence another moment before Terese folded her hands on the table and looked at her. "Want to tell me what's going on or do I have to drag it out of you? Again."

Kiera lifted her gaze, ready to play dumb, but tears rushed into her eyes. It took several tries before the words came out. "We broke up."

Terese stared at her. "What? When?"

"The night after the funeral."

"I don't understand. You're crazy about each other."

Kiera looked down at her hands clenched in her lap. A tear splashed onto her fingers, followed by another. "It had been coming for a while, Tess."

She snorted. "I don't believe that. What happened?"

A vision of the blonde girl wrapped around an unresisting Peter flashed through her mind. Her brain seemed stuck on that image. "He auctioned himself off on a date. Part of it was…" Grief had a stranglehold on her throat. "It would end with a romantic breakfast together."

"No way." Terese shook her head. "Peter wouldn't do that."

"I saw him on TV describing the date. And the girl that won—let's just say she was ready to start the date right then." She swiped at the tears on her face and leveled her gaze on her friend. "I've had enough. I can't do it anymore."

"Oh, hon." Terese reached across the table to grasp her hands. "I'm so sorry. I know how much he loves you. I hope this tour is worth what he's given up."

"He's so focused on being a celebrity, nothing else matters."

"He's going to wake up one of these days and realize it's all gone."

"Maybe." She already had.

"What is wrong with you, Theisen?"

Peter blinked at Bill's irritated voice. "What?"

"I asked what's wrong with you. You haven't been the same since you came back from Minnesota."

"Oh."

"Did you have a fight with Kiera?"

He shrugged and went back to the mindless card game. "You could say that."

Bill pulled a chair out from the table and dropped into it. "I'm guessing you broke up."

He shrugged again, his jaw settling into its familiar clench. "You guess right. So now you can be happy that nothing will interfere with my rise to superstardom."

Sarcasm resonated in the silence.

"I don't have anything against Kiera, but as long as you were focused on her, you weren't putting one hundred percent into your career."

"Well, there's nothing to distract me anymore." Except that he thought about her every minute, dreamed about her, ached to hear her voice. He'd dialed her number a hundred times in the last week, only to hang up before it rang.

Bill stood and patted Peter's shoulder as he headed toward the door. "It'll get easier with time. And there's plenty coming at you in the next few weeks. That will help."

He stopped, holding the door open. "By the way, I asked the front desk to give Madelyn a key to your room so she can get in here if we need something for a show or a meeting. You okay with that?"

Did it matter? He shrugged and went back to the cards. "Whatever you think is best. You're the boss." *I'm just the singing piece of meat you hung out to dry.*

After a long pause, the door closed. Peter dropped back against the chair and released a short breath. "That's just great. Now Kiera will think I'm sleeping with Maddie too."

An hour later there was a light rap at the door and Maddie let herself in. "Peter?"

"Yeah." He didn't look up until she had taken Bill's place at the table.

"How you doing?"

"Fine."

She studied him for a moment then pulled an envelope out of her purse.

"Here."

He made no move to reach for it. "What is it?"

"You'll like it, I promise."

He took the envelope and pulled out two tickets. Turning them right side up, his eyes went wide. He lifted his gaze to hers, his mouth open. "Seriously?"

She smiled.

"Wow. Front row seats to NightVision. How'd you pull this off?"

"I called in a favor." She lifted a shoulder. "I've been working in publicity for a long time. I've got lots of connections."

He chuckled. "A long time, hmm? Started when you were twelve?"

"I'll have you know I'm going to be thirty next month."

"You are not." She barely looked twenty.

"I know. I look like a teenager." She giggled. "That comes in handy sometimes. But I'm happy to show you my driver's license, if you want."

"I believe you." His eyes narrowed. She was pretty. Not Kiera-pretty, but pretty in her own way. "So, do you like NightVision?"

"Who doesn't?"

"Want to go with me?"

"Peter, I didn't get you the tickets so you'd take me. You can take anyone you want."

No, he couldn't. "I want to take you."

Pink filled her cheeks, a hint of shyness in her smile. "Well then, yes. I'd love to go."

"Okay. Next Saturday. NightVision. Front row." He fingered the tickets, touched by her action. "Thanks, Maddie."

"You're welcome." She sat back in the chair, her smile deepening.

He pushed the guilt away. He was a free man now. He could hang out with anyone he wanted.

– 38 –

"You're the biggest hypocrite I've ever seen."

Kiera stared at the ugly words on her computer screen, tears blurring the text. The new print ad campaign had started Monday, and this was the fifth email she'd received from different people, all with the same message: she was a fraud—a phony who misled kids and lived the shallow lifestyle she preached against.

Peter had accused her of this same thing and she'd reacted angrily. The truth hurt. While he'd been open about his desire to pursue a celebrity life, she preached against it but then went back to living it. Just to pay the medical bills, she'd said. They'd been paid in full weeks ago.

"I have no right," she whispered. Reality felt like a kick in the teeth. While she believed wholeheartedly in the message of *One of Me*, her double life had come to light. She wasn't surprised. Some part of her had been expecting a backlash. If she continued modeling, she'd have to stop presenting *One of Me*. If she chose to hold on to the curriculum, she'd have to tell Kyle she was through with the jobs.

She wandered through the empty old house that creaked in the howling wind. Icy air snuck in through the windows and around doors that needed new weather stripping. Standing in the kitchen dimly lit by the outdated light fixture, she leaned back against the counter.

Her gaze roamed the familiar room where she and Buck had enjoyed countless meals, decorated cookies, carved pumpkins, and played cribbage with Peter. It was a wonderful old house in desperate need of updating. If she gave up the modeling, there'd be no money left for repairs. Perhaps she should sell it—

"No!" She pushed away from the counter. It was hard enough navigating each day without her father. Letting go of this house would be letting go of him permanently.

She went back to the computer and reread the email. They were right. Until she lived a life that exemplified what she taught, she couldn't stand before them and tell them how to live. She lifted her gaze to the *One of Me* binder on the top shelf, then stood and took it down.

Flipping through the material, she smiled. She'd had such great conversations with so many kids. Seeing their faces light up, hearing them talk about their desire to follow God and make positive changes that would affect their future—countless memories that would stay with her forever.

She blinked hard against the tears. There would be more moments like that someday, more opportunities to make a difference in kids' lives again. But right now she needed to fix up her childhood home. She would focus on that and someday, when the house was the way she thought her father would have wanted it, she'd resume those meaningful conversations.

Pulling open the bottom drawer, she set the binder inside with trembling fingers. She'd send out emails in the morning to cancel upcoming presentations.

It was one more in a growing line of endings in her life. She couldn't take any more.

"Kiera, I'm worried about you," Kyle said, leaning against the door frame.

She looked up from tossing the salad for her unexpected guest and frowned. "Why? Did someone have an issue with the last shoot?"

He chuckled. "No one has ever had an 'issue' with any of your work. As usual, you knocked their socks off. They can't wait to release it. No, it's not about work. It's about you."

"Uh-oh." A crooked smile touched her mouth. "I'm in trouble with the boss."

"I'm not your boss and you're not in trouble. I'm a friend who's concerned."

"Thank you. Now take a seat. This is almost ready." She heaped salad on two plates, added diced chicken, green grapes and cashews, and set one in front of him. Settling into the opposite chair, she put her napkin in her lap and gave him her full attention. "Okay, my friend. Lay it on me."

His mouth twitched. "Are you going to listen or are you just humoring me?"

"Both."

He leaned his forearms on the table, the smile disappearing from his blue eyes. "It's only been three weeks since your dad passed, but somehow you've managed to continue your presentations and model full time. You're the most professional, focused person I've ever worked with."

Not quite. "Thank you."

"And it's going to kill you."

"Modeling or dealing with kids?"

He chuckled and took a bite of salad, shaking his head.

"I hope I'm getting a raise. I sound amazing."

"You *are* amazing."

She squirmed under the intensity of his gaze.

He set his fork down. "You're the most incredible woman I've ever known. And I think you know I'm having a hard time keeping this relationship strictly business. But that's for another conversation."

She pushed the spinach around on her plate, waiting for the heat in her cheeks to fade.

"What I'm concerned about is how you're coping with your grief. You're so thin and when you're not working, you're so sad. I want to know how I can help."

Tears sprang to her eyes. *Bring my father back and I'll be fine. And while you're at it, could you find Peter for me too?*

"I'm okay, Kyle. There's no way to hurry this process along. I just get up each day and put one foot in front of the other." She forced a smile. "I appreciate your support. And I promise I'll eat less salad and more ice cream, okay?"

He studied her silently, a light in his eyes that made her think he was going to come around the table and—

"Fine." He turned his attention to his meal. "I just want you to know I'm watching. If I think it's getting to be too much, I'm going to pull the plug and force you to rest."

"Yes, sir." After another bite she said, "Anyway, you'll be glad to know I've cancelled my *One of Me* presentations for the time being."

His head came up. "Why?"

She shrugged. "Modeling doesn't mesh well with the message. When I finish updating the house, I'll quit modeling and focus on the presentations." She picked through her salad, feeling his eyes on her.

"It's good to know you won't be pushing yourself so hard."

Peter wouldn't have let her quit. Their relationship, yes. *One of Me*, no. She straightened and kept her tone light. "So you see? I'm taking perfectly good care of myself."

He gave a snort and shook his head. "You are irritatingly independent, you know that?"

"It's how I've survived this long."

"But you're missing some great opportunities to connect with the people who love you by not letting them closer than arm's reach."

Peter's face jumped to mind and she blinked. She'd pushed him away when she needed him most, and he'd left with barely an argument. "Some of those very people have let me down harder than if I'd never let them close in the first place."

His eyes narrowed. "Not all men are like Thomas or Peter."

She sat silent. *He knows?*

"I heard about the breakup on the news."

"Well, maybe all men aren't like them, but right now it's easier depending on myself." She took a long drink of water.

He stabbed at his lettuce and chewed with gusto. Kiera winced at his frown. He'd become such a good friend, but she just didn't have it in her to let it go beyond that.

"Okay, it's time we have some fun." His fork clattered to the plate and he turned to rummage through his suit coat hanging on the back of the chair. He slid a white business envelope across the table toward her.

"What's this?"

"An invitation to a night on the town. In Los Angeles."

She pulled out two tickets and read them aloud. "'The Twentieth Annual Belle of the Ball Extravaganza. An evening of entertainment, world-class cuisine and silent auction. Presented by the California Heart Health Institute.' Oh, look at the entertainment! Raina is one of my favorite singers. And Charlie is fabulous too."

"It's *the* event of the season. Black tie, ball gowns, the whole nine yards."

Her heart picked up speed and she smiled. "I've heard of this but never been to it."

"Now's your chance. It's in two weeks. I'm thinking we can fly in that morning and home Sunday afternoon. I can get two hotel rooms booked."

Her smile widened. "This sounds wonderful. But are you sure you want to take *me*?"

A smile lifted his lips. "There's no one else I'd even consider taking. You'll love it. So is that a yes?"

She nodded. "Yes. A definite yes."

The knock at the hotel room door made Kiera's heart jump. She smoothed her hair and opened the door. Kyle stood holding a single red rose, a glittery ribbon dangling from the stem. His mouth fell open and he breathed a single word as he stared at her. "Wow."

Heat filled her face and she managed a smile. "Hi. Come in."

He stepped into the room, still staring, his dimples deepening. His white shirt gleamed beneath the black tuxedo. The cerulean blue handkerchief poking up from his pocket matched his eyes.

"Kiera, you're gorgeous. That's an incredible dress."

"Thank you." She clasped her hands in front, breathless beneath his frank admiration. Unwilling to wear the green dress Peter loved, she'd worn something completely different—a black halter gown. Its tiny lines of silver thread and long slit on the left created a simple yet more sophisticated look, more…Kyle than the green one.

"I haven't been to an event like this for a long time. I hope I'll fit in."

"Fit in?" He moved closer and lifted her chin to smile down at her. His height made her feel petite. She looked into eyes that sparkled with laughter. "I've been to plenty of these, so trust me when I say you will definitely be the belle of the ball. You're setting the bar out of reach in that dress."

"Thank you." She looked away, jittery with anticipation and an unexpected sadness.

He stepped back and handed her the rose. "I'm afraid this looks paltry next to you."

"It's beautiful. Let me put it in water." When she returned, a black cashmere wrap in hand, he was still smiling. "Stop it," she scolded. "You're making me self-conscious."

"Get used to it." He settled the wrap over her shoulders, his voice at her ear. "Just remember who your date is when all the men try to steal you away."

She forced a laugh that sounded breathy and silly. "You'll be stuck dragging me home at the stroke of midnight, when I'll turn back into plain ol' me."

He offered his arm. "The party awaits, Cinderella."

Outside the hotel, a black limousine gleamed under the street lamps. Kiera glanced at him with a laugh. "You thought of everything."

"I want this to be an evening you'll never forget."

The ride to the event passed quickly as he shared stories of previous galas. She let her hand rest in his as the car glided through the busy city. Stepping out of the limousine, she was blinded by the flashes that went off. She'd forgotten the energy that accompanied events like this. Kyle tucked her hand in the crook of his arm and they smiled their way into the building.

In the lobby, her name was called from the crowd. "Kiera!"

Christine hurried over and pulled her into a hug. “It’s so good to see you, darling girl. You look gorgeous.”

“So do you. How are you? How’s married life?”

Christine waved a perfectly manicured hand, her numerous bracelets sparkling under the lights. “Everything is simply wonderful. I’m thrilled you came back to the business. The world missed your amazing presence.”

“I doubt anyone knew I was gone. I’ve enjoyed being back.” Now she could add liar to her growing list of unappealing attributes. When had she bought back in so completely? Perhaps she’d never really let it go.

Kyle put his hand to Kiera’s back. “We should head in to find our seats. Christine, we’ll see you inside.”

“You kids have fun.”

The ballroom was aglow with the sparkle of massive chandeliers and warm with the aroma of hors d’oeuvres. The music of a string quartet floated over the hum of hundreds of voices.

For as many events as she’d attended as a spokesmodel, and those she’d attended with Thomas, this one reached a new level of elegance and star-studded attendance. A movie star couple glided past, even more beautiful in person than on the big screen. When the man’s gaze met hers, she blushed under his wink.

Kyle took her elbow as he whispered, “I don’t care if he’s the President of the United States, he’s not getting near you tonight.”

“Don’t be silly. With that gorgeous woman on his arm, I can’t imagine he’d look anywhere else.”

“People do unexpected things with a drink or two in them.”

As he led her into the mass of people, she kept a smile plastered to her face. It took only a few moments for her to lose track of names as he introduced her to this distinguished man, that lovely older woman glittering in diamonds, numerous couples.

“Do you know everyone here?” she asked as they moved toward their table.

“It’s all about connections, Kiera.”

People continued to greet him, turning interested expressions toward her.

Some handshakes were hearty and welcoming, others limp enough to make her want to shake life back into her fingers. She sipped her glass of sparkling water and watched as Kyle laughed with a couple he had introduced as old friends.

He wore his blond handsomeness easily, relaxed under the attention, looking interested in each person he spoke with. He was bright, funny, and charming. His Christian faith was strong, his values set, his warmth almost enough to heal her wounded heart. Almost. Maybe someday she could care for him as more than a friend.

He leaned close. "Looks like we'd better get to our table or we'll miss the first course. Having fun?"

"I am," she said, surprised. "This is a fascinating event."

There were three other couples at their table next to the stage. Conversation was spirited and filled with laughter as they enjoyed bowls of lobster bisque. Kyle doted on her, made her laugh, and admired her with a glow in his eyes that rattled her composure.

The emcee was a well-known comedian who kept his act clean. He poked fun at the attendees, politicians, and his wife, then introduced Raina, a country singer Kiera had long admired. To be this close was a dream come true. She applauded heartily when the woman finished, then shared an excited smile with Kyle.

When the emcee returned to the mic, he announced a change in the lineup that left Kiera unable to breathe. The ballroom went dark, then the spotlight illuminated Peter's long, lean frame, microphone in hand, smiling as applause thundered.

The musicians started a melody that sent memories washing over her. His adorable excitement at hearing this—his very first song—on the radio. He'd called from Detroit early in the tour, awed laughter in his voice; they'd talked for nearly two hours. Talking had been easy then. *Life* had been easy.

She closed her eyes. The song was as familiar as breathing. She wanted to memorize his voice, the sensations that bubbled up from their hiding place deep within.

Applause broke the spell and she opened her eyes to find him staring down at her. Then he blinked and looked away, thanking the audience for their kindness in letting him fill in for his friend Charlie.

He sang two more songs off the album. She was unable to look away, afraid if she blinked he'd disappear. With the opening notes of the last song, her heart flew into an erratic rhythm, tears knotting her throat. It was her song. Their song.

Peter strolled down the stairs to wander among the tables. He sang with a new depth and maturity in his voice, smiling as he shook hands, never missing a beat. As the song headed toward its climax, he stopped beside her and reached out a hand.

She let him draw her to her feet. The grasp of his fingers was achingly familiar, sending the thrill of their old connection through her like a burst of sunshine. The spotlight narrowed to focus on them. There was nothing outside the shaft of light, nothing beyond his handsome face, his dark eyes smiling at her, the warmth of his touch.

The song drew to a close and he reached up to wipe a tear from her cheek as the audience roared its approval. Pulling her into a hug, he whispered, "I miss you, Kiki." Then he was gone, moving back to the stage where he shared a laugh with the emcee. He waved and bowed in acknowledgment of the crowd's extended applause, then dipped his head to Kiera before disappearing behind the curtain.

As the salad course was served, the women at the table giggled through comments about her being singled out by "that gorgeous man." She had no breath to respond. Kyle sat stiff and silent beside her.

The program continued and she clapped at what she hoped were appropriate times, trying desperately to process the emotions coursing through her. How could her heart respond so quickly, so traitorously, to his voice and touch? Where had the anger gone? What had she been so angry about?

A wild mosaic of memories marched through her mind. Their first meeting, laughing together, sharing long walks and iced tea. She clenched her hands, trying to capture the warmth of his fingers, the electricity that still raced up her arms.

For a frantic moment she couldn't breathe and she closed her eyes. *You're fine. Deep breath in, slow breath out. It's okay. He's gone.* Tears burned her eyelids. The thought echoed in the silence of her heart. It had been a moment of magic, a chance to remember something beautiful. Now she was here, in a different life. With a different man.

Opening her eyes to focus on her date, she was surprised to see him frowning at her. No, past her. A familiar tingle swept through her and she turned her head slowly. Peter's dark eyes met hers from where he sat at the next table. And she'd thought she couldn't breathe before.

– 39 –

Peter watched Kiera turn toward him, waiting for their eyes to meet, praying she wouldn't leap to her feet and run away. He hadn't taken a full breath since seeing her beautiful face from onstage. Now those green eyes connected with his, blinking then narrowing as they stared at each other in the darkened room.

Applause shattered the moment and she turned back to the stage. Her profile revealed a clench to her jaw, a hard swallow, a sparkle in her eyes that looked like tears. He wasn't sure if he should laugh or cry. Probably both. He'd almost run out the door with her at the end of her song—to some place far from the stages where they spent their time, from the cameras that tracked them, from the people who demanded too much.

"Peter?"

He met Maddie's questioning gaze. "Hmm?"

She cocked her head. "You okay?"

"Yeah." He nodded. "Just starving." *For Kiera.*

She smiled and glanced at her watch. "Main course should be coming up in three minutes."

"You know what time we're eating?" Of course she did.

Dimples appeared. "We have a plane to catch. I'm just trying to stay on schedule."

The house lights came up and conversation sprang to life around the room. Waiters in crisp white tops and creased black pants filed in balancing round trays. Peter dug into his meal. He wasn't hungry but he'd do anything to keep from staring at the beautiful redhead.

The couple on Maddie's right introduced themselves and conversation turned to Peter's concert tour. He didn't want to talk about the tour. He wanted to talk to Kiera. Alone. Right now.

Maddie dove in with exaggerated details about life on the road, and he stayed busy downplaying her stories. Her hand on his arm was like a branding iron and he shifted enough to pull away without being obvious.

He could barely swallow the prime rib, didn't taste the potatoes Maddie raved about, and shook his head when the dessert tray came out. She asked again if he was okay. His curt dismissal cast a shadow across her face and he winced.

Moments after the orchestra started the first song, Kiera and Mr. Glitz headed for the dance floor. Peter watched them go, the lump in his throat cutting off his air. She should be dancing with him.

"Let's dance!" Maddie's enthusiastic suggestion yanked his attention back to the table like a dog on a leash. He started to protest, but the pleading light in her eyes stopped the words, and he let her tug him from his chair. Midway through the second song, they paused for the photographer, then Maddie continued chattering as they moved around the dance floor.

Her monologue allowed him to wander back to dancing with Kiera at Christmastime. The evening had been magical. She'd looked gorgeous, he'd cleaned up pretty well, and they'd been ecstatic to have that time alone. Nothing had existed outside the two of them.

"What's so funny?"

He looked at Maddie. "What?"

"You're smiling. I thought you'd be hollering about too many things on your plate."

"Oh. No." Memories of Kiera always made him smile. Unless they made him cry. "I just appreciate how you keep so many plates spinning at the same time." Man, he was good at lying. When had that happened?

Her eyes twinkled. "It's my job. Oops, there's my phone." She pulled it from her shiny black purse. "It's the call I've been waiting for about next week's radio interview. I'll be back to finish our dance, okay?"

Peter watched her hurry away then went in search of the bar. Too bad he didn't drink. He could use a shot of something strong right now. He ordered a Coke on the rocks. Nothing like drinking alone, especially when the woman who haunted his dreams was somewhere in this very room with another guy.

Drink in hand, he headed back toward the table. His heart did a backflip when he saw Kiera sitting alone, watching the couples on the dance floor. He slid into the chair beside her and waited for her to turn.

Surprise lit her face. "Peter!"

"Sorry. Didn't mean to startle you."

"I didn't expect…I thought you left." She smiled shyly. "Your songs were beautiful."

"Thanks. I'm glad you were here. Especially for the last one." The urge to touch her made his fingers twitch.

In the awkward silence that followed, he watched the couples gliding by. "Do you…would you dance with me?"

She turned wide eyes toward him, eyebrows pinched upward. She looked like he'd asked her to run away with him. Maybe he had. "Kiera?"

"Shouldn't you be dancing with your date?"

Her words threw cold water in his face. "She's not my date, and she had to take a call. What happened to *your* date?"

"I think he's on the same call." She glanced around. "I'm assuming Bill's here tonight?"

"He stayed in the hotel. He hasn't been feeling good lately."

They looked at each other a moment longer. Heart pounding, Peter put out his hand. After a second's hesitation, she put hers in it. He tightened his grasp around the familiar fingers.

On the gleaming dance floor, he wrapped her in his arms and they melted into the crowd. Neither of them spoke, they simply smiled at each other. A happiness he hadn't felt in months swelled in his chest. She was his, at least for the moment. Why had he ever let her go?

The song ended and the dancers applauded the band. Kiera remained close beside him, leaning lightly against his arm. A slower song started, and he raised an eyebrow and held out his arms. She came into them willingly. Hypnotized by the gentle music and the possessiveness that swept over him, he tightened his arms and she nestled against him. He was sure now it was a dream, but that was okay. It was the best dream he'd had in months.

"Hey." He needed to see her face, look into those eyes that made his insides go crazy.

She lifted her head, her expression peaceful. "Hmm?"

His heart pounded in time to the music. "You are still the most amazing woman in the world to me."

Longing filled her face and a smile softened her mouth.

"I meant what I said before. I've missed you." At some point they'd stopped dancing. He drew a finger along her jaw, summoning all his strength to keep from kissing her. Their eyes met. "Every. Single. Day."

"Ohhh." Her sigh wrapped around his heart.

Tears sparkling, her chin quivered. "I…know. Peter, I was so—"

"Here you are." Maddie's voice cut between them as sharply as if she'd physically shoved them apart.

Peter was slow to pull his eyes from Kiera's. "Oh, hey, Maddie. Did you get things taken care of?"

"I did." She looked at Kiera with a steely expression he'd never seen before. Then it was replaced by a bright smile, her professional, take-charge face. "I'm back to finish our dance."

Over her shoulder, he saw Whatshisname weaving through the tables toward them. Kiera's fingers tightened around his, pulling his attention back to her. Her wide eyes pleaded for something.

Talk to her.

And say what? I have to dance with Maddie even though I'd rather run out the door with you? She pushed me out of her life, remember? She chose him.

She would hate a scene standing in the middle of the dance floor. She'd never forgive him for making a spectacle of her the way Thomas had. He released her fingers one at a time.

"Here's my gorgeous date." Kyle's voice joined the clamor in Peter's head.

His gaze moved from Maddie's frown to the challenge on Kyle's face to the sadness on Kiera's. She wasn't his anymore. No matter how much he wanted it to be different.

"Here she is." The words choked him and he swallowed against the burning grief that rose as he let her go. *My beautiful lady...*

She turned her face away, put her hand in Kyle's and walked out of his life again.

It was a struggle to stay upright as Kyle led her back to their table. She tried to chat normally with the other couples, forcing words from a throat tightened with tears. Her mouth ached from keeping a smile in place. She wanted to go home. Back to that time when it was just her and Buck, and Peter who had completed their family.

But Peter didn't want her. He wanted the dark-haired girl. He'd handed her back to Kyle fast enough once that girl showed up. He'd said he missed her but now she realized it was just something he said to all the women. Except the little assistant that he spent his days with. Maybe even his nights.

"Ready to call it a night?" Kyle's breath was warm against her ear.

She nodded. "All this excitement has given me a headache. Are you sure you're ready to go?"

"This is longer than I usually stay," he assured her.

They said goodbye to the couples at their table before Kyle took her hand and led her through the crowded room. Minutes later they were gliding back to the hotel in their limo. She rested her head against his shoulder, glad he remained silent.

In the hotel, he stopped in front of her room and held out his hand. She handed him her key card, surprised when he went into the room ahead of her. Stopping beside the mahogany armoire, she slipped out of her shoes with a tired sigh. "That was a wonderful evening, Kyle. Thank you for taking me."

When she turned around, he was standing close behind her. Her breath caught at the intensity on his face. He pulled her into his arms. "You were the most beautiful woman there, just as I predicted. You make it impossible for me to breathe."

Before she could respond, he leaned down and kissed her.

She stood unmoving. His kiss was gentle at first, then searching, demanding a response. She waited for thunder and lightning. None came.

He drew back and held her gaze as if looking for an answer to an unspoken question. Then he released her and turned away, running his hands through his hair. He looked sideways at her. "It's no use, is it?"

She frowned, unable to form a coherent thought.

He faced her and folded his arms. "You're not over him."

Warmth blazed through her and she looked away. How could she answer that? After tonight, she knew she would never be "over" him. But she was trying to move on. "I'm not over the hurt, if that's what you mean."

"Would you get back together with him if he asked?"

She bit her lip. Would she? Based on the feelings that had swept through her as they danced, the answer would be a resounding "yes!"

"No." She'd want to, but she wouldn't. Twice bitten, she was done with serious relationships for a while, perhaps forever. And never again with someone living in, or even near, the spotlight. "Maybe if I explain what's happened in my past, it would help."

"I'd appreciate that."

She settled on the edge of the sofa and smoothed the silky fabric of her dress over her knees. He sat beside her and stretched an arm along the back of the couch. Retelling her experience with Thomas wasn't nearly as painful as it had been when she told Peter, because the second half of her story was now more difficult to tell.

Kyle sat quietly as she talked, the crease between his eyebrows the only hint of his emotions. As she reached the breakup part of her story with Peter, she kept her tone matter-of-fact to hold the tears back. "The relationship was dying a slow death until we made some decisions that were not the best. For either of us."

She was quiet for a moment. "What I've learned is that I don't pick the right men. So I'm just not willing to put myself out there again. At least, not anytime soon."

Kyle shifted on the couch to face her. His deep frown surprised her. "You see these relationship issues as your fault?"

She shrugged. "I don't pick the right guys."

He released an irritated snort. "Kiera, it's not about you picking the right guys. It's about them *being* the right guys. We all have a choice in how we treat people, how we behave. It's not someone else's fault when I do something stupid. It's mine.

"Honey, look at me." He waited until she did. "You are God's masterpiece. And in that dress you are an exceptionally gorgeous masterpiece. But even dressed in rags, you would still be more valuable than gold, more beautiful than diamonds."

The familiar words from Scripture that she'd quoted in her presentations both stung and soothed.

He leaned forward. "I want you to hear me on this. Your worth is not tied up in Thomas or in Peter or in me. Your worth is tied to the God of the universe. The only opinion that should ever matter is His. What you told the kids through *One of Me* also applies to you."

She soaked in the passionate words that were a balm to her heart. Her smile was shaky. "Thank you. That's the reminder I need right now."

"I'm happy to remind you whenever you need it. You are an incredible woman who I'm honored to know. And to have fallen for in a big way." When she started to speak, he put a finger to her lips. "I'm not going to push you into anything, Kiera. You've come off a couple of lousy breakups and you need to take it slow. I can do that.

"As long as you don't kick me out of your life, I'm happy to be your friend. For now anyway." His crooked smile was sweet. At least he wasn't demanding more than she had to give. "We don't know what the future holds, but I can hope, right?"

She nodded, a slow smile lifting her lips, loosening the clench in her jaw. "We can both hope. I have a lot to think and pray about." Praying would be a good idea. She seemed to have forgotten how. "Thank you for a wonderful evening, and for being such a good friend."

"I'm not through caring about you, Kiera Simmons, or hoping that you'll realize what a fantastic, amazing guy I am."

The wiggle in his eyebrows made her laugh. "I already know that, Mr. Matthews."

His expression sobered and he put a finger under her chin. "Then hopefully God will use that to make you fall for me like I have for you."

How she would love for that to happen. "Maybe He will."

He stood and pulled her to her feet and into his arms, pressing a gentle kiss to her forehead. "Goodnight, Cinderella. You were the belle of the ball."

He was such a nice man. Why couldn't she have fallen for him instead? She forced a smile. "That's because I went with a prince."

– 40 –

Settled at the kitchen table, Kiera stared at the Monday evening news program, her fork halfway to her mouth.

"Music industry giant William Djerf, III was found dead in his New Orleans hotel room this morning. The fifty-year-old agent and publicist was known to be a shrewd businessman with numerous A-list clients, including new singing sensation Peter Theisen."

A photograph of Peter, Bill, and the dark-haired assistant appeared on the screen. "Djerf and Theisen, shown at a recent charity event in Atlanta, had returned to New Orleans from Los Angeles to prepare for Theisen's upcoming concerts in that city. Those concerts have been cancelled. No word on if or when they will be rescheduled. An investigation is underway as to the cause of death."

Kiera stared at the TV a moment longer then reached for her phone. Voice mail. "Peter, it's Kiera. I just heard about Bill and I'm stunned. How are you holding up?" She closed her eyes, aching to be there with him. "I'm sure you're devastated."

After a few more bumbling words, she hung up and sat staring out the kitchen window. Yet another reminder of how quickly life could change. *Lord, wrap your arms around him.*

She moved mechanically through the evening washing dishes, dusting, doing a load of laundry. Hoping the phone would ring. When she came up from a quick trip to the basement, a tone from her cell phone signaled a message. Disappointment shot through her. In those few moments, he'd called.

"Hey, Kiera. Thanks for your message." His familiar voice was quiet and strained. "I'm in shock like you. We got back to the hotel about 3 a.m. Sunday and went right to our rooms to crash. Everything seemed okay yesterday during rehearsal. He's been pretty stressed lately but that's nothing new, although he'd been complaining about not feeling good. After dinner last night, I just went to my room. I didn't know anything had happened until the police showed up at my door this morning."

He released a long breath. She could picture him running a hand through his curls, dark eyes filled with tears. The way he'd looked the night he'd left her.

"I've been identified as a person of interest." He gave a snort. "Like I'd kill off my own manager. I guess they have to question everyone but I seem to be number one on the list since I've spent the most time with him lately. And I guess I was the last to see him alive."

There was a new hoarseness in his voice; he sounded exhausted and angry. She clutched the phone to her ear to bring him closer.

"So anyway, they'll be watching me. Do what, I'm not sure, but they told me I need to report my whereabouts all the time. Not hard to do. Just look for me on a stage somewhere. Finding the stage is the biggest problem. I'm in New Orleans at the moment, but I have no clue where I'll be next week. We cancelled this week's shows but there might be something on Saturday."

There was a heavy silence. "I'm tired, Kiera. Just…tired. The shows are harder, trying to keep my energy up all the time. Bill said he had a few things in the cooker for this summer that wouldn't be as grueling as running around the country like this. It always sounded like such a cool life, but now that I'm living it, I'm not impressed. It's not what it looks like, but I guess you already knew that."

Her heart ached at the regret in his words.

"I almost fell off the stage when I saw you in L.A. You looked…amazing. As always. I hope things are going well for you." He gave a sharp laugh. "Well, I don't hope things are going well with Whatshisname, but I hope everything else is going well. I've seen your picture in a couple new ads so it looks like you're keeping busy.

"How are Terese and Jason? Hey, the wedding's coming up pretty soon, isn't it? Man, I wish I could be there. What?" She heard a muffled female voice in the background. Peter sighed. "Yeah, okay. Kiera? I have to go. Sounds like they have more questions about Bill. Thanks for your call, Kiki. It was really great hearing your voice."

The message ended and she sat still, holding the phone to her ear. She could see him sitting in a hotel room somewhere answering questions from investigators with serious faces and monotone voices. She wanted to run all the way to New Orleans and tell them he had nothing to do with Bill's death. But he had the pretty assistant to do that now.

She saved his message then dialed his number. When it went yet again to voice mail, she hung up, turned off the kitchen light and dragged herself up the stairs for bed.

The weeks following Bill's death were filled with interviews and endless questioning by the New Orleans police. Maddie kept Peter on schedule and in place. She was Bill in a dress but with an adoring smile his manager had never worn. She was his constant companion, quick with a compliment or word of encouragement.

Now in the final weeks of the tour, the concerts were more draining than energizing. Bill's dogged determination to help him—*make* him—reach his dream of stardom just might kill him before the tour ended.

There was a persistent rasp in his voice now that added a sexy element to some songs but was annoying in others. Maddie made an appointment with an ear, nose, and throat specialist when they arrived in San Francisco.

"Peter Theisen?" A woman in flowered scrubs held a manila folder in one hand.

Maddie stood with him and he frowned. "Maddie, I can handle a doctor's appointment on my own."

"But I can take notes—"

"No!" She flinched and he glanced around the waiting room, softening his tone. "I'll tell you exactly what he says, don't worry."

Her mouth drooping, she sank back into her chair. He turned away, kicking himself for overreacting. She was just trying to be helpful, especially in Bill's absence.

The doctor was pleasant and thorough. He took his time looking in Peter's throat with several different instruments while Peter concentrated on not gagging. He pulled Kiera's face to mind and focused on the photo shoot. He could smell the lake water, hear the seagulls, taste the kiss.

"Well, Mr. Theisen. I have some good news."

He crashed back to the present, relieved to close his mouth. He wiggled his jaw back and forth. "That's what I want to hear."

The man leaned back in his chair and crossed his legs. "I see no reason to suspect cancer."

Peter's eyebrows shot up. That hadn't even been a consideration.

"You've developed vocal nodules. Apparently you're a singer?"

He nodded, wondering why he'd assumed this man had heard of him. *Get over yourself, Theisen.*

"Vocal nodules and polyps are a result of several things. The first thing we look for is carcinoma, which is obviously the most serious issue. I don't see anything that would lead me in that direction. What I do see are nodules on your vocal cords.

"Vocal cords are folds of mucous membrane in the larynx." He held up two fingers parallel to each other and wiggled them. "They're long, thin bands that vibrate to make sounds so we can be heard when we speak, sing, scream, and so on. One end of these bands is attached to the front wall of the larynx. The other end is connected to tiny cartilage near the back wall.

"Nodules are growths that develop when we strain or overuse our voices. You don't look like a rock star kind of singer, who develops what we sometimes call 'screamer's nodules.' I'm thinking yours have developed from overuse followed by little time for rest."

"I've been on the road since September without much of a break."

"That would explain it. For professional singers, teachers, people who do extended presentations, rest is needed between performances to allow the vocal cords to recover. You have nodules on both cords, what we call the false and true vocal cords. That tells me that what you need is rest and lots of it."

Rest? There was no time, although it sounded pretty good right now. "What happens if I don't?"

"Eventually you might need surgical intervention. If you continue the strain, it could end your career."

"Would it help if I whisper?"

"No. Whispering strains the vocal cords just like screaming. When you talk, use a normal tone, like you are now. Singing should be off-limits for a minimum of three weeks, followed by a checkup to see if the nodules are decreasing."

"Any other options?"

The doctor chuckled. "I see that *not* singing is going to be an issue for you, Mr. Theisen."

"I have a tour to finish. I'll have lots of time for rest after May first."

"Hmm." He glanced at the calendar on the wall behind him. "That's about a month from now. Hopefully by then the nodules won't have increased enough to totally prevent you from singing. Any chance you can cut down on the schedule between now and then?"

Peter shook his head. "Not without making a whole lot of people unhappy. But then, they'll be unhappy if I can't sing, either."

The doctor scribbled something on a pad and handed it to Peter. "I'll have Cindy bring in a few sheets with some basic throat and neck exercises that might help reduce stress and tension. I'd be happy to see you again in May for a recheck. Good luck with the tour."

In the waiting room, Peter handed Maddie the information sheets. "See? Even better than notes."

She scanned them, frowning. "You're not supposed to sing?"

"Or talk, for that matter. I told him I had concerts until the first of May and then I can rest my vocal cords."

"And until then?"

He looked down at the prescription paper in his hand. "Talk as little as possible when I'm not performing. Lots of warm liquids and do the exercises on those sheets. And there's no cancer."

Relief filled her face and she smiled. "Good. That was my first concern. We'll get you all sorts of rest come May. In the meantime, you'll just have to listen to *me* talk. I think I like this prescription."

Peter followed her into the elevator. "I don't know what you'll do if you ever develop nodules."

She giggled and fluttered her hands. "I'll learn sign language and make everyone crazy that way, instead."

The doors shut on their laughter.

– 41 –

"Are you serious?"

Kiera stared at Kyle as they faced each other in her living room.

"Unfortunately, very serious."

"But I thought they liked the photos. The ad turned out great. I heard it's getting a fabulous response." Nausea rose up like a wave.

"The ad *did* turn out great, Honey. They're worried about future ads. And frankly, they're concerned about your health."

She turned away and stood at the window, squinting against the spring sunshine that poured in. They didn't want her back. She'd never been rejected by a client before. By Thomas and Paisley and Peter, but not by a client.

Kyle turned her to face him and took her hands. "It's not forever, Kiera. Just until you put some weight back on."

"I would if I could."

"Have you been to the doctor?"

"Yes. Full physical, just like you ordered. Everything's normal. I'm not sick, I don't have thyroid issues, and my blood work came back negative for every disease known to humans and small animals."

He grinned. "Good to know we can rule out rabies."

"I'm sorry if this messes things up for you."

"Kiera, this isn't about me. It's about making sure you're healthy." He squeezed her fingers. "I've been worried."

She offered a vague smile and pulled away to perch on the arm of the faded couch. She knew exactly what was wrong and it had nothing to do with blood work or X-rays or any other medical procedure. It was a heart issue.

Kyle squatted before her and set his hand on her knee. "I have an idea that I think you'll like."

She forced a smile at the hopeful excitement lighting his face.

"How about a cruise over Easter? It will be after Terese and Jason's wedding. We can make it a four-day weekend. Warm sun, white sand beaches and tons of good food. You can sleep the whole time if you want, or we can sit on lounge chairs sipping margaritas." He lifted his eyebrows. "We can even play bingo with the seniors. What do you think?"

A cruise sounded lovely. Especially over Easter. Facing this first holiday without her dad, while Terese and Jason were honeymooning, had haunted her dreams. Mark had been adamant that she join the rest of the family, but she didn't think she had the strength.

"It sounds wonderful," she said. "Can I think about it for a few days?"

Disappointment flickered as he nodded and stood. "Sure. I'll check out some choices. Where would you like to go? The Bahamas? Caribbean? Mexico?"

"You decide. I just need some time to think about it. Thank you for watching out for me."

He put a finger under her chin, studying her face for a long minute. "I'll always watch out for you, Kiera. You're in my blood. I'll do whatever it takes to make you happy."

The light in his eyes poured guilt into her heart. If only she could care for him the way he seemed to care for her. He was a dear man, a good friend. Maybe a cruise on blue waters under a warm sun would change that.

The week of the wedding kept Terese and Kiera running with last-minute details. Saturday morning, the sky was a brilliant, cloudless blue. The mid-April air was fresh and warm. Daffodils and tulips stood tall, lifting their brightly colored heads to drink in the sunshine. Even the birds were singing more cheerfully than usual.

Kiera declared it was a day of rejoicing even in heaven and wondered aloud why it wasn't a national holiday. Terese agreed as she sat at the mirror in the church basement, applying her makeup. They giggled and finished the last of their primping amidst happy chatter.

Vanessa and Ashley, Terese's closest friends from the church, were the first two down the aisle. Kiera followed, sharing a smile with Jason before taking her place at the front of the church.

The music changed and the doors opened to reveal Terese beside her father. She was stunning in a strapless ivory wedding gown, tiny pink flowers woven into her black hair. Jason beamed, bouncing on his toes as she floated toward him.

Kiera kept her smile in place. Could her heart burst from bittersweet joy? Her father should be sitting in the second row with Peter beside him. He would be as proud giving her away as Terese's dad looked. She pressed her quivering lips together to keep the flood of emotion at bay.

The ceremony was simple and moving. They'd chosen a special song that spoke of friendship and love, soaring dreams and a bright future. Pastor Kurt sang with smiling energy and infectious joy.

For Kiera, it was a moment of happiness that her lonely, battered heart sorely needed. Before the recessional began, she found Kyle among the crowd and smiled at his wink. The sit-down dinner was delicious, the dance more fun than she'd had in a long time. After Terese and Jason left the reception amidst a burst of rose petals, Kiera sank into a chair and slid her sandals off to rub her feet.

Kyle dropped beside her and loosened his tie. "What a day, hmm?"

She managed a tired smile. "Everything was perfect. Terese looked gorgeous. I've never seen Jason look so handsome. I thought he was going to bust some buttons when she came down the aisle."

He laughed. "He sure looked happy. They both did. And you were the most beautiful maid of honor ever."

"Oh, hardly. But you are very sweet." They shared a smile before she pulled her shoes back on and stood. “Now for the cleanup.”

Kyle stood and reached for her hands, lacing their fingers together. “Are you sure I can’t change your mind about the cruise?”

She’d told him no a few days ago. Now tempted to throw caution to the wind and say yes, a tiny warning niggled at the back of her mind. She’d ignored it too many times and reaped the consequences.

Releasing a deep sigh, she shook her head. “I would like to say yes, but… it’s just not the right time. Can I have a rain check?”

With a crooked smile he pulled her close, hooking his fingers together behind her. “I won’t say I’m not disappointed, but I understand. Of course you can have a rain check.”

She rested against him, eyes closed, trying hard to feel something other than simple contentment. He was offering her the world on a platter. What was wrong with her?

It was the right offer but the wrong man.

Peter’s voice continued to deteriorate. It was probably good Bill wasn’t around to hear it; he’d have demanded Peter stop being dramatic. Only six concerts remained, but it was questionable whether he could do them all. They’d cut out songs that required too much of a stretch to his normal range. The show was now just over ninety minutes, down from two hours, but even then he was exhausted from trying to make enough acceptable sound.

He left the Seattle hotel one morning as sunlight spilled over the quiet city. A dull heaviness lay on his heart. He was tired after almost nine months on the road. Exhausted actually. But he should be dancing down the sidewalk after seeing so many of his dreams come to life. Singing on national television, recording with music icons he’d idolized, performing a great show with adoring crowds at his feet.

He’d learned from one of the best agents in the business and had a pretty assistant keeping him on the same soaring path. So what was his problem? Standing at the corner, he looked across the street at the lighted hand that told him to wait. That's what life felt like now, he was waiting for…something.

As the light turned green, he noticed a large, stately church just beyond it. He was drawn across the street and up the wide expanse of steps that led to ornate wood doors. Sunlight glinted off tall stained glass windows; vines crawled up the weathered stone walls.

An unexpected memory seared his heart, making him hesitate at the doors—standing beside Kiera at Faith, singing, worshipping… He pulled on the wrought iron handle. Inside, the open sanctuary doors beckoned and he crossed the empty foyer and slid into the back pew.

Silence settled over him like a warm hand placed gently on his head. He closed his eyes and let the peacefulness soak into his parched soul. Tears burned up his throat and he raised his eyes to focus on the rough wood of the cross hanging behind the altar.

With so few concerts left, he had an overwhelming urge to walk away from all of it. Music critics had gone from hailing him as the next superstar to wondering if he had the power to carry a full concert. He tried to let the criticism roll off, knowing they were right. He wasn't the powerhouse he'd been in September.

Kiera's words rang through his mind. "At first I was like you," she'd said, "thinking there was something out there in the great big world calling my name. But it was home that was calling. The bright lights and the attention were a smoke screen, keeping me from seeing what I'm really meant to do."

Canoeing on the lake with her that warm summer day, he'd known he was supposed to sing, to perform, to find his way in the world of entertainment. He'd worked hard to make that a reality. His singing, until recently, had continued to improve. He could now put on a decent show. He loved performing and he was good at it. But he wasn't happy.

He leaned his elbows on his knees and propped his forehead against clenched fists. Burning shame filled him. He'd done things and made choices because he wanted to be famous. Well, he was famous now, with more money in the bank than he dreamed possible after only his first tour. Yet his heart continued to ache, missing Kiera like it was just yesterday that she'd sent him away.

The sigh that lifted to the vaulted ceiling was deep and long. Last summer in Minnesota had been far happier than all these months on tour combined. Not even an amazing career could beat being wildly in love, enjoying new friends, and reveling in his renewed faith.

He lifted his head to stare at the cross. *That's what's wrong, isn't it? When I left Minnesota, I left you and everything that matters behind. I got too busy to work with Joel or even spend time in Scripture, and I've been floundering ever since.*

Come to me, all you who are weary and burdened, and I will give you rest.

Jesus' words that he'd read months ago in Scripture resonated deep in his spirit. His heart leaped in response. He was exhausted physically, but it was the weariness in his soul that burdened him most.

He slid to his knees and bowed his head, letting the tears cleanse his aching heart. It was so obvious now. He wouldn't find what he truly needed on a stage or from adoring fans or even in Kiera. This was where he'd find it, right here on his knees.

Forgive me, Lord. I've let it all come before you. But I know now it's meaningless without you. I'm not much, Father. I may not even have a voice with which to praise you, but my heart can still sing. I want to come home. I want to be yours, only yours.

The silence that followed pulsed with energy as an inexpressible joy bubbled up from deep inside. He lifted his hands as *thank you* resounded in his soul, in the sweetest melody he'd ever heard.

An hour later he pushed open the heavy door and blinked against the sunlight. Filled with a joy he'd been sure was lost, he rejoined the waking neighborhood with a fresh perspective.

It was time to go home.

– 42 –

At the end of the final concert, Peter stood arm-in-arm with his friends and bandmates. He squinted into the lights and thanked the enthusiastic audience. After the cheers had subsided, he spoke again.

"This has been an amazing journey. There are so many people to thank it would take all night. But those who have given the most to the *Road to Love* tour are right here on stage with me.

"The commitment of these people has been astounding and humbling. They put their own lives on hold to travel the country with me. Without them, I wouldn't be here." He turned his back to the audience to face his friends. "Thanks, you guys."

The crowd came to their feet to join his appreciation. The ovation was long and enthusiastic. The small group high-fived each other and shared back-slapping hugs and a few tears.

"And," he continued, "there's a young woman who has kept us on our toes, in the right places and on the right schedule. Madelyn Birning, come out here, please."

From where she stood at the side of the stage, she gave a start and shook her head quickly, sliding backwards. Jeff took a few quick steps to capture her hand and propelled her to Peter's side while the audience clapped.

Peter put an arm around her. "Thanks is hardly the right word for what she's done for me and this tour. Maddie stepped up in a big way when we lost our friend and fearless leader, Bill Djerf. We're indebted to her for her hard work, long hours, and dedication to the tour. So thanks, Maddie."

After he hugged her, she was besieged by the band. Her smile was wide and grateful as she hugged each of them.

"We have one more song for you tonight. It's my favorite. It's titled 'Hearts Entwined,' but I call it 'Kiera's Song.'" He'd looked forward to closing the tour with this song that held precious memories. He had started this journey with Kiera constantly in mind and was glad to end it the same way, singing her song with a smile in his heart.

As the melody faded into the evening, he bowed and waved to the audience. "Goodnight, everyone. God bless."

And with that, the *Road to Love* tour officially ended. He couldn't wait to get offstage. He had a phone call to make.

Cheerful birdsong welcomed Kiera to a dazzling morning as she started breakfast. She turned her phone on and checked voice mail. Peter's raspy voice stopped her mid-stir, egg white dripping from the whisk as she stared blindly out the window.

"Hey, Kiera. It's Peter. I just wanted to see how you're doing. I know how much I miss Buck, so I can imagine this has been a brutal spring for you. I hope you're okay. I wanted to tell you that we just finished the last show of the tour about thirty minutes ago. I wish you could have been here. Bill would've been proud. And we ended the tour the way we started it, with your song. Even with this worn-out voice, it was the best I've ever sung it. The crowd loved it."

In the silence, she dropped the whisk and clutched the phone tighter. *Please don't hang up. Not yet.*

"Oh, and I wanted to tell you they just wrapped up Bill's investigation. Turns out he'd had a heart issue for a number of years, and he died from a massive heart attack. He was constantly popping pills." He sighed. "Too bad he thought mixing them with all that beer was a good idea.

"Yeah, so…umm… I just wanted to say thanks. I couldn't have done this without you. Your support and your…care…got me on the road. I never did a show without thinking about you."

Tears dripped down her face.

"Well, I just wanted to let you know how much I appreciate what you did for me. You sacrificed a lot. More, I suspect, than I'll ever know." He sighed. "Take care, Sweetheart."

Holding the phone to her chest, she closed her eyes, seeing his smile, feeling his arms around her. Her heart ached with the longing she'd learned to live with. The tour was over. But while it changed everything for him, nothing changed for her. He'd achieved his dream. Did she even have one left?

"You're what?" Maddie stared at him across the room.

"I'm going to take the summer off." He'd dreaded having this conversation. "Since I have to rest my voice, I'm leaving tomorrow for the cabin to just hang out and maybe write new songs."

She continued to stare at him.

"Maddie, I need the break. This tour was beyond anything I could have imagined. But I feel like the walking dead. I'm tired."

"Of course you are." She sat taller and gave a firm nod. "The cabin sounds like a wonderful place, so spending time there is a great idea. Do you need me to get our tickets? I'll get a rental car lined up. Mark would like to meet with you in July to start planning the next album. I can work from the cabin for a bit, no problem."

She tapped her chin with a pen. "Another idea I had was a cruise. How about after a few days at the cabin we take a cruise and spend some time relaxing on the beach? Oh, wait. That reminds me." Her brown eyes sparkled. "I have a friend who owns a condo in Cabo San Lucas. I'm sure he'd let us borrow it for a while." She made a note in her portfolio. "I'll call—"

"No."

She waved a hand. "Don't worry. I've stayed there before."

"Maddie, stop. I don't want to go to Mexico."

"Oh." She frowned. "Okay. Well then, let's go with the cruise idea. I'll just check—"

"Maddie, listen to me!"

Her fingers stilled, her gaze lifting slowly. He released a short breath. *Give me the right words, Lord.* He softened his tone. "I'm going to the cabin alone. For the summer."

She looked at him, silent.

"I'm tired. No, I'm burned out. But more than that, I think God is calling me to do something else. Maybe sing different music."

"Sure. It's great to try different styles. I'm sure Mark will be happy to work on something—"

"I'm done recording for a while. I'm done touring. I need a long break before making any decisions. I know we should have talked about this earlier, but with all the end of the tour stuff going on, there was never time."

He sat down beside her on the couch. "Maddie, you're awesome. I thought that before Bill died, but since then—wow. You stepped into his big shoes and made them your own. It's been incredible to watch. But now that the tour is over, and I'm not doing another one for who knows how long, I don't need an assistant. I don't think I even need a manager at this point. I just need time to regroup and figure out what God wants me to do next."

"Of course you need a manager. Everyone with your talent needs one." She said it matter-of-factly but her chin quivered.

Oh, don't cry. "I might, once I know what's next for my career, but for now I don't." He pulled an envelope from his back pocket and held it out. "This is for you, to help you get started in your new career. I know you've talked to a few of Bill's clients so I think you've probably already started, but I wanted to thank you and do my part to get you up and running."

She leaned away as if it held the plague, her dark eyes narrowing. "It's okay to fire me, Peter. It's how it works in this business. You don't have to pay me off."

"I'm not! This is the last of your salary and a bonus from the tour. You earned every penny. But it can't possibly be enough to compensate for everything you've done for me these past months."

"I did it because I wanted to."

"I know. And you're good at it." He set the envelope on top of her papers. "You're going to make a huge difference in the music world, Maddie. I'm grateful that I got to be part of you reaching the next rung on your career ladder. I can't wait to see where you go from here."

"I guess…I just assumed we'd go up the ladder together."

He stood and moved away with a shrug. "I may not even stay *on* the ladder. I'm so tired I can't think about it. But there's no way I'll let you sit around waiting for me. You've got too many other plates spinning."

"So this is it? We just shake hands and say adios?"

It had been him asking that of Kiera when she brought the ax down on his heart. He struggled to stay in the present moment. "For now. I hope you'll consider representing me if I do decide to take the next step in my career. You'll be the first person I call."

She fingered the envelope. "You know I fell for you right at the start." The quiet words were filled with regret.

He'd guessed as much. But he'd never be able to return the sentiment. "My heart is still too banged up after Kiera to be ready for another relationship."

"A girl can hope."

"The right guy is out there for you. A guy who can be focused completely on you and how terrific you are. People like me—we're too selfish to focus on anyone but ourselves. You deserve better than that. And I hope you'll hold out for it."

She chewed her bottom lip. "I'm not sure they come any better than you."

"Oh, they do. Trust me on that." Probably by the tens of thousands.

– 43 –

"Thanks for holding. This is Pastor Joel."

Peter almost hung up. The humiliation of explaining the mess he'd made of his life since they'd last talked was paralyzing. "Joel, it's...Peter Theisen."

"Peter! It's great to hear from you. How are you?"

"I'm good. The tour ended last week so now I can breathe."

"I'll bet it's been crazy."

"That would be a good start to describing it. Is now a good time to talk?"

"It is. I have the next hour free. Let me shut my door and we can get caught up. So where are you now?"

"At the cabin. I got here last night." His eyes rested on poignant reminders of Gram in the kitchen—her favorite dish towel, the old spice rack. "I can't tell you how great it is to be back."

"I want to hear all about it."

The warmth in Joel's voice gave Peter the courage to share openly about his choices and struggles of the past year. Joel responded to his halting confession with compassion, and Peter soaked in the godly counsel like a man who'd been wandering in the desert.

He released a slow breath as the conversation wrapped up. "You've given me a lot to think about. It may take the whole summer to think it through."

Joel chuckled. "Take it one day at a time, my friend. The fact that you're willing to look back before you move forward says a lot about you."

"Yeah. Like I'm a slow learner."

"Emphasis on the learner part. Let's get started where we left off on the Bible study. And when you're ready, we can meet for lunch. How about we talk tomorrow at eleven?"

After hanging up, Peter sat still on the couch, phone in his hand, a tiny light flickering deep in his heart. Joel's gentle questions had pointed him inward, to the source of his decisions and behavior.

As hard as it would be to face what he'd done with his life, the spark of hope was being fanned into a flame. Finally he was on the right path.

"Kiera, I'm worried about you." Joel's words echoed Kyle and Terese.

Settled across from him in his office, she met his gaze squarely. "So am I," she acknowledged. She'd been floundering for so long. She needed Joel's counsel, especially in the absence of her father.

He leaned back in his chair, studying her. "If you could do anything right now, with no limitations, what would you do?"

Run away. The words leapt to mind. But it wouldn't accomplish anything. The pain would simply follow. She shrugged.

"Come on. I know you better than that. Tell me what your first thought was." His eyebrows lifted. "I'll wait until you're ready."

Yes, he would. She sighed. "Run away."

"Okay. To where?"

"Nowhere in particular. Just…away from here."

"From what?"

She'd forgotten how perceptive he was. "From you at the moment."

His chuckle relieved her tension. "You're free to leave, as you well know."

Kiera reached deep inside for a scrap of courage to respond honestly. She'd sought him out for this very reason—like Tess, he wouldn't let her get by with anything less than the truth. And she desperately needed help to escape the black vortex she was in.

"Okay. From…modeling. From missing my dad." Tears filled her eyes. *From missing Peter.*

He nodded, fingertips tapping together. “You’ve been through a couple of really rough years.”

She focused on the flowering crabapple tree outside his office window.

“With Buck gone, the bills paid off, and the house fixed up, what do you *want* to do?”

The bright faces of the teens she’d worked with sprang to mind. But who would hire her? After a great start, she’d dropped right off the radar. Like she had in Peter’s life.

“I’d like to start up *One of Me* again,” she said quietly.

“Great idea. It’s an amazing program, Kiera. And I’m not just saying that,” he added, when she looked back to him. He grinned. “You know *me* better than that.”

She did. He meant what he said. If he thought she could start it up again, then maybe she could.

“What else?”

Her heartbeat ramped up as their gazes held. He wasn’t going to stop until he’d dragged it all out of her. “This will sound crazy but I’ve been kicking around the idea of starting a fishing camp for inner-city kids. To honor Dad.”

“I like that. And we both know Buck would.” He waited. “Anything else?”

“I’d like to apologize to Peter.” The words hung before her, a surprising revelation.

“For?”

“For letting my pride get in the way of our relationship. I should have told him about the money, about why I made those choices.” She sighed. “He deserved better from me.”

Joel folded his arms, a thoughtful frown on his bearded face. “It was a rough time for both of you.” He was quiet for a long moment. “I have an idea to get you started moving again.”

“I’ll take it.”

He laughed. “Maybe you should hear me out first.”

She smiled in return. “I’m all ears.”

“I think you need to get away from here, like you said. Friends of ours own a small resort up on Gull Lake and they've set aside a small cabin for this very reason."

Gram's cabin was on that lake.

"I'd like you to take some time up there on your own. To rest and listen for God's direction. To let Him heal the pain in your heart and mind. There've been so many demands on you over the past year, I think you need to find your way back to who you are, who God is calling you to be."

Alone up north? It was frightening. And exciting. When had she ever relied solely on herself? "For a week or so?"

"For the summer."

Her eyes widened. *All summer?* What would she do alone up there? Ideas rained over her. Revamp *One of Me.* Go for walks. Gain weight. Spend time with God. A sudden longing caught her breath. Time with God.

He set his elbows on his desk. "Let me call my friend and see if the cabin is open. We have a standing agreement that I can send people up there for respite and there's no charge. It's their way of giving back."

She nodded and he picked up the phone. The odd flutter in her heart felt almost like hope. Maybe there was a way out of the darkness after all.

Kiera settled into the rustic lakeside cabin with an unexpected sense of contentment. She hung up the last shirt and looked around the cozy bedroom. A bed, a dresser, a small table. The simplicity suited her. She was glad she'd taken Joel's suggestion. It felt right to be here alone. Just her and God.

Last night, she'd cried for all that she'd lost, but this morning the veil of grief lifted with the morning sun. She looked out at the lake, watching sunlight dance over the ripples, and smiled. This was exactly where she was supposed to be.

The days fell into a comfortable routine. Rising early, she ate breakfast at the kitchen table, working on the Bible study Joel had designed for her. Then she'd head out on a walk to mull over what she was learning. How she'd missed these quiet times with God.

By the fourth day she'd drummed up enough courage to drive past Peter's cabin. She wasn't sure what she'd do if he were actually there, but the need to release the sadness and longing tied up in the memories was stronger than her fear.

As the log cabin came into view, her heart thundered in her chest. The cabin was dark, with curtains drawn. No sign of life. Releasing a sigh, she stopped the car and relaxed against the seat. She studied the familiar lines of the cabin and allowed bittersweet memories to surface. Buck's fishing stories over dinner on the deck, the intense cribbage tournament.

Her gaze drifted past the cabin to the lake and the fire pit. Again, the familiar quiver as she remembered their first kiss against a backdrop of gentle thunder. The view blurred. Such beautiful memories, such an amazing love scarred by fear and pride, muted by angry words, colored by jealousy. They hadn't realized what they had until they let it shatter into pieces.

She put the car in gear and pulled away from the cabin one last time.

Kyle called at the end of the week during her morning hike. "I'm glad I caught you," he said, "but it sounds like you're out walking."

"Just finishing. It's a picture-perfect morning here. How is it where you are, wherever that is?"

He chuckled. "I'm in New York this week. Can't say it's ever picture-perfect here, but at least it stopped raining."

"Hopefully all this sunshine will make it across the country to you."

"I'm counting on it. So how are you? Feeling settled?"

"I am. It's wonderful to be away, to have time to think."

"Does that mean you've made a decision?"

The contract he'd sent was buried at the bottom of her suitcase. When she'd told him last month about her idea of starting a fishing camp in Buck's memory, he'd suggested she model full time for a year to get the funding established. The idea made her nauseous. "To be honest, I haven't even thought about it. Sorry." She'd tried, but her mind refused to focus.

"No worries. You're there to rest and get reenergized."

"And gain some weight."

"That too. All I care about is you being healthy and happy, Kiera."

The declaration slowed her steps. He was a dear man, a good friend. But now, having been on her own just this one week, it was clear he would never be more than that.

"Kyle…" The sudden pounding in her heart wasn't from the hike. "Being up here, away from everything, has already helped me see things more clearly. I really don't know if I'll do any more modeling. Ever."

"That's okay. I don't need a decision right now."

"I know. It's just…I don't want you waiting for me. I'm trying to listen for God's direction, and I have a feeling it's going to take time."

He was quiet for a long moment. "Kiera, I truly want you to be happy. If God isn't calling you to modeling, you won't be." He cleared his throat. "And if He's not changing your heart about me then…I'll deal with it."

"You deserve to be happy too."

"I won't be if it's at your expense. As much as I've prayed for you to fall for me, I can accept His answer. I've seen the writing on the wall for months. I just kept hoping it would change."

In the silence, Kiera looked up at the cloudless sky. The relief in her heart was all the answer she needed. *God, put the right woman in his life. Soon.*

"Well, I'd better run," he said. "I've got a meeting with Richard in twenty minutes and I'm across town."

"Tell him hello from me. I'm heading into town for groceries."

"Throw a package of cookies in the cart in my honor. We'll talk again soon, okay?"

"Okay." She stood still for a long moment. *Thank you for putting such a wonderful man in my life, Lord. And please, put someone just as wonderful in his.*

Twenty minutes later she zipped down Highway 77 toward the grocery store in Baxter. It was all so familiar and yet brand new. She was on her own, Just her and God for a whole summer. It was terrifying and exhilarating.

In the store, she hooked a green basket over her arm and wandered through the produce area. Stir-fry sounded good. A yellow pepper in hand, she paused as a memory of Peter's first visit home during the tour made her smile. They'd made stir-fry with Terese and Jason.

So many happy memories and so many heartbreaking ones. She shook her head and selected a different pepper. Up here, in the fresh air and sunshine, only happy memories were allowed.

She turned and started. The person who'd provided the majority of happy *and* sad memories stood ten feet away, staring at her with wide dark eyes. The pepper rolled off her fingertips into the basket.

Peter was more gorgeous than she remembered. Taller. But she'd never forgotten how his eyes crinkled at the corners when he smiled. Like he was now. And what that smile did to her heart.

He took a few steps toward her, shaking his head. "If we've ever had a God-moment, this would be it."

"That's the only thing that would explain it." Her heart banged around her ribs like a crazed animal.

They both spoke at once. "What are you doing here?" "When did you get here?"

Kiera giggled. "You first."

"So when did you get here? And where are you staying?"

"Earlier this week. I'm staying at that little resort not far from your cabin. The Lone Pine? Friends of Joel own it."

"Great little place. How long will you be here?"

She shrugged. "I've got the cabin until August 23rd, but they're flexible with when I head out. I may go back earlier or stay a few extra days."

"You're by yourself?"

"I am. And very happy to be alone, I have to admit."

His smile deepened. "Me too. I need time to get some things figured out."

His voice was deep and gravelly. She put a hand to her throat. "Your voice…"

"Vocal nodules. From overuse. I'm not allowed to sing for the next few months, and I have to keep my talking to a minimum."

"Wow. I'm sorry."

"I'm not. When I don't feel like talking, I just point at my neck." He pointed a finger at his neck, frowned and shook his head.

She laughed. "Ah. The universal sign for vocal nodules."

His handsome face lit up. "Hey, I didn't know you were familiar with it."

They stood smiling at each other until she asked, "So how long are you staying?"

"Until I know what God wants me to do next. I told Him I'm not moving until He makes it clear what my next step is."

Her eyes narrowed as she studied him. He looked serious. "Aren't you planning the next tour or album?" Why did she ask that? She didn't want the answer.

"Nope. I'm going to spend the summer resting my voice, writing songs, and getting my head on straight. No tour plans at all. Maybe ever."

Hopefully the smile on her face wasn't as goofy as the one in her heart. "Sounds kind of like my summer, although I don't think I'll try my hand at songwriting."

They were quiet another moment. Peter rubbed the back of his neck and studied his feet.

She switched the basket to her other arm and straightened her shoulders. "Well, I'd better finish my shopping." She took a step back, her smile fading. How many times did she have to say goodbye to this man? "It was great seeing you, Peter. Really. I'm glad the tour went well." The words squeezed through her tight throat. "Hopefully some quiet time up here will repair your voice."

"Thanks." He swallowed hard and gave a nod. "It was great to see you too, Kiki."

The nickname pinged her heart. "Okay. Well, maybe I'll see you around this summer."

"Yeah. Maybe."

With an awkward wave, she turned back toward the produce. She blindly handled the tomatoes, waiting for him to walk away. Out of her life. Again.

When a sideways glance confirmed he was gone, she lifted her face and blinked back the tears, scolding her heart for its wild flutter. If she were going to run into him again, she'd need to get her feelings under control. At the moment, that seemed impossible.

By the time she checked out and left the store, she'd put the lid firmly back on her warring emotions. It had been a pleasant surprise to see him again, a relief to know he was doing well and that he was here alone. Seeing him with his pretty assistant would have sent her running back to the Twin Cities.

"Hey, Kiera!"

She turned so quickly from loading the groceries into her trunk, she dumped the contents. Peppers rolled one way, zucchini another.

Peter jogged up and stopped before her. "Hi again."

"Hi. Again." Her heart kicked into its ridiculous dance.

"I was wondering..." He licked his lips. "We haven't had a real chance to, you know, get caught up and hear about life and what's been happening. Or not happening. Or...whatever."

She held back a smile. This was the Peter she'd fallen in love with.

"I was thinking maybe we could, you know, have coffee. Sometime this summer maybe? This week or next. Or whenever you want. If you want."

Her brain screamed an objection while her head nodded. "That would be nice. I have the same cell phone number, so call when you have some free time."

A smile released the crease between his eyes and he bobbed his head. "Great. That'd be great. Okay then." He stepped backward and bumped into the car parked beside hers. "Well... talk to you soon."

Kiera cried all the way back to the cabin, the joy and pain of seeing him again spinning her thoughts into chaos. The summer looked a whole lot different as she returned from her simple grocery run. Peter was back in her life.

– 44 –

It was three days that felt like three weeks before he called, suggesting coffee and a walk through town. The initial awkwardness faded as they strolled, shopped, and chatted. She kept her conversation light, careful not to bring up anything from the past. He seemed to do the same as he talked about songwriting and getting to finally sleep on his own schedule.

The following weeks morphed into a routine of morning walks, afternoons going their separate ways, then evenings of cribbage, roasting marshmallows in the fire pit, or quietly reading side by side.

Kiera reveled in the friendship that developed in these simple, easy hours together. His respectful distance warmed her heart and raised her trust. She was more relaxed in his presence than she had ever been with anyone, including him.

One rainy mid-June evening, they relaxed in her cabin, the room lit only by the cozy fire. She swung her legs sideways over the arm of the chair and faced him. “What were you expected to do when it came to publicity?”

He shrugged. “Mainly give a great show every night. Afterwards, no matter how tired I was, I did the meet ’n greet and the photo ops. I enjoyed it for the most part. I was glad for the chance to thank people for paying to see the show or buying the CD. But it didn’t take long for me to catch on to how Bill wanted it to work.”

“Which was?”

His deep sigh filled the room. “He told me once that my job was to provide the fantasy material for women. I remember him saying something like I had to sell myself in order to sell the album." He frowned at the fire. "I hated that idea. I just wanted to sing. I didn't want to be a piece of meat."

He turned his frown toward her. "I was so stupid. So naïve. But I thought Bill knew everything. So I tried to do what I was told. It cost me more than I could have imagined."

It was the first time in their weeks together that he'd referred to their failed relationship. Her heart caught in her throat as their gazes held.

"When he hired Maddie, it was just another voice telling me where to go, what to say, how to act. I enjoyed a lot of the tour experience, but there was always something in the back of my mind saying, 'I didn't sign up for this.'

"I made choices that were foolish, that hurt you and Buck. But they were *my* choices. As much as I tried to blame them on Bill or Maddie or the tour or whatever, it came down to me. I've been living with the consequences ever since."

The fire crackled in the silence. His confession was a hammer to the ceramic protecting her heart. She'd never expected to hear words like these from him, and it filled her with sadness for what they'd let slip away.

He stood and moved toward her, reaching out a hand that she took automatically. Pulling her up, he held her hands in a gentle grasp, rubbing his thumbs across her knuckles.

"Kiera, I've enjoyed spending time with you these past weeks. I wish this was how we'd started a year ago. I can share things with you I've never shared with anyone else."

She managed a shaky smile, locking her knees so they wouldn't buckle.

"To be honest…I'm falling for you in a whole new way."

His confession nearly dropped her back into her chair.

His trembling fingers tightened around hers. "I don't expect that you feel the same, but one thing I decided when the tour ended was that I was done playing games. From now on, I'm going to be as open and honest as I know how. It's a process God is teaching me, and it's been pretty humbling at times."

She bit her lip. Would she be able to learn that as well?

He rubbed the bridge of his nose before continuing. "I know how much I've enjoyed being together again, and I think…it seems like you have too. So I'm hoping you maybe want to keep going?"

His question rang in the silence. She nodded.

"Good. That's good." His brow relaxed. His crooked smile faded. "But…for us to go to the next level, there's a lot more to talk about. Together. I can't do it alone." He rolled his eyes. "Obviously."

She smiled.

"We have a lot of ground to cover, lots of stuff that needs to be said to get to a new place. I think some of it could be painful."

Her heart melted at the uncertainty on his beloved face. She couldn't walk away now even if she wanted to. Maybe if she faced the past with him, if she could admit to her own issues as well, they could build a future together. "Is it okay to say I'm scared?"

He brushed his fingers against her cheek. "I'm scared too. I'm such an idiot when it comes to you. But if we make God the foundation for everything we do, it will work out." He pulled her gently into his arms. "I'm in it for the long haul, pretty lady."

She rested in his familiar embrace. "I'm in too."

Settled on a grassy hill overlooking the lake, Kiera faced Peter. It had been easier listening to him talk about his shortcomings than to face her own. "I knew Kyle was falling for me, but it felt good to be cared for. I needed you so much when Dad died. But you weren't there. You couldn't be. Kyle was."

His eyebrows lowered but he remained silent.

"Dad warned me before he died. He said I was vulnerable with you gone so much. At the time, I just laughed at the idea. I'd never thought of myself as vulnerable, but…" She sighed and picked at the clover spread around them. "He was right. And yet, I've never felt anything more than friendship toward Kyle. Ever. If we're being honest, I have to admit I tried." She lifted a hesitant gaze to his. "I should have put the brakes to it long ago."

"He's in love with you?"

Warmth filled her face but she kept her eyes on his. "He's never said so straight out, but he's been pretty clear about wanting to build a future together."

His frown deepened. "You're sure you aren't in love with him."

"Positive."

"Could you be someday, if you gave it more time?"

She watched a duck skim across the lake as it landed. Romantic love just wasn't what she felt for Kyle. She shook her head. "No. I love Kyle as a dear friend. He was so kind to my dad, and he's looked out for me all these months. But it will never be more than that. When he called shortly after I got here, I told him not to wait for me."

His brow relaxed and his mouth quivered, like he was trying not to smile. She hoped she liked his answer as much. "So tell me about your relationship with your assistant."

It seemed he left nothing out. Several times she held her breath to keep the tears at bay, but she was relieved to hear that it had been no more intimate than her relationship with Kyle. An emotional closeness, yes, but nothing beyond that. She didn't like it, but she understood it.

"So I'm going to ask you the same questions. Is Maddie in love with you?"

He met her gaze and nodded. "She never said the words but yes, I think so."

"You aren't in love with her?"

"Not at all."

"Could you be?"

He took the same amount of time giving thought to her question. "No."

"You realize there are hundreds, if not thousands, of pictures of you two? And to the world, including me, it has looked like you're in love."

He nodded, his expression serious but not defensive. "I know. I'm sorry for that. Really sorry. Maddie is going to be a great manager. She saved my rear a few times by stepping in to put the right spin on something careless I did. I was always open about my feelings for you, but I don't think that mattered to her."

He slid closer and reached for her hands. "I do not love Maddie as more than a friend. We were never…you know…intimate, nor was I with any woman, including the girl at the auction."

Kiera flinched and tried to pull her hands away, but his grasp tightened.

"Of all the stupid things I've done this past year—and there are many—that was by far the worst. And I have no one to blame but myself. God even told me not to do it, but I listened to Bill instead."

"Did you have the date?" She hated how small her voice sounded.

"No. I sent her a note saying my schedule was just too busy to spend more than an hour with her, and I paid her what she'd bid. I never heard back from her but I can tell you, Bill was steaming mad."

A smile tugged at her mouth.

He squeezed her hands. "So what else do you want to know? Ask away."

There was a question yet to be answered, one that still haunted her when she dreamed of a future with him. She pulled her hands away, clasping them together. His answer could make or break their relationship. "Why didn't you come back?"

"When?"

"When we broke up." Pain from that night washed over her like it was yesterday.

"You kicked me out!"

"I *needed* you but you just walked away. You said you weren't going to give up on us, but you never came back."

He stared at her, a pained crease between his eyes. "That was the worst night of my life. I'd been walking around with so much guilt—about the auction, and not getting back to see Buck before he died. I'd made a promise to him at Christmas, but I'd already messed up. Everything was falling apart and I couldn't figure out how to fix it."

He stood and moved a few feet away to stare out at the lake. "I'd been mad about your modeling, and I was jealous about Kyle. When you said you were done with us, I didn't know what to do. I was so shocked I couldn't think straight.

"I meant every word I said that night, but on the plane back to wherever

I was going, I figured what you really wanted was to be with him, and that's why you broke it off. It was the only thing that made sense to me at the time."

He kicked at the scraggly grass under his feet. "I called you at least a hundred times those first weeks, but I always hung up before it went through. I was a zombie during the concerts. I forgot words, messed up the order of the set. I actually started crying during a couple of songs. People thought it was a great act, but I was dying inside."

He lifted his head and met her tearful gaze. "I learned to live with it, but I've never gotten over it. I'm sorry for hurting you, for letting my ego keep me from going back into the house to make it right between us." He dropped down beside her and reached for her hands again. The regret in his eyes touched her heart.

"Sweetheart, I am so sorry for everything I did that hurt you this year. I'm sorry I took the easy way out and blamed you for things." With a gentle finger, he wiped away the tear that slid down her cheek. His dark eyes glittered and his voice had an extra raspiness. "I'm sorry I wasn't there for you when Buck was dying. I'll never get over that."

She gave a slight nod, biting her lip to keep the flood of tears back. She'd never expected to hear words of apology like that. It took several tries to respond. "I've always prided myself on being self-sufficient, being able to take care of myself. I thought it was because I didn't want to cause problems for anyone else, but God has been correcting me on that. Pride has long been my downfall, but I've refused to see it because it was easier to pretend I was in control."

"I think we all do that."

"But I've turned it into an art form. I'd rather struggle to come up with my own solution than admit to someone I need help. It's thanks to Terese that our friendship has survived this long. She's the only one who hasn't let me get away with that stuff."

He nodded. "She's a good friend."

"The best." She folded her arms. "I was humiliated after the Thomas fiasco, and then doubly so when I got fired. I'd decided I wouldn't let anyone close again after that, but then you came along."

"Sorry."

She smiled. "It was divine intervention. I'd have closed myself off for good if God hadn't put you in my life. Even so, I couldn't get to a place of trusting you. I pushed you away so many times when what I really wanted was to lean on you and let you in.

"I knew the life you were heading into. Even dealing with Dad's cancer, I should have been more supportive of you. I made it about me instead and that was wrong."

Admitting the truth was as painful as it was freeing. "You were under so much stress and I only made it worse." Her trembling fingers touched his cheek. "I'm so sorry, Peter."

He took her hand and pressed a kiss to it. "We were both under unbelievable stress, Sweetheart."

A wobbly smile touched her mouth. "I want to admit here and now, out loud, that it's okay for me to say I need help." She stood and lifted her arms, turning slowly in a circle. "Hey, world! Sometimes I, Kiera Simmons, don't know what to do. Sometimes I even need help. I don't have all the answers, and guess what? That's okay! And sometimes I need a kick in the pants to stop being so selfishly independent."

She dropped back onto the log, filled with an unexpected relief. There. She'd said it out loud.

"I'd be happy to do the pants-kicking," he said with a wink.

She laughed then grew serious. "It won't be easy," she warned. "I don't give up old habits easily."

"I can handle it. Me and God, we make a good team."

She studied the face of this man she loved so much, and the last of her fears dissolved. Finally she got it. She was safe and loved, free to be the person God created her to be. Flinging herself into his arms, she released the pain that had built over the past months and soaked in the strength and reassurance of his arms wrapped securely around her.

When she leaned back to wipe her face, she was surprised to see him wipe away his own tears. He grinned self-consciously and shrugged, an eyebrow lifted. "Think we've covered enough for today?"

They burst into relieved, happy laughter. As they caught their breath, he stood and pulled her to her feet. "Let's go get some lunch and continue this later. I'm starving."

– 45 –

Peter's voice grew stronger as the last of the tour's tension evaporated under the healing summer sun. Kiera was blooming before his eyes. New color filled her face, her eyes sparkled with laughter. She announced triumphantly that she'd put on a few pounds. They celebrated with chocolate-covered doughnuts.

Sitting by the fire near her cabin one evening in early August, Kiera finally shared the real reason behind her return to modeling. "When it all fell apart, Terese told me to tell you," she admitted, eyes glued to a distant object across the water. "I should have but…I thought I could handle it. I never wanted your money. I just wanted *you*. But since you were so busy, I decided I'd fix it myself."

She was right. He'd been too busy for her much of the time. Vague memories stirred—interrupted conversations after which she'd pulled away from him a little more. Why hadn't he seen it? "You know I'd have helped you however you needed it."

"I know. I should have trusted our relationship more, trusted *you* more." She reached for his hand. "Can you forgive me?"

"I already have." He pulled her close and they sat quietly, watching sparks fly upward into the night sky. A loon's lonely cry echoed across the still water.

"So looking beyond this summer," he said eventually, "what do you want to be doing?"

She snuggled against him. "Staying right here for the rest of our lives."

He tightened his arms. "That can be arranged. But at some point you're going to want to get up and do something. In the ideal world, what would that be?"

She was quiet so long he wondered if she'd dozed off.

"I know what I don't want to do ever again. Model. I'm done with that life. I was offered a contract to go full time, and I brought it out here to pray about it." She moved out of his arms, stood, and pulled folded papers from her back pocket. "Want to help?"

He joined her and accepted several of the sheets. As she tore hers into shreds, he glanced through his. The modeling contract. With Kyle's signature at the bottom. Joyful relief ballooned in his chest as he shredded the papers into tiny bits.

Kiera's laughter rang out as she tossed her handful into the air over the fire. His pieces mingled with hers, sparking into tiny flames before being consumed. Then she stood quietly for a moment, gazing into the fire, and his heart stopped. Did she already regret that moment of impulse?

The smile she turned toward him was reassuring in its joy. "And that's that," she said, brushing her hands together.

"Amen."

They settled back onto the log, wrapped in quiet relief.

"I'd like to put my energy back into *One of Me*," she said. "But I've also been thinking about starting some kind of fishing camp for inner-city kids to honor Dad. Call it Buck's Fishing Camp or something."

The pain of Buck's absence still made him flinch. "He'd love it. Have you figured out how to get it going?"

"I've done a little research. I'll get serious about it when I get home."

It was something they could do together to honor Buck. "I think we should work on that this fall. Check around, send out feelers. Whatever will make it happen. I think it's a great idea, Kiera."

She shifted to look up at him, tears sparkling in the firelight that bathed her face. "Thank you."

He smiled and pressed a gentle kiss to her temple.

There was a peaceful silence before she asked, "What would you do in the ideal world?"

"It won't be going back on tour, that's for sure."

"Really?"

"It's not the kind of life I want. And I don't believe it's what God wants for me."

"You say that now, but once you're rested and you can start singing again—"

"I'll find another way to share my music. I'm serious, Kiera. Just like I knew I wasn't cut out to be a cruise ship crooner, I'm not cut out to spend months away from home bouncing from city to city. I love doing concerts, but no more long tours. It's just not going to happen."

Her heart burst into joyous color and she snuggled against him with a tiny, "Yay."

He chuckled. "That's how I felt when I made the decision. Like someone rolled a boulder off my chest."

"What will you do if it's not touring?"

"Find a way to help kids get involved in music. Whether it's through singing, songwriting, teaching them to play an instrument or run a soundboard. Whatever they'd be interested in."

"That sounds wonderful."

"I can't wait to get back to Faith to hear more of their worship music. With all the music I listen to, nothing has touched me like the songs we sang at church. I want to be part of that, whatever that might look like."

"I love it."

He hugged her. "Me too."

As the fire died down and the evening drew to a close, Peter hated to leave her. These months together had changed his world. She was the one person who would keep him grounded and focused. He couldn't go forward in life without her beside him.

A plan formed as he drove toward his cabin. *God, give me the courage. And don't let me mess it up.*

A week later they enjoyed a light lunch in brilliant sunshine on his deck. At least it seemed Kiera enjoyed it. Peter's stomach was so tied in knots he was afraid the food wouldn't stay down. When she commented on his lack of appetite, he quipped that the beautiful woman sitting across from him was all the sustenance he needed. She rolled her eyes and finished his fries.

They filled their water bottles and set off on a leisurely hike. Getting to their secret spot hot, sweaty, and stinky was not the ambiance he had in mind. Conversation was easy, laughter abundant as they crested the hill hand in hand. A warm summer breeze rustled through the leaves, setting the clover swaying and nodding. An eagle circled lazily overhead. At the far side of the pond, several deer trotted back into the woods.

"This is my favorite place in the world," she sighed.

"It's our own special hideaway." They settled on the log where they'd sat a full year earlier, and he slid his arms around her. "Being here makes me feel like we have a future that stretches as far as we can dream."

She leaned back against him. "I love that image."

In the silence, he licked his lips, sure she could feel his heart pounding. "Kiera, I need to tell you something."

"That sounds ominous."

"When we met, my goal was to be famous. Not for anything noteworthy like ending poverty or finding a cure for cancer. Just because I liked to sing. I wanted to make a boatload of money and feel like I was important.

"I reached my goal, but only because of the people who helped me along the way. I could never have achieved it on my own, but I was too self-absorbed to know that at the time. God introduced me to an amazing woman and blessed me with good friends, a faith mentor in Joel, and a life coach in your dad. I had the best manager in the industry and was surrounded by top-notch musicians. I had the best of everything."

He sighed, resting his cheek against her hair. "But I found out the fame didn't matter. None of it did—not the money, the perks, or the attention. I'd been so focused on the goal, I lost sight of the journey. I turned my back on my faith, my friends, and the woman I will never stop loving.

"I had to lose almost everything to figure out what really matters. It was only then that I realized what my rush to fame had cost me. Now that I've had time to myself away from the paparazzi and the spotlight—and even you—I've found my way back to a God who never stopped waiting for me to come to my senses. And you and I have been able to develop the relationship we couldn't a year ago.

"The other night, when we talked about dreams in an ideal world, I told you I want to help kids get involved in music. I've realized it's more than that—I'd like to introduce kids to Christian music and help them experience God's love. The new songs I've written have a deeper focus, and I'm discovering what it means to use my music to glorify God.

"But it's not just about me. I want to help you take *One of Me* all over the country because you have a message kids need to hear. And I want to be part of starting the Buck Simmons Fishing Camp."

Get on with it, Theisen.

He slid off the log and lowered to one knee, watching her eyes go wide. There, in their secret place, he asked the question he'd dreamed of asking for a year. "Kiera Marie Simmons, will you marry me?"

She stared at him, a trembling hand to her mouth, her beautiful green eyes locked on his. And for an endless moment he waited, unable to breathe or move or speak.

"Seriously?" she choked out.

Was it that big of a surprise? "Of course."

"Yes, I'll marry you. Yes!"

Thank you, God. He got to his feet and pulled her up, then took her face in his hands. "I love you, Kiki. I always have and I always will."

The paths of her tears sparkled in the sunlight. "I love you, Peter. Forever and for always."

He drew her into a kiss filled with sunshine and salty tears, clean lake air and promises of the future. And on the breeze that danced around them, he heard the melody of Kiera's Song.

For I am convinced that neither death nor life, neither angels nor demons, neither the present nor the future, nor any powers, neither height nor depth, nor anything else in all creation, will be able to separate us from the love of God that is in Christ Jesus our Lord.
Romans 8:38–39

Gratitude Beyond Words

One of the most amazing parts of my writing journey has been encountering the people God put in my life along the way. Here are just a few who have helped make this book possible.

Thank You to…

Mike, the love of my life – my encourager, supporter, and main squeeze. Thanks for 34 years of laughs. **Camry and Nate, Aaron and Rosanna** – my cheerleaders along this bumpy path. **"Special K"** – who knew being Gramma would be such a hoot?

Sue, Mark, Steve, Linda, Scott, Nan, Dad, and all the "kids" – I wish everyone were as blessed with siblings, nieces, and nephews as I've been.

Mary, Jon, Danny, PJ, Dave, and all the "kids" – extended family who have encouraged me every step of the way.

The Moms Group – Gail, Nancy, Ruth, Susan, Theresa, and Wendy. There are no words to thank my BFFs for decades of love, support, and laughter. Lots of laughter.

The Marriage Group – Sue and Wayne, Mary and Kevin, Nancy and John, Lynne and Don. Can't imagine life without this group of amazing, godly men and women.

And to…

These writerly people who have improved my writing, encouraged me through the valleys, and celebrated every victory, big or small. What a privilege to create alongside them.

Nina Engen – an amazing editor and even more amazing friend.

Karen Anderson – my patient graphic designer friend.

Andrea Cox – my copyediting friend and fellow writer.

MN-NICE – An ACFW chapter of the most encouraging, supportive, caring individuals ever.

Sharon Hinck – for a sweet, God-inspired friendship (and for not letting me quit).

The Crit Group – Brenda, Carol, Chawna, Michelle, Sharon, and John. Brainstorming, writing, editing, and laughter. What could be better?

The Maple Grove Critique Group – Ann, Barb, Sharon, and Zenith. Sharing this journey with you has been fun AND informative.

The Open Door Writers Group – Karen, Vanessa, Doug, Nina, Jeff, Thomas, Tim, Colleen, Julie, Autumn, Mary, Dave, Bill. What a joy it's been to learn together (while eating M&M's and popcorn).

Midwest Fiction Writers – the group that got me started. Special thanks to Ellen and Liz for the laughs and encouragement.

Suzie Johnson and Narelle Atkins – writing partners across the country and the world. Couldn't have done this without you.

My beta readers – especially Diana, Stephanie, Amy, Brenda, Beverly, PJ, and Camry. You ladies rock!

About the Author

Stacy Monson writes stories that show an extraordinary God at work in ordinary life. A member of ACFW (American Christian Fiction Writers), she is the current secretary and past president of MN-NICE, as well as the area coordinator for Minnesota. Residing in the Twin Cities, she is the wife of a juggling, unicycling physical education teacher, mom to two amazing kids and two wonderful in-law kids, and a very proud grandma. You can learn more about Stacy and her books at www.stacymonson.com.

CPSIA information can be obtained
at www.ICGtesting.com
Printed in the USA
LVOW13s2103150117
520989LV00007B/435/P

9 780986 124518